SQUEEZE ME

SQUEEZE ME

CARL HIAASEN

ALFRED A. KNOPF   NEW YORK   2020

THIS IS A BORZOI BOOK
PUBLISHED BY ALFRED A. KNOPF

www.aaknopf.com

Knopf, Borzoi Books, and the colophon are registered
trademarks of Penguin Random House LLC.

Library of Congress Cataloging-in-Publication Data
Names: Hiaasen, Carl, author.
Title: Squeeze me : a novel / Carl Hiaasen.
Description: First edition. | New York : Alfred A. Knopf, 2020.
Identifiers: LCCN 2020018516 | ISBN 9781524733452 (hardcover) |
ISBN 9781524733469 (ebook)
Subjects: LCSH: Political fiction. | GSAFD: Humorous fiction.
Classification: LCC PS3558.I217 S69 2020 | DDC 813/.54—dc23

This is a work of fiction. All names and characters are either invented or
used fictitiously, and the events described are mostly imaginary. However,
the proliferation of Burmese pythons throughout South Florida—and their
indiscriminate feeding habits—are accurately represented.

Jacket image: Python skin texture. VectorStock
Jacket design by John Gall

Manufactured in the United States of America
First Edition

In memory of my brother Rob

GET A GRIP

ONE

On the night of January twenty-third, unseasonably calm and warm, a woman named Kiki Pew Fitzsimmons went missing during a charity gala in the exclusive island town of Palm Beach, Florida.

Kiki Pew was seventy-two years old and, like most of her friends, twice widowed and wealthy beyond a need for calculation. With a check for fifty thousand dollars she had purchased a Diamond Patrons table at the annual White Ibis Ball. The event was the marquee fundraiser for the Gold Coast chapter of the IBS Wellness Foundation, a group globally committed to defeating Irritable Bowel Syndrome.

Mrs. Fitzsimmons had no personal experience with intestinal mayhem but she loved a good party. A fixture on the winter social circuit, she stood barely five feet tall and weighed eighty-eight pounds sopping wet. Her gowns were designed on Worth Avenue, her hair-and-makeup was done on Ocean Boulevard, and her show diamonds were cut on West 47th Street in Manhattan.

Kiki Pew's guests at the White Ibis Ball were three other widows, a pallid set of roommate bachelors and one married couple, the

McMarmots, whose clingy devotion after four decades of marriage was almost unbearable to observe. Kiki Pew spent little time at her table; a zealous mingler, she was also susceptible to Restless Legs Syndrome, another third-tier affliction with its own well-attended charity ball.

The last person to interact with Mrs. Fitzsimmons before she vanished was a Haitian bartender named Robenson, who under her hawk-eyed supervision had prepared a Tito's martini with the requisite orange zest and trio of olives speared longitudinally. It was not Kiki Pew's first cocktail of the evening. With cupped hands she ferried it from the high-domed ballroom into sprawling backyard gardens filled with avian-themed topiary—egrets, herons, raptors, cranes, wood storks and of course the eponymous ibis, its curly-beaked shadow elongated on the soft lawn by faux gaslight lanterns.

Inside the mansion, the other guests gathered for the raffle, which, for a grand prize, offered a private cruise to Cozumel that would inevitably be re-gifted to the winner's college-age grand-children in time for spring break. Alone with her vodka, Kiki Pew Fitzsimmons wended through the maze of bird shrubbery toward a spleen-shaped pond stocked with bright goldfish and bulbous koi. It was upon that silken bank where Kiki Pew's beaded clutch would later be discovered along with her martini glass and a broken rose-colored tab of Ecstasy.

The venue for the event was known as Lipid House, which in addition to its Mizner-era ballroom featured two dining halls, a cavernous upgraded kitchen, a library, a piano room, a fitness center, twenty-five bedrooms, nineteen-and-a-half baths, an indoor archery range, and Waterford hand-sanitizer dispensers in every hallway. Among Kiki Pew's retinue only the McMarmots were sober enough to organize a search, assisted somewhat perfunctorily by members of the service staff. It wasn't uncommon to find a missing party guest snoring on a toilet.

The door-to-door hunt for Mrs. Fitzsimmons interrupted an unsightly entwinement in a north-wing bedroom—the chromium-haired heiresses of two separate liquor fortunes, tag-teaming a dazed young polo star from Barcelona. Wordlessly the searchers turned away and moved on. There was no trace of Kiki Pew in the building.

The McMarmots proposed interviewing the bartender, but he was already gone. Robenson always endeavored to get off the island before midnight, unless he could hitch a ride with a white friend. Driving alone, Robenson had been pulled over so many times that he now paper-clipped his employment documents to the sun visor of his Taurus, for easy retrieval when quizzed by the Palm Beach cops.

The Fitzsimmons search party moved outdoors and boarded golf carts to scour the walled ten-acre estate. Because the area around the koi pond was faintly lit, no one spotted Kiki Pew's purse on the bank. After a fruitless hour spent calling her name, the McMarmots extended a theory that she must have drunk too much, forgot about her waiting driver from the car service, walked the quarter-mile home, and passed out. Kiki Pew's other companions embraced this scenario, for it also would explain why she wasn't answering her phone.

Nobody notified the authorities until the next morning, after Kiki Pew's housekeeper found her bed untouched, the cats unfed. Meanwhile, at Lipid House, the supervisor of the grounds crew was instructing his workers to mow carefully around the small purse, martini glass and the tiny broken pill on the grass.

The chief caretaker of the estate met the police at the gate and escorted them to the scene. It appeared to the officers that Mrs. Fitzsimmons had consumed half the tablet and either decided to have a swim, or accidentally toppled into the pond.

"Can you drag it ASAP?" the caretaker said. "We've got another event tonight."

The officers explained that the body of water was too small and inaccessible for a full-on dragging operation, which required motorboats. Shore divers were summoned instead. Groping through the brown muck and fish waste, they recovered numerous algae-covered champagne bottles, the rusty keys to a 1967 Coupe de Ville, and a single size-5 Louis Vuitton cross-pump, which the McMarmots somberly identified as the property of their missing friend.

Yet the corpse of Kiki Pew Fitzsimmons wasn't found, which perplexed the police due to the confined location. The sergeant on scene asked Mauricio, the supervisor of the Lipid House grounds-keepers, to continue watching the pond for a floater.

"Okay. Then what?" Mauricio said with a frown.

Katherine Sparling Pew began wintering in Palm Beach as a teen-ager. She was the eldest granddaughter of Dallas Austin Pew, of the aerosol Pews, who owned a four-acre spread on the island's north end.

It was there, at a sun-drenched party benefiting squamous-cell research, that Katherine met her first husband. His name was Huff Cornbright, of the antifreeze and real-estate Cornbrights, and he proposed on their third date. They were married on Gibson Beach at Sagaponack, Long Island, where the Pew family convened every summer with tenuously managed rancor. *The New York Times* chron-icled the Cornbright-Pew wedding with six colorless paragraphs and a scrapbook-worthy photograph of the joyful couple. Katherine used the occasion to unveil her chipper new nickname, a custom among post-debutante women of a certain upbringing.

Huff and Kiki Pew Cornbright settled in Westchester County, producing two trendily promiscuous offspring who made decent grades and therefore needed only six-figure donations from their parents to secure admission to their desired Ivies. The family was jolted when, at age fifty-three, Huff Cornbright perished on an autumn steelhead trip to British Columbia. Swept downstream while wading the Dean River, he foolishly clung to his twelve-hundred-dollar fly rod rather than reach for a low-hanging branch and haul himself to safety.

Kiki Pew unloaded the Westchester house but kept the places she and Huff had renovated in Cape Cod and Palm Beach. His ample life-insurance policy paid off both mortgages, which had outlived their usefulness as tax deductions. Meanwhile, the Cornbrights' now-grown sons had found suitable East Coast spouses to help liquefy their trust funds, freeing Kiki Pew to spread her wings without feeling the constant eye of filial judgment. She waited nearly one full year before seducing her Romanian tennis instructor, two years before officially dating eligible men her age, and four years to re-marry.

The man she chose was Mott Fitzsimmons, of the asbestos and textile Fitzsimmonses. A decade earlier he'd lost his first wife to an embolism while parasailing at Grand Cayman. Among prowling Palm Beach widows Mott was viewed as a prime catch because he was childless, which meant less holiday drama and no generational drain on his fortune.

He was lanky, silver-haired, seasonally Catholic and steeply neo-conservative. It was Kiki Pew's commiserative coddling that got him through the Obama years, though at times she feared that her excitable spouse might physically succumb from the day-to-day stress of having a black man in the Oval Office. What ultimately killed Mott Fitzsimmons was nonpartisan liver cancer, brought on by a stupendous lifetime intake of malt scotch.

Kiki Pew was consoled by the fact that her husband lived long enough to relish the election of a new president who was reliably white, old and scornful of social reforms. After Mott's death, with his croaky tirades still ringing in her bejeweled ears, Kiki Pew decided to join the POTUS Pussies, a group of Palm Beach women who proclaimed brassy loyalty to the new, crude-spoken commander-in-chief. For media purposes they had to tone down their name or risk being snubbed by the island's PG-rated social sheet, so in public they referred to themselves as the Potussies. Often they were invited to dine at Casa Bellicosa, the Winter White House, while the President was in residence. He always made a point of waving from the buffet line or pastry table. During the pandemic lockdown, he even Zoom-bombed the women during one of their cocktail-hour teleconferences.

News of Kiki Pew's disappearance at the IBS gala swept through the Potussies faster than a blast sales alert from Saks. The group's co-founder—Fay Alex Riptoad, of the compost and iron ore Riptoads—immediately dialed the private cell phone of the police chief, Jerry Crosby, who assured her that no resources would be spared in the effort to solve the case.

"We've already issued a Missing Persons bulletin to the media," the chief said. "I asked the state to do a Silver Alert, but—"

"Anybody can get a Silver Alert, even on the mainland," Fay Alex sniffed. "Isn't there a premium version for people like us? A Platinum Alert, something like that?"

"Silver is the highest priority, Mrs. Riptoad. However, it's only for seniors who go missing in vehicles." Crosby had learned the hard way never to use the term "elderly" when speaking with the Palm Beach citizenry. "Since Mrs. Fitzsimmons wasn't driving the other night, the best they can do is a Missing Persons bulletin."

Fay Alex said, "You didn't give out her real age to the media, did you? There's no call for that. And which picture of her did you post?"

"We're required to list the age provided by her family. One of her sons sent us a photo from a family gathering on Christmas Day."

"A *morning* picture? Oh, dear God." Fay Alex groaned; noon was the absolute earliest that Kiki Pew allowed herself to be seen by civilians.

When the police chief inquired if Mrs. Fitzsimmons was known to use psychoactive drugs, Fay Alex threatened to have him sacked.

"How can you even ask such a vicious question?" she cried.

"A pill was found among your friend's belongings, next to the fish pond. Actually, part of a pill. Our expert says it was bitten in half."

"For heaven's sake, Kiki was on blood-pressure meds. Who isn't! She kept hers in a cute little Altoids tin."

The chief said, "The fragment we found wasn't high-blood pressure medicine. It was MDMA."

"What in the world are you talking about?"

"On the street they call it Ecstasy, Mrs. Riptoad."

"Ecstasy!" she yipped. "That's the most ludicrous thing I've ever heard. Kiki Pew, of all the girls, wouldn't have a clue where to get something like that."

In fact, Kiki Pew Fitzsimmons knew exactly where to get something like that—from her tennis pro, with whom she had resumed bi-weekly lessons soon after Mott passed away. Kiki enjoyed the MDMA high, which lasted for hours and kept her energized even after too many drinks. She had come to believe that the pill gave her a strategic edge at posh island functions, where most attendees began to fade and ramble by nine-thirty, ten at the latest.

"One bad side effect of the drug," Jerry Crosby explained to Fay Alex Riptoad, "is a sensation of overheating. Users tend to feel hot and sweaty even when it's chilly outdoors. That might explain why Mrs. Fitzsimmons went into the water—to cool off."

"Then where's the body? I seriously doubt the koi ate her."

"The pond is very murky. It's possible our divers couldn't see her under the surface. We'll know for sure in a day or two, when . . . well, we'll know."

"Kiki Pew is *not* a druggie," Fay Alex re-asserted, "and I won't listen to another word of this insulting rubbish. Here's a radical idea, Jerry: Just do your fucking job. Find her!"

That evening, the Potussies gamely dressed up and gathered at Casa Bellicosa. They left an empty chair where Kiki Pew Fitzsimmons usually sat, and ordered a round of Tito's martinis in her honor. Other club members stopped by the table to express support and seek updates.

"Oh, I'll bet our little Keek is just fine," one man said to Fay Alex. "She probably got confused and wandered off somewhere. My dear Ellie does that from time to time."

"Your dear Ellie has Stage 5 dementia. Kiki Pew does not."

"The onset can be subtle."

Fay Alex said, "Let's all stay positive, shall we?"

"But I am," the man replied, canting an eyebrow. "Being mixed-up and lost is *positively* better than being dead at the bottom of a fish pond, no?"

During the yard crew's lunch break, Mauricio noticed that one of the large standing mowers had been abandoned, its throaty motor idling, on the Lipid House croquet lawn.

"Where the hell is Jesús?" Mauricio shouted to the others. "He knows he can't leave the Hoosker there!"

Hoosker was the crew's nickname for the big Husqvarna stand-on, twenty kick-ass horses and the sweetest turning radius in the trade.

"Jesús he gone," said one of the men.

"What do you mean gone? He just quit and walked off?"

"Not walk. He run."

"What the fuck," Mauricio said. "Which way did he go?"

The man pointed.

Mauricio stared. "What are you saying—he climbed the damn wall?"

"He just jump from Hoosker and haul ass," the man said. "I don't know why, boss."

Mauricio walked over to the tall stucco wall and examined the fresh scrapes in the ivy showing the path of Jesús's hasty ascent.

"Crazy fool," Mauricio muttered. Then to the others he yelled: "Move that hot mower and get a hose on those treadmarks! *Ahora!*"

Ten miles away on the mainland, in a neighborhood of modest duplexes, Jesús's wife knew something was wrong the moment he walked in the door.

"What is it?" she asked.

"They're going to fire me, Gloria." He told her everything, the words spilling out.

"*Dios mío!*" she cried. "What did Mauricio say?"

"I spoke to no one."

"But you've got to go back and warn them!"

"I can't do that, Gloria. You know why."

"The police are there? I don't understand."

Jesús shrugged dismally. "They are searching for that missing woman."

Gloria fell silent. Her husband was undocumented. He could be in serious trouble if police detectives started interviewing the yard workers at Lipid House. Maybe they'd ask to see a visa, maybe they wouldn't.

These were perilous times. Jesús's young brother, Esteban, was currently in government custody awaiting deportation. The week after Christmas, he'd been detained during the pre-dawn raid of a 7-Eleven in Wellington, handcuffed by armed ICE agents while he was repairing the Slurpee machine.

Gloria fixed a ham-and-pork sandwich for Jesús. She asked if there was a chance to save his job.

"No way," he answered morosely. "I left my mower with the engine running."

"In gear?"

"God, no! In neutral."

"So then, that's good. There's no damage done," his wife said.

"But it was parked on that bentgrass lawn where they do the croquet."

"What is croquet, Jesús?"

"Where they chase the colored balls around with hammers. The grass is soft and *muy caro*."

"Oh, no!"

"I was scared," he said. "So I just jumped off the machine and—"

"But you're sure about what you saw?"

"Yes, Gloria. It's something I will never forget."

"*Es horrible.*"

"Why do you think I ran?"

Jesús pushed his sandwich away after two bites. His wife made the sign of the cross as she whispered a prayer.

Somebody knocked at the door. "Are you there, Jesús? Open up!"

It was Mauricio. Gloria let him in and went to the bedroom, leaving the two men alone.

Jesús said, "I'm sorry, boss."

"The catalytic converter on the Hoosker, it burned a damn patch on the croquet field."

"You can take it out of my last day's pay."

Mauricio shook his head. "No, I told Teabull it was a mechanical problem."

Tripp Teabull was the chief caretaker of Lipid House, and he understood nothing about the exhaust systems of stand-on mowers.

"Did he believe you?" Jesús asked.

"*Por supuesto.* They're already re-sodding the lawn."

"Thank you, boss."

"Tell me what happened, and maybe you still have a job."

Jesús said, "It doesn't matter. I can't ever return to that place."

Mauricio, who was aware of the plight of Jesús's brother, promised to deal guardedly with the police. He said, "There's no reason to give out your name."

"It's not only that, boss. I can't go back there again because of what I saw."

"I need to know."

"You'll say I'm crazy."

"I'm the head groundskeeper. Or did you already forget?"

"If I tell you . . ." Jesús looked up at the wooden crucifix on the wall. Then his chin dropped.

"Was it the missing woman you saw?" Mauricio asked.

Jesús shuddered and said, "Sort of."

TWO

The Otter Falls subdivision was on the westernmost outskirts of Boca Raton. A small drab gatehouse marked the entrance. The young, thick-tongued guard said nobody named Angela Armstrong was on the vendor/contractor list. Angie said she wasn't a vendor/contractor; she was a specialist.

"What's that in the back of your truck?" the guard asked.

"Capture noose. Bungie cords. Road kennel."

"I meant the gun."

"Gas-propelled rifle. Shoots tranquilizer darts."

"For real? No effin' way."

"Doubt I'll need it today," Angie said. "A man named Fleck left a message asking me to come right away. Unless there's another Otter Falls around here . . ."

"This is the only one I heard of."

"Wild guess: No otters and no waterfall."

The guard rubbed his fleshy chin. "It's just that Mr. Fleck didn't call and put your name on the list."

"That's because he didn't have my name," said Angie. "All he had was a number."

Drowsily the guard shook his head. "Sorry. It's the rules."

"I believe you're baked."

"What! No way."

"Sir, there's a vape pen in the pocket of your uniform."

The guard sheepishly moved the pen out of sight. "I am *totally* legal," he said. His mouth had gone dry. "I got my state card and everything. The weed is for migraines."

Angie smiled. "I'd get stoned, too, cooped up all day in this glorified outhouse. But at least they gave you a/c. Some of these homeowners' associations, they're so cheap they make the guards roast in the heat."

"I can't let you in. That's how the dude before me got fired."

"Understood. So, if Mr. Fleck calls up asking where I am, please tell him you did your job and turned me away." Angie put the truck in reverse. "Also, tell him good luck with that raccoon."

As Angie backed up, the stoner guard scrambled out of the booth waving at her: "Yo, ma'am, wait! I didn't know that's why you were here."

She poked her head out the truck. "The noose wasn't a clue?"

"The Flecks are in Building D, number 158." He raised the gate and motioned for the specialist to drive through.

"Rock on," Angie said as she drove past.

Jonathan Fleck was pacing the sidewalk in front of the townhouse. His wife and kids had barricaded themselves in an upstairs bedroom while the wild raccoon ransacked the kitchen.

"It must've broke in through the back door," Fleck said as he led Angie inside.

The living room was neat and newly renovated. White walls and pale furniture made it feel less cramped. Fleck was dressed up for a legit job—navy slacks, white shirt, club necktie. Obviously the guy worked Saturdays, so Angie figured he must be in sales—new cars maybe, or household audio components.

Fleck took out a handgun, which he passed to Angie saying, "I couldn't do the deed myself. Truth is I've never fired this thing."

It was a Glock nine, of course, the favored armament of modern white suburbanites. Angie made sure the safety was on before placing the weapon on a hallway table. She went back to her truck, rigged the capture noose and put on some long canvas gloves.

"Can I watch?" Fleck asked.

"No, sir. You get hurt, I lose my insurance."

"All right. But at least can I ask how much is this gonna cost?"

"Four hundred dollars," Angie replied.

"You're shitting me."

"Five-fifty, if it's a female with little ones."

"Unbelievable," Fleck muttered. "You take plastic?"

"Effortlessly."

The pudgy raccoon sat splay-legged on its haunches, finishing a Triscuit. It growled at Angie while nimbly plucking another cracker from the box. The animal's furry dome of a tummy was evidence of a prolonged feast. The kitchen was a wreck—the cabinet doors had been flung open, the countertops strewn with rice, raisins, dry macaroni, granola, flour, pistachios and Lucky Charms. A half-eaten blueberry Pop-Tart extruded from a toaster that the raccoon had unplugged and dragged to the floor.

Angie noticed the animal eyeing her long-handled noose.

"Sorry, *compadre*," she said, "but we gotta take a ride."

From the hallway came a voice: "Don't you need to shoot it so they can test for rabies?"

"It's not rabid, sir. Just cheeky."

Behind Angie, the swinging kitchen door moved. It was Fleck, holding the damn Glock again.

He whispered, "I thought you could use some backup."

"Back your ass up those stairs," Angie told him, "and wait with your family."

Transferring the raccoon to the truck was, as usual, a clamorous enterprise. Plenty of bare-fanged snapping and writhing—Angie's trousers saved her shins from being shredded. Afterward the Fleck children emerged with upraised phones to snap photos of the sulking intruder inside the transport kennel.

Angie shook off her gloves and processed Fleck's AmEx with her mobile card reader, which rejected it on three attempts.

"Your chip slot isn't working," Fleck protested.

"It works fine," said Angie.

"Then there's some sort of screwup by American Express." Fleck was striving to appear more irritated than embarrassed. "I'm afraid I don't have four hundred in cash on me. Will you take a personal check?"

"Don't even go there."

"So . . . what happens if I can't pay you right now?"

"What happens is I re-deposit this unruly creature in your domicile."

"You're joking, right?"

"No, Señor Fuckwhistle, I am not."

"I went from 'sir' to 'Señor Fuckwhistle?'"

Angie put on her gloves again. "I didn't come here to get stiffed. This bad boy's going straight back to the kitchen."

Fleck bolted inside to fetch his wife's MasterCard, which sailed through Angie's reader on the first try. Angie promised to email a receipt.

After departing Otter Falls, she drove all the way to the Seminole reservation at Big Cypress. There were closer places to have staged the release, but she enjoyed the long ride across the blond saw grass marsh. It was a rare stretch of South Florida interstate with a view that wasn't savagely depressing.

Angie took the Snake Road exit and continued north to an area with lots of tall timber and relatively few hunters. When she reached down to unlatch the door of the carry kennel, the raccoon huffed at her. She stepped back and saluted as the animal grumpily walked into the woods. In a perfect world, it would never again catch the scent of a Pop-Tart.

For a while Angie cruised slowly along the back roads of the reservation, hoping to see a panther or a bear. She didn't get home until seven-thirty. Joel was sitting in her TV chair watching a PBS special about calving glaciers.

"I thought this was your dad's weekend," said Angie.

"He asked me to skip his turn."

"Ah. The equestrian must be visiting."

"Actually, they're living together now," Joel said.

"Well, well."

"And she can't ride for a while. She got thrown and cracked her pelvis."

"Ouch. What's your old man going to do for fun? Or should I say who?"

"She's getting around pretty good. You want a drink, Mom?"

Joel fixed her the usual, a tall gin-and-tonic. He showed up every other weekend, as if there was court-ordered custody sharing. He and Angie joked about it. She felt good that her grown ex-stepson still cared enough to hang out with her. A while had passed since Joel's father, Dustin, had divorced her. It had happened when Angie still worked for the state.

The kid had been a senior at FSU when she left for prison, fourteen months at Gadsden Correctional. On Angie's orders, Joel didn't visit. Soon after graduating, he moved back south and began alternating weekends between his dad's place in West Palm and Angie's apartment in Lake Worth. Sometimes he brought along a girlfriend, and sometimes the girlfriend showed promise.

"Tell me some stories," he said to Angie.

"Well, let's see. I had a fragrant morning in Margate, your basic dead opossum-under-a-porch. Next call was two feral cats behind the funeral home in Coral Springs, then a raccoon at a townhouse in West Boca."

"Dumpster coon?"

"Break-in artist. Big sucker, too."

Joel, who'd majored in business, had helped Angie Armstrong

set up her critter-removal company, Discreet Captures. He'd even ordered magnetized signs for her truck, though Angie removed them because people kept flagging her down to ask if she was one of those TV bounty hunters.

Joel said, "Let's grab dinner."

"I need to clean up first."

He pinched his nose and said, "Take all the time you need."

When Angie stepped out of the shower, her phone was ringing. The caller ID showed the 561 area code. A man on the other end identified himself as "Tripp Teabull, with two P's." He said he managed the Lipid estate in Palm Beach.

Angie asked, "Did Mr. Lipid die and leave me some money?"

"Not *that* kind of estate. It's a private compound on the island."

"So you would be the caretaker."

"Manager," Teabull said tautly. "We need you out here right away."

"It's late, sir, and I have a dinner date," Angie said. "Tell me what you've got."

"What we've got is a nightmare."

"No offense, but everyone who calls me says that."

"Does everyone who calls offer you a fee of two thousand dollars?"

Angie stepped back into her dirty khakis.

"The address, please," she said.

She drove up the driveway of Lipid House and pulled into the valet line. Moments later a brawny, brick-headed fellow in a pale tuxedo approached her truck and asked to see her invitation.

"I have none, sir."

"You must be at the wrong place. This is the Stars-and-SARS event." The man wore an ear bud, and a peanut microphone clipped to his lapel. He said, "Please turn this vehicle around and leave."

Angie said she'd been summoned by the manager of the estate. "He made it sound like an emergency," she added.

Brick Head relayed this information to his lapel and awaited instructions. Dutifully he stayed beside the pickup as Angie inched forward in the valet line. Ahead of them, couples were emerging with varying degrees of fragility from limousines, hired sedans and private luxury cars. Angie noted an absence of SUVs, which are impossible to exit gracefully in formal wear. All the women wore long gowns; evidently the men had been ordered not to deviate from tuxes.

Finally Brick Head tapped on Angie's windshield and said, "Mr. Teabull wants you at the service gate right away. You'll definitely need to turn around."

But Angie was too far along for that; in her rearview glowed a train of headlights stretching all the way to the road. Brick Head attempted to create a gap in the line, but the hunched white-haired driver of the Jaguar glued to Angie's bumper refused to yield, defiantly rolling up his window when the security man approached.

The procession moved slowly toward the portico, where an elaborate ice sculpture spelled out "Stars for SARS!" above a foaming neon-blue fountain. Brick Head slipped into the shadows as Angie's pickup—caked with swamp mud from the raccoon transport—began attracting comments. When she braked to a stop beside the ice sculpture, the valets reacted with wary reserve. None ventured forward, so Angie cranked up the radio and waited.

A person that could only be Tripp Teabull appeared, roughly shoving one of the valets toward the truck. As soon as Angie stepped out, Teabull hustled her away from the curious guests.

On the veering golf-cart ride through the topiary, she asked, "Who are tonight's 'stars'?"

"Pardon me?"

"I know SARS is the disease, but who are the stars?"

"Technically SARS is not a disease, it's an illness," Teabull said. "The stars? Well, let's see—Dr. Oz, Jack Hanna, Ann Coulter, and a former Mrs. Ron Perelman. They're all on-site this evening."

Angie whistled. "*That* is a recipe for crazy."

Teabull parked beside a pond that was dimpled by cruising goldfish. Instead of yellow crime tape, purple velvet ropes had been strung through brass stanchions to secure the area to be avoided. Patrolling the perimeter were Brick Head and several other body-builder types. At Teabull's command, one of the guards unclipped a segment of the cordon so that Angie and the caretaker could enter. They crossed a soft flawless lawn to a corner of the property illuminated by triangulated mobile floods. The powerful white beams were fixed high in a lush old banyan tree.

Teabull pointed needlessly with his own puny flashlight. "See?"

"Impressive," Angie said.

"How quickly can you get that thing out of here? We've promised the guests a nighttime croquet match. The glow sticks are already fastened to the mallets. Where's the rest of your team?"

"I don't have a team, sir."

Teabull gave Angie the same up-and-down she always got, being female, five-foot-three and barely a hundred pounds. Usually she didn't need assistance on a job. This time would be different.

She said, "I'll come back in the morning with some help. Meanwhile don't let that sucker out of your sight."

Teabull blanched. "No, we can't wait! Whatever needs to happen, make it happen *now*."

Angie was staring up at one of the largest pythons she'd ever seen, and she'd seen some jumbos. This one had arranged its muscular length on a long horizontal limb. The reptile was deep into a post-meal stupor; a grotesque lump was visible halfway between the mid-section and tail.

"Anybody missing a goat?" Angie asked.

"Mauricio will help you handle this," said Teabull, and introduced the head groundskeeper.

Mauricio looked as if he'd rather be in the front row at a German opera. He told Angie that one of his mowing crew had spotted the giant snake in the tree that afternoon.

"It hasn't moved an inch since then," he said.

"We're hoping the damn thing is dead," Teabull added anxiously.

"Oh, it's the opposite of dead," Angie informed him. "It's digesting."

The trunk of the ancient banyan presented a dense maze of vertical roots. Angie wasn't wearing the right shoes for such a slippery climb.

"I'll need an extension ladder," she told Mauricio, "and a pistol."

From Teabull: "Absolutely no gunfire at this event!"

"Well, we're looking at about eighteen feet of violent non-cooperation," Angie explained. "The recommended approach is a bullet in the brain."

"Hell, no! You'll have to do it another way."

"Then *you* will have to find another wrangler."

The band had started playing—Cuban music, a well-meaning tribute to the Buena Vista Social Club. Soon the guests would be twirling drunkenly all over the grounds. Teabull wore the face of a climber trapped on a melting ledge.

"Five thousand cash," he whispered to Angie. "But we're running out of time."

Angie put a hand on Mauricio's shoulder and said, "Sir, would you happen to have a machete?"

The Burmese python is one of the world's largest constrictors, reaching documented lengths of more than twenty feet. Popular among amateur collectors, the snakes were imported to the United States legally from Southeast Asia for decades. But because a hungry baby python can grow into an eight-foot eating machine within a year, owners often found themselves having second thoughts. Consequently, scores of the pet snakes were set free.

Only in southern Florida did the species take hold, the hot climate and abundance of prey being ideal for python reproduction. A relatively isolated population exploded to a full-blown invasion during the early 1990s, after Hurricane Andrew destroyed a reptile breeding facility on the edge of the Everglades. The storm liberated fresh, fertile multitudes, and today the Burmese is one of the state's most prolific and disruptive invasive species. An adult female can lay as many as ninety eggs, which she will encircle and guard from predators.

Like all constrictors, pythons encoil their prey, squeezing the breath out of it. By disengaging their jaws, the snakes are able to swallow animals of much larger girth, which are typically consumed head-first. In this way the furtive intruders have decimated native Everglades wildlife, including marsh rabbits, raccoons, otters, opossums, and full-grown deer. Adult Burmese pythons will even drown and devour alligators. To the chagrin of suburban Floridians, pythons will leave the wetlands to travel long distances. Frequently they are discovered prowling residential neighborhoods, the signal clue being a sharp dip in the cat population.

To stem the onslaught, authorities have recruited both lay hunters and experienced reptile handlers by offering hourly wages and bounty payments that escalate per foot of snake. While the frenetic capture videos are wildly popular on YouTube, the removal program has so far proven to be biologically inconsequential. Although hundreds of pythons have been caught and removed, biologists believe that many thousands more are still on the loose, mating insatiably.

Despite their startling size, individual specimens aren't easy to find. Their skin is lightly hued, with chocolate-brown patches creating puzzle-board patterns similar to that of a giraffe. Even the beefiest of pythons can be astonishingly well-camouflaged in the wild, and experts cite their "low detectability" as a primary challenge for hunters.

"Where the hell did it come from?" Tripp Teabull grumbled about the one in the tree. "And why did it show up here, of all places?"

"Sir, you've got a pond full of slow, dumb fish. However, *that*"— Angie cocked her trigger finger at the exceptional lump in the python—"is something else."

Mauricio and a co-worker arrived with a ladder that unfolded to twenty feet. With Angie's assistance they notched one end into a cabled tangle of banyan branches directly beneath the quarry, which remained motionless.

"You think there's more of those fuckers around here?" Mauricio asked.

Angie said this was the first one she'd ever heard of on the island. "What do you suppose she ate?"

The groundskeeper exchanged a tense glance with Teabull. "How do you know it's a she?" he asked Angie.

"The biggest ones always are."

"Then maybe she didn't eat anything," Teabull cut in. "Maybe she's just pregnant."

Angie chuckled. "Sir, that's *not* a baby bump."

Scientists in the Everglades have implanted transmitters in captured pythons and released them to help locate "breeding aggregations," groups of randy males that communally cavort with a lone large female. That telemetry tracking has led to the interruption of many amorous assemblies but, so far, it has failed to stop the epochal march of the species. Although many pythons were found dead one winter after a rare hard freeze, the hardy survivors rebounded and—thanks to natural selection—produced new generations able to withstand colder temperatures. Nonetheless, Palm Beach County, which on some January nights experiences temperatures in the thirties, was believed to be safely north of the invaders' comfort zone.

"We should fill in that damn koi pond," Teabull said, "if that's the big attraction."

Angie asked him if any domestic animals were allowed to roam the grounds of Lipid House. Teabull said absolutely not.

Mauricio spoke up. "We got a few iguanas. Everybody's got iguanas."

"Have any neighbors complained that their pets have gone missing? Like maybe a Rottweiler," Angie said, "or a miniature pony."

"That's not funny," Teabull snapped.

"Sir, I'm serious." Angie's habit of saying "sir" was the result of a childhood rule imposed by her father, whose own father had been a career Marine. She said, "These snakes feed only on live prey. Are you sure no animals have disappeared in the neighborhood?"

Teabull shot another uneasy look at Mauricio before saying, "I'll ask around."

Angie turned to the groundskeeper. "All right, let's see that blade of yours."

Because of their gluttonous threat to Florida's shaky ecological balance, all captured pythons are supposed to be euthanized. A gunshot is the most humane way, but another state-approved method is decapitation by machete. The one that Mauricio loaned to Angie Armstrong was practically new.

Teabull said, "One more thing, Ms. Armstrong. Could you please move that thing off-site before you kill it?"

"Sir, I'm loving your sense of humor."

"There are nine hundred guests here tonight!"

"Okay, we'll do it your way," Angie said. "But I'll need four of your strongest security guys to help me wrestle it out of the tree. My experience is that large men are often terrified of snakes, so please find me a crew that isn't. FYI, their tuxedos are going to get trashed big-time. A python that size shits like a fire hose."

As he eyed the immense silent presence up in the banyan, Teabull reconsidered his position. Trying to take the beast alive would turn into a spectacle. The wrangler was right—an inconspicuous removal would be possible only if the snake was limp and unresisting. In other words: dead.

Teabull sought assurances from Angie that the act could be carried out quietly, and with a minimum of gore.

She said, "I'll try not to bloody your landscaping."

Her tone rankled the caretaker, whose priority was to prevent guests from learning of the reptile's presence on the property. The fallout would be devastating.

Hosting parties, weddings and fundraising galas such as the White Ibis and "Stars for SARS" was a lucrative industry in Palm Beach. Competition among mansions had always been intense, but it had turned cutthroat after the social drought inflicted by Covid-19. This was supposed to be the season of the big rebound. Owners of old island estates were counting on event revenue to offset their overhead—parabolic property taxes, criminally priced hurricane insurance and six-figure landscaping fees. Half the fucking pool boys drove Audis.

Sponsors of charity balls were seldom fazed to learn that the one-night rental fee for Lipid House was a quarter of a million dollars, not including custom catering. However, rumors of goliath pythons could wipe out a season's worth of bookings. The five grand that Teabull had offered the female wildlife wrangler was a bargain; the trust that owned the estate had been prepared to pay ten.

Still, the machete and all its messy possibilities made Teabull nervous. In particular he was fretting about that dowager-sized lump in the snake.

"So, you'll be cutting off its head," he pressed Angie Armstrong, "and that's all, correct? No further chopping."

"Sir, I'm not fixing cutlets. I'm neutralizing an invasive."

Angie hated to kill anything, but the magnificent python had signed its own warrant. Dead or alive, it would be delivered to wildlife officers. The next stop was a biologist's dissection table. Angie expected to collect no bounty for the specimen because Palm Beach was outside the state's hunt-for-pay zone.

"We've moved your vehicle to our rear gate," Teabull informed her, "to expedite the departure phase. Is there anything else you need?"

"A backhoe would be swell," Angie said.

Teabull hoped she was joking. "I'll leave you to your work," he said, receding into the cover of the topiary.

"Wait—what about my money?"

"Your fee will be in the console of your vehicle, Ms. Armstrong."

"Just call it a pickup truck, sir. That's what it is."

But Teabull had already slipped out of earshot. Mauricio steadied the ladder while Angie climbed.

The machete was sharp. It worked fine.

THREE

The Cornbright spawn arrived the following morning at their missing mother's house. They were met by Fay Alex Riptoad towing the police chief, whose presentation was brief: The statewide Missing Persons alert had generated a dozen false sightings and one random marriage proposal, in the event Kiki Pew was found alive. Other tips, none especially promising, were being pursued.

At Mrs. Riptoad's instruction, the chief didn't tell the two Cornbrights about the half-eaten Ecstasy tab found by the pond. He likewise avoided the subject of the tennis pro, who'd been interviewed and cleared of suspicion. (At the time of Kiki Pew's disappearance, young Constantin was entertaining one of the other Potussies aboard a chartered Falcon, somewhere in the skies between Jackson Hole and Lantana.)

"We're doing everything possible to locate your mom," Jerry Crosby said to the Cornbright sons. "Did either of you speak with her that day?"

The answer was no, although each claimed to have left voicemails on her cell phone. That was bullshit, as the chief well knew, for Kiki

Pew's Samsung had been found in her purse. The device held no messages from Chance or Chase.

Both had distanced themselves from their mother after she married Mott Fitzsimmons, who perceptively viewed his stepsons as lazy trust-fund sucklings. Following Mott's death they and their families began turning up in Palm Beach more frequently, usually on short notice. Their wives were gratingly deferential, their children unremarkable in every aspect. Kiki Pew feigned a doting attitude though she never embraced the role of grandmother. As for her sons, she remained wary of—and occasionally amused by—their competitive campaigns to re-connect.

On some level, Chance and Chase cared about their mother and were alarmed by her disappearance. However, their emotions were also steered by the knowledge that their deceased stepfather had left no lineal descendants. That meant his wealth had streamed directly to the already-loaded Kiki Pew, whose only heirs were Chance and Chase themselves. It couldn't be presumed that the windfall from Kiki Pew's future passing would be divided evenly, for she evaded the subject in family conversation. As a result, her sons had been jockeying artlessly for her favor since the day Mott Fitzsimmons died.

"Was your mom a good swimmer?" the police chief asked.

On this topic the Cornbright brothers disagreed. The tie was broken by Fay Alex Riptoad, who bragged that her friend was "quick as a harp seal" in the lap pool at Casa Bellicosa.

Jerry Crosby excused himself and drove to Lipid House, where he was perturbed to find nobody watching the koi pond. He walked the shoreline and observed schools of chubby fish lolling near the surface, but no deceased widow.

Had it been summertime, the chief thought, a corpse would have surfaced by now. However, today's forecasted high was only sixty-eight degrees, which meant it was cool enough at the bottom of the pond to forestall post-mortem bloating. A new diver was summoned to do a second search. She, too, came up empty-handed except for a be-slimed magnum of Dom.

Crosby was puzzled. If Mrs. Fitzsimmons didn't drown, then what the hell happened?

Soon the caretaker Teabull appeared, saying he'd been at meetings off-property all morning. He blamed the head groundskeeper for failing to station cadaver scouts around the water.

"Nobody on the staff has come across anything unusual?" Crosby asked.

"So far, no." If questioned on this point later, Teabull would argue that, in Florida, a snake in a tree could hardly be classified as a police matter. The whole damn peninsula was crawling with reptiles.

He said, "We had had the usual level of security here for the Ibis Ball—team of six, all ex-military. One of them used to bodyguard for Pink."

"Really?" The police chief actually smiled. "I'm a big Floyd fan."

"Not Pink Floyd. Just 'Pink.'"

When Crosby stared back at him blankly, Teabull said, "She's a major female recording artist. Huge. Point is, no intruder could've slipped past our team. The property was totally secure on the night Mrs. Fitzsimmons turned up missing."

The chief nodded though his gaze kept drifting to the koi pond. "Let's say she's not in the water, Mr. Teabull. What do you think could've happened?"

"Maybe she decided to leave the grounds and walk . . . wherever."

"Wearing one shoe?"

"She'd had numerous vodka drinks and a dose of Ecstasy. I've seen people with less crap in their system strip naked and bark at the moon."

"But your security guys—"

"Their job is to keep uninvited individuals out of the event—not to stop our guests from leaving," the caretaker said. "Besides, Mrs. Fitzsimmons had a driver waiting. They would have assumed she was heading for her car."

This time Jerry Crosby didn't nod. "So let's say she makes her way to the street, starts walking for unknown reasons in an unknown direction and then . . . something really bad happens. In *this* neighborhood—the most crime-free zip code in forty-eight states."

Teabull frowned. "This is the new reality. No place—even the island—is one hundred percent safe anymore."

In his python panic, the caretaker hadn't coached himself for the possibility that local law enforcement might devote extra effort to the case of a missing Potussy. The police chief seemed annoyed to see there were no video cameras mounted on the grounds.

"Surveillance devices would make the guests uneasy," Teabull explained. "This isn't a Nordstrom's at the outlet mall. Nobody's stealing our flatware, Chief Crosby."

Which was totally untrue. Some of the town's richest geezers were avid kleptos. Pocket-sized shit disappeared from Lipid House during every gala—the Sumatran teak cocktail forks, Baccarat salt shakers, scotch-infused toothpicks, even the fucking porcelain coasters. The problem had gotten so bad that Teabull now replaced purloined valuables with cheap knockoffs, and instructed all catering firms to double-count their knives and spoons before departing.

The chief said: "We've interviewed all the other nearby property owners. Nobody saw Mrs. Fitzsimmons in the neighborhood during or after your event."

Teabull forced a chuckle. "That's not surprising. Everybody's in bed or passed out drunk by nine."

Crosby said most of the residents had home-security systems with high-resolution cameras. "Once we collect all the tapes, we'll basically have the whole street covered for that night, from several angles."

"Well, there's a lucky break." Teabull suppressed an impulse to vomit in the ferns.

The chief put on his sunglasses and fished the car keys from a pocket. He said, "So far, Mrs. Fitzsimmons hasn't shown up in any of the videos we've reviewed. There's no indication she ever got outside these walls."

Teabull wanly made a one-armed motion toward the goldfish pond. "I'll make sure Mauricio posts some men along the bank."

"Please do that. It's unusual for us to make two dives in a private body of water and not locate the victim. Mrs. Riptoad gave you my direct number, right?"

"Yes, of course. Twice, actually."

As he watched Jerry Crosby drive away, Teabull was clammy and gut-sick. He felt much better after making a phone call.

Joel had gone back to his father's house, though not before cleaning Angie's apartment and re-stocking the kitchen. She turned on the television, muted the volume, removed a fresh syringe from the refrigerator, kicked off her clothes, and gave herself a tetanus shot in the hip.

Goddamn opossum.

She should have worn the canvas gloves. Rookie mistake, reaching barehanded into a crevice of a hoarder's cluttered attic. Contrary to popular lore, cornered opossums don't always play opossum; this one had sunk its teeth into Angie. For a professional wildlife wrangler, getting chomped by one of nature's slowest, most nearsighted creatures was embarrassing.

My own damn fault, Angie thought, buttering her punctured left forearm with antibiotic cream. She'd released her captive in an orange grove near Bluefield. It was a calmed critter now, as was the hoarder.

Angie's phone rang, as it usually did at six p.m. Her nightly death threat.

"Hello, Pruitt," she said.

"Listen, bitch, I'm gonna hunt you down and rip out your fucking spleens!"

"Only got one, pal." Last night it was her livers, also plural.

"Yeah, then after? I'm gonna chop off your legs and feed 'em to my dogs!"

"Not the Bichon, for God's sake," Angie said. "They've got tiny stomachs, Pruitt. Give 'em to that big-ass Labradoodle instead. Name's Fritz, right? Feed 'em to Fritz."

"Fuck you, lady! Your time's up."

"Have a pleasant evening, sir."

Pruitt was the reason Angie had lost her job as a wildlife officer and gone to prison. One spring evening, while Angie was patrolling the lee shore of Lake Okeechobee, she watched aghast through binoculars as an obviously drunken fuckstick drove an airboat over a baby deer standing in the shallows.

The fuckstick was Pruitt, and he wasn't too intoxicated to circle back and collect the dying fawn for dinner. As soon as Pruitt unsheathed his butcher knife, Angie moved in for the arrest.

Then—somewhere between the crime scene and the boat ramp—Pruitt lost one of his hands by forcible trauma. Angie told the paramedics that her prisoner had slipped the zip ties and jumped overboard, startling a large alligator. Pruitt's version of the incident was quite different. He claimed that Angie had sought out the reptile, into whose gaping maw she'd inserted Pruitt's left fist, the one that had been holding his knife.

Angie eventually resigned, pleading guilty to one felony count of aggravated assault and one misdemeanor charge of illegally feeding wildlife. The gator in question was a popular dock denizen nicknamed Lola. Over the years she'd received so many chicken bones and marshmallows from clueless tourists that she eagerly approached every occupied vessel she saw, expecting a handout.

Which is literally what she got, in Pruitt's case.

Ironically, the amputation served to benefit the poacher when he went to court for killing the deer. Not wishing to be viewed as a hard-ass on the handicapped, the judge sentenced Pruitt to probation and a token $100 fine. However, his beloved airboat was confiscated, and that—more than the missing hand—fueled his ongoing fury toward Angela Armstrong. Every new call displayed a different area code and phone number, Pruitt being skilled at spoofing caller

IDs. His punctuality was also impressive, and somewhat uncharacteristic of redneck whack jobs.

Still, after so much time and still no attempts on her life, Angie found it hard to take the man seriously. She did, as a precaution, keep tabs on Pruitt's whereabouts, job status, bank loans and registered vehicles. Fortunately she still had data-savvy friends at the sheriff's office. The info on Pruitt's dogs came from veterinary vaccination records.

Angie showered and drove to Applebee's with an eye on her rearview. Nobody followed her. She sat in a corner, and ordered a salad and iced tea. When the server inquired about the bandage on her arm, Angie told him she'd had a gaping skin biopsy. It was a line devised to end the conversation, yet instead it elicited an overlong monologue in support of homeopathic cancer remedies. Angie made a mental note to wear long-sleeved shirts in public until the opossum bite healed.

She skipped dessert and returned home. The door was unlocked, the apartment ransacked.

Angie sighed and said, "Well, fuck a duck."

For years her stepson had told her she was a dumbass for renting on the first floor, even if it saved seventy bucks a month. Still, this was the first successful break-in. Entry had been achieved at the rear of the building, through a bathroom window. A glossy imprint of the burglar's large right sneaker was visible in the tub.

By the time the cops arrived, Angie had taken inventory. Her main concern was the money from the Lipid House python job, five thousand in fifties. The cash sat untouched, inside a white box marked "Wound Care" that Angie kept in a cabinet under the kitchen sink.

The only items missing from the apartment were her laptop and checkbook.

A Taser that she hid under the mattress was on the floor, near the foot of the bed.

"Do you own a firearm?" one of the officers asked.

"I do not, sir," Angie said.

"How come? Everyone on this block's got a gun."

"Multiple guns," the other cop added.

Angie shrugged. "I'm a convicted felon."

Amused, the cops looked at each other.

"And your point is . . . ?" one said to Angie.

"I know the law."

"All that means is if you had a firearm and it got stolen, you wouldn't tell us."

"Probably not. However, if I did own a firearm, why would I bother keeping that lame-ass bug zapper?" Angie motioned toward the Taser.

The officers conceded the point, but they ran her name and D.O.B. anyway, checking for warrants. Angie didn't mind; she was clean.

When she asked if the cops planned to dust the apartment for fingerprints, they showed her a discarded medical glove that they'd found on the sidewalk. "Your visitor didn't leave any prints," one of them said. "Doesn't mean he was a pro. Any shithead watches *CSI* knows to use these."

"But there's only one glove."

"Which he dropped by mistake, I'm sure. The other one's probably still in his pocket." The officer handed a copy of the burglary report to Angie and said, "You got insurance, right?"

"Not much, sir."

After the cops were gone, Angie grabbed a flashlight and went outside to see if the burglar had left any clues behind the building. She was looking for more that pointed to Pruitt. A search of the area beneath the broken bathroom window revealed only shards of glass.

But when Angie looked inside a nearby dumpster, she spotted her checkbook discarded among the trash bags. She climbed in to retrieve it.

The blank checks were untouched though, oddly, the register in which Angie wrote down her payments and check numbers was missing. It would be useless to an ordinary burglar.

Angie called Joel and said, "Somebody busted into the apartment. Came in through the bathroom window, but please don't be a smartass and sing the song."

"What have I been telling you? Rent that place on the third floor!"

"All he took was my laptop."

"Not the art collection?" Joel said.

"Walked right past the Chagall. Go figure. Anyhow, I was thinking maybe you should stay away from here for a while."

"Why? It was probably just kids. Your neighborhood has a very active chapter of the Future Felons of America."

Angie said, "There's a possibility my six o'clock stalker is taking it to a new level. I'd feel better if you weren't in the target zone."

"You mean Pruitt? Come on, burglary isn't his M.O."

"The cops found only one glove."

"Right or left?"

"Right."

"Damn," said Joel.

"I can still meet you out for dinner on our weekends."

"But who's gonna clean your apartment, Angie?"

"I bet there's a tutorial somewhere on Google."

Joel said, "Then at least get your cheap ass off the first floor. Promise?"

"Love you, kid. Good night."

Angie nailed a sheet over the window before sitting down to pee. She went to bed with the Taser positioned on her nightstand. As she sometimes did, she thought back to the regrettable night that she'd fed a piece of Pruitt to Lola the alligator. Most of all, she remained dismayed by the fact that the reptile had been shot afterward and sold to a hide tanner—the state-proscribed fate for gators that lose their fear of humans. Lola was now somebody's handbag, while Pruitt was sporting a state-of-the-art polymer prosthetic that cost $6,000. Angie had paid for the device out of her own pocket, in compliance with the court order. Her listless defense lawyer never sent a bill for his fees, which she later learned were paid by an anonymous benefactor. Angie figured it was somebody from PETA, which had publicly denounced the judge for handing out such a light sentence to a poacher of baby deer.

She fell asleep anticipating another enigmatic dream. Tonight's feature starred the commander-in-chief himself. Angie had been summoned to Casa Bellicosa to unfasten a screech owl from the presidential pompadour, which the low-swooping raptor had mistaken for a road-kill fox. When Angie arrived, the commander-in-chief was lurching madly around the helipad, bellowing and clawing at the Velcro skull patch into which the confused bird had embedded its talons. The owl was still clutching a plug of melon-colored fibers when Angie freed it. Swiftly she was led to a windowless room and made to sign a document stating she'd never set foot on the property, or glimpsed the President without his hair. A man wearing a Confederate colonel's uniform and a red baseball cap stepped forward and hung a milk-chocolate medal around Angie's neck, after which she was escorted at sword-point out the gates.

She awoke with renewed certainty that Carl Jung was full of shit. Dreams meant nothing—nonsense farted by a restless subconscious.

Angie spent all the next day removing a population of fruit-eating bats from the stately but vulnerable bell tower of a Lutheran church in Hobe Sound. She caught a career-high total of seventeen, which she released at dusk in a public park before driving home exhausted. Dinner was a microwave pizza. After one glass of wine Angie pitched into bed still smelling of bat piss.

It was a rare dreamless sleep, mercilessly interrupted by the goddamn phone. Groping in the dark, Angie by mistake snatched the Taser from the nightstand and with a hot crackle she fired both barbs into her pillow.

On the second swipe she found her cell.

"Is this Ms. Armstrong?"

"Who are you, sir?"

"This is Johnny Sanford at Safe N' Sound. I'm the co-owner."

Safe N' Sound was the warehouse yard on South Dixie Highway where Angie rented storage space.

"May I ask what time it is, Mr. Sanford?"

"Uh. Three-fifteen a.m."

"So this will likely be unwelcome news," Angie said.

"Our security service called. Your space is K-44, right?"

"Yup." Angie sat up in bed. "I assume it wasn't a false alarm."

"Not this time."

"Well, fuck."

"They used a bolt cutter on the padlock," Sanford said.

"How many other units got hit?"

"Just yours."

"I feel special."

"How fast can you be here?" Sanford asked. "The police have some questions."

I'm sure they do, thought Angela Armstrong.

FOUR

The marriage had been Angie's first and only. Dustin was twenty-one years older, smart, charming, and self-confident. He was also, in her eyes, arrestingly youthful. Although he listed his occupation as a life coach, most of his income came from modeling in TV commercials for a chicory-based edible called Luv Buzz, a trendy though medically unproven treatment for male fatigue and depression.

Angie first met him when she was sent to his house to sedate a confused black bear. Lured from the woods by the scent of the chicory gummies, the animal had broken into Dustin's garage and gobbled a thirteen-pound bag. It was in a manic state, hurling itself in all directions and emitting a piteous croak, by the time Angie arrived. She had to fire three times before getting a dart in the wild-eyed bear, and by then Dustin's cherry Targa was totaled. He remained phenomenally calm, even philosophical, despite an unsatisfactory exchange of phone calls with his insurance company.

Angie married him six months later, and loved him until the day he bailed. She adored his son, too. Joel's mother, Dustin's first wife, had died after sinking her golf cart in a lake during the inaugural member-guest tournament at the Jupiter Glades Country Club. The toxicology report showed she had enough Xanax in her blood to etherize a sumo wrestler.

Joel was a toddler when the tragedy happened. He was ten when his father introduced her to Angie, who was attracted to the idea of an instant family; in her teens she'd lost her own mother to cancer, and had no brothers or sisters. Her father hadn't spoken to her since the day she'd quit his veterinary practice, the same morning a cocker spaniel died while Angie was removing a ping-pong ball from its stomach. Surgically she hadn't done anything wrong, and it wasn't the first animal she'd lost on the table. The dog was old and had heart problems, but watching the life-light fade from its eyes crushed Angie worse than any other experience. She couldn't figure out why this time and not the others, but she knew she was done.

The state of Florida was pleased to give her a job as a wildlife officer. Being overqualified did not elevate her prospects for a proper wage, but over time Angie saved enough money to repay her father for the tuition to veterinary school. He never responded except for cashing the check. Later, when she went to prison, she didn't bother writing him. By then she was single again, Dustin having dumped her a few years before she fed Pruitt's hand to the alligator.

Angie sometimes wondered if they'd still be married had she stuck with those damn yoga classes. God knows she tried. The crowded, windowless studios made her claustrophobic, and that mandatory loop of Eastern chimes was so annoying. Why the fuck couldn't they play Pearl Jam?

"I'm not cut out for this, Dustin," she'd said after one blazingly sweaty Bikram session. "Serenity is overrated."

He didn't get angry; that wasn't his style. Instead he took up with one of the community's freshly divorced, self-discovering female yoga fanatics that traveled in packs, ever-alert and lithe as meerkats.

Looking back, as Angie too often did, she regretted overlooking other signal differences between Dustin and herself. For one thing, he disliked being around animals; he claimed their presence interfered with his meditations. Joel would have loved to own a dog or a cat, but dear old dad wouldn't even buy the kid a hamster. That, Angie knew, was a red flag missed.

One time Dustin had chased after a small garter snake in the yard, swinging at it frantically with a 24-inch carbon steel crowbar. He'd missed the snake completely but pulverized three toes on his right foot.

Angie was reminded of the incident by the sight of a similar crowbar—definitely not her ex-husband's—on the floor of her rented storage unit. This one had been used to snap the hinges on the lid of the freezer.

"What's inside that black bag in there?" the cop asked. He happened to be one of the same pair who'd answered the burglary at Angie's apartment.

"Dead coyote," Angie replied.

"And *that* thing?"

"Juvenile otter."

"What the hell?" the cop's partner said, with exaggerated disgust.

Angie explained that she was in the business of removing so-called nuisance wildlife from human environs. The coyote had been shot by a horse trainer, and nobody at the stable wanted to handle the corpse for fear of rabies. As for the poor little otter, it had failed to outrun a pit bull mix owned by an eccentric obstetrical nurse in Greenacres.

"Most of my trade is alive," Angie felt compelled to add.

"Then how come you collect the dead ones and freeze 'em?"

"I don't collect them, sir. There's a place way out west, some woods near Loxahatchee, that's where I bury them. It's a long drive, so I usually wait until I've got a full truckload."

The cops said they'd never met a woman in her line of work. Without comment Angie acknowledged that most critter-removal companies were owned by men.

Mr. Sanford wasn't much help. To the police he proclaimed: "I had no idea she was using our premises for this!"

"Oh, Johnny, that's bullshit," Angie said. "When your grand-daughter's pet bunny croaked, who showed up on my doorstep with the shoebox?"

Sanford lowered his eyes and licked his mustache. The first cop said to Angie: "You're on an epic bad-luck streak, ma'am. Any chance this incident was connected to the break-in at your apartment?"

"The thought crossed my mind."

"What else you keep in this freezer?" the second officer asked in a serrated tone. "Maybe a leafy green substance?"

"No, sir," said Angie. "There's only one item missing, by the way."

"Which would be . . . ?"

"A dead Burmese python."

"No shit? How big?"

"Eighteen feet, eleven inches." Before unspooling the tape mea-sure, Angie had laid out the Lipid House specimen in the parking lot and carefully aligned the severed head with the neck.

She added, "One person couldn't carry it alone."

The first cop snorted. "Then how the hell'd a girl your size drag it in here all by yourself?"

"Two sturdy youths from the neighborhood agreed to help me. Ten bucks each," Angie said. "I told them it was a rubber prop from a movie set. Otherwise they wouldn't come near it. Somehow it fit in the bottom of the freezer."

The second cop asked where the python had been found.

"The island of Palm Beach," said Angie, "winter enclave of the sun-drenched one-per-centers."

"How'd the damn thing die?"

"I decapitated it with a machete."

The first cop frowned again. "That's some sick shit."

"It's a state-approved method of euthanizing, sir. You can check it out online."

"Wait—so whoever broke in and stole your dead snake, they jacked the head, too?"

"They did not." Angie leaned over and from the deepest corner of the freezer lifted a bulging clear baggie.

"Get that goddamn thing away from me!" the second cop yelled, as his partner thrust the crime report into Angie's free hand.

Then they were gone.

The lead burglar's name was Uric. His helper was a dull-eyed fuck-wit who worked cheap, basically for cigarettes and Yuengling. The helper wished to be called Prince Paladin. He sat listening to his jams in the grimy paneled van while Uric entered Angie Armstrong's apartment through the bathroom window.

"It's not there," Uric reported crossly when he returned.

The Prince yanked out his earbuds. "So, whassat mean? We don't get paid?"

"You know anything about computers? Never mind. Dumb question."

"What's so 'portant about a croaked snake?"

"I got no idea," Uric said. "What I do know is that these rich-ass fucks get into some super weird shit. I heard some stories, Holy Christ-ola."

The Prince snorted and said the only good snake was a dead one.

Uric drove to a mall, parked in front of the Target and leafed through Angie's checkbook registry. On the 15th of every month she wrote a $118 check that was recorded as "storage rental." Unfortunately, she didn't include the name of the company in those entries.

The Prince said, "Shit. We got nuthin'."

"Bro, I need you to keep the faith."

"How come? Oh. I get it. 'Til we find the snake."

"Also, could you shut the fuck up?"

Uric opened Angie's laptop. He was locked out of the email server, and he couldn't crack the password. It was aggravating. He suspected that the storage company invoiced electronically, which would have provided both the name and address. After several minutes he gave up, got out of the van and placed the laptop beneath a rear tire of a Suburban LTZ parked beside him.

The Prince said, "How come you did that?"

"To crush the damn thing. What else?"

"But that's, like, what they call 'destroying stolen property.'"

"There's no such crime, Prince. The stealing is the part that's against the law."

"Maybe the chick just dumped the snake in a ditch."

Uric said, "No way."

Angie Armstrong had intended to deliver the giant python to a state laboratory. Tripp Teabull had shared this intel with Uric during their phone conversation, before they settled on Uric's fee. For some reason, Teabull didn't want the monster corpse donated to science.

The Prince hopped out and retrieved the laptop. He asked Uric to read through Angie's check register again and see if there were any men's names. Uric found an entry for a $250 check that said: Joel/birthday. The Prince tried "Joel" as a password, adding combinations of double numerals that might be associated with a likely year of birth. No luck.

"Try '69,'" Uric said.

"Seriously? Not even bikers use '69' in their passwords anymore."

"I do, asshole."

The Prince tapped in the numbers. "Nope, not it. Hey, what does this chick call her business?"

"Discreet Captures."

"D-I-S-K-R-"

"No, Your Highness." Uric spelled it for him. "And don't put a space in."

"Yo, score!"

Uric grinned—maybe he'd underestimated this bozo. "Give it here," he said, reaching for the laptop.

Scrolling through Angela Armstrong's inbox, he spotted a recent email from Safe N' Sound Storage. The company's South Dixie Highway location was displayed at the top of the bill, along with the number of Angie's warehouse unit: K-44.

The following afternoon, Uric ambled out of the Safe N' Sound office with a short-term rental contract for unit K-39, and a punch code for the security gate. After dinner he and the Prince stole a white Chevrolet Malibu from an alley behind a discount liposuction clinic. They spent the next stretch of time watching *Game of Thrones* repeats in some careless fool's unlocked condo.

At two-thirty in the morning they returned to the warehouse yard. Uric put a sun mask on his face and used a long-armed bolt cutter to sever the wires on the video cameras mounted at both ends of the K corridor. The inexpensive padlock on Angie's unit succumbed with a clap like a .22.

There was little of value inside except a chest freezer, also locked. The Prince used a crowbar to pop the lid, cursing at the sight of the unbagged, headless python coiled like a psychedelic fire hose. Uric teetered backward.

Although both men were strong and tall—the Prince in his slides stood six-three—they were anxious about transporting the frozen reptile. Their main concern wasn't the weight—somewhere north of a hundred-and-fifty pounds was Uric's guess, judging by the length and the whopping lump in its belly—but rather it was their mutual aversion to snakes of any size.

Uric had dropped one of his latex burglary gloves after leaving Angie's apartment. He'd meant to swing by CVS and steal new pairs for him and the Prince, but he'd forgotten, so they used rags to mummy-wrap their hands. The python's rigid circularity allowed the thieves to thread it like a tractor tire on a length of loose fence pipe. With cautious half-steps they advanced their frosty load down the K corridor and out the doorway to the parking lot, where they found themselves challenged by the Malibu's limited trunk space. The Prince was dripping like a plow mule by the time they got the morbid popsicle stowed.

Once they were back on the road, the Prince said to Uric, "Yo, drop me off at that titty bar on Hypoluxo."

"Drop you *off*?"

"Yeah. Ain't we done for the night?"

"No, bro, we ain't done," said Uric. "But I agree we deserve some titty time."

Fay Alex Riptoad was having a golf lesson at the Breakers. From a distance Police Chief Jerry Crosby watched drearily. His only thought: *What the fuck is she wearing?*

Fay Alex's shorts, shoes and golf glove were the same shade of lime as the Gatorade with which the chief had rinsed the tobacco from his mouth, back when he played Double-A baseball. Almost all his teammates dipped. Their star closer, a gregarious lefthander named Nuckley, got oral cancer at age thirty-four. By then he was working for Geico at the regional level; fit, married, father of three. They cut a tumor the size of a Bing cherry from under his tongue, and eighteen months later he was dead. Jerry Crosby missed the funeral because he was still on road patrol at the time, and his corporal wouldn't give him the day off. It didn't escape Crosby's notice that the corporal was also hooked on dip—Skoal, which had been Nuckley's favorite brand. The irony was less infuriating than the karmic unfairness that had claimed the cheery southpaw while allowing the ass-wipe corporal to sail on, rolling that perpetual plug in his cheek, spitting the brown juice-crud into a coffee mug on his desk.

Crosby's own dream of a major-league career had ended with blown-out knees. He married a high-school girlfriend and for a long time worked as a foreman at her family's citrus packing plant in Sebastian. The groves eventually were sold to a Brazilian fashion model seeking unlimited tons of grapefruit pulp for a dye-free exfoliating scrub that she was trying to launch. Crosby's favorite uncle, a cop, talked him into joining the Rockledge city force. He discovered he enjoyed small-town law enforcement. When his wife was offered a good paralegal job down in Wellington, Crosby sent his application to the police department in gilded, fussy Palm Beach. He'd never set foot on the famous island but he knew that violent crime there was rare, which was his wife's only stipulation. The rest of South Florida, she said, was a damn shooting gallery.

And, as Crosby expected, Palm Beach wasn't a hotbed of felony activity. The day-to-day challenge was trying to deal with a pampered, demanding, half-paranoid citizenry. It took a while for Crosby to adjust, but he advanced up the ranks due to an innate politeness, whiteness, and lack of a redneck accent. Since becoming chief, he'd also been well-served by an uncommon immunity to condescension.

He'd given up all forms of tobacco after his pal Nuckley died, though these days he kept a bong hidden in his office for the occasional crisis. It was the best way to unwind from absurd stress in an absurd town. Once the mystery of Katherine Fitzsimmons's disappearance was solved, the chief planned to celebrate with the blinds drawn.

"Jerry! Come over here!" From the driving range, Fay Alex Riptoad was signaling with what appeared to be a lofted iron.

Crosby began the uncomfortable walk, drawing the usual stares from other club members. The Breakers employed its own agile though low-key security team, and calling uniformed officers to the property was discouraged except when incidents became unmanageable. Delivering an update on a Missing Persons investigation didn't qualify as an emergency, but Fay Alex set her own rules. As the chief approached, she shooed away the golf pro, whose relief was manifest in each departing stride.

"Give me the latest. Let's hear it," demanded Fay Alex, her sun-spotted claws planted imperiously on the grip end of what was now identifiable as a Callaway nine-iron, its shiny blade embedded in the spongy grass.

The chief said, "We collated all the videos from security cameras in the neighborhood. There's no sign of Mrs. Fitzsimmons, or anyone resembling her, walking the streets during the critical time frame."

"And what about the koi pond at Lipid House?"

"We've done two dives, Mrs. Riptoad. No remains have been recovered."

"Suppose we call that good news, shall we? Kiki Pew's boys are a wreck. The grandchildren, as well." Fay Alex unplugged the nine-iron from the emerald turf and placed it in her golf bag. "And what about the Missing Persons alert? Any new tips?"

The police chief thought: *Why couldn't we do this on the phone?* Standing among the candy-hued golfers, he felt like the proverbial turd in the punch bowl.

"Mrs. Riptoad," he said.

"What is it, Jerry?"

"Do you know how many people Mrs. Fitzsimmons's age go missing in Florida? They get disoriented. Light-headed. Confused. They wander off. Or just get in their cars and start driving. Sometimes they even go to an airport, buy a random ticket and board a plane."

"Your point being?"

"Each time that happens," Crosby explained, "worried relatives notify the authorities, who send out a bulletin like ours, which gets some media attention for a short while. Then, a few days later, another missing-senior alert is issued for someone new . . ."

Fay Alex made no effort to hide her disdain. "Surely they've got a ranking system. You're telling me what—that some senile retired shoe salesman who stumbles away from a retirement home could knock someone as important as Kiki Pew off the top of the list?"

"We've had no leads that could be considered credible."

Fay Alex, crossing her damp matchstick arms, said, "Ah, then you *did* receive some tips!"

"Just one."

"I haven't got all day, Jerry."

Which was horseshit, he knew. Fay Alex had all day, every day.

He said, "Some tourist in Macau claimed to have had his palm read by a woman who looked like Mrs. Fitzsimmons. She spoke fluent Portuguese and wore an opal stud in her left nostril. The tourist had been smoking opium, by the way—"

"Enough, for Christ's sake. Eeeeee-nough." Fay Alex laser-drilled the chief over the rims of her oversized shades. "In other words, you've got nothing. Zilch-o."

"It appears she never stepped off the grounds of Lipid House," he said.

"Come on. You still think she got trashed and fell in the pond?"

"I didn't say that. Our job is to eliminate the obvious scenarios, and there's no evidence she ever left the party. No video, no eyewitnesses."

"Not a party, *not* a party," Fay Alex groused. "A charity ball."

"My advice to the family is post a reward. That always reboots media interest, and it might shake loose some helpful information."

"Information such as what? My God, you're not actually suggesting there was oh, what . . . do you people call it?"

"Foul play," the chief said.

"Foul play, yes. Here on the island? Get serious."

Jerry Crosby didn't live on the island. He lived miles away on the mainland, in a western municipality that grandly called itself Royal Palm Beach.

No beach, of course, and all the royal palm trees got there on a truck. Yet the chief really liked the town—lovely parks, excellent schools. Last July 4th, there were post-pandemic fireworks, a Skynyrd tribute band and a bass fishing derby.

"What kind of reward do you suggest?" Fay Alex Riptoad asked.

Crosby said the larger, the better.

"How large? Fifty thousand? A hundred?"

"That should be plenty."

"Fine, Jerry. I'll speak to the boys." Fay Alex unfolded her arms and peeled off the lime golf glove. "You think Kiki Pew's dead, don't you?"

"With each passing day, it seems more likely. I hope I'm wrong."

"The Potussies are having lunch today at Casa Bellicosa. I'll not mention your fears about foul play. *Possible* foul play."

"There's no point," the chief agreed. "Not yet."

Most days, Angie Armstrong liked her job. She chose to believe she was extending the life expectancy of every creature that she relocated from a traffic-clogged suburb to a safe, quiet place. She was aware that some of her transportees—raccoons, in particular, which adapted ingeniously to life among humans—didn't appreciate being moved to a habitat where there were no garbage cans to pillage.

Angie felt that all wildlife was better off in the true wild, or the nearest thing to wild that still existed in a state with twenty-two million humans. She felt childishly hopeful every time she opened a travel kennel and watched her relieved captive scamper into the scrub, out of sight. Angie would usually stay for a while, shutting her eyes, listening closely until all she could hear was sweet pure silence; then she'd get in her truck and drive back to the city.

No removal calls had come in all morning, leaving Angie time to sit around wondering why anyone would go to the trouble of stealing a headless reptile from her storage freezer. Pruitt had been her prime suspect in the apartment break-in—until the warehouse job happened. Appraised together, the two crimes pointed to a more complicated motive than the vengeance fantasy that was driving the ex-poacher.

Angie assumed that her laptop and checkbook entries had led the apartment burglar to the storage unit. Maybe the creep was looking for dope or valuables, but the fact remained that he'd swiped the dead python—and he couldn't have done it alone.

While she was fixing breakfast, Angie's attention was drawn to a breaking story on the local TV news: The family of a missing elderly woman was offering $100,000 for information leading to her whereabouts.

It was a strikingly large sum, so Angie wasn't surprised to learn that the lost woman was a winter resident of Palm Beach. Her name was Katherine Pew Fitzsimmons, age seventy-two.

Such disappearances weren't uncommon in South Florida, though few families could afford to post six-figure rewards. Angie assumed that Mrs. Fitzsimmons, like many of the elderly who went missing, struggled with Alzheimer's or some other dementia. Perhaps her family had asked the authorities not to publicize that. An accompanying photograph showed the woman wearing a droopy Santa hat and posing in front of a Christmas tree.

The newscaster concluded his report with a detail that made Angie flip her omelet into the garbage pail and reach for the phone—Mrs. Fitzsimmons had last been seen the previous Friday night at a charity event on the grounds of Lipid House. Only twenty-four hours later, Angie was called to the estate to remove the gorged Burmese python.

Mystery solved: The lump was the missing widow. Had to be.

She made three rapid-fire calls to Tripp Teabull but he didn't answer, so she ran to her truck. The drive up the interstate to Southern Boulevard was painless, but after leaving the highway Angie began encountering roadblocks—a sure sign that the President was either in town, or on the way.

Angie doglegged northbound on Dixie to the Royal Park Bridge, crossed over to the island, and doubled back down South County toward Lipid House. From the front, the place looked deserted. She made a slow roll past the forged black gates before circling the block. Finding the rear service entrance open, she parked between two supernaturally shiny landscape trailers. Stepping out of the pickup, she was assaulted by the high-pitched din of mowers and gas-powered hedge trimmers. Evidently the bird-themed topiary was being re-sculpted into chessboard pieces, in advance of another gala.

Passing through a regiment of sweaty lawn workers, Angie counted four men in straw hats spaced around the shore of the koi pond, as if serving as sentries. Eventually she spotted Mauricio, the groundskeeper, wearing industrial earmuffs and sprawled in the shade of a massive strangler fig. He got up and led her to an out-building where badminton rackets hung on paneled walls and lacquered croquet mallets, arranged by color, lined the floorboards.

Sliding the earmuffs down around his neck, Mauricio said, "What brings you back to this side of the bridge?"

Angie said she needed to speak with Teabull.

"He's off-property today. Whassup? Don't tell me they shorted you on the pay."

"No, sir. It's about Mrs. Fitzsimmons."

"Who?"

"The woman who disappeared from here the night before Teabull called me to come get the python from the tree," Angie said.

Maurice got fidgety. "What about her?"

"You're in a tricky position, loyalty-wise. I totally understand. But somebody stole that Burmese. They broke into my warehouse unit."

Mauricio reacted with a baffled grunt. "Who'd want to jack a dead twenty-foot snake?"

"Actually, it was eighteen-eleven. My first question was why. The second was how they knew it was me who had the remains. Did you mention my name when you told people about the euthanization?"

Mauricio raised his hands. "The *what*?"

"When I chopped off its head."

"Are you kiddin'? I didn't even tell my wife. Mr. Teabull, he was hard-core about that. The whole staff got the same order: 'Don't say a word about what happened.'"

Angie picked up a red croquet mallet and let it swing by the tip of the handle from her fingers, like a pendulum. "Looks brand-new," she said.

"They get polished every week. Even the mallet heads."

"Every week? This *is* a whole other universe."

"Anybody can take the ride. All you need is money."

Angie made a baseball batter's swing with the mallet before

returning it to the rack. She said, "The missing woman's family is offering a big reward. It was on TV today."

"Like how much?" Mauricio asked.

"Hundred grand." She was watching closely, but his expression didn't change. "Look, Mauricio, we both know what really happened to Mrs. Fitzsimmons. So does Tripp Teabull with two P's."

The groundskeeper wheeled and stalked out the door. Angie caught up. As they walked past the pond, she said, "Your lookouts are just for show, right? Because she would have floated up by now."

"You need to leave, Ms. Armstrong."

"Know why that python got stolen from me?"

"Probably for the skin is all. To make boots, belts, crap like that."

"No, sir, they stole the snake," Angie said, "because they knew I was taking it to scientists who were going to slice it open and find what was inside. And that would have created some seriously shitty publicity for this place, actually for the whole island. 'Giant Reptiles Picking Off Helpless Palm Beach Widows!'"

"We're done," Mauricio snarled sideways. He said nothing more until they reached Angie's pickup. Then: "You were a smart girl, you'd go back to the mainland, bank the five grand you got for this job and keep your crazy-ass theories to yourself."

Angie said, "Let me explain something. In addition to ripping off my storage unit, at least one of these cockheads—whoever they are—broke into my home, my personal domicile. Try to appreciate the indignity I'm experiencing, the sense of violation."

"I'll let Mr. Teabull know you stopped by."

"Excellent," said Angie. "And feel free, sir, to tell him my line of inquiry."

FIVE

Mockingbird's motorcade was only ten vehicles long. It was short compared to her husband's, but still she hated the attention it attracted, the way people on the streets stopped to gawk. Some waved; some flipped her off. One time, riding to the island from the airport, she saw a young man stick out his tongue and grab his crotch as her armored stretch Cadillac rolled past. He wasn't even one of the regular protesters; he was a U.S. postal carrier, in uniform.

And, actually, kind of hot.

Since then, Mockingbird tried not to look at the people lining the motorcade route. After visiting a special-needs school in Liberty City, she'd spent a few hours listlessly shopping for blouses at Bal Harbour. Her Secret Service detail had phoned ahead and arranged for her to enter the stores through a rear entrance. The best shops offered private fitting rooms, so Mockingbird had no interaction with other customers. Most of them likely didn't know she was there.

Now the motorcade was speeding back toward Palm Beach. Mockingbird's husband would be flying in soon for a round of golf, followed by a private dinner with Saudi royalty that the First Lady would definitely not be attending—her call, not the President's. Mockingbird had chosen to spend the evening with two girlfriends from New York; one taught hypothermal sex exercises in Chelsea, and the other was a retired model who married and divorced professional baseball players, usually infielders.

Soon after exiting the interstate, Mockingbird's security procession braked to a full halt, which was unusual. She heard the agents in her car communicating by radio in cool, practiced tones to those in the vehicles ahead and behind.

"What's going on, Keith?" Mockingbird asked.

"There's an unexpected delay ahead of us, ma'am."

Unlike other First Ladies, she chose not to be addressed as "Mrs." Keith said he had to call her something, so "ma'am" was their compromise.

"It doesn't appear to be a threat," he said. "We expect the police to clear the situation any minute."

Other agents from the escort materialized on foot to surround Mockingbird's limousine. The formation blocked her view.

"Is it a car accident?" she asked, removing her sunglasses.

"No, ma'am. It's an animal in the road."

Mockingbird figured that somebody's dog had gotten off its leash and was running loose. She put her glasses back on, and settled in to wait.

Keith said, "The President has been informed of the situation."

"Did the President sound like he gave a shit?"

"It shouldn't be much longer."

"All right, Keith."

At first, she had disliked the code name chosen for her by the Secret Service. Then she'd watched a YouTube video about actual mockingbirds, which were crafty, graceful, and melodious.

Like me, she thought. *Once upon a time.*

The President's Secret Service code name was "Mastodon." He loved it.

"Perfect!" he'd boomed when he was told. "Fearless, smart, and tough."

And enormous, she'd said to herself. *Don't forget fucking enormous.*

On only his second day in the White House, the President had ordered his chief of staff to arrange a trip to the National Zoo for a close-up look at a real mastodon. The chief of staff wasn't brave enough to tell the President the truth, so he cooked up a story that the zoo's beloved mastodon herd was on loan to a wildlife park in Christchurch, New Zealand. The President had scowled, muttered something about "those snotty Kiwis," and soon gotten sidetracked by another daft notion.

"Is it a dog in the road?" Mockingbird asked Keith, who was positioned in the front passenger seat.

"No, ma'am, it's a snake."

Mockingbird scooted forward. "Really? What happened? I want to see!"

"I don't have that information," said Keith, using two fingers to snug the fit of his earbud. "There's no danger whatsoever. The snake is very large, but it's dead."

Mockingbird leaned left and right, peering through the bullet-proof windshield, trying to see around the other agents.

"How do they know it's not just sleeping?" she asked.

"Because the head's been removed, ma'am."

"Can't we get closer? Please, Keith?"

The agent said, "They're taking some pictures. I'll show them to you later."

"That's not the same." Mockingbird sat back, frowning. "Not at all."

She enjoyed nothing about being First Lady, but she felt especially smothered by the ironclad timetables upon which each day was structured. Once inside the limousine, she was captive cargo—no spontaneous detours, no carefree changes of plans. How often does a person get the chance to see a humongous headless serpent?

"But you said there isn't any danger, Keith. So why can't I just—"
"Buckle up, please, ma'am. We've been cleared to proceed."

Looking back, Uric would admit they should have dealt with the
dead python *before* getting trashed at the titty bar.

The name of the joint was Prime Vegas Showgirls, which the
Prince after four bourbons complained was false advertising; a
flame-haired dancer with whom he'd been chatting had confided
that she'd never been west of Tallahassee. Meanwhile Uric allowed
himself to get bewitched by a rangy Russian brunette with a Jiminy
Cricket tattoo on each of her dimpled butt cheeks. The conversation
between dance numbers was appreciably less monotonous than the
choreography.

Hazy hours passed, and a coral sun was peeking over the horizon by the time the empty-pocketed burglars emerged from the
strip club. Yet even Prince Paladin, who was more wasted than Uric,
grasped the problem.

"Oh shit," he said. "Now we gotta ditch that fuckin' snake in
broad daylight."

"Chill your drunken ass. I know a place."

But, in truth, Uric couldn't think of another safe location. The
remote rock-mining pit where he'd planned to dispose of the reptile
in the dark would now be open, bustling with dredges, cranes and
dump trucks.

Had he been sober and clear-thinking, Uric wouldn't have been
steering the stolen Malibu—its tail end sagging under the heft—
toward the busy, heavily policed island of Palm Beach. He would
have been racing in the opposite direction, toward a landfill or a
cane field.

Lipid House was quiet. Uric parked under the arched stucco portico. Although he'd done several jobs for Tripp Teabull, he had never
been invited to the estate. Likewise the Prince had never seen a real

mansion up close. No one approached the car, so the men got out and waited in the shade.

"Dude, the trunk's leakin'," the Prince observed.

Uric dolefully studied the slow drip coming from somewhere under the Malibu's rear bumper. The goddamn snake was melting.

"It's gonna stink," the Prince said.

Uric slapped him in the nuts. "This is all your fault, draggin' me to that lame-ass bar."

The doors opened and out walked Teabull wearing charcoal slacks, loafers, and an Oxford shirt with the cuffs rolled up. He stared coldly at the men, glanced at the Malibu, and then with open palms raised his arms. Silently he mouthed the words: "What the fuck?"

They all clambered into the car, which Uric drove to the back of the property. Teabull told him to park in the golf-cart shed.

Uric said, "We need to unload the snake. You got any ideas?"

Teabull kicked open the passenger door and practically rolled out of the car. "The damn thing's in the trunk? The deal was—Are you serious? Are you dicking with me?—because the deal was you bury it way out west, somewhere it'll never be found."

The Prince said, "Yo, they was complications."

Uric added, defensively, "Shit, the hardest part of the job got done. We found the motherfucking snake and we stole the motherfucking snake."

Teabull was livid. Mauricio had told him about Angela Armstrong's visit—and how much she already knew.

"Why in God's name did you bring it back *here*?" he yelled at the two hired thieves. "All you had to do was call."

"Phone died," said Uric, which was the truth. There was no charger in the stolen Malibu.

"You guys reek of booze," Teabull croaked. "Are you drunk?"

The Prince said, "We *were* drunk. Now we're just hungover."

Uric told Teabull to focus on the problem. "Think hard, bro. There's gotta be a place around here to drop this load."

"On the island? Are you insane? This is Palm Fucking Beach."

Teabull pointed one of his loafers at a puddle widening beneath the car. "Don't tell me the gas tank's leaking. This shed'll blow like a napalm bomb."

The Prince said, "Don't worry, man. That ain't gasoline."

"The snake was in a deep freeze when we jacked it," Uric explained.

A hot surge of nausea wobbled Teabull. "So you're saying it's . . . thawing?"

Uric offered to pop the trunk. "Then you can see with your own damn eyeballs that we really got this thing."

"Don't open it! I believe you."

In almost a decade as the caretaker-manager of Lipid House, Teabull had smoothed over—and covered up—many difficult situations arising from the bad behavior of club members or their guests. There had been thefts, fistfights, unsought nudity, indiscreet sex, drug overdoses, rowdy vandalism, and one felony stabbing (a surgeon wielding a Wusthof steak knife had forcefully attempted to remove a benign but unsightly mole from the neck of his carping father-in-law).

Still, no member in good standing had ever expired on the estate, at least officially, during Teabull's coolheaded tenure. Thanks to his friendly relations with first-responders, even the indisputably deceased victims of heart attacks on the property were rushed to a nearby emergency room for a convincing charade of resuscitative efforts before the official pronouncement of death—purposely delayed by hours—was issued. The hospital, not Lipid House, would be listed as the location of demise.

Teabull pondered the steep challenge now facing him. Not only had Katherine Pew Fitzsimmons, society matron and presidential fan-girl, perished on the grounds, but her once-removed, half-digested corpse was now back at the scene, reheating inside the dead monster that had devoured her. Teabull longingly thought back to the great job offer he'd turned down last season—managing a Waspy

Cape Cod yacht-and-tennis club where the average member's age was only fifty-six. The climate there was way too cold for pythons or boa constrictors or whatever the fuck had gobbled Kiki Pew.

"Stay with the car. I need to make a call," he said to Uric and his idiot sidekick.

Not far down A1A, near the Par-3 golf course, a Venezuelan currency trader had torn down an old mansion and was currently pouring the foundation for a new 28,000-square-foot villa that he would occupy three weeks a year, at most. Teabull was on good terms with the supervisor of the concrete project, who had done some work at Lipid House.

When the man answered his phone, Teabull said, "Hey, Jackson, when do your guys break for lunch?"

"Twelve-fifteen is our usual."

"Take 'em all to the crab shack. It's on me."

"You're so fulla shit."

"No, I'm serious," Teabull told him. "I'm buying for the whole crew today."

"What's the catch?" the concrete man asked.

"You cut me a sweet break on the formwork for our driveway last year. Billed us the residential rate instead of commercial."

"Yeah, I remember. No biggie."

"So this is me saying thanks. Who else is working on that site today?"

The concrete man said, "Nobody. Just us."

"Then you should take a whole hour," Teabull suggested. "Try the tuna poke. It'll blow your mind."

He returned to the seeping Malibu, wrote down the address for Uric and told him exactly what to do. He explained that the deepest pours would be the load-bearing footers for the outside walls. "If you can't find anything wet enough, leave the premises immediately."

"My life motto," said Uric.

"You've got shovels?"

The Prince said they were in the back seat. Uric asked Teabull if he'd brought their money.

"What a comedian. Ha, ha, ha," the property manager said. "When the job's done is when you get paid—and it's a long damn way from being done."

He scowled at the puddle swelling beneath the car. The drip of foul fluids had become audible.

"You need to get the hell outta here," Teabull said.

"Where? We got, like, three hours to kill," the Prince complained, tapping the face of his wristwatch.

"I don't care where you go. Pick a beach. Find a dog. Throw him a fucking Frisbee, whatever. Just get this damn car off the property."

Uric and the Prince drove to the luncheonette at Green's Pharmacy, ordered breakfast, and sat at the counter for the rest of the morning. Like most burglars, they looked night-worn and skittish. Still, nobody asked them to move. Shortly after noon, they departed for the villa-under-construction near the Par-3. There they scouted for signs of workers or other possible witnesses, but saw no one.

Uric parked the Malibu between a pair of rotund mixing trucks. The drivers were gone, but they'd left the drums turning to keep the compound loose. Uric and the Prince prowled around the property, checking inside the ground frames to find the freshest pour. One long section of concrete, the base for an east-facing wall, was still wet. When the Prince tossed a rock, it landed with a plop. Just for kicks, he lobbed another one.

Uric ran to the car and backed it flawlessly as his partner directed him to the closest dumping position. The men then snatched the shovels from the rear seat and began digging in the wet cement and aggregate, creating a hole that seemed plenty deep for corpse concealment. Once the site was ready, the interment would have to be completed swiftly, before the concrete began to harden.

Neither Uric nor the Prince was ready for the sight that assailed them when they opened the trunk of the Malibu. The thawing python hadn't exploded so much as unzipped, exposing the reason for the lump in its belly—crumpled, corkscrewed remains of a slight, silver-haired woman cloaked in a pale gown.

"Oh f-f-fuck," gasped Uric, a sentiment repeated more emotively by his sidekick, who commenced to wail and puke.

The stench was otherworldly. Uric covered his mouth and nose, and struggled to remain steady. Now he understood why Tripp Teabull had hired him to snatch the dead snake: There was a dead rich lady inside of it.

Uric knew she was rich because, in addition to expensive-looking clothes, she wore diamond earrings the size of Cheerios and a string of small, creamy-pink pearls. Removing them was a gooey chore that ended with Uric snapping the necklace and sliding the pearls into his hand. Bitterly he wondered how—while killing a whole morning at Green's drugstore—he'd forgotten to purchase hospital gloves in anticipation of reptile gore.

As he pocketed the moist jewels, Uric kept his back to the Prince, who was down on both knees, forehead in the dirt. When Uric turned around, he barked, "Dude, get in the fucking game!"

Together they hoisted the bony heap from the Malibu's trunk and placed it into the fresh hole in the concrete.

"Now there's no room for the snake!" the Prince bleated, violently wiping his hands on his pants.

Uric said, "It doesn't matter anymore. Don't you see?"

But the Prince got so freaked that Uric made him sit in the car. Working alone with his shovel, Uric hastily covered the misshapen body and smoothed the surface on the footer. The concrete crew, returning from a long lunch of crab cakes, didn't look twice at the white car speeding away from the construction site, nor did they glance at the faces of the driver and his companion.

"So, let's hear your next genius move," the Prince said.

Uric wasn't in the mood for sarcasm. "What's your problem, dickface?"

"I never touched a dead body before is my problem."

"Chill your pussy ass out." Uric stomped the accelerator. "The worst part's over. We are home-fucking-free."

He was wrong.

Late that night, after too many Captain Morgans, he and the Prince would resume a protracted argument about which of them had shut the Malibu's trunk—or, more precisely, which of them had shanked the task of shutting the trunk.

Following a tense dinner at KFC they'd returned to their squatter's condo and were planted in front of the television when the eleven o'clock news came on. The top story was about the First Lady's motorcade being delayed en route to Palm Beach that afternoon, due to the presence in the roadway of a headless Burmese python. Grisly video focused on the burst predator, stretched across two lanes.

The scene was surrounded by wry-looking cops and tight-lipped Secret Service dudes wearing sunglasses and three-for-one suits from JoS. A. Bank. Visible in the background were the red-striped gates of the railroad crossing that the Malibu had vaulted doing fifty-plus miles per hour, a tooth-cracking jolt that had stunned the car's unbelted occupants and sprung the unsecured lid of the trunk, resulting in an ill-timed launch of the decomposing snake carcass.

At the end of his story, the TV reporter quoted a White House spokesperson saying that the First Lady was never in danger, and that the motorcade had proceeded to Casa Bellicosa with no further delays. Law-enforcement authorities were said to be investigating how the python ended up on the First Lady's route.

"I bet they already found the car," the Prince said dejectedly.

"Oh, right. At the bottom of that canal? No way, José."

"You were the one in charge of lockin' the trunk!"

"Bullshit. I was in charge of buryin' the body," Uric said. "You're the one supposed to close the trunk. A retard baboon couldn't screw up a job that simple."

The dead woman's pink pearls and diamond earrings remained in a front pocket of Uric's pants. He considered the gems a well-earned bonus, and couldn't think of one good reason to mention them to his partner.

"Can I ask why the hell you call yourself Prince Paladin?"

The Prince said, "That was my stage name. I was in a reggaeton band."

"A what?"

"Before I started dealing pills."

"X?"

"Naw, Vicodins mainly."

"And then . . . ?"

"Then I got busted. This was up around Pittsburgh."

Uric said, "So, how come you're out already? You beat the rap?"

"I wish. Did six months and three days."

"All you got was six months?" Uric snatched the TV remote away from the Prince, who was flipping through channels like a gacked-up chimp. "Six months for opioids? Jesus, did you have to blow the judge? Or just let him blow *you*?"

The Prince shrugged and reached for the rum bottle.

"Oh, now I get it," said Uric. "The feds cut your time 'cause you flipped. You rat-fucked your friends."

"They weren't no friends a mine. And don't come down on me, bro. Sometimes you get in a situation, you gotta do whatever it takes."

"That's a true statement, Your Highness." Uric finished his drink and stood up. "Sometimes you do."

SIX

Angie Armstrong was at the hair salon when her phone began to ring. Her eyes were closed and Mike Campbell's cosmic guitar solo from "Runnin' Down a Dream" was playing in her head.

The man holding the sharp scissors happened to be an ex-boyfriend of solid character. They'd broken up over religious differences; he was a re-enlisted Catholic, and Angie refused to set foot in church—any church, not just his. Baptist, Lutheran, Presbyterian, it didn't matter. She was not a fan.

"Under what circumstances," she'd mused to Martin the hairdresser one Sunday morning in bed, "could you envision Jesus Christ, a humble carpenter, hawking rosaries at the Vatican Gift Shop?"

That ended their relationship, except for Angie's monthly haircut. These days they mostly talked about the sorrowful plight of the Marlins or Dolphins.

"Your phone," Martin said, snipping briskly.

"I know." Angie opened her eyes.

"Well, answer it."

"That would be rude," she said, "interrupting an artist at his craft."

"What's rude is your choice of a ringtone."

"Gaga?"

"It's the words."

"*Shut* up!"

"'Pornographic dance fight?'"

"You, who worshipped Prince," said Angie, "are complaining about naughty lyrics?"

Martin snipped faster and louder. "Babe, are you fond of your earlobes?"

"I've been told they're cute."

"Then answer that stupid phone."

The caller ID showed a 202 area code, which was Washington, D.C. A man on the other end identified himself as Agent Paul Ryskamp from the United States Secret Service. He sounded legit.

Angie's first thought was that Pruitt, her nightly phone harasser, had gone off the rails and called her in as a threat to the vacationing President.

But it wasn't that. "We're contacting you about a large snake in our possession," the agent said. "You might've seen it on the news."

"I watched basketball last night. Heat and Mavs went to overtime. What type of snake?"

"Burmese python. Been dead for a while."

"No problem. A hundred dollars plus gas and tolls," Angie said. "Sounds fair."

"I'm curious, sir, how such a specimen ended up in the custody of your particular agency."

"Me, too," said Ryskamp. "When can you be here?"

"Washington?"

"No, Ms. Armstrong. We've got an office in West Palm."

The Secret Service kept an unmarked suite in a downtown office building, from which agents had a distant view of Casa Bellicosa across the Intracoastal Waterway. The space had been selected not for its proximity to the presidential getaway, but rather because the landlord donated half-a-million dollars for media commercials supporting Mastodon during his impeachment trials.

Paul Ryskamp was waiting for Angie in the lobby. She didn't pick him out as an agent immediately because he wore board shorts and an untucked, pineapple-themed tropical shirt. With sun-streaked hair and a Gulf Stream tan, he looked more like a tiki bar mixologist-in-training. She guessed he was in his late forties.

They rode a private elevator to the Secret Service offices. In the kitchen area stood a double-door refrigerator from which the shelves had been removed. Crammed inside the chilled space was an oversized burlap bag, knotted at the top. Ryskamp helped Angie pull the unwieldy load to the floor.

"I'll take it from here," she said.

Three other male agents wandered in, dressed in standard street-fed fashion. They joined Ryskamp in a semicircle around Angie and the hefty parcel.

The knot was too tight. Angie took out a small knife.

"May I?" she asked Ryskamp.

"God, by all means."

Angie sawed off the knot and opened the neck of the bag.

"Holy shit," she said. "I know this snake."

She unfurled the mammoth Burmese and arranged its reeking limpness along the tile floor. The other agents, their faces now as gray as their suits, exited the area.

"Something's missing," Angie remarked.

Ryskamp said, "Uh, yeah? The head."

"No, sir, I've got the head. Something else is gone."

"How can you tell it's the same snake?"

Angie showed the agent a cell phone photo from the Lipid House incident. "The skin is identical," she explained. "Each python's color pattern is unique."

"This one doesn't have a big lump in its belly like the one in your picture."

"Exactly. That's our mystery—what happened to the phantom lump? A.K.A. supper."

Ryskamp smiled. "Let's go down the street and grab a drink. You can tell me the whole story."

"First we'll need a large box," Angie said, "and a shit-ton of ice."

The same night as the White Ibis Ball, eighty miles on the other side of the Gulf Stream, a thirty-two-foot boat departed the Bahamian island of South Bimini on a beeline for the coast of Florida. The vessel was overloaded with twenty migrants plus the captain, but the chop was light, the ride smooth. Powered by twin 350s, the boat moved very fast. Nobody got seasick.

At half-past two, the darkened craft nosed onto a beach across the road from the Palm Beach Country Club. The silent, anxious passengers descended one by one from the bow and began to run. They carried gym bags or backpacks, and not much else. There were six Haitians, five Hondurans, three Chinese and six Cubans, each of whom had paid $8,000 cash to the smuggler.

For all but one of the travelers, the sprint across the sand would be their first footsteps inside the United States. However, a twenty-five-year-old man named Diego Beltrán was returning to a familiar place. He'd earned a bachelor's degree in Latin American studies from the University of Miami before going home to Tegucigalpa after his student visa expired.

After seeing his two favorite uncles shot dead by police at a political rally, Diego decided to return to Florida as soon as possible. Knowing the asylum-application process would be slow and complicated, he drove past the U.S. Embassy and straight to the airport. From there he flew to Nassau via Havana, hopped the mail boat to Bimini, and the following afternoon was sitting at a waterfront bar buying bottles of LandShark for a no-name smuggler with a speedboat.

Diego was the last to debark when they landed on the crystal shore of Palm Beach. He knew by the pattern of the skyline where they were, and how difficult it would be for the others to blend in. When he reached A1A, he turned and saw that the smuggler's boat was already gone. Diego listened to the fading growl of its engines as he pressed his back against the trunk of a tree on the golf course.

Before dawn, he undressed and rinsed off in the fairway sprinklers. He waited to drip-dry before donning a Bon Jovi tee that matched his black jeans and black high-tops. Diego was only five-eight, but his upper arms and shoulders were ripped. Clean-cut was the impression he aimed for; before leaving the Bahamas, he'd shaved his beard and neatly trimmed his black hair.

As the sun rose above the ocean, he walked along the road with an unhurried yet deliberate gait. He didn't want to look like someone who'd just crossed the Gulf Stream on an outlaw's midnight run; he wanted to look like an average guy carrying an average backpack on his way to an average job. Maybe he drove a delivery truck for the florist. Maybe he stocked the aisles at the boutique grocery. Or maybe he even worked the cabana shift at the Bath Club, serving chilled mimosas to crepe-faced old millionaires reeking of designer sun block.

All that mattered to Diego was that nobody paid him any attention. He walked a long way, peeking between the tall sculpted hedges of white stucco mansions grander than anything he'd seen in Miami. He crossed a drawbridge over the Intracoastal and paused to watch a dreamlike procession of southbound yachts, each trailing a seam of froth.

As soon as his shoes touched the mainland, Diego felt safer. He hoped his fellow migrants would make it safely off the island as well. He'd advised them to scatter and go solo, but those traveling with siblings or cousins were unlikely to do that. The Cubans had rides waiting, but the rest of the boat people were on their own. Diego never expected to lay eyes on any of them again, although he would.

On his first day he lucked into a job at an industrial park—a small factory that manufactured rainbow-colored beach umbrellas.

Several of the workers shared rooms at a local roach-friendly motel, so Diego rented himself a cot between two easygoing Nicaraguans. Almost everyone on the umbrella crew was illegal, like him, but he stood out because of his flawless English. The factory's manager, an African American named LeVonte, immediately tapped Diego as a bilingual conduit to the other migrants.

Not long after his arrival, while walking to the factory one morning, he stopped at a railroad crossing to wait for a freight train to pass. It took so long that Diego was afraid he'd be late for work. The moment the last car rolled by, he darted around the warning gates to hurry across the tracks. That's when he spotted a small bright object among the rock ballast in the gutter between the ties.

The object was as pink as cotton candy, smooth though not perfectly round. It looked like a natural pearl, though Diego had never seen one that color. He placed it in his pocket wondering how such an exotic-looking gem—real or fake—had ended up on a railroad bed. It seemed like a sign of good things to come.

But later that same day, Diego was pulled off the stitching line by LeVonte, who whispered, "Tell everyone do not panic, and do *not* fucking run. These dudes got major guns."

"Who?" said Diego.

The dudes with guns were officers from ICE, the U.S. Immigration and Customs Enforcement agency. They were so surprised by Diego's fluency that the female agent who interviewed him triple-checked on her laptop to make sure he wasn't legal before seating him in the ICE van. An hour later he was being processed at the benignly named Broward Transitional Center, a for-profit prison owned by pals of the governor who got a $20 million government contract to lock up and feed undocumented aliens.

In the line of detainees ahead of him, Diego recognized two Haitian women and a Chinese teenager who'd been on the same speedboat from Bimini. They looked downcast, rumpled and hungry. As badly as Diego felt for himself, he felt worse for them.

When he got to the front of the line, his pockets were emptied and inventoried: seventeen dollars in U.S. currency, the key to a motel room, two packs of peppermint chewing gum, and one lustrous pink sphere that Diego no longer believed to be a lucky charm.

Still, on the day he was unexpectedly transferred from immigration detention to the county jail, Diego wouldn't make the connection between the railroad pearl and his ominous change in status from asylum seeker to murder suspect.

Uric saw no downside to killing Prince Paladin. The unreliable fuckhead couldn't be trusted to keep quiet about the python heist, and he'd rat out Uric in a heartbeat if the cops ever braced him. That was his history.

Another factor in Uric's thinking was the mind-blowing $100,000 reward put up by the family of the old lady who'd gotten swallowed by the snake. Uric went on the Palm Beach Police Department's website and closely read the press release. The money was being promised to anyone "providing information that leads to the safe return or whereabouts of Katherine Pew Fitzsimmons." Uric focused on the word "or," which signified to him that a dead body was as valuable as a live one.

While there would be no happy return of Mrs. Fitzsimmons, Uric could definitely provide the details of her whereabouts. In his mind he tinkered with a script for his phone call to the anonymous tip line, settling on this:

I heard about that sweet old lady that's gone missing. Other night at a titty bar I met a dope dealer name of Prince Paladin, he got wasted and started bragging how he offed some rich bitch on the island. He told me he hid her body in concrete at a construction site near a golf course on south A1A. Maybe it was all bullshit, but I'm putting it out there, anyway, in case it was actually him that did it. I'm sure the old lady's family would feel better to get her back, no matter what.

When Uric placed the call, he was assigned a number-and-letter code as identification. Confident of claiming the huge reward, he wrote out the sequence on his left wrist using a black Sharpie.

Although he was demonstrably smarter than Prince Paladin, Uric still wasn't bright enough to see that pinning a front-page murder on a soon-to-be-deceased partner wouldn't cause the police to stop investigating. Likewise he failed to realize that mentioning the titty bar on the tip-line recording was both unnecessary and problematic.

Cops enjoy interviewing strippers, who are often funnier and more forthcoming than fully dressed witnesses. Eleven nude dance clubs were licensed in the county, and Prime Vegas Showgirls happened to be first on the list compiled by the two detectives assigned to check out Uric's tip. Inevitably, they were drawn to the six-foot Russian dancer with matching Jiminy Cricket tats. Without hesitation she identified a mug shot of Prince Paladin—whose real name was Keever Bracco—as one of two white customers that had blown all their cash at the club on a recent night.

One detective said, "Tell us about the other guy."

"Black hair, brown eyes," the dancer recalled. "He was the man that paid for champagne. He really liked me." She pointed with a jade mica fingernail to the center of her forehead. "Was dimple right here."

"A dimple?" the other detective said. "You mean a scar."

"Did not feel to me like scar. More like hole."

"Was the man tall or short?"

"Yes, tall," she said.

"American or Latino?"

"Yes, American."

"Did either of them say their names?"

"I don't remember names," the dancer lied.

By then, Uric—whose forehead indeed bore a noticeable divot— had already strangled Prince Paladin, chained fifty-five pounds of barbells to the corpse and sunk it in the same canal where he'd dumped the stolen Malibu, another move no master criminal would make.

Now Uric needed some cash to tide him over until he collected the Fitzsimmons reward, so he drove his van to a safe pawn shop in West Palm. The owner was a misshapen cretin named Giardia, who habitually wore a cranberry tuxedo jacket to conceal his shoulder holster.

When Uric placed the dead woman's diamond earrings on the counter top, Giardia scooped them up and humped like a badger toward his vile-smelling office in the rear of the store.

"What the fuck, bro? You tryin' to get me busted?" he whinnied at Uric, who'd followed him into the room. "Shut the goddamn door."

Uric said, "Chill your fat ass. Those earrings were my mom's. I mean before she died."

"Right. And your mom, she was Jackie Onassis?"

"Her name was Inga, and she was a goddamn saint."

Giardia held the diamonds up to the bulb of a gooseneck lamp, salaciously turning them with his fingers, marveling at the rich sparkle. "Don't tell me how you got hold a these. It doesn't matter," he said, "because I *cannot* move 'em. Whoever they belong to, she's already called the cops."

Uric smiled. "No, she hasn't."

"I'd have to be insane to do this," said the pawnbroker, though he seemed in no hurry to hand back the earrings.

"How many carats?" Uric asked.

"Don't even go there. I'll give you five grand for the pair. Take or leave. And use the back door, bro."

"Wait. I got more."

Uric removed the snake lady's pearls from his pocket and lined them up like rosy marbles on the pawnbroker's desk.

"Also your mom's?" Giardia needled.

"From her favorite necklace. The chain got broke, I'm sad to say."

"Only thing is, they're, like, all different kinds a pink. What is *that* one—magenta? And half of 'em, they ain't even round."

What a scammer, Uric thought.

He said, "Those are conch pearls. They're s'posed to look that way, and you know it. Want 'em, or not? I went online and did the research, my man. They're super rare—guess how much Carter's sells a conch-pearl ring for?"

"Who?"

"Carter's. It's only the most famous jewelry store in all New York."

Giardia chuckled acidly and clicked his brown teeth. "You mean *Cartier's.*"

"Fuck you."

"I'll give you eight hundred for all of 'em."

"Yeah, yeah. Whatever."

"I only count eighteen," Giardia said, rolling the pearls into his right palm. "That's a queer number for a necklace."

"Well, you would know."

"Did you keep some for a girlfriend?"

"Yeah. Your little sister." Uric assumed that any lost pearls were in the trunk of the Malibu, at the bottom of the canal.

"Just give me the damn money," he snapped at the pawnbroker.

Mockingbird lay up to her neck in the bathtub. She wore silver seahorse earrings and fresh rose-colored lipstick. Her long auburn hair was pinned into a bun, and her unpainted toes peeked over the marble sill. She turned off the water jets and reached for her Cosmo. It was the third of the evening. She wasn't keeping track, but somebody on the staff undoubtedly was. They kept track of everything.

Almost.

Her bathroom had a westward view, overlooking the Intracoastal Waterway. Mockingbird put on her favorite Dior shades to watch the sun go down over the mainland. She left them on after darkness fell.

"Yo, Keith," she called out. "Where are those snake pics?"

"On my phone," replied a voice from the other side of the door.

"I want to see!"

"Soon as you're done, ma'am."

"No, Keith, now."

Keith Josephson's real name was Ahmet Youssef, one of the sharpest young agents in the satellite detail assigned to protect the President's wife. His father was a Syrian Muslim but his mother was Boston Irish, so Ahmet had been raised Catholic. Professionally, the Youssef surname had become problematic because of Mastodon's festering distrust of Muslims—and anyone looking or sounding like they *might* be Muslim. To avert a blowup, the Secret Service had created a new neutral-sounding identity for Ahmet Youssef a week before he joined Mockingbird on the campaign trail. Ahmet had been shocked and offended, yet he'd said nothing; the agency offered a solid future, and Mastodon wouldn't be president forever.

The ID switch had worked splendidly. On Keith/Ahmet's first trip aboard the campaign plane, Mastodon had expressed no curiosity about his heritage, commented enviously on his skin tone and demanded the name of his bronzing product. Caught off guard, Keith had lied and said he favored tanning beds.

"Agent Josephson, where are you?" Mockingbird sang out from the bathroom.

He entered sideways, averting his eyes as he edged past the makeup table toward the tub. It wasn't the first time that the First Lady had been naked when she summoned him.

"Would you like a towel?" he asked.

"No, I'd like to see those pictures."

"My phone case isn't waterproof."

"I'll be careful, Keith. Give it to me, please."

Mockingbird sat upright, the bathwater dripping in soapy rivulets from her breasts. The walls were plated with gold-lace mirroring, which from several angles gave Keith an unavoidable, glorious view. He gave her the phone. She kept her sunglasses on.

"My God, that thing's a beast!" she exclaimed. "Even with no head."

"Burmese python. It was a messy scene."

"What's all that goop?" she asked, tapping one of the images on the screen.

"The intestines, ma'am. And other organs, I imagine."

"Where on earth did it come from?"

"This particular species has spread all over the Everglades," said the agent, unsuccessfully trying to stare at anything other than the First Lady's body. "We're not sure how this one ended up where it did."

Mockingbird laughed. "Are you kidding? It just crawled there, of course. That's what snakes do. Then it got killed by a car, obviously."

"No, ma'am. The head was removed with a sharp object, possibly a sword or a machete."

Mockingbird scrolled back and forth through the graphic sequence of photos. She said, "It's gross but also kind of exciting, yes?"

"We're in Florida. This is what goes on."

"Maybe it's more. Maybe it's an omen."

"Of what, ma'am?"

"We'll see. Here, catch," she said, tossing him the phone. Then she rose in the tub and let her hair down.

He held his breath. "*Now* may I get you a towel?"

"How long 'til my girlfriends arrive for dinner?"

"Twenty-six minutes."

"Plenty of time, right?"

"Yes, ma'am. Probably."

"So. Are we going to do this or not?"

"It's up to you."

"You're funny," she said, plucking off her shades. "Lock the door, Agent Josephson. And take off your gun."

SEVEN

Special Agent Paul Ryskamp was a good listener but a poor liar.

"I believe you, Ms. Armstrong."

"No, sir, you do not. And call me Angie."

"I don't know much about snakes, but it sure looked big enough to eat a small person."

"The part about burglars stealing it from my storage unit? There's an actual police report. Same shitbirds who tossed my apartment."

Again Ryskamp said, "I believe you."

"Even though I never actually saw the woman's body?"

"Just a lump in the python, right?"

"Correct," Angie said. "As I said, the burglars were hired for one reason—somebody didn't want the state lab to dissect that animal. I'm betting on Teabull, the caretaker at Lipid House."

"Because he was afraid the bad publicity would hurt his event business. Makes sense to me."

"Admit it. You're just playing along."

The agent said, "No, I'm keeping an open mind."

"Knock it off. Wasn't I up-front about my hitch in prison?"

"I already knew about your felony record. And you probably knew I knew."

"Every word I've told you today is true."

"Our mission at the agency," said Ryskamp, "is to protect the President and his family. At this point we're confident the dead snake wasn't deliberately placed in the road to block the motorcade, and that it posed no danger to the First Lady. Consequently, that's where my professional interest in the python ends. I'm sorry."

"But what about Mrs. Fitzsimmons?" Angie asked.

"Finding her body is a matter for the local authorities. It's a dark, weird narrative, for sure."

"No shit. Sir."

"Thanks for the beer," the agent said.

After he was gone, Angie sat frowning at the empty bar stool. Nothing could be done for the deceased socialite, wherever her mortal remains might be. But those goddamn burglars, Angie thought, ought to be held accountable for what they did. Meanwhile the bad-luck reptile reposed in a cardboard appliance box packed with dry ice in the bed of Angie's pickup. The Secret Service, she'd discovered, does not pay in cash. Ryskamp had left her with a four-page voucher request and a promise that a check from the U.S. Treasury would appear in Angie's mailbox after the paperwork was processed.

Which meant at least three months.

The bar was on busy Clematis Street in downtown West Palm. Angie had parked on a side road several blocks away. As she approached her truck, she noticed that the tailgate was down. Three skinny figures stood in the back, struggling to lift the appliance box. As Angie crept up behind the truck, she thought it wise that the state of Florida no longer allowed her to carry a firearm. She slammed shut the tailgate, hopped to the driver's seat, jammed the key in the ignition and stepped on the gas. Two of the would-be thieves got launched immediately; the third hung on until Angie took a corner at high speed, the airborne asshole waving a defiant middle finger in the moments before his face impacted a stop sign.

Angie stopped at her apartment and took the bagged python head out of the freezer compartment of the refrigerator. Then she drove to her secret burial ground near the Loxahatchee Slough and dug a round pit. When she opened the cardboard box, she was enveloped by cool tendrils of smoke curling up from the chunked dry ice. She backed up the truck and, using a cattle rope, dragged the snake corpse out of the box, off the flatbed and into the grave. The head went in last.

An hour later she was home, standing in the shower. After the hot water ran out, she got dressed and called Joel about meeting for dinner. He said he was going out with his father and the equestrian girlfriend.

"Her pelvis must be healed. It's like a miracle," Angie remarked.

"You mean healed enough for *that*? I wouldn't know."

"I suppose he's still infatuated."

Joel, who was maddeningly neutral, said, "Dad's just Dad."

"Does she limp now?"

"Would that make you feel better?"

"Elated, I'm ashamed to say."

"You need to meet a new guy," Joel said, "soon as possible."

"I'm on it," Angie said.

On a whim, she changed from jeans and flats to a black dress and heels, brushed her teeth and headed for a Mediterranean restaurant called Nikko, which was on the island and therefore out of her price range. The drive up from Lake Worth was neither scenic nor speedy, but Angie was accustomed to mad interstate traffic. Besides the Greek salad, the main attraction at Nikko was a hazel-eyed assistant manager named Spalding, who'd been helping Angie practice her flirting. Spalding had a killer accent, and plausibly presented himself as South African. He'd been unattached since breaking up with the college-age daughter of covid refugees who'd packed up and moved the clan back to Connecticut.

Angie was surprised to see Spalding texting alone at the bar in Nikko's. She took the seat beside him and asked if he was on a break.

He looked up and smiled. "I'm not working tonight, Lady Tarzan."

He'd tagged her with the annoying nickname because of her line of work. She tolerated it only because she liked him.

"You're probably waiting for a rich babe in a leather micro-skirt," she said.

"Nope. Flying solo."

"Hard to believe."

"I'll even buy you a drink," Spalding said, "because I'm celebrating."

"Life in general?"

"A new job. Tomorrow I start at Casa Bellicosa. The pay sucks, but at least I don't have to leave the country."

There'd been an issue with his work visa—a minor traffic stop, during which police spied a half-smoked joint in a cup holder.

Spalding said, "My manager here tried to get the problem smoothed over, but no luck. Then one of the Ukrainian dishwashers told me that if you get hired at the President's club, magic things happen to your immigration status. And that, Lady Tarzan, is exactly how it went down. Apparently they're desperate for fair-skinned foreigners who speak perfect English. No tats allowed, however. They actually did a full-body check."

"With that visual seared in my mind," said Angie, "I'll take a Bombay-and-tonic. Two limes."

"I'm down for that. Tell me about your day in the fearsome sub-urban jungles."

"The highlight? I interacted like a responsible citizen with the United States Secret Service."

"Stop right there," Spalding said. "That word 'interact'—if you were trying to pick me up right now, I'd think you were a total nerd and walk away. We've had this chat before, Angie. If you're going to tell a story to a hot guy, tell it in a way that brings him to the edge of his seat. Or the edge of . . . whatever."

The waiter arrived with Angie's drink. She squeezed the limes, tasted the gin and said, "Okay, how's this: *I spent the afternoon hanging with the Secret Service . . . ?*"

Spalding laughed. "Much better!"

"They gave me a large dead python to transport. Eighteen-footer."

He grimaced. "Again, let's hit the pause button. You know I'm not a snake person."

"I can't talk about it, anyway," Angie said in a fake whisper. "This case reaches to the highest levels of government."

Spalding raised his eyebrows. "Now *that's* a pretty tasty line."

"Seriously. I've been warned not to discuss it."

"With bold men at bars?"

"With anybody, anywhere."

"Bullshit. You can trust me." Spalding gave her a scheming wink. "By the way, the Secret Service? That's who cleared me for the server job at the presidential Casa. Fingerprints, photos, birth certificate, heavy-duty background."

"They didn't care about the pot bust?" Angie asked.

"Seriously? A hundred bucks says the First Lady vapes like a fiend."

"I were her, I'd go straight for the needle."

"Christ, I'm starved," said Spalding, flipping open the menu. "But first, let me respond to your 'rich micro-skirt' comment. I ever meet the right girl, I won't give a shit if she's dead broke and dressed like she works in the opal mines."

Angie smiled. "Does that mean I've got a chance?"

"With me? Probably not. However, as your social coach, I'm just saying all guys aren't dying for long legs and old money. Somewhere out there waiting for you is a cool, emotionally mature, sexually adventurous reptile freak. Meanwhile I'm ordering the swordfish and starting with stuffed mushrooms. Are you in, or out?"

Driving home after dinner, Angie found herself facing a river of brake lights on I-95. She darted off the ramp at Southern, crossed back to the island and turned south on A1A. It appeared to be a smart move; traffic was light. Angie rolled down her windows—she loved the sound of the ocean breakers, the taste of salt on the breeze. Offshore were the lights of a long ship, probably an oil tanker headed

for Port Everglades. She wished she could afford a waterfront apartment; waking up to the sight of the Atlantic would add at least ten
years to her life.

Soon she spotted a cluster of police lights ahead, and the cars in
front of her began to slow. She assumed it was a DUI checkpoint,
and felt clever to have stopped at one drink. Getting closer, though,
she saw it was a full-blown crime scene at a flood-lit construction
site near the Par-3 golf course. As her truck crawled past the commotion, Angie counted six cop cars (four marked, two unmarked),
an ambulance, three TV satellite vans, and a long black SUV from
the medical examiner's office.

Behind the fluttering yellow tape trudged two burly workers
caked with concrete dust. Their faces pulsed in red and blue as they
walked past the squad cars. Angie noticed that each of the men was
lugging a demolition jackhammer.

"Bad gig," she said to herself.

Then she drove home to catch the news on TV.

Early the next morning, the police chief met with the Cornbrights
to deliver the sad news: Kiki Pew's remains had been found. The
death was definitely a homicide, though the cause had yet to be
confirmed.

"Then how do you know it was murder?" Chase asked.

"Because her body had been concealed under fresh cement," Jerry
Crosby replied.

Muted gasps followed.

Chance raised his right hand to say: "Maybe Mother tripped and
fell in. The McMarmots said she was heavy into the Don Julio that
night."

"I thought it was Tito's," his brother cut in.

"This wasn't an accident. I'm sorry," said the chief.

Fay Alex Riptoad arrived, dressed for tennis and ruddy-cheeked

81

from her sunrise lava scrub. When she noticed the Cornbrights sniffling, she folded her sunglasses and demanded a recap from Crosby. Immediately his eyes began to well up, not from the circumstances but rather from Fay Alex's noxious choice of perfume.

"Jerry, what kind of monster would do this!" she cried. "Kiki Pew didn't have an enemy in the world."

"Don't worry. We'll catch him." Crosby spoke with more certainty than was warranted. His town had a lower murder rate than Antarctica's, and consequently his staff lacked the experience of most South Florida detectives, for whom heinous homicides were a routine occurrence.

"What on earth was the motive?" Fay Alex said. "For God's sake, we need answers. We're suffering here, Jerry. We're *mourning*, and you're not helping one damn bit." She grabbed a Kleenex box and forcibly passed it among the Cornbrights.

The chief told the group about the hotline tip that led to the discovery of Kiki Pew's body at the residential construction site near the Par-3.

Fay Alex said: "Isn't that where the crazy Nicaraguan is building that ghastly house? He's probably mixed up in all this."

"The property owner is Venezuelan," Crosby noted, "and he won't be back from Caracas until April."

"How convenient."

"The hotline caller identified a suspect, Mrs. Riptoad. Every officer from here to Key Largo has his name and mug shot. It's only a matter of time before we find him."

"Well, who is he, Jerry? Who, who, *who*?" Fay Alex brayed.

"A convicted narcotics dealer. All of you will be the first to know when he's in custody." The chief turned to the Cornbright sons. "Unfortunately, in the meantime I need someone to come with me and I.D. your mother's body."

Chance said, "How come? I mean if you already know for sure it's her."

"We need a family member to make it official."

Chance shook his head no. Chase did the same. Their wives simultaneously paled and declined.

Fay Alex Riptoad spoke up. "I count as family, Jerry. I'll do it."

The offspring of the late Katherine Pew Fitzsimmons gratefully approved the proxy. On the ride to the county morgue, Fay Alex complained to Crosby about the lack of a makeup mirror on the passenger-side visor. He told her to prepare for a difficult experience.

Fay Alex said, "I sat in on my first husband's vasectomy. How could this possibly be worse?"

"Why would you want to watch that kind of surgery?"

"To make sure the horny bastard went through with it. By then he'd already knocked up our Lamaze teacher."

Crosby thought: *This is what I get for asking.*

He said, "Mrs. Riptoad, what you're about to see won't be anything like that."

And it wasn't.

The layout of the Venezuelan's future mansion was expansive, but the police who'd searched the construction site were guided by a distinctive stench that led them to a Z-shaped crack in a rectangle of recently poured concrete. As it turned out, Tripp Teabull was wrong—the footers were not deep enough to permanently entomb a decomposing corpse, even a diminutive one.

Before entering the autopsy room, Fay Alex was given a hospital mask and protective glasses. Crosby expected her to break down at the sight of her dead friend, but Fay Alex remained stoic and upright, her whitened fists clutching the steel table for balance.

"Mrs. Riptoad, is that the person you know as Katherine Fitzsimmons?"

"Yes, it's Kiki Pew," she said, her voice thin but unbroken. "Dear God, what'd they do to her?"

"The medical examiner took preliminary X-rays. Most of her ribs are broken. He believes she was grabbed around the chest and asphyxiated by someone extremely strong. The lineal patterns of small punctures from her head to torso—he's not sure what caused those. He says he's never seen wounds like that before."

"When is the autopsy?"

"This afternoon."

The chief waited for Fay Alex to back away, now that the gruesome task was completed. Instead she leaned closer to her friend's body. "Where's her damn jewelry, Jerry?"

"I, uh . . . what jewelry?"

"An absolutely breathtaking conch-pearl necklace, and those diamond earrings Mott gave her the Valentine's Day before he died."

"You're sure about that?"

"I saw them with my own eyes, Jerry. You think I'd forget what she was wearing that night?" Fay Alex had done a pop-in at the White Ibis Ball before dashing to another big-ticket gala, the annual benefit for Psoriatic Gingivitis.

"Be right back," Crosby said. He moved to the other end of the room and called the medical examiner. The answer he received was the one he'd expected.

When he returned to the table where the late Mrs. Fitzsimmons lay agape, Fay Alex hadn't backed away. "Please tell me," she said, "that Kiki Pew's jewels are safe and sound in the coroner's vault."

Crosby shook his head. "Nothing's been removed from the body since it was found. There wasn't any necklace or earrings."

"So the killer stole them."

"Looks that way, yes."

"Isn't that what you people call a 'promising lead'?"

"It is," the chief replied tightly. "Thank you, Mrs. Riptoad."

"You're welcome, Jerry. Now get the fuck *on* it."

EIGHT

The most desirable sea mollusk on the planet is the queen conch, too scrumptious for its own good. Once abundant throughout the shallows and coral reefs of South Florida, the slow-growing snail was nearly wiped out by fritter-crazed divers in the 1970s. Domestic harvesting of the species was outlawed.

Today, the United States consumes eighty percent of all commercially sold conch. Most of it comes from the Bahamas and Caribbean islands, where the spiky, porcelain-lipped shells are plucked from the bottom one at a time by free divers. A small pick or screwdriver is used to punch a hole in the tip, severing the tissue connecting the animal's tough, coiled body to its mobile lair. The flesh—a slimy, unappealing muscle—is then pulled from the shell and tenderized with a mallet. The noisy ritual may be witnessed by anyone fortunate enough to be visiting an island when a conch boat pulls up to the dock. Lucky tourists may be offered bags of the fresh cutlets, to be immersed in the nearest fryer or diced into a salad.

A queen conch that reaches five years in age might weigh several pounds. About one of every ten thousand *Strombus gigas* specimens produces a small colorful pearl, the gastric equivalent of a glamour kidney stone, though only a very small percent are gem quality. The calcareous masses are discovered by fishermen when the conch is removed from the water and dislodged from its shell. Many pearls have a pink hue; others are shades of yellow, brown or salmon. A precious few feature a striking flame-like pattern. Some of the pearls are oval, some are elongated. Perfectly round ones are absurdly rare.

Conch pearls appeared first in Edwardian jewelry and later in Art Nouveau pieces popular during the early twentieth century. Interest ebbed after World War I with the rise of Art Deco, and for a long time afterward the international market was negligible. If you were in the conch trade, the money was in the meat. The pearls were peddled locally as inexpensive souvenirs.

But in the late 1980s, commercial interest in the gems resurged and the prices began to rise. Conch divers from Bermuda to Belize became more attentive when extracting the otherwise homely mollusks. In 2012, Sotheby's auctioned a 1920s-era enamel bracelet made with diamonds and conch pearls for $3.5 million. It wasn't long before Cartier, Mikimoto and Tiffany began designing expensive conch-pearl pendants, earrings and rings. The shape, size and coloration of the pearls influence the price at dockside in Freeport, as well as in the shops of Manhattan. Exceptionally radiant specimens can fetch as much as $15,000 per carat.

None of these facts were known to Diego Beltrán. Nor was he aware that the bubblegum-colored ball that he'd picked up from the gravel between two railroad ties had been catapulted from the open trunk of a stolen Malibu jouncing across the tracks carrying a deceased, headless python.

Now Diego's pearl was being rolled between the thumb and hairy forefinger of a middle-aged police detective, who asked, "Where'd you get this?"

Diego told him.

"Bullshit," the detective said. "Where's Keever Bracco?"

"Who?"

"Prince Paladin, your partner. I guess you want to play games."

"Never heard of him," said Diego. He pointed at the pearl. "What's *that* got to do with this?"

"It's from a stolen necklace, Mr. Beltrán. By the way, where'd you pawn the diamonds?"

"What diamonds?"

"The *victim's* diamonds, you cocksucker."

Diego was thunderstruck. "What victim?"

He and the detective sat facing each other across a bare table in a dreary taupe interview room that smelled liked Clorox and boiled urine. The night before, ICE officers had removed Diego from the immigration lockup, slapped on the handcuffs, placed him in a government car, and transported him to the county jail. No reason was given.

Diego was unaware that the Palm Beach police had sent insurance photos of a homicide victim's missing jewelry to all major law-enforcement agencies, and that the ICE agent who'd first booked Diego remembered the exotic little pearl among his meager belongings. Nor could Diego foresee that the commander-in-chief of the United States would soon take an ardent interest in the case because the wealthy victim had belonged to an all-female political fan group. Diego likewise couldn't know that the President would become animated—almost giddy—when informed that one of the suspects in the elderly Potussy's death was an illegal Hispanic immigrant who was rounded up at a factory only a few miles from the crime scene. The story line would jibe splendidly with one of the President's favorite fake-populist narratives: The nation was under siege by bloodthirsty hordes charging like rabid wolverines across the borders.

Diego said: "I swear I didn't steal anything from anybody."

The detective told him a prominent resident of the island had been kidnapped, robbed, and barbarically killed. She'd been wearing diamond earrings and a necklace made of rare pink pearls, one of which bore a constellation of faint saffron freckles.

"Just like yours does," the detective added acidly.

"Can I take a look?" Diego held out his hand.

The detective wouldn't give up the pearl. "You'd need one of those special magnifying glasses to see what I'm talking about."

"A jeweler's loupe."

"That's right, smartass. Don't worry, it's the same damn pearl as in the picture."

Diego didn't believe him. "I want to call a lawyer, please."

"Oh, Christ, here we go," the detective sneered, "like you're some kind a regular citizen."

"I went to college in Miami."

"But you re-entered the country illegally on a smuggling vessel from the Bahamas last week. True or false? Spoiler alert: We've already interviewed some of your fellow passengers."

"Yes, I admit I was aboard that boat."

"Same night our victim disappeared, not far from where you and your people snuck ashore. Was His Highness the Prince of Percocets waiting for you at the beach?"

Diego slid lower in the chair and rubbed his eyes. "I want to call a lawyer," he said again.

"Well, of course you do, *amigo!*"

Angie didn't care about the frail-hipped equestrian girlfriend, but she remained bitter about the way Joel's father had left her, with no warning or discussion. One afternoon, four women—all strangers wearing camo yoga leggings—had swept into the marital residence to haul away her husband's belongings and loot the kitchen.

After snatching the coffee maker, the last of them paused at the door and nodded equably.

"Namaste *this*, bitch," said Angie, raising both middle fingers.

Later she discovered that one of the yoga mafia was her husband's mistress, the equestrian.

On the day the divorce was finalized, Angie stopped her ex outside the courtroom and said, "I just want you to be happy, Dustin," which wasn't true. She wanted him to be regretful, lonely, riven with guilt and self-doubt.

It was a deplorable attitude, and Angie was ashamed by its longevity. Her friends said she'd feel differently as soon as she found somebody new, somebody special. So far, she'd met not one male soul that she'd found dazzling. Her friends said that she should be more outgoing, that she was setting the bar too high, that she was too judgmental, too cautious, too literal.

"Maybe I'm not emotionally available," Angie would tell them, "but at least I'm polite."

She didn't want to get married again, though she would've liked a relationship that lasted longer than four dates. It was always disheartening when the conversation ran dry—that graveyard stillness at the end of dinner, so unforgiving that you could hear a widower buttering a French roll at the next table.

Angie's friends tried to rally her with tales of crazed inconsequential sex, but in her experience such a thing didn't exist. Even a half-drunken fuck inevitably got misread by one or both parties as commitment. By now Angie knew the script, which usually stalled in the second act.

Nothing romantic was in progress when the virus pandemic struck, so her social calendar had not been noticeably impacted. Now that people were dating again, she was trying to move forward with a more receptive attitude. She was getting ready for a rare night out, in brand-new jeans, when a TV bulletin announced that the body found in Palm Beach had been positively identified as Katherine Pew Fitzsimmons.

The police chief had called a press conference to reveal that the woman had been robbed of her jewelry and brutally slain. Angie figured that the burglars who stole the python from her warehouse unit had removed the victim's valuables before hiding the corpse. In her view, such coldblooded shitsuckers deserved to be punished like murderers, not just thieves.

The TV newscast replayed video taken where the body had been found. Angie had seen the footage the night before, and recognized the scene as the construction site she'd driven past on A1A.

She phoned her date, whom she'd met only once previously, for coffee.

"I'm really sorry," she said, "but something urgent just came up."

"Like what? Urgent how?" His name was Jesse, and originally he was from Queens. Now he worked at Merrill Lynch in Boynton Beach.

"It's work-related," said Angie.

"Can I come with?" Jesse knew she relocated wild animals for a living; she'd shared a few of her better stories over coffee at Starbucks.

She said, "Not tonight. Maybe another time."

"This is way rude."

"I don't mean to be. It's a business emergency."

"Unbelievably rude, Angie."

"Seriously?"

"My ex used to pull this kind of shit all the time."

"Well, I wish I could say I'll make it up to you."

"What does *that* mean?"

"Bye." Angie put down the phone like it was a hot poker. Right away it started ringing. The caller ID displayed a number supposedly in Ketchum, Idaho. Angie didn't know anyone in that area code.

"Hello, Pruitt," she said.

"Why the hell do you answer if you know it's me?"

"You're late tonight. It's six-thirty-seven."

"Fuck you, bitch. *Your* time is up!"

"Is one of the dogs sick?" Angie asked. "Is that why you're late—you just got back from the vet's?"

"Stop talkin' shit," Pruitt snapped.

"I know the Bichon struggles with gout. It's been a tough road, hasn't it? Lots of emotional ups and downs."

"Hey, cunt, I'm going to blow up your stupid pickup truck with you inside."

"Pruitt, listen to me. A one-handed amateur should *not* be dicking with live explosives. That prosthesis is fine for routine household tasks—washing dishes, folding laundry and so forth—but not wiring a bomb. Just a thought."

"Anyway, who the fuck told you about my dogs?"

"Gotta run," said Angie. "Have a peaceful evening, sir."

She couldn't reach Paul Ryskamp by phone, so she drove to the hangout bar in West Palm. Along the way, she noticed the roadblocks were down; that meant the President was gone. Angie thought Ryskamp might be unwinding with some of his agent friends and, sure enough, he was.

Angie walked up and said, "You look positively lethal in that suit."

"What are you drinking?" Ryskamp asked.

"Nothing."

They moved to a table in the corner. Angie asked Ryskamp if he'd heard the news about Mrs. Fitzsimmons.

The agent nodded. "Your alleged python victim. It's a bummer."

"Not alleged. She definitely got eaten. Then whoever stole the snake from my warehouse put her body under two feet of concrete."

"Like I told you before, it's a local case. We don't investigate that kind of crime . . . whatever you'd call it."

Angie said, "They took her damn jewelry. I'd call that robbery."

Ryskamp tapped his beer mug. "The way the statutes are written, I'm not sure you can 'rob' a dead person that you didn't kill yourself. Stealing from a corpse is probably grand theft."

"Suddenly you're an attorney?"

"Not suddenly. Georgetown Law, class of '98."

Angie shrugged. "Okay. Decent school."

"It is."

"You want me to admit I'm impressed?"

Angie was well aware that the Secret Service didn't normally investigate burglaries and body snatchings. All she wanted from Ryskamp was a little help. She knew that, because of the President's frequent presence at Casa Bellicosa, the Palm Beach police regularly shared information with Ryskamp's office.

"What else do the cops know?" she asked him.

"I'm not supposed to—"

"Talk about it? Let me point out that your agency would still have a large mangled reptile in its Sub-Zero, if not for me. Sir."

"Call me Paul, okay? And it's not a Sub-Zero, it's a fucking Kenmore. But I agree—you were punctual and efficient."

"Don't forget 'discreet.' As advertised."

"Very discreet," Ryskamp said good-humoredly. "All right, here's the latest from the locals, which you did *not* hear from me. They're looking for one suspect and interviewing another guy as a possible second."

"Who's got him?"

"Immigration, technically. But they moved him over to the county lockup."

"Do they have a solid ID?" Angie asked.

"We're waiting to confirm."

"What about the first dude?"

"His name I've got."

"Outstanding. I'll take it." Angie reached in her bag for a pen.

"What the hell are you going to do?" the agent asked.

"Assist my law-enforcement brethren."

"Don't. I'm serious."

"Oh, stop worrying," said Angie. "It's not your case, remember?"

Uric used a burner phone to dial the hotline, in case the cops were tracing the calls. Nobody ever picked up, so Uric left several recorded messages saying he was ready to claim the $100,000 reward, since it was his tip that had led authorities to Mrs. Fitzsimmons's body. At the end of each call Uric carefully recited his confidential code—the numerals and letters were still visible in Sharpie ink on his wrist because he hadn't bathed since disposing of Prince Paladin.

Surely the old woman's relatives intended to pay in cash; sending a check or wire transfer would require that the tipster provide an ID, defeating the whole point of an anonymous hotline. Uric figured that, once he connected with an actual human, he'd be given directions to the family's bank. There he would simply show his wrist to a teller and collect his hundred grand.

He'd spent the night in the back of his van, the odor so foul that it kept him awake. He looked forward to buying something newer after collecting the Fitzsimmons reward. For now he was suffering at a Walmart, parked among the vehicles of other budget-conscious overnighters—mostly in RVs and pop-up campers. Although Uric still had some of the pawn money from the dead lady's jewels, he chose not to waste it on a hotel room. Staying in the Walmart lot was free.

To kill time he wandered the aisles of the store, luridly appraising listless housewives while loading his shopping cart with pet diapers, hoverboard batteries, orchid-scented sun block, fluorescent cross-trainers, candied pomegranates and other useless crap. He abandoned the cart at the deli counter after ordering a pepperoni-and-meatball hoagie. Outside, in the parking lot, he watched a young couple nearly come to blows trying to squeeze a giant flat-screen television into their two-door Honda.

Uric popped a Coors Light and unfolded a stolen lawn chair next to his van. He pulled out the burner phone, dialed the hotline again and was pleased to hear a living person named Judith Asher answer. She sounded friendly, sharp and helpful. After Uric provided his call-in code, she confirmed that his other messages had been received and passed along to the police, as well as to the family of the late Mrs. Fitzsimmons.

Uric said, "Cool. So how long till I get paid?"

"I don't have that information right now. You'll have to keep checking in."

"Here's a better idea. Just call me as soon as the money's ready."

"I'm sorry, but that's not possible," Judith Asher said. "To protect the privacy of our tipsters, we don't file any phone numbers. You should try back on this line in a few days."

Uric was irritated by her reply. "A few *days*? Why so long, Judith? Is there a problem?"

"I don't have that information."

"Are you fuckin' serious? The cops wouldn't never have found that old lady's dead body weren't for me. There wouldn't be no big fancy funeral 'cause her kids wouldn't have a damn thing to put in the coffin!"

"Sir, there's no cause to use profanity. I wish I could help, but I'm just a volunteer. You really need to call back in a couple days—"

"Okay, okay. Whatever." Uric took a deep breath. "I'm sorry, Judith. Really I am. By the way, you've got, like, a perfect voice for this line of work. Can I ask, are you single? Because you *sound* single. Hello? Judith?"

At the moment Uric's hotline hottie hung up on him, Palm Beach Police Chief Jerry Crosby was standing in the oak-paneled billiard room of Kiki Pew Fitzsimmons's house, waiting for her sons to finish a monotonously unskilled game of eight-ball. Fay Alex Riptoad was present in her self-appointed role of family adviser, and she was engaged full-throttle.

"What did the tipster sound like on the phone?" she asked the chief.

"Late twenties, early thirties."

"No, Jerry, I'm talking about his color. White or black?"

"He's got a mild Southern accent."

Fay Alex nodded. "So we can rule out the Hispanics. That helps."

Crosby said no, his detectives couldn't rule out anyone based on telephone recordings.

"The issue right now is what to do about the reward money, Mrs. Riptoad. Whoever this person is, it was his information that led us to Mrs. Fitzsimmons. All the other tips we got were garbage. Now, is he telling the truth about hearing it from the killer at a bar, or was he involved in the crime himself? That's our concern."

"Duh," said Fay Alex.

Either Chase or Chance finally scratched, ending their inept duel. They both slapped their cue sticks down on the pool table, gouging the burgundy felt.

"Do we really have to pay this guy?" Chance asked. "A hundred grand's a lot of dough."

His brother said, "Yeah, what's he gonna do—sue us for it? Our mother just died, for God's sake."

The chief, who was experienced at interacting with overbred dolts, crafted a simple path for the Cornbrights:

"The media's already asking if the reward's been claimed. If you don't pay up, they'll want to know why—and, if there's not a damn good reason, you can expect major PR blowback. Here's what I rec-ommend: Stall for a few days to give my detectives time to work up some assailant profiles, then you put out a press release, pay the reward and we'll see if the evidence trail leads to anyone who matches up with the caller."

Chance glanced at Chase, who shrugged one shoulder. "The whole hundred thousand?" he asked.

"It's not my money," said Crosby. "But it's not my reputation, either."

He was talking about the family's status on the island. Being pegged as welshers would cost the sons of Kiki Pew some valuable social points.

Fay Alex, who wished not to be tainted by association, urged Chase and Chance to cough up the dough. "Otherwise you'll be all over social media, and not in a good way. Think about your wives and children. Palm Beach is a hideously small town. This is a legacy issue."

The brothers mulled the problem. Eventually Chance said, "Mother probably would want us to pay the reward."

"Yes, but not necessarily *all* of it," added Chase.

Fay Alex stewed, her taut cheeks turning color.

Jerry Crosby was looking out a window at the immaculate green yard, where a lawn worker's leaf blower had caught fire. The worker calmly heaved it in the swimming pool and ambled away.

"Here's another idea," Crosby said, turning back to the group. "Give the phone tipster half the money now, and promise to pay the balance in a couple weeks. You can tell the media you're acting on the advice of the police."

The Cornbright brothers agreed in an instant. Relieved to be unburdened, they departed for an early lunch at the Alabaster Club, leaving the chief alone with Fay Alex in the billiard room. She continued fuming about Chase and Chance:

"They're whining about a lousy hundred thousand bucks—my God, Kiki Pew spent more than that every year on stem cells! And did her boys even once ask about the progress of the murder investigation?"

The chief said, "Not that I heard."

"Well, *I'm* asking, Jerry. Is there anything new? Anything at all?"

"My detectives are interviewing a young man who had a pink pearl in his possession. We believe it belonged to Mrs. Fitzsimmons. The kid claims he found it on the railroad tracks, which we're not buying."

"Obviously. Come on."

"Right now we're trying to connect him to Keever Bracco, the drug dealer identified by the anonymous caller as the one who killed your friend."

Fay Alex paused to consider the momentous development. "This new suspect," she said, "the man with Kiki Pew's pearl, I assume he's in jail?"

"Immigration busted him. He came by boat from the Bahamas the night she disappeared."

"Oh, dear Lord." Fay Alex wrung her well-moisturized hands. "What's the bastard's name, Jerry?"

"Diego Beltrán. However, we're not ready to release that—"

"Diego?"

"Correct."

"I knew it! I *knew* it had to be one of those horrible Hispanic caravan people."

"No, I told you he arrived by sea," the chief said uselessly. "The investigation is still in the early stages. We haven't charged him with anything yet."

"What on earth are you waiting for? I *cannot* believe the non-sense I'm hearing." Fay Alex was practically levitating with distress. "Suppose this thug gets out of jail and flees back to . . . I don't know, whatever shithole he came from."

"Honduras, Mrs. Riptoad. But he's not going anywhere, trust me."

"I bet he's MSNBC. They'll try to bust him out. Happens all the time. Don't you pay attention to the news?"

The chief didn't need to ask which network she'd been watching. He said, "We've got no evidence Beltrán is a gang member. And it's MS-13, not MSNBC."

"Hell, you know what I mean," Fay Alex growled. "And I don't care if he's chairman of the Cozumel Kiwanis Club, his lying brown ass belongs in maximum security. Make it happen, Jerry!"

She executed a fluttering, pinched-face departure. After so much time on the island, the chief was unfazed by melodrama but keenly tuned to political pressure. He decided it would be a good idea to sit down with Diego Beltrán, one-on-one.

NINE

When Germaine Bracco returned from a productive road trip to Beckley, West Virginia, he found stuck in his door the business cards of two police detectives. Germaine didn't bother unpacking; it was time to move. He pulled a second suitcase from a closet and stuffed it with the remainder of his clothes and personal belongings, including an unlicensed .38 he'd stolen from the handbag of a patient who'd fallen asleep on the table, her ears bristling with needles. Germaine was a self-taught acupuncturist with no legitimate credentials but many faithful clients. He didn't want to abandon them, yet there was no choice.

He flung open the door, picked up his suitcases, and found the way blocked by a small woman with an ash-blond ponytail. She was holding a pole tipped with a slender noose.

"Where you going, Germaine?" she said.

"Move out of my way."

"I'm not the police."

He said, "I've got a plane to catch."

"Where's your brother?" the woman asked.

Germaine swung the suitcases trying to knock her aside. When he regained consciousness, he found himself sprawled on the kitchen floor with the noose around his throat. It was loose enough to let him breathe, but not slack enough to let him fit his fingers under the coated wire.

The ponytailed chick sat on the countertop beside the microwave looking down at him. She had pinned him with the pole and was tapping the soles of her hiking shoes together, like Dorothy in her damn ruby slippers.

"Where's your brother?" she repeated.

"Which one? I got three."

"Prince Paladin."

"Who?"

"Keever. The one the cops are looking for."

Germaine said, "I dunno. I been outta town."

His voice was scraping and distorted, like one of those undead fuckers in a zombie movie. "What the hell's this all about—the car? Then go on, strangle me, 'cause I don't know shit about that."

"My name's Angie Armstrong," the woman said. "This pole is designed to humanely secure wild animals, and I've never hurt one. It's all about controlling the tension on the noose wire, see? If I tug a little too hard from this end—"

"Stop! Holy Christ, just stop."

"You mentioned a car."

"They stole a Chevy Malibu. The dumbass texted me a picture. I wasn't even here, I's in West Virginia. And I can prove it, too."

"I believe you, Germaine," said the woman named Angie. "You were at a pill mill, restocking for your customers. This, while awaiting trial on similar charges in Tennessee. Or is it Arkansas? Anyhow, I'm guessing you need the money to pay your lawyers, but still, it was poor judgment. Who was riding with your brother when they jacked the Malibu?"

"I got no idea."

The noose tightened. Germaine perceived a fuzzy gray curtain descending slowly behind his eyelids.

"Stop! Fuck!" he hacked. "Dude's name is Uric. He and Keev, they work together sometimes."

"So your brother calls him 'Eric,'" the woman said.

"He says it more like *your-ick*. I only met the dude once, so don't ask me his last name."

"Did he speak with an accent?"

"Just normal 'Merican," Germaine said. "How'd you know about the pills?"

"After you blacked out, I opened your suitcases. Found your stash and also the handgun, which, being a convicted felon myself, I was careful not to touch."

"You're a con? No way."

"Yes, sir."

"Bullshit. Look at you!"

"I fed a man's hand to an alligator. He was a bad guy, but nonetheless it was an overreaction. I did fourteen months at Gadsden and today I'm a model citizen."

Germaine didn't know much about the prison at Gadsden, but the gator story didn't seem like something a person could make up on the spur of the moment. "What is it you want from me?" he asked.

"Your douche brother and his partner broke into my apartment," said the woman named Angie, "and then my storage unit. They stole something important."

"So, you want it back."

"Not anymore. I just need to know who they were working for."

Germaine squirmed. "Maybe they workin' for theyselves."

The woman slid off the countertop, stood her full weight on Germaine's chest, and stared down the pole, straight into his watering eyes. Since his arms were free, he considered punching her legs out from under her—but what if she didn't let go of the noose when she fell? It might snap his goddamn neck.

She confirmed the risk, explaining that Germaine didn't possess the natural layer of fur that protected the necks of raccoons, otters, skunks and so forth while being subdued with that particular device. When she demanded to see the photo of the stolen Malibu, Germaine took out his phone and handed it to her. She stepped off his chest but ordered him to stay down.

"I'll ask only once more," she said, so softly that he cowered. "Who were they working for when Keever texted you this picture?"

"All he told me was they took a job from some dude on the island."

"Meaning Palm Beach."

"Guess so," Germaine said.

"Was the man who hired them named Tripp Teabull?"

"Keev didn't tell me a name, I swear to God."

"What kind of job?"

"I don't never ask my brothers 'bout they bidness, they don't ask 'bout mine."

"Really? You guys don't even share stock tips?"

"That's no lie."

"Why does Keever call himself Prince Paladin?"

"That's from when he had a band."

"Before he started dealing?"

Improbably, Germaine found himself thinking: *This crazy bitch is rockin' those baggy khakis, just like the dead crocodile dude's wife on TV.*

The woman must have read his mind, because suddenly she gave a firm yank on the noose. It elicited from Germaine a sound that one might hear from a coyote with stage-four COPD.

After he regained his breath, she asked, "Where's your brother now?"

"No clue. Half the time he lives in his damn van."

"I bet the cops are all over that. Speaking of which, they catch you on the road with suitcases, they'll assume you're running because you know what Keever did. They might even think you're in on it."

"But I don't know shit about shit!"

The woman slackened the noose, and Germaine sat up gingerly. "You work for a zoo?" he asked, tracing a forefinger along the wire mark that encircled his throat.

"Nope. Independent contractor." She held the pole on one shoulder, like a batter waiting on-deck. "The time you met Uric, where was that?"

"Titty bar in west county," said Germaine.

"Which one?"

He laughed. "Like you would know the place."

The woman raised the capture stick and positioned the slip noose on the crown of Germaine's head. She said, "Are we starting over again? Is that really what you want?"

He spat a curse and told her the name of the joint. "You don't fuckin' scare me," he added, slapping the pole away.

"Of course not, Germaine. You outweigh me by a hundred pounds."

"Hey, I'm watchin' out for my little bro is all. What is it they say he did?"

"A murder," said the woman named Angie.

"No. Effing. Way. Keev wouldn't never kill nobody."

"Well, I don't know about 'never,'" the woman said, "but in this case he happens to be innocent. The victim was already deceased by the time he got to her."

"So you're sayin' Keev's been, like, framed?"

"Yes, sir. An anonymous caller told the cops your brother was the killer."

"Motherfucker!" Right away Germaine felt better about giving up Uric's name.

Angie advised him to cooperate fully with the police, then she said goodbye. Later—speeding up the interstate to St. Augustine, where there was an opening for an acupuncturist at a faux Tibetan holistic clinic—Germaine realized that the pretty woman with the skunk noose had failed to return his cell phone.

Which was stolen, anyway, so who gives a shit.

———

The surviving Potussies gathered for lunch at their traditional round table in the Poisonwood Room (the dining wings at Casa Bellicosa were named after native Florida trees). Fay Alex Riptoad was the last to arrive, bearing intel that the lobster-guava tapenade was no less than three days old and should be avoided. Likewise for the "fresh" Chilean sea bass, which was actually flash-frozen tilefish from Galveston.

In honor of their fallen sister-warrior, the Potussies left one chair empty and a Tito's martini on the place setting. They arranged themselves by habit. Clockwise from Fay Alex sat Dee Wyndham Wittlefield, of the bauxite and lanolin Wittlefields; Kelly Bean Drummond, of the processed-soy Drummonds; and Dorothea Mars Bristol, of the aerospace Bristols (defiantly unrelated to the denture-paste Bristols). On Fay Alex's right was Deirdre Cobo Lancôme, of the dolomite Cobos and windstorm-insurance Lancômes; Yirma Skyy Frick, of the personal-lubricant Fricks; and, gloomily, the unoccupied chair of the late Kiki Pew Fitzsimmons.

The average age of the surviving Potussies was 71.3 years, and their cumulative wealth approached half-a-billion dollars. They were presumed to be dependable Christians, although it was a rare Sunday morning when they were able to detail their faces in time for church. Collectively they'd divorced four husbands and outlived nine others. Only two of the women were currently married, and by choice neither resided in the same area code as her spouse.

Ever since a ping-pong mishap had felled their only Roman Catholic member, the Potussies had steered to less strenuous hobbies such as golf and duplicate bridge. They wintered in Palm Beach mainly for the sunshine, gilded charity circuit and cosmetic surgery advances, but what bonded them as a unit was their unshakable devotion to the perpetually besieged President. Throughout the long deep-state witch hunt—the doctored Minsk defecation video, the phony tax-evasion probe, the counterfeit porn-star diaries, the bogus Moscow skyscraper investigation, the hoax penile-enhancement scandal, the fake witness-tampering charges, and both fraudulent impeachment trials—the Potussies had remained steadfast, vociferous, adoring defenders.

It was more than political loyalty; it was cultish fervor, with Casa Bellicosa as the opulent shrine of worship. There, in the darkest of times, the group would make a swooshing entrance wearing haute floor-length renditions of the Stars and Stripes, and Edwardian coiffures spangled with red, white and blue baubles. Led by Fay Alex Riptoad (or, as a stand-in, Kiki Pew Fitzsimmons), the women moved in an adulatory procession, exfoliated chins held high. On one much-discussed occasion, they boldly displayed—upon preternaturally taut, polished cleavages—matching henna tattoos of POTUS's resolutely pursed, fondly retouched visage.

Other Casa Bellicosans weren't embarrassed by the flamboyant fan group; just the opposite. The President had many die-hard supporters who preferred to demonstrate their allegiance in more subtle ways such as writing six-figure checks to political-action committees, or loaning out their private jets for the discreet delivery of certain presidential "friends." (Except for official trips and White House events, the First Lady was seldom seen with her husband. It was well known they slept in different quarters. Her aloofness grated on the Potussies, who found POTUS enormously attractive and in any case deserving of intimate companionship. They were, of course, also miffed by the First Lady's non-negotiable avoidance of the Palm Beach society scene.)

Fay Alex Riptoad waited until the others got their drinks before she told them the big news about the investigation of Kiki Pew's death.

"I've been fully briefed by the police chief," she began. "One man's in custody, and they're hunting for another."

"Who did they arrest?" asked Kelly Bean Drummond and Dorothea "Dottie" Mars Bristol simultaneously, though a full octave apart.

Fay Alex sipped her peach Melba mimosa.

Sighed.

Set down her glass.

Touched a linen napkin to the corners of her lips.

With both hands gripped the edge of the table.

Leaned forward, mostly with her neck, like a mildly arthritic condor.

"The man is Hispanic," Fay Alex hissed, "*and* illegal."

The other Potussies variously recoiled, moaned, or gasped. Immediately they began croaking out questions, most of which Fay Alex was unable to answer.

"This much I do know," she said. "His name is Diego something-or-other, and they found one of Kiki Pew's pearls in his pocket when they caught him."

"Oh, dear God, no!"

"That greasy heathen!"

"Monster!"

"One of her pink pearls?"

"Oh, yes," Fay Alex confirmed, "from the necklace she was wearing the night of the White Ibis."

A discussion produced the unanimous sentiment that court trials in such brutal cases were a waste of public tax dollars, and that the culprit should be dragged by his hairy nut sack straight from the booking desk to the death chamber.

"Do not pass Go!" erupted Deirdre Cobo Lancôme. It was a quip favored by one of her late husbands, who'd heard it from a squash partner who worked as a Human Resources specialist, laying off middle-aged executives.

"Does POTUS know about this Diego person?" asked Dee Wyndham Wittlefield, whose close friends were required to call her "Dee Witty."

Fay Alex said she wasn't sure if the President was aware of the latest developments. "Although I'm sure he'd be keenly interested," she added. "He was quite fond of Kiki Pew."

"As he is of us all," said Dee Witty. "And this sort of foreign-bred . . . *fiend* is exactly what he's been warning us about. Murderous invaders, rapist clans and so forth. I will definitely be speaking with my brother."

Dee Witty's brother Barnette was a presidential confidant, one of seventeen lawyers working full-time to suppress, mislead or discredit ongoing investigations of the executive branch. Barnette Wittlefield met with the commander-in-chief every morning at four-thirty a.m. bringing news of the latest subpoenas along with four bags of Egg McMuffins.

"That's a good idea," said Fay Alex. "POTUS listens to Barney. A phone call from the Oval Office would fast-track this Diego character to the flaming gates of hell. It's the least we can do for our dear, sweet, magnificent friend."

She raised her mimosa. "To Kiki Pew! To justice!"

The other Potussies, moist-eyed, joined in the toast.

In truth, the President didn't know Katherine Pew Fitzsimmons from any of the other lacquered weekend warriors. Casa Bellicosa was always stocked with fans who applauded on cue every time he appeared—so many worshipful faces that the leader of the free world couldn't possibly remember them all.

He did, however, occasionally pay attention to the things Barnette Wittlefield told him at four-thirty in the morning.

Diego Beltrán was surprised that the police chief came alone to interview him. The man listened to the whole story without once interrupting.

Then he said, "Diego, can you show me the railroad tracks where you say you found the pearl?"

"Yeah, sure. I offered to take the detectives there, but they weren't interested."

"Well, I am," said Jerry Crosby.

"Do I have to wear handcuffs?"

"Yup. There'll be another armed officer riding with us."

Diego said, "Don't worry, I'm not running."

"No, you don't strike me as stupid."

"You mean because my English is so good."

Crosby smiled. "That's got nothing to do with it. I know plenty of English-speaking morons."

With his wrists cuffed in front of him, Diego was placed in the caged back seat of the chief's SUV. The other cop, a county sheriff's deputy, sat up front with the chief. Diego gave directions to the railway crossing. Crosby pulled off the road near the striped warning gates and switched on his red-and-blue roof lights. Diego led him to the section of tracks where he'd picked up the pink pearl.

The deputy stood in the middle of the crossing with his arms up, stopping the cars, while Diego and Crosby walked side-by-side, scanning the debris in the gravel between the ties. Crosby didn't seem to be faking an interest, and he caught Diego off guard by suggesting they split up to cover more ground.

"Sounds good," said Diego warily.

"But try to run off, and you'll be visiting one of our modern emergency rooms."

"I get it. Can I ask what we're looking for?"

"Anything," the chief said, "that might make your story remotely believable."

There was a cloudless sky, no breeze and a bright sun. If it had been August, ripples of heat would have been rising from the steel rails. Diego's eyesight was sharp. Between the ties lay a sooty scattering of coins, soda straws, batteries, unmatched socks, condom wrappers, bottle caps, moldy wine corks, bird skeletons, used syringes, bent needles, copper BBs, Styrofoam cups, a rusted harmonica, a large fish hook, a turtle shell, a partial set of vintage dentures, and a filthy baby's mitten.

Diego had no intention of touching anything; none of the items had any clear connection to his predicament. He looked up when he heard the deputy holler. Warning bells rang from the crossing gates. Diego stepped back and waited while a mile-long train passed between him and the police chief. Diego didn't even consider running. After the last freight car rolled by, he saw Crosby beckoning from the other side of the tracks.

When Diego crossed over, he found the chief holding a plastic fixture bearing the stylized letters *SS*.

"What is it?" Diego asked. "Some Nazi thing?"

The deputy, an auto buff, explained that the *SS* stood for Super Sport. "That means it came off a Chevy. We've got a guy can find out the exact make and model."

"But what's a car logo got to do with my case?"

Crosby said, "Maybe nothing. But *this* little beauty was lying in the rocks underneath it."

With his other hand he held up a small pink sphere.

Diego Beltrán sucked in his breath and said, "No shit!"

"My reaction exactly," said Crosby.

On the ride back to jail, Diego closed his eyes and propped his head sideways against the rear window. After a while the police chief and county deputy started speaking low, thinking Diego was asleep.

"You didn't hear about that?" the deputy was saying. "I was workin' traffic for the motorcade. It was all over the TV and Facebook."

"When did this happen?" Crosby asked.

"Few days ago. I can't believe you didn't know."

"Was the President in the car?"

"Naw, but his wife was. The route was blocked off for, like, fifteen minutes. But those Secret Service, they know how to button down a scene."

"All because of a dead snake?" Crosby said.

"You shoulda seen the size of the damn thing. Twenty-footer, at least—and that's with no fuckin' head."

"And you're sure it was at the same railroad crossing?"

"Positive." The deputy shook his head and laughed. "What're the odds, right?"

"Actually, that's a damn good question," said Crosby.

In the back seat, Diego Beltrán kept his eyes closed. While he was entertained by the deputy's tale of the mutant headless snake in the road, his thoughts kept returning to the pink pearl that the chief had collected from the tracks. It was solid proof that Diego was telling the truth about where and how he'd found his own pearl—and that he'd had no involvement with the robbery and murder of the old lady on the island.

Diego was confident he'd be freed from jail the next morning and taken back to the immigration detention center, where he would join the others and resume work on his asylum application.

In a place like South Florida, such heart-bound faith in the justice system could best be described as quaint.

TEN

Angie said, "Tell the truth. As a man, do you find any of this arousing?"

Spalding answered carefully. "Not at all."

"The dancing's awful, the music sucks, the drinks are piss."

"It's a strip joint, Angie."

They were seated among the late-nighters at Prime Vegas Showgirls. Angie had asked Spalding to come along as backup. Nonetheless, she had three times been approached by couples asking hopefully if she was bisexual.

"It's the khaki thing," Spalding said. "You should've worn a skirt."

"I told you, I was working late."

"So was I, Lady Tarzan, but you don't see me in my damn butler suit."

A performer who called herself Karma paused at their table to offer a private dance. Angie gave her five bucks and showed her a mug shot of Keever Bracco, which the woman pretended to study. "Nope, never seen him before," she murmured with a medicated smile, and wandered on.

Angie had already scoped out the stage-side bar patrons; in the dim reddish light, almost all of them in some way looked like Keever Bracco. She had little hope that the dancers would be much help, particularly if he was a good customer. It was also possible that Germaine Bracco had lied to her about the name of the club where he'd met his brother and the man known as Uric.

To Spalding she said, "Tell me about the new job."

"The lily-whitest place I've ever worked. Practically everyone's on visas from the Eastern bloc—it's like a Romanian *Hell's Kitchen*."

"What does the staff say about our commander-in-chief?"

"Check this out: His Secret Service code name is Mastodon."

"Could've been worse," said Angie.

"The guy drinks between eighteen and twenty-one Dr. Peppers a day, room temperature only. And right before bed, every single night, he eats an entire Key Lime pie topped with Chantilly cream."

"Glorious!"

"And there's this one dude on the payroll," Spalding went on, "his only job is to disinfect and tune the President's tanning bed."

"Eewww."

"Yeah, times ten."

"What about the First Lady?"

"They say she's nice, but super lonely," Spalding said. "Supposedly she's banging one of the agents who's guarding her. The prevailing sentiment is, 'You go, girl.'"

"Keep a diary, please. By the way, this is the worst gin I've ever tasted."

"It's a strip joint, Angie."

A tall raven-haired dancer approached the table. With a heavy Russian accent she said her name was Farrah Moans. She wore see-through platform heels and a satin thong exposing matching tattoos on each buttock. This time Angie laid a ten-dollar bill next to Keever Bracco's photo.

The dancer eyed it and asked, "Are you also police?"

"Seriously?" Spalding rolled his eyes toward Angie. "Look how she's dressed."

Farrah Moans plucked the money off the table and folded it into the V of her thong. "Police too ask me about this person. But the other one, his friend, he liked me. Had big dimple here." She pointed.

"The middle of his forehead?" Angie said.

"Yes, the forehead."

"Was his name Uric?"

The Russian held out her hand. Angie took a ten from Spalding and handed it to the dancer.

"Uric, yes. Was him," she said.

"Last name?"

Again Farrah Moans put out her hand.

Angie frowned. "Come on, sister. We're out of cash."

"I really like your top," the dancer said, stroking one of the sleeves.

Spalding laughed. "That's a total burn, by the way."

"No. Top is fresh," said Farrah Moans.

Angie's shirt was a short-sleeved khaki with a smudge of squirrel shit on the collar. The "Discreet Captures" logo was stitched in forest-green thread above the left breast pocket.

"It's too small for you," she said to the dancer.

"No. Is just right."

"Fine. You're the one in show business."

Angie took off the shirt and handed it to the Russian, who lit up and said, "Last name of Uric is Burns. B-U-R-N-S. He wrote it on dollar bill for me. Also his phone number."

"Which you didn't save."

"Why would I keep? One dollar for what?" the stripper mused. "Also he is not my type."

Angie self-consciously covered her chest. Farrah Moans inquired about the bandage on her left arm.

"Animal bite," Angie said, hoping the customers at the next table couldn't hear her over the music.

"You mean was a man? Why did he bite you?" the dancer asked.

"It wasn't a man. It was a marsupial. Did you give Uric's name to the police detectives?"

"I tell them I don't know."

"Why did you hold back?"

"Because when it's for free, I don't remember things so good."

"If either of these bozos come back, call me," Angie said. "Next time I'll bring you some swamp boots." She handed one of her business cards to the Russian, who put it with all the dollar bills in the waistband of her thong.

Spalding kept his eyes away from Angie's cleavage by focusing on the dancer's butt: "Sweetheart, are those Jiminy freaking Crickets?"

"Yes!" Farrah Moans spun and bent over to show off her ink. "I love so much the Disney World!"

Then she put on Angie's shirt—the fit was snug, but it didn't matter because she left the front unbuttoned. On clacking heels she marched to the stage, scissored herself to a brass-plated pole and began twirling.

Nobody in the strip club even glanced at Angie in her T.J. Maxx bra as she and Spalding hurried out through a side door.

As he did every Saturday morning, Uric Burns went to the farmers' market and shoplifted organically grown produce. Blueberries were his fave. He gobbled them by the fistful on the drive to Lipid House, where he wheeled through the open gates and parked his van under the portico. He wasn't worried when two square-jawed security guys approached and told him not to move.

"I'm here to see Mr. Teabull," Uric said.

"Stay right where you are."

It was when Uric heard the sirens that he tensed up. *Oh fuck oh fuck oh fuck . . .*

But it wasn't the cops coming to arrest him for ditching the old lady's body.

A line of late-model black SUVs, led by police on motorcycles, wheeled into the driveway. Uric wasn't an attentive follower of current events, but as a criminal with loads of idle time he watched enough TV to recognize the long-legged hottie stepping from one of the Escalades:

It was the First Lady of the United States. She wore wide movie-star shades, a clingy print dress and matching heels. Her hair was perfect.

Uric tried to imagine this sleek gorgeous woman hopping into bed with a person as soft and mountainous as the President. Uric wasn't seized by a feeling of disgust or even pity, but rather a forensic sort of curiosity about how the sexual act itself was choreographed. She would need to perch on top, obviously, because the missionary position would result in crushed organs and suffocation. Maintaining her balance in the absence of a saddling device would require the skills of an aerialist. Uric wondered if the Secret Service supplied a spotter—possibly the tall dark-skinned agent who was leading the First Lady's entourage into the mansion.

Once she was safely swept out of public reach, the other agents dematerialized and the commotion subsided. When Tripp Teabull walked out of the entrance, he glowered at Uric's dirty van.

"Move that piece of shit outta here!" he barked.

Uric said, "Let's us go for a ride."

"Are you joking?"

"Okay. Be a douche." Uric yanked the keys from the ignition. "Call a fuckin' tow truck. I can wait."

Teabull got in the van, and soon they were southbound on A1A. Uric lighted a cigarette and rolled down his window. Teabull wouldn't stop yammering. *Where the hell are we going? I've got the tri-county Hep-C benefit tonight! What's this all about? Where's your dumbshit partner?*

"You owe me money," Uric cut in, "for the snake job."

The caretaker seemed relieved. "So that's what this is all about? Come on, man, the damn thing ended up in the middle of the road. That wasn't our deal."

"Wait—you're not gonna pay me?"

"No, no, of course I'll pay. All I'm sayin' is . . . okay, forget it. Turn around and go back—I've got the cash in my office."

Uric tapped his cigarette ash on Teabull's lap. "Check out all the poon on the beach. Too bad they don't allow topless."

"The fee is eight thousand dollars," said Teabull, "just like we agreed. Split it with your buddy however you want."

"But eight grand, see, that was just for jackin' the snake. You conveniently forgot to tell me there was a dead fuckin' body inside of it, which is a major add-on. Hey, look, we're almost there . . ."

Teabull stayed silent as the van passed the Par-3 golf course. Moments later Uric stopped on the shoulder of the road beside the billionaire Venezuelan's future mansion. The construction crew had padlocked the chain-link gate; a shredded ribbon of yellow police tape fluttered from one of the fence poles.

Uric shut off the ignition, grinned and said, "Scene of the crime, bro."

Teabull was on edge but also aggravated. Years of abusing minimum-wage staff had conditioned him to vent unsparingly. He said, "The only reason they found her was because you guys fucked up the concrete. It's your own goddamn fault!"

Uric punched him in the face. "The bill doubled," he said, "on account of the dead granny in the snake, plus all my extra manual labor. I hope you got sixteen grand in your office. Oh shit, dude, look at you."

He used a dirty towel to dab the blood from Teabull's mouth and nose.

The caretaker sniffled and said, "Chill out. I've got your damn money."

Uric waved the rag. "And I got *your* damn DNA. You better hope

I don't accidentally on purpose drop this bloody rag where they dug up the old lady. You want a tour of the property?"

"No! Christ, no."

"Okay. Your loss." Uric pulled his door shut. "Did I tell you I got a hotline number to the cops, with my own special code?"

Teabull wiped his face with a sleeve. "Unbelievable. You, a police informant?"

Uric slugged him again. "I'm not a motherfuckin' informant, I'm a tipster. Also known as a 'information broker.'"

Teabull pinched the bridge of his nose and tilted his head upward. "Take me back to Lipid House. I've got to meet with the caterers."

"And pay me, don't forget," said Uric.

"Right. And pay you."

Filomena Ricci was still hobbling days after the surgery, two liters of fat vacuumed from her chubby knees at a cost of $159. The once-in-a-lifetime bargain had been brought to her attention by an unsolicited email promising perfect results and a speedy recovery. The storefront clinic wasn't far from Filomena's apartment, so she drove there for a consultation with the surgeon, who—despite speaking not a word of English and wearing a black beret during the meeting—seemed otherwise professional and reassuring. Through a stroke of luck, his operating schedule happened to be wide open that afternoon, so Filomena agreed to undergo the liposuction then and there.

The procedure had taken longer than expected, and the results were the opposite of flawless. Filomena's kneecaps looked like rotting grapefruits. Everybody who saw them urged her to sue. On Instagram she posted grisly before-and-after photos, and within an hour she'd been contacted by a dozen law firms. One offered to send their top malpractice ace, and that's who Filomena assumed was ringing her doorbell.

The visitor was wearing a suit, but he wasn't a lawyer. A badge on his belt identified him as a detective from the sheriff's office. He glanced first at Filomena's crutches and then at the fluid-stained compression sleeves on her legs. She was disappointed when he didn't ask what had happened to her.

"Are you Filomena Ricci?" he asked.

"Why? What's wrong?"

"You're listed as the registered owner of a white 2014 Chevy Malibu SS."

Filomena chortled, "Praise God! You found it."

The car had been stolen from an alley behind the surgical clinic while she was getting her fat sucked.

"Boo! Hey, Boo!" she shouted to her boyfriend. When there was no answer, she started thumping the floor with one of her crutches. "Boo, get your ass in here! Hurry up, they found Margie!"

That was their nickname for the car—Margie the Malibu.

The detective said, "It was at the bottom of a canal, Ms. Ricci."

Filomena stopped banging the crutch tip. "What're you sayin'?"

"Your vehicle was under twenty feet of water. It's totaled."

"Fuck me!" Filomena exclaimed. She wouldn't get a nickel from the insurance company; her policy had been canceled months earlier for nonpayment.

From down the hall came a muffled: "What's goin' on, Filly? I'm on the can."

"Take your time, Boo," Filomena called back, "and open the damn window."

The detective said the Malibu had been discovered by a fisherman whose boat anchor snagged on the front bumper. In Florida, canals are the favored dumping choice for auto thieves; a tow company specializing in such retrievals had hauled out Filomena's precious Margie.

"Take a look at this please," the detective said. He showed her a picture of a scowling, narrow-eyed man in an orange jumpsuit.

"Who's this?" she asked. "Is he the asshole stole my Malibu?"

"You don't know him?"

"Hell, no."

"His name's Keever Bracco," the detective said. "The diver who hooked the chains to your car found his body in the same area of the canal."

"You mean dead?"

"Oh yes."

To Filomena it made sense. "So this shithead, first he hotwired Margie, then he accidentally drove his sorry dumb ass into the water and drowned. Ten bucks says he was textin' one of his punk peeps and not watchin' the road."

"That isn't what happened. Mr. Bracco was strangled. Whoever did it sunk his body with barbells."

"Sweet Leaping Jesus!"

"He's a prime suspect in a murder on Palm Beach. The police all over the state have been hunting for him."

Filomena was flabbergasted. *A murderer?*

The detective said, "Right now they've got nothing that connects Bracco to the theft of your car. It's probably a coincidence his body ended up in the same canal. He's a convicted felon, a dope dealer, and they make lots of enemies, Ms. Ricci. We're just doing routine follow-up."

Relieved, Filomena caught her breath and said, "Look, I never heard that man's name and never seen him before in my life. *Never!* Swear on my stepdaddy's grave."

The detective seemed to believe her. He gave her the phone number for the impound lot, in case she wanted to sell the Malibu for scrap.

Filomena sagged cheerlessly on her crutches. "Man, I just put in some brand-new Alpine speakers I bought on eBay. What if, like, I took a hair dryer and worked on 'em real slow at high heat?"

The detective was genuinely sympathetic. "Alpines rock. That's what I've got in my Mustang," he said. "But they're definitely not waterproof."

"Listen, okay? Do me a favor. You ever find the bastard that did this to my Margie—"

"We'll call you first thing, Ms. Ricci."

Later that afternoon, Paul Ryskamp and the other senior agents gathered in front of the flat-screen in the secure briefing room to watch Mastodon conduct an impromptu press conference on the 18th green of a Maryland golf course that bore his name, though it was owned half by a Swiss bank and half by a cross-dressing Russian oligarch.

"Anyone see this coming?" Ryskamp asked.

"Hell, no," was the consensus reply.

"So, who told him and why?"

"It was Barney Wittlefield."

"That Dartmouth dipshit."

"No, he's Princeton. His sister was friends with the dead woman."

"Small fucking world," said Ryskamp.

Up on the TV screen, Mastodon was wearing a vast beet-colored golf shirt that hung on his upper frame like an Orkin termite tent. His long-billed cap had been yanked down tight to keep his hair-piece moored to its Velcro moonbase during gusts of wind. Facing a hastily assembled battery of cameras and bobbing microphones, he somberly announced that on the previous fairway he'd been briefed by the attorney general about a serious matter.

"As many of you know," he said, "there was a horrible, horrible crime committed recently in Palm Beach, not far from the Winter White House. The victim was a fabulous woman, a dear close friend of mine, named Katherine Fitzsimmons. Fantastic people. Fantastic family." Here he paused for a fake fond smile. "Those of us who knew Katherine best," he added, "we called her Kikey Pew."

Ryskamp put his hands to his ears. "Did he really just say *Kikey* Pew?"

"Not our problem," cackled one of the other agents. "This is why his press secretary gets the big bucks. Shit, I'd rather piss off the Hell's Angels than the Anti-Defamation League."

Live from his golf links, Mastodon rambled on: "But today I've got some really, really terrific news. One of the thugs involved in this sick crime has been found. His name is Keefer or Keever Bracco, A.K.A. Prince Palindrome. They say he was a notorious drug dealer with a long rap sheet. Bad guy. Very bad guy. The worst. My people at the Justice Department tell me he was executed by his own partner to silence him about the abduction and murder of Mrs. Fitzsimmons."

Please, somebody, shut him up, thought Ryskamp. The Palm Beach police must have given some version of the Bracco scenario to Barnette Wittlefield's sister, who delivered it to her brother, who fed it to the President along with his predawn McMuffins.

"Today I'm happy to report," Mastodon rumbled on, "that the magnificent people of Palm Beach are safe again. We now have the second murder suspect in custody. His name is Diego—we'll get you the last name later, but the first name is definitely, one-thousand-percent Diego. Tragically, this predator entered our country illegally on the same night Mrs. Fitzsimmons disappeared, and not far from where she was last seen alive. He was captured later in a lightning sweep by our amazing border security forces. That's when they found a jewel belonging to Kikey Pew in his possession, an incredibly rare gem. They tell me the island people call it a conch pearl."

The President rhymed conch with "haunch."

"It's 'conk,'" Ryskamp said under his breath, but no harm done— the "island people" would get a laugh out of it.

The agent was also relieved to have heard nothing in Mastodon's announcement that threatened to complicate his own job. Even with the possible involvement of an illegal migrant, the murder of Katherine Fitzsimmons was strictly a local homicide case. The FBI or ICE might offer assistance, but there was no angle that would require the expertise of the Secret Service . . .

Until the President cocked his head, flared his nostrils, puffed his scrotal cheeks and declared:

"Unfortunately, the tragic death of Mrs. Fitzsimmons appears to be much more sinister than just the usual kidnapping and robbery. I've received some very disturbing information about *Señor* Diego, a very *malo hombre* who I'm told is from Honduras, a country infested with violent street gangs. But, folks, what happened in Palm Beach wasn't an ordinary street crime. It seems Diego and his accomplice, the late Mr. Broccoli, might have targeted Mrs. Fitzsimmons not because she was rich, elderly and slow, but because she was a dear friend of mine and very active in a women's political group that has proudly and loudly supported this presidency—especially my crusade to secure America's borders. In other words, it's very possible—and I say possible, because we're not ready to release all the details—but let's call it an extremely high probability that the brutal murder of Kikey Pew Fitzsimmons was an act of political terrorism aimed at me and my administration."

Ryskamp stared numbly at the screen. He was the only one in his office who knew that Mrs. Fitzsimmons had actually been killed and eaten by a snake. The other agents offered their usual assessment of the President's melodramatic performance.

"This is a show of the shit variety," one remarked.

"He's a pathogen," sighed another.

Mastodon railed on a while longer, making air quotes with his stubby doll fingers whenever mentioning the name Diego, and thundering that this was exactly the bloodthirsty breed of invader that the White House had been warning the nation about.

"They're storming across our wide-open borders to prey on our most precious citizens! Women, children—and now helpless, rich, old patriots like Kikey Pew Fitzsimmons. Well, my fellow Americans, guess what. This stops now! It ends here! No more Diegos! You have my solemn word as your president. No more Diegos!"

With Arthurian flair, Mastodon thrust his custom-made Ping

putter toward the heavens. He kept it high as he parted the press corps and moved toward a line of parked golf carts.

Ryskamp turned off the TV and sat down to wait for his phone to ring.

"Maybe he'll forget about it in a few days," one of the other agents said hopefully. "That happens a lot."

"Not this time. No way."

"You think he could be right about this Diego kid being involved in the old woman's death?"

Ryskamp looked up with a rueful smile. "Don't you get it? It doesn't fucking matter whether he's right or not. That's the scary part."

ELEVEN

Chief Jerry Crosby dry-heaved twice over his laptop while watching the President's press conference. Afterward he phoned the county sheriff, who confirmed that Keever Bracco's weighted corpse had been discovered in a waterway by a tow crew salvaging a stolen Chevy Malibu. The sheriff said he knew of no link between the car and Bracco's murder, adding, "Who dumps a body in the same canal where he sunk a stolen car? You either lock the body inside the damn trunk, or you go bury it somewhere far away. What a moron."

"But it's probably true that Bracco was murdered by his partner," said the chief, "to shut him up. That's the only part of the President's story that didn't sound like horseshit."

He reminded the sheriff that Diego Beltrán couldn't have killed Bracco because Beltrán had been in custody for days. "He had nothing to do with the death of Katherine Fitzsimmons, either. I'll bet my badge on it," Crosby said.

The conch pearl that the chief had found on the railroad tracks was in a baggie on his desk.

"What gang was our fearless leader yapping about at his press conference?"

"No fucking clue," the sheriff replied. "If I find out anything, I'll let you know."

Crosby was sickened by the cynical motives of the President's conspiracy theory, and also by the damage caused. Diego Beltrán had been indicted, tried and convicted in a breezy golf-course rant. Finding an untainted jury anywhere but the North Pole would be impossible.

Nobody in the chief's circle of island insiders was able to explain how this toxic carbonation of shit got uncorked, but soon he had his answer. There, streaming on a local news feed, appeared Fay Alex Riptoad. She was aglow from the salon and sporting a Stars-and-Stripes brooch the size of a Philippine fruit bat. A male reporter asked if she was worried that she and the other Potussies were being targeted, like poor Kiki Pew.

"All of us are taking the threat very seriously," Fay Alex said. "It's a sad, sobering day for this great country. But, just like our brave President, we will never *ever* be intimidated by ideological terrorists."

Crosby had only himself to blame. He was the one who'd told Fay Alex about Diego Beltrán's arrest, though he'd had no warning that the information would be shared with the White House, woven into a bizarre xenophobic plot, and then trumpeted to the entire world. The facts of the case remained sparse and cloudy. Even the killing of Keever Bracco could be linked only by suspicion to the anonymous hotline tip about the death of Katherine Fitzsimmons. Nor had any evidence surfaced placing Bracco in Palm Beach on the night of the crime—or in the unlikely company of young Beltrán, a fresh-off-the-boat immigrant.

Yet demonstrators galvanized by seething talk-radio hosts had already gathered outside the county jail on the mainland. Some carried handmade signs, while others waved ineptly knotted lynch nooses.

All were chanting, "No more Diegos! No more Diegos!"

It was rampaging imbecility, and possibly unstoppable.

Crosby trudged into his office bathroom, where he scrubbed the taste of bile from his mouth. Only one person was waiting outside in the small lobby—a pretty, green-eyed woman wearing a ponytail and the unlikeliest of Palm Beach attire, long outdoor khakis with grass stains on the knees. She introduced herself as Angela Armstrong and said she was a wildlife-relocation specialist. The chief thought she didn't look big enough to arm-wrestle a squirrel, but the logo on her shirt advertised a company called "Discreet Captures."

"We specialize in humane techniques," she added, "whenever possible."

"I'm sorry, but you've caught me at the worst possible time. It's crazy busy around here today."

"Yes, sir, I bet. We should go somewhere quiet and talk."

"Look, Ms. Armstrong, I'm not trying to be rude but—"

"It's Angie, please." She reached up and put a hand on his shoulder. "I promise you want to hear what I've got to say."

Crosby was caught off guard by her directness. Also, those eyes.

He heard himself ask, "All right. What's this about?"

"The late Katherine Pew Fitzsimmons. Specifically, the true and unusual nature of her death."

Oh Christ, thought Crosby. *Another escapee from Loonyville.*

He said, "Somebody's already put in a claim with the victim's family for the reward. Now, I've really got to run. Late for a meeting—"

Angie blocked his juke to slip past her. "I don't want a goddamn reward," she said. "And don't you dare brush me off."

"Okay, sorry." Crosby stepped back. "Tell me what you've got."

"For starters, it was no coincidence they found Keever Bracco's body in the same canal as that stolen car."

The chief remained wary but was now intrigued. "What's the connection between Bracco and the Malibu?" he asked his visitor.

"You're whispering, sir, and there's nobody here but us."

"Yes or no—do you know who killed Mrs. Fitzsimmons?"

"It's not a 'who,'" said the woman named Angie. "May I call you Jerry? Come on, Jerry, I'll buy you a beer."

Uric Burns was still angry about the last phone conversation when his cell started ringing. The caller's number had a blocked ID, but Uric answered anyway.

"Did you get this shit straightened out?" he barked.

A woman was on the other end. It didn't sound like Judith from the tipster hotline. Uric had just cursed at her and hung up after learning that the rich snake lady's relatives would only cough up half the promised reward. Judith had said the other half would be released after the police investigation was finished.

Fifty thousand dollars was still a shit-pile of money, more than Uric had ever made on a single job, and the sensible move would be to grab it and vanish. But he resented being jerked around, and the sweet scent of that other fifty grand held sway over his judgment, which wasn't razor-sharp to begin with.

Uric didn't consider his stubborn stance as one of shortsighted greed, but rather as a principled effort to collect something that was rightfully his. He hoped his outburst had worried the hotline operations office, though the woman had yet to identify herself as a representative.

"Are you, like, Judith's boss?" Uric demanded.

There was a pause. "Yes, that's right," replied the woman, who had introduced herself as Miss Baez. "I'm her supervisor."

"Then she must've told you I want *all* the reward money right now, not just half. That was the goddamn deal. So it's a real bad idea for that old lady's family to pull any last-minute bullshit. They'd never a found her, weren't for my tip. And I been straight with you guys from day one. I always acted in—what the fuck do lawyers call it?"

"Good faith," said the woman on the other end of the line.

"That's it. Good faith!"

"Sir, I understand how you feel."

"Really? Then go tell your people I want the whole hundred grand."

"Consider it done," Miss Baez said. She read off the address of a SunTrust branch near the Kravis Center and told him to be there Monday morning at ten a.m. She added, "There'll be some paper-work regarding the withdrawal of the family's funds, but your iden-tity will remain protected."

"Secret from the cops, too, right?" Uric asked.

"Well, of course."

"Fan-fucking-tastic!"

"It's good we got this settled," said Miss Baez, "for the family's sake as well as yours."

Something occurred to Uric. "Yo, how'd you get my number?"

"Excuse me?"

"Judith said you people don't save phone numbers and that's how come she couldn't ever call me back. But *you* just called me."

Miss Baez said, "To preserve the confidentiality of tipsters, we don't log incoming phone numbers until we've selected the proper recipient of the reward money, which in this case is yourself. That's why we kept your number. Judith should've explained that part."

It made enough sense to Uric. He was grinning like a chimp that picked a padlock at a banana warehouse.

"Yo, tell Judith I'm sorry I yelled at her," he said, "and thanks for your help. I'll see you at the bank tomorrow."

"Oh, I won't be there personally," Miss Baez told him, "but you're very welcome."

Uric tossed his cell on the passenger seat and high-fived himself. Jauntily he bounded out of the van, which Tripp Teabull had made him leave in the truck shed at the back of the estate. A security goon with a black muscle shirt and a head like a shoebox led him through an unmarked doorway and up a flight of stairs to a small office where Teabull awaited. He had cleaned the crusted blood from his swollen nose.

"Done with all your important calls?" he asked Uric snidely.

"Strictly business, my man."

"What's so damn funny? Are you high?"

"How come I need a reason to smile? It's just another beautiful fuckin' day in paradise."

Teabull glared. "Seriously, Mr. Burns."

"*Seriously*. Blue skies, bright sunshine, all that happy Florida shit. So, just hand over my sixteen grand for the snake job, and you won't have to look at my smiley face no more."

"Well, about that . . ."

"Well, *what*?" Uric said.

Then he heard the door close behind him.

They got a table on the outside patio at the Brazilian Court. Angie didn't mind that other women, recharging with cocktails after their ruthless shopping forays on Worth Avenue, kept staring at her outfit. She rolled up her left sleeve to show off her opossum bite. Nobody took the tables on either side of them.

Jerry Crosby ordered a beer. Angie got a gin-and-tonic.

"Start from the beginning," he said.

"You might want to take notes."

"Not here I don't."

"Understood," said Angie, and gave him the whole story: euthanizing the enormous python at Lipid House; the burglary of her apartment and the subsequent theft of the frozen reptile from her warehouse unit; the pickup call from the Secret Service, which had confiscated the mangled snake—minus the lump—from a road on the First Lady's motorcade route; Angie's visit to Germaine Bracco, from whom she'd learned about the stolen Chevy Malibu; the nude bar that the Bracco brothers had patronized, where Angie had obtained the name of Keever's accomplice; her phone chat with Uric Burns, who thought she was calling from the tipster hotline . . .

Crosby intently listened, ignoring his beer. Angie wasn't sure if he believed her or not. She encouraged him to call Special Agent Paul Ryskamp at the Secret Service, because Ryskamp knew her to be a truthful person.

"I'm sure you've got a million questions," Angie said.

The chief started to respond, then merely shook his head.

She took out Germaine Bracco's cell phone and showed him the photo of the stolen car that his idiot brother had texted to him. "It's the same one they pulled out of the canal, a 2014 Malibu Super Sport. Same busted left front headlight."

"A Super Sport?"

"Yes, sir."

The plastic SS logo that Crosby had picked up on the railroad tracks during his field trip with Diego Beltrán had come from a 2009-2014 Malibu Super Sport, according to an auto forensic expert. Crosby said nothing to Angie Armstrong about the logo, the second pearl, or the fact that he'd found both of them near the spot where the python had ended up in the road. He had a pretty good idea of what had happened.

"What's your background?" he asked Angie.

"I was trained as a veterinarian," she said, and waited for the curious look she always got. Then:

"After that, I was a wildlife officer, until I went to prison for assaulting a poacher." Angie checked her watch. "In fact, he'll be calling shortly to threaten my life. No biggie, happens every night. But, getting back to Mrs. Fitzsimmons, may I summarize? I'd feel better if we went over this stuff one more time. I mean, since you're not taking notes."

"Have faith," said the chief.

"It's just you seem sort of . . . well, baffled by the information."

"The information being that a well-known member of Palm Beach society got strangled and eaten by a giant snake during a charity gala, and no one saw it happen." Crosby smiled dryly. "I wouldn't say I was baffled. I would say taken aback."

On Angie's own phone was a photo of the Burmese in the banyan tree, the round bulge in its midsection glinting in the camera's flash. Crosby asked how she killed it.

"Machete."

"And then you put it in a freezer because . . . ?"

"For the state lab, as required. Obviously Mrs. Fitzsimmons's body would have been found during the dissection procedure, and the publicity would have been a disaster for the Lipid House. So my guess is that Teabull hired these two geniuses—Bracco and Burns—to steal the dead python from me and get rid of it. They fucked up big-time. The damn thing ended up in the middle of a busy road, and poor Mrs. Fitzsimmons, minus her jewelry, wound up in concrete. The only living victim of this five-star cluster fuck is Diego Beltrán who, thanks to the President, is being crucified for a crime he didn't do."

Crosby was nodding though Angie couldn't tell if he was totally on board, or just being polite.

"Here's the main thing," she told him. "At ten o'clock Monday morning, Uric Burns will walk into a bank not far from here thinking he's about to collect $100,000 for leading your police department to the remains of Mrs. Fitzsimmons. He's a tall white dude with a freaky dimple in the center of his forehead—I'll bet there's a mug shot or two you can pull. Point is he bears no resemblance to the pictures I've seen of Diego Beltrán. This is only a suggestion, Jerry, but when Burns shows up in that bank lobby, you should probably have someone waiting to arrest him. Because not only did that maggot burglarize me *twice,* he stole a dead widow's jewelry and quite likely killed his own partner so he wouldn't have to split the money."

Crosby asked Angie for the name and location of the bank. She wrote it on a napkin.

He said, "The way you tricked Burns, that's pretty slick. How'd you set it up?"

"Dumb luck. I got his number off his brother's cell. When I called today, he'd just hung up on somebody at the Fitzsimmons hotline.

He assumed it was them calling back, and right away goes off on a tirade about the family jerking him around over the reward money. All I had to do was play along."

The chief smiled. "Greed makes people stupid. We like that."

He was looking at Angie in a way that usually would have triggered her letch radar, but he seemed like a decent guy. Nonetheless, she made a point of eyeing his wedding band long enough for him to notice her noticing.

"What happened to your arm?" he asked.

"Didelphis virginiana," she said. "Possum nailed me."

"Know what? If I could trade this homicide case for an infected opossum bite, I'd do it in a heartbeat."

"Once Uric Burns is locked up, you need to call a press conference and let Diego off the hook. Because you know he's innocent. Right, Jerry?"

In the breast pocket of Crosby's uniform was the little pink pearl he'd found on the railroad tracks. He took it out and held it up for Angie to see.

"Ah ha! Now it's your turn to tell *me* a story," she said.

"When the time's right."

Lady Gaga interrupted—Angie's phone ringing. This time the spoofed caller ID showed a South Dakota area code. She said, "That's my six o'clock stalker. Wanna say hi?"

The chief reached for her phone. "Sure, why not."

Mockingbird had never heard of conch pearls until her husband mentioned them during his press conference, which she was forced to watch while on a treadmill at Casa Bellicosa. The gym had been cleared out for security before the First Lady arrived, but every muted television in the place was tuned to Mastodon's golf-course monologue about Kiki Pew Fitzsimmons, complete with word captioning. Having dodged the haughty Potussies as a group, Mockingbird couldn't recall if she'd ever met the dead woman. She was, however, intrigued by her husband's depiction of the stolen jewels.

After finishing her workout, Mockingbird hurried upstairs and went online to research the pearls; they looked delicate and sensuous, glistening in the dark wet palms of Bahamian boatmen. The First Lady wondered why at least one of the Hadids or even Gwyneth hadn't tweeted about these trendy tropical gems. Fluidly she scrolled through the websites of Tiffany and other high-end jewelry stores, most of which offered small selections of handmade pieces. However, in the advertisements, the individual pearls appeared puny and pallid.

An aide dispatched by Mockingbird to scour Worth Avenue located a pair of conch-pearl earrings styled by Mikimoto. The sales clerk couldn't say for certain where in the Caribbean the mother shells had been harvested, so Mockingbird passed without even asking the price. She wanted only wild island specimens.

There was a light triple-knock on the door, and Agent Keith Josephson appeared. He was escorting a server who bore a silver tray holding a plate of avocado slices, a modest wedge of Belgian cheese, seven fried kale chips and a tall glass of room-temperature papaya juice. The name pin on the young man's uniform said "Spalding" and, beneath that in smaller letters, "Cape Town." It was a practice at Casa Bellicosa to include the hometowns of the employees—not to honor their diverse backgrounds so much as to reassure club members that the staff was being recruited from cultures that were educated, tidy, and unthreatening.

When Mockingbird spotted the young man's name pin, she said, "Spalding, do you have conch shells down in Cape Town?"

The First Lady had never before spoken to him, so Spalding's response betrayed a touch of the jitters. He said, "Actually, South Africa is world-famous for its sea shells. The beaches are covered with them. People come from everywhere—"

"Yes, but only queen conchs make pearls this color." She repositioned her laptop to show him the pictures.

"I can follow up on that for you," he said. "My little brother dives at Jeffreys Bay."

"That's so kind of you. Let me know what he says, please." Mockingbird gave him the smile that she saved for men who'd been led to believe she was icy and stuck-up.

Spalding was appropriately charmed. He took his time laying out the First Lady's lunch selections on the coffee table.

"Keith, I need to speak to you," she said to the Secret Service man, "after you take Spalding wherever he needs to go now."

"Of course, ma'am."

Mockingbird closed her laptop, popped a kale chip in her mouth and, while chewing, said, "My afternoon schedule has changed. I told Leena to push the disabled Girl Scout awards back an hour because I need some personal time."

"I'm on it," said the Secret Service man, who didn't look like a "Keith" to Spalding. He looked Middle Eastern, though he spoke with an American accent.

He led Spalding down the hall and waited beside him until the elevator arrived. Spalding stepped inside, pressed the button for the first floor, and nodded goodbye. Before the doors began to close, Agent Keith turned away and strode briskly back toward the First Lady's private quarters.

Spalding peeked out of the elevator. From behind, it appeared that the Secret Service man was loosening his necktie.

TWELVE

Winter residents of Palm Beach inevitably return north forever, either in caskets or urns. Funeral services for Kiki Pew Fitzsimmons were held at her Cape Cod estate, where she'd wanted her ashes scattered.

The Potussies chipped in to charter a mid-sized Citation with a well-stocked minibar. They were plastered by the time the jet touched down, though Fay Alex Riptoad pulled herself together enough to speak movingly at the podium under the lawn tent. Chance and Chase Cornbright were up next, dressed in matching cashmere top coats. They stood side-by-side reading alternate paragraphs from a eulogy that scrolled on a teleprompter laced with black crepe. The Potussies agreed that Kiki Pew would have been embarrassed by her sons' torpid performance.

Mastodon didn't attend the chilly seaside event but he sent the Vice President, who'd never met Katherine Fitzsimmons but warmly praised her as a martyred patriot. The VP then launched into seven-and-a-half minutes of stock diatribe about the immigration crisis, citing Kiki Pew's death as worst-case proof of the dark menace lurking on the edge of America's borders. If the other mourners were bothered by the naked political exploitation of their friend's funeral, they didn't let on. Several chased down Sean Hannity to have their prayer cards autographed before he boarded a Fox helicopter back to Manhattan.

The town of Palm Beach sent an elaborate flower wreath but no official representative. Council members feared setting a costly precedent; scores of prominent part-time residents died every season, and the municipality's modest travel budget would be sapped by April if the mayor and his wife flew north for every funeral.

As the last crumbs of Kiki Pew Fitzsimmons were being sprinkled from a New England bluff into the Atlantic Ocean, Palm Beach Police Chief Jerry Crosby sat twelve hundred miles away watching videotapes of the back street leading to the service entrance of Lipid House. The footage had been recorded by a security camera at a neighboring generic mansion, but the owner had been vacationing in Bali when Mrs. Fitzsimmons vanished. Once he returned to town, he voluntarily turned over digital files holding a week's worth of surveillance loops.

The images were of better-than-average quality, and Crosby immediately advanced the time-stamped sequence to the night of the White Ibis Ball. Angela Armstrong's python hypothesis could be dismissed if Kiki Pew had been recorded alive and well, departing the Lipid House grounds through the rear gates. The videos showed a flurry of party trucks, florist vans, and catering vehicles, but no lone person could be seen leaving on foot from the service driveway from sunset until dawn. Crosby clicked on fast-forward to the end of the file, speeding through the herky-jerky frames until he noticed one particular car turning into the back entrance:

A white Chevy Malibu Super Sport, arriving on the third morning after Mrs. Fitzsimmons disappeared.

It stayed less than an hour. The broken front headlight was easy to spot when the Malibu pulled out, driven by a white male. A companion, also white, sat on the passenger side. The chief froze the video, but the car's grimy windshield made it impossible to positively identify the occupants as Keever Bracco and Uric Burns, whose most recent mug shot—complete with dented forehead—lay on Crosby's desk near the railroad conch pearl.

Unfortunately, the recovered Malibu had already been cubed for scrap. The county's overworked auto-theft squad had elected to spend zero time searching for microscopic evidence in a vehicle that had been submerged for days in murky water. A corpse in the back would have piqued their interest, but the Malibu's trunk was empty. "Except for a mudfish," the owner of the impound lot had told Crosby.

And no one, of course, would have found it noteworthy that the SS insignia was missing from rear end of the vehicle.

Another item on the chief's desk was the Fitzsimmons autopsy report. Kiki Pew was ruled to have died from asphyxiation caused by massive trauma from an unknown source or sources. She was drunk at the time of her death, and blood tests additionally revealed a .18 g/L plasma concentration of the drug MDMA, commonly known as Ecstasy. Because she had been purposely entombed in concrete, the coroner's speculation about her final hours did not include the scenario of a random reptile attack. In any event, testing a victim's skin and garments for digestive python enzymes had not yet become standard post-mortem procedure in Florida.

Finally, stacked on Jerry Crosby's desk beneath the autopsy findings, was a file detailing the short, peculiar criminal record of Angela Christine Armstrong. The case had received almost no publicity because the media paid little attention to wildlife agencies, the poaching of a deer being of less interest to the public than gang shootouts at the county fair.

If a regular road cop had forcibly severed the limb of a criminal suspect and fed it to an alligator, it would have sparked an uproar. Yet, because Crosby had a soft spot for animals, he found himself empathizing with Angie as he read her account of the airboat incident. In the court transcripts, Pruitt came across as an unrepentant asshole, the same impression that the chief had taken away from their short exchange on the phone, while he and Angie were at the Brazilian Court.

"Ms. Armstrong says you call every night and threaten her," Crosby had said to Pruitt.

"And who the hell are you?"

The chief had told him.

"Bullshit," was the one-handed stalker's response. "You're just another loser she's boning. Better break it off now, dude, unless you want to end up as dead as her."

"Every one of these calls you make is a felony."

Pruitt, taunting: "There's no way to trace 'em, so they'll never catch me. Now put Angie on the line, Chief Dicklicker, or whoever you really are."

Crosby had hung up and asked Angie if she wanted to press charges.

"Not necessary. I keep tabs on him, Jerry."

"You know where he lives? What kind of car he drives?"

"As of last week, yes."

"And you've got a gun at home? Just in case."

Angie had smiled. "I'm a felon, remember? No bang-bang allowed."

The chief seldom met women who made him wonder what it might be like to be single again, but Angie Armstrong was one who did. The voice, the eyes, the attitude. He chased from his mind whatever adolescent fantasy was forming; after all these years, Crosby was still crazy about his wife.

Before leaving his office, he locked away Angie's arrest file and the thumb drive containing the Chevy Malibu video. Then he went to scope out the SunTrust bank branch where Uric Burns was due to arrive the following morning with the aim of collecting $100,000 from the Fitzsimmons family tipster fund.

Joel came by Angie's apartment to watch the Heat-Bulls game. He brought tortilla chips and a bowl of sketchy guacamole. At halftime Angie received a call from man who identified himself as the manager of a country club in the western part of the county. He said there were mice in the kitchen.

"We don't do mice, sir," she told him.

"Please? I can't get anybody else out here on a Sunday. Your website says twenty-four-seven service."

"Our website also says we don't remove and relocate house rodents. We find it not to be worth the trouble and expense. Just go buy some traps at Home Depot."

The manager said, "Would three thousand dollars make it cost-effective?"

Angie asked him to hold on. When she whispered the details of the ridiculous offer, Joel said, "Jump on it. Miami's already down by nineteen."

"Maybe they'll make a run."

"Sure, and maybe Jennifer Lawrence will show up topless at my front door. Take the gig, Angie. I'll go with you."

The man on the phone gave her directions to the club, Loxahatchee Downs. Angie had never heard of the place. Joel said it was new: Golf, tennis, equestrian, sporting clays and a six-figure membership fee.

Angie stacked some small box traps in the truck and waited for Joel to finish texting his latest girlfriend, who in her fifth leisurely year at UF had switched majors again, this time from art history to philosophy. The move in no way improved the young woman's employment prospects, but Angie kept her doubts to herself. Joel usually came to his senses.

The sun went down during the drive to Loxahatchee Downs, way out in cattle country. Surrounded by pines and palmetto scrub, the clubhouse and facilities weren't visible from the road. Angie would have missed the turnoff had it not been for the lighted sign above a one-lane entrance. Beyond the closed gate was a winding, unlit road.

Joel looked up the club's website on his phone and learned that the grand opening was three weeks away. When Angie tried to call the manager back, she got a recording that said no such phone number was in service.

That fucking Pruitt, she thought.

Before she could back up, a car with its headlights off pulled in behind her truck, blocking the only way out. The driver was wearing a rubber Mitch McConnell mask.

"Run," Angie said to Joel.

"What?"

"Get your ass into the woods. *Now!*"

Something landed with a metallic bang in the bed of her pickup.

"Joel!" she yelled.

"Okay, I'm going."

"Keep your head down."

"No shit."

Angie jumped out the door and sprinted. The moment she heard the explosion behind her, she wondered if it had been a mistake to let Chief Jerry Crosby speak with her stalker. Instead of being scared off, Pruitt had snapped.

With no light, Angie ran at a cautious jog, weaving through the tall pines, palmetto thickets and moon shadows. The long khakis protected her arms and legs, but random twigs and thorny vines clawed at her face. She wasn't concerned about running up on a wild animal because she'd dealt hands-on with every species from bears to rattlesnakes. However, she was worried about Joel, who had no experience with nighttime transit in deep woods. When her cell began ringing, she pulled it from her pocket and knelt behind a tree. Joel was on the other end of the line.

"Tripped over a damn log," he reported. "I'm pretty sure my ankle's broken."

"How far'd you get from the road?"

"I dunno. Maybe twenty yards."

"That's all?" said Angie. "Then keep your voice down. He's gonna hear you."

"The prick already took off. Can't you see the flames?"

"No, but I smell smoke."

"That's your truck burning," Joel said.

"Well, I'm not surprised."

"Whatever he threw at us went off like a grenade."

"Probably homemade."

"That's still fucked up, Angie."

"Stay where are you are. Don't move," she told him.

"Duh. I actually can't walk."

"I'll find you."

"You won't need a flashlight," Joel said. "It's a big-ass fire."

Paul Ryskamp spent part of his Sunday afternoon interviewing Diego Beltrán at the county jail. Despite the uptight presence of a lawyer from the Public Defender's Office, Beltrán seemed eager to answer questions from the Secret Service agent, who came away convinced that the young Honduran had no role in the death of Katherine Pew Fitzsimmons. Ryskamp expected the Palm Beach police chief to confirm Beltrán's exculpatory revelation that the chief had found a second conch pearl along the railroad tracks.

Later, at the office, Ryskamp gathered the other agents and handed out the Potussies directive from the head of Mastodon's security detail.

"These are all elderly white females," one agent observed as he skimmed the roster, which included dates of birth.

"That's correct," Ryskamp said. "Mastodon requested that each of these individuals receive round-the-clock protection, beginning tomorrow. Washington has promised to send us warm bodies to fill the shifts."

"Does Washington understand how ridiculous this is?" asked another agent, reflecting the mood of the room.

"Of course they understand," said Ryskamp. "No one's pretending this assignment is anything but a colossal waste."

"Paul, what does 'Potussies' even mean?"

"It stands for 'POTUS Pussies.' The name might suggest they've got a sense of humor, but I'm told they take themselves quite seriously. They're infatuated with Mastodon, and they're getting a ton of media since his press conference."

A third agent spoke up: "The deceased woman—has anyone got a speck of evidence she was really murdered by terrorists? Or that the Guatemalan kid they busted, Diego Whatever-the-fuck, is connected to a radical cell?"

"The answer to both questions is a hard no," said Ryskamp. "And the young man is from Honduras, not Guatemala. I just spent two hours interviewing him."

"So where did Mastodon come up with this crazy conspiracy shit?"

"He just pulled it out of his ass, like everything else. Plays huge with his fans."

"Paul, how long do we have to hang with these old birds?"

"The memo says indefinitely, but that could also mean short-term."

Ryskamp was trying to sound an optimistic note, for he was sensitive to the demoralizing effect of Mastodon's antics. As a price for her silence, one of his West Coast mistresses demanded to be met by the Secret Service every time she flew into Dulles. The ride to the White House always included a leisurely stop at a luxe mall in Chevy Chase, where the woman would hang full shopping bags on the arm of whichever miserable agent had been assigned to accompany her. If nosy GAO investigators ever asked to examine the duty logs, that particular guest of the President would show up as a visiting niece of the Taiwanese ambassador, not the twice-divorced manager of a wine bar in east San Francisco.

After Ryskamp ended the briefing about the Potussies, a female agent named Jennifer Rose stayed behind in the room. She told him she had something to report from Casa Bellicosa.

"Just a rumor, but you need to hear it," she said.

Ryskamp closed the door. "Is this a security issue?"

"Potentially. There's a new hire on the wait staff, a South African named Spalding. Yesterday I overheard him tell another server that Mockingbird is having a 'super-sloppy hot affair.' He claimed he saw the man."

"The First Lady's sleeping with someone here in Palm Beach?"

"Worse. On the property."

"Oh, fun."

"Up at the White House, too," Jennifer Rose said. "According to the kitchen gossip, it's a traveling hump fest."

Ryskamp wouldn't have been shocked if the story checked out, but there was a limit to what could be done. Mastodon and Mockingbird were seldom in the same room, much less the same bed. Regardless of whom they were screwing, the Secret Service's mission was to keep them safe from harm. Keeping them safe from scandal was supposed to be somebody else's job.

"The rumor's strictly from Spalding?" he asked Agent Rose.

"It's been floating around, but this was the first time I picked up the name of the supposed boyfriend."

"So who is he? We'll need a background check right away."

"Actually, we won't," said Jennifer Rose.

"We've already got a file on him?"

"Everything, Paul."

"Uh-oh."

"The First Lady's lover is Agent Josephson. Supposedly. Allegedly."

"Great. Cute. Perfect." Ryskamp banged a fist on the desk. "*Fuck!*"

"At least he's not one of yours," Jennifer Rose said. "Still, I figured you might want to kick it up the ladder—"

"Whoa." Ryskamp raised a hand. "Has anyone actually witnessed Mockingbird and Agent Josephson in the act?"

"Of fucking their brains out? Not that I'm aware."

"Kissing? Holding hands? Exchanging sultry glances?"

Agent Rose shook her head. "But we haven't questioned any of the staff yet."

"And we sure as hell ain't gonna start now," said Ryskamp.

"What about Josephson?"

"I'll have a talk with him, Jen."

Among the other agents it was common knowledge that Josephson was actually Ahmet Youssef. They also knew why his name had been changed.

"You're not in his chain-of-command," Jennifer Rose pointed out.

"True, but I *am* in the brotherhood of men who've made astoundingly poor decisions about women."

She smiled and asked Ryskamp if he'd be joining the after-work bitch session at the bar on Clematis. He said no, he was going home to watch a hockey game.

But as soon as she left, he locked the door, took out a calculator, and began working up the numbers for an early retirement.

Joel's ankle was sprained, not fractured, but he still scored a full-siren ambulance ride to the hospital. Angie's pickup was charred to a husk, smoldering on bare rims. A sheriff's deputy who gave her a lift back to Lake Worth said Pruitt would be arrested soon; officers were staking out his apartment building.

As soon as she got home, Angie emailed pictures of her burned pickup to the insurance company. She had a tricky job scheduled for the next morning—a momma skunk with four kits had taken up residence in the backyard of a retired Wall Street broker and his wife, who together had fled to a suite at the Breakers. The couple lived in a gate-with-a-guard community, so Angie planned to rent a truck and attach the magnetic "Discreet Capture" signs that Joel had designed for the pickup. Fortunately, not all her wrangling equipment had melted in Pruitt's firebombing; at home she kept a spare pole for noose jobs, and plenty of extra traps and transport kennels.

Spalding called and asked to meet for a late drink. Angie said she was too tired.

"But I got some face-time with the First Lady! Don't you want to hear about it?"

"Maybe later. Like on my death bed."

"In person she's super hot," Spalding went on excitedly, "even hotter than her modeling pictures. And she smells just incredible."

"A grateful nation thanks you for your service."

"And, yo, I'm ninety-nine-point-nine-percent sure she's shagging one of her Secret Service guys!"

"Really? I heard it was Orlando Bloom."

"Hey, what's with the snark?"

"Sorry," Angie said. "Somebody blew up my pickup tonight. I'll call you in the morning."

After hanging up, she realized she was no longer interested in having sex with Spalding; he'd never made a move, and now the window had closed. It was nothing he'd said or done; possibly the allure of his accent had worn off. Maybe it was that simple.

Jerry Crosby had given Angie his private cell number, so she texted him saying that Pruitt had torched her truck. Because of the late hour she didn't expect a reply, yet the phone rang almost immediately.

"What the hell happened?" Crosby asked.

"I got a call from a fake number with a fake mouse emergency. Pruitt must've been waiting when I got there. He threw a Molotov cocktail in the back of my pickup. The worst part was my stepson was with me."

"Are you guys okay?"

"We jumped out and ran like hell," Angie said. "Joel sprained his ankle. The truck's fried."

"When did this happen?"

"Couple hours ago."

The chief said she was lucky to be alive. "Did you get a look at his face?"

"No, he had one of those freaky Halloween masks. The county's got deputies waiting at his place right now."

Crosby said, "Waste of time. They won't find him."

"How do you know?"

"Because he's already in jail."

"What? Hold on. Since when?"

"Nine-thirty this morning," said Crosby. "I had him picked up for threatening a law enforcement officer. That phone call at the restaurant yesterday—it pissed me off, Pruitt's shitty attitude. And you were right, he was easy to find. Same address as his driver's license."

Angie was stunned. "So it wasn't him who burned my truck."

"Nope. He's been locked up all day."

"Then what the fuck, Jerry?"

"Do you have any enemies that are into firebombs?"

"At least one, obviously. But I've got no idea who it is."

"Call me if you get a name," the chief said.

Before lying down in bed, Angie groped under the mattress and took out the Taser. It looked like a Hasbro toy. She placed it on the nightstand, turned off the light and lay on her side with a pillow tucked between her knees, like when she was a little girl.

She slept poorly, awakened by a nightmare in which she was wearing a gossamer ball gown and climbing a snarled old banyan tree. Perched in the topmost bough was a one-eyed roaring bear, and the bear's eye was a rosy pearl.

Angie sat up panting in the darkness, and told herself again that dreams don't mean a damn thing.

THIRTEEN

Strangling Prince Paladin was by far the worst crime Uric Burns had ever committed, and he was pleased with himself for not feeling bad afterward. Strictly business, as Michael Corleone would say. The second *Godfather* was Uric's favorite movie. Next on the list was *Scarface*, even though Pacino's accent was fucked up. Uric knew plenty of tough Cubans, and none of them talked that way.

Prince Paladin was the tallest partner Uric had ever had, but he was otherwise dull and forgettable. He'd never mentioned that his real name was Keever Bracco, and Uric wouldn't have remembered it, anyway. They had only been working together a few weeks before the fateful python job.

The men had first met at Giardia's shop, where Uric was unloading a stolen scuba tank and the Prince was pawning a stolen Blu-ray with *Avatar* stuck in the disc feed. They began chatting, and Uric said he had a break-in planned that night in Gun Club Estates.

"Need a driver?" Prince Paladin asked.

"Can you lay off the weed?"

"Yeah, for three hundred bucks."

"Two-fifty," said Uric. "And if you show up stoned or drunk, I'll pulp your balls with a claw hammer. Hit the shower, bro. You smell like a fuckin' grow house."

The Prince stayed sober behind the wheel, and Uric emerged from the burgled house carrying four AKs, a half-dozen loaded handguns and an antique crossbow that brought a rare smile to Giardia's blighted face. Uric ended up paying the Prince the full three hundred he wanted, which predictably he blew on chronic. He was an okay driver, a semi-diligent lookout, and strong enough to move jumbo household appliances. The break-in at Angela Armstrong's apartment had been the pair's fifth job together, which in the realm of petty street crime practically made them an old married couple. For Prince Paladin, the divorce was harsh. He never saw it coming.

Uric Burns's path to a life of crime had been untraditional. He grew up in an unbroken home with hardworking, affectionate parents, and an older brother who seldom picked on him. In high school, Uric made Bs and Cs, played intramural soccer, and worked on the yearbook. He had plenty of friends and dated three nice girls, one of whom favored him with a surprisingly skilled hand job after the senior prom. There was nothing in Uric's past—no abuse, abandonment, family alcoholism, trauma, or tragedy—that would have caused anyone to predict he would one day quit his Furniture/Bedding sales job at BrandsMart to become a break-in artist, car thief, shoplifter, freelance shitbird and, ultimately, a killer.

In reality, Uric's transition from working-class citizen to career felon was nothing more mysterious than unbound laziness, and the appeal of setting his own casual hours. He thought of himself as canny and cautious, for he'd never been shot, knifed or even diddled in the county jail. The unusual cleft in his forehead was of mundane origin; it came from the corner of a hurricane shutter that a previous cohort, wrecked on meth, had heedlessly tossed from a third-story landing. Uric knew he could have been killed, and the dent in his skull was a daily reminder of the risks posed by choosing unreliable partners. As soon as the Prince had revealed himself to be weak of resolve, a potential snitch, Uric saw him as a ticking time bomb. End of story.

Such was Uric's pride in his own survival instincts that he was embarrassed to have walked into Tripp Teabull's trap at Lipid House. Fright would have been a more useful reaction, but Uric acted super cool. He was confident he could talk his way out of the situation, though he'd barely gotten started when Teabull told him to shut the fuck up. The two muscle-shirted dudes who hauled him downstairs were even less interested in conversation.

During the long, uncomfortable ride, Uric began to comprehend he was in deeper-than-usual shit. The feeling would grow stronger with each passing hour. It wasn't the first time he'd pissed off the person who had hired him, or been stiffed after a job. It wasn't even the first time he'd been locked in a car trunk for a night.

It was, however, the first time anyone had strung a rope around his neck and led him like a lame horse across a bridge. The nervousness changed to relief when he saw his own white van parked on the other side. That meant the goons weren't going to kill him; they were just going to kick his ass and let him go.

Tripp Teabull hated the sight of Uric's filthy Dodge on the property, and he probably didn't want Uric coming back to get it. That would explain why he'd ordered the van brought to the bridge.

Sweet, Uric said to himself. *Least I won't have to hitchhike home.*

Which was the second-to-last thought to enter his mind.

The last was: *Aw fuck.*

Teabull had been awaiting a call from Angela Armstrong ever since Mauricio had told him about her unannounced visit. With Uric and the Prince now gone, Teabull believed that the young wildlife wrangler was the only person out of his sphere of control who knew the true circumstances of Kiki Pew Fitzsimmons's death at Lipid House. When Angela failed to make contact after a few days, Teabull decided to send a preemptive message. He hired a reputable Hialeah arsonist to drive to Palm Beach County and firebomb Angela's pickup truck. The explosion was to be ignited in her presence, maximizing the psychological impact.

Afterward, Teabull met up with the torch artist in the parking lot of a Walgreens.

"Well?" Teabull asked.

"Easy peasy."

"Did she freak out?"

The arsonist chuckled and showed his rubber mask to the caretaker.

Teabull grimaced. "Mitch McConnell?"

"Scary shit, right? The store was all out of Nixons. You got my money, *chico*?"

Teabull had not ordered Angela Armstrong killed because—unlike the death of Uric and his dipshit partner—hers would have drawn plenty of police and media attention. He hoped she was sharp enough to connect the burning of her truck to the Fitzsimmons matter, and would be deterred from future meddling.

If not, she still had no way of proving what had really happened to Kiki Pew Fitzsimmons. Without the testimony of the python thieves, Teabull thought, nobody would ever believe Angela Armstrong.

He was wrong about that.

At dawn on the morning after the firebug-for-hire bombed Angie's pickup, Palm Beach Police Chief Jerry Crosby sat watching and re-watching street-cam video of a white 2014 Malibu SS jouncing at a stupid speed over a railroad crossing. The impact popped a plastic logo off the car and flung open the trunk. Out flew a flexible mass that resembled an intricately embroidered hawser; it uncoiled in midair before landing in the middle of the street on the other side of the tracks.

The Malibu kept going. Moments later, a line of flashing lights approached from the opposite direction—a ten-vehicle motorcade, mostly black SUVs, which rolled to an organized stop. Motorcycle cops followed by armed men in plain suits swarmed both lanes to surround the road obstruction, which was unidentifiable in the video. Crosby knew what he was looking at: an enormous headless snake. He wondered which of the SUVs was carrying the First Lady of the United States.

After hiding the thumb-drive of the video, the chief drove to the SunTrust bank. His stakeout team was already in place—six officers in three unmarked sedans, and a pointlessly masked sniper on the roof. Inside the lobby, the branch manager and tellers waited anxiously, coached on how and when to duck.

Ten o'clock came and went. No sign of Uric Burns. At eleven sharp Crosby's cell phone rang. It was Angie Armstrong.

"You got him?" she asked.

"Not yet. He's late."

"Shit. *Shit.*"

The chief said, "Maybe he chickened out."

"Impossible. Nothing would scare that moron away from a hundred grand. If you told him it was powdered with anthrax, he'd still show up."

"Then where the hell is he, Angie?"

"Something major must've happened. Something not good."

"We'll give him till noon," Crosby said.

"Don't bother. If he's not there by now, he's not coming."

She was right. Uric Burns wasn't on his way to the bank. He was hanging dead from a weed-choked bridge in a bankrupt development called Blue Pelican Shoals.

The bridge, which connected two of the bare subdivided tracts, crossed a tea-colored drainage canal that for marketing purposes had been renamed Soldier's Creek. Stocked with feisty peacock bass, the waterway was popular with local fishermen, one of whom had made an errant cast and snagged the pants zipper of Uric Burns, whose body had theretofore gone unnoticed due to the short length of the homemade noose. The dead man wasn't swinging above the water but rather appeared cinched to the bridge rail, his slack form resting high against one of the support columns. Attached to his crotch by two #1 treble hooks was a bullet-shaped bass lure called a Zara Spook, realistically painted to mimic a native leopard frog. The lure was connected by thin braided line to a rod and reel belonging to a teenaged boy who was skipping school.

The boy looked up from the canal bank to see what he'd snagged, dialed 911, cut his line with a knife, and walked away. It was the third dead body he'd found while fishing, but such was the reality of a childhood spent outdoors in Florida. It was a testament to the teen's passion for angling that he'd never considered getting a new hobby.

"You're not one of my lawyers," Diego Beltrán said to the woman.

"I lied to get in here."

"Why?"

"I have a personal interest in this case," Angie said.

"Your hand's bleeding."

"I punched out a guy."

"Just now? Who?" Diego asked.

"One of the demonstrators."

"Right in front of the jail?"

"He got up in my face," Angie said, "which was rude."

"Those screamers are out there all day and night. I can hear 'em from my cell."

"No way. These walls are too thick."

"Then I hear 'em inside my head," said Diego, "which is even scarier."

"Well, the one I hit—he's in the back of an ambulance with a headache and a splint on his nose. I'm betting he's done for the day."

"Who are you, anyway?"

Angie introduced herself and told Diego the whole story. He said he didn't believe it.

"Which part?" she asked.

"The mega devil snake, for starters."

She showed him the cell-phone photos of the dead Burmese, her ransacked apartment, her burgled storage unit and her burned pickup truck.

"No offense," said Diego, "but you don't look like someone who wrestles wild animals for a living."

"Actually, this is the only pants suit I own. The briefcase is a prop, obviously. Found it at the Dollar Tree."

"How's a fake lawyer with a fake briefcase going to help me?"

Angie warily nodded toward a corner-mounted fisheye camera, which Diego had already spotted.

"Are there microphones, too?" he whispered.

She shook her head. "Not allowed. This room is for attorney conferences."

"And, now, *fake* attorney conferences. So are we pretending you can get me out?"

"As in free?"

"Back to ICE detention," Diego said.

He knew the immigration case wasn't going to disappear, and he doubted that even his real lawyers could win a petition for asylum. Given a choice, he'd rather get deported to Tegucigalpa than rot in a Florida jail with a lynch mob outside.

Angie said, "The only state charge against you is possession of stolen property. That's usually a low-bail offense, which means the feds are pressuring the cops to keep you locked up here. "

"The stolen property being that one little pearl I found? *Dios mio.*"

"Honestly, the jewelers association should give you a lifetime achievement award. Retail prices doubled after the President mentioned your conch pearl in that press conference."

Diego felt beaten down. He rubbed his eyes and said, "How did this even happen to me?"

"Bad luck. You happen to be the brown-skinned Fiend-of-the-Month. Your mug shot's all over Fox and CNN. The White House wants you alone in a cell with real bars, not a fenced courtyard with picnic tables and soccer games."

"I get that. So, what's your secret plan?"

"The priority is to get you exonerated," Angie said. "*Officially* exonerated, if possible, but otherwise we go to the media. That would be me telling everything I know about the Fitzsimmons case—starting with the fact that you couldn't possibly have killed the woman that night because she was already dead by the time you came ashore."

"But you never saw her body, Ms. Armstrong."

"No—and it's Angie—but I saw the lump. And those snake pics I took, don't you think the *Palm Beach Post* would put one on the front page, along with my harrowing first-person account? But we don't make that move unless the cops and prosecutors won't back down."

"They know I'm innocent. They *know*." Diego told Angie about Chief Crosby discovering another conch pearl on the same railroad tracks.

She said, "Yeah, he showed it to me."

"Then how is it possible I'm still sitting here?"

"Because the whole country thinks you're a political terrorist, knocking off rich old white ladies who love the President. A hard ugly mood has taken hold, and you're the metaphorical bug under the boot heel."

"Squashed flat."

"Not just yet," said Angie, sliding her chair forward. "Tell me everything you told the police chief."

"I told it to the Secret Service, too."

"So now tell it to me, beginning the night you and the others got off the boat."

"What's the point?" Diego said wearily.

"I'd like to hear the story in your own words."

"Meanwhile, the dude in the cell next to me, he got busted for doing a llama on the ranch where he works."

Angie said, "Okay, yes, that's truly awful."

"It wasn't even *his* llama. You get what I'm saying? He took the damn llama on a date!"

"We'll get you out of here, Diego."

"I'm so over this. Not that I don't appreciate what you're trying to do, but I'm sick of talking to people and then nothing happens. *Nada.*"

"Just one question, then," said Angie. "Do you know Keever Bracco or Uric Burns?"

"No!" Diego practically shouted. "Jesus Christ."

"Never met 'em?"

"No, no, and no! I already told Chief Crosby, and also the Secret Service man."

Angie said, "I believe you. I do."

"That's what they told me, too, but I'm still here. Me and the llama fucker. Sometimes he falls asleep jacking off in the sink. You get the visual? And yet after all this I still want to be an American, which is insane."

"Try to hold on, Diego."

"What are my other options?"

Angie rose to leave. "If any of the deputies ask, I'm your lawyer's paralegal."

"Don't forget your pretend briefcase."

"Hey, did it not work like a charm?"

"You hear those crazies chanting out there?" he said.

"The protesters?" Angie asked.

"Yeah. Who else." Diego closed his eyes to listen.

"Honestly, I don't hear them."

"Well, I can," he murmured. "All day, all night."

She met Spalding for a late lunch at the crab shack on the island. He brought along a co-worker named Christian. Angie was annoyed when friends tried to set her up, especially if the friend trying to set her up was somebody with whom she'd once plotted having sex.

Christian was from Denmark and naturally spoke flawless English. He was handsome enough—bleach-toothed, blond and blue-eyed—but he was too short. Angie's ex-husband stood six-one, and she'd grown accustomed to feeling a chest against her cheek during stand-up hugs. The young Dane was only five-seven in thick-soled Rockports. Angie knew that having a height requirement for prospective dates was shallow criteria but—in the words of Emily Dickinson, Selena Gomez and Darius, the guy who sprayed her apartment for roaches—the heart wants what it wants.

Spalding said that Christian worked the winter season at Casa Bellicosa.

"Guess what his job is, Angie?"

"Pastry chef?" She could be clumsy when aiming for polite conversation.

"God, no." Spalding laughed. "Chris, tell Lady Tarzan what you do."

"I service the President's personal tanning beds," Christian said, raising his beer mug in a wry self-toast.

Angie was intrigued. "And how does one secure such a prized position?"

"I worked for the manufacturer in Hamburg. One day the Secret Service called and said they needed a technician to take care of two new Cabo Royales—those are our premium models—one here in Palm Beach, the other at the White House."

"I assume those machines were custom-built," Angie said.

"I can't really talk about that, but . . ."

"Like, big enough for a manatee."

"No comment," said Christian, grinning. "The pay was good, and they promised free health insurance, including dental. So right away I said yes. Two visas arrived the next day, one for me and one for my fiancée. Unfortunately, she got homesick after a few weeks and went back to Germany—"

"If you don't mind me asking," Angie interrupted, "how does one 'service' a tanning bed? Meaning what exactly is involved?"

Christian explained he was responsible for checking the fan, capacitors, relay contacts, timer, gas springs, hinges, and ultraviolet lamps.

"And cleaning the whole Cabo after every use," he added with a queasy wince, "Wiping down the surfaces, and all that."

Spalding piped up: "He's got some blood-curdling tales. Tell her what you found that one time in the canopy chamber."

"No, do *not* tell me—" Angie tried waving him off, too late.

"An extra-large Depends," Christian reported mirthlessly, "burnt to a crisp."

Angie said she wasn't hungry anymore. The tanning-bed specialist apologized. He asked if she was seeing anyone.

"I'm sure Spalding told you I'm not," she said.

"I didn't know if I should believe him."

"This time you can. Other times, no."

"Screw both of you," said Spalding. "I'm stepping out for a smoke."

When they were alone, Christian made the rookie mistake of looking Angie in the eyes and saying, "Tell me about yourself."

"You're joking."

"All right, then I'll start. I just turned twenty-nine, my parents own a chain of coffee shops in Copenhagen, I've got two older brothers—"

"Hold it." Angie made a slashing motion across her neck.

"What, really?"

"I'm sorry, but you're not my type."

He blinked in slow motion, like a frost-stunned lizard. "Harsh," he said.

"No, Chris, it's merciful honesty. I'm not *your* type, either."

"How can you know that already? We haven't even gotten our entrées."

Angie felt a bit guilty, even though Christian had met her only twelve minutes ago and therefore couldn't credibly claim that his feelings were hurt.

Still she said, "You're right. Let's see how it goes. I'll text Spalding and tell him to leave us alone."

"Oh. Cool."

"Yeah, he can eat at the bar. That smartass."

"Thank you, Angie."

Lunch was fine. Christian ordered fried shrimp and crab cakes, and didn't make a mess. He seemed good-natured and earnest. Twice he made her laugh.

But, alas, he didn't grow any taller.

So when the police chief texted Angie asking her to hurry to a place called Blue Pelican Shoals, she lay a twenty on the table, and said farewell to young Christian with a handshake. On the way out, she cut through the bar to alert Spalding that his Scandinavian friend might need some cheering up.

FOURTEEN

The bright afternoon was cool and windy. Angie put on a fleece.

Agent Ryskamp wore a slate hoodie, jeans and black sneakers. Jerry Crosby showed up in the long-sleeved version of his chief's uniform. It was the first time the two men had met, and they were deep in conversation when Angie arrived.

The purpling corpse of Uric Burns still hung from the bridge abutment. Photographers clambered around like coked-up marmosets. Every agency wanted its own set of photos—the Secret Service, the FBI, the sheriff's office, the medical examiner's office, the Palm Beach cops, even the U.S. Marshals. An unprofessional air of amusement was elicited by the colorful fishing lure hooked to the zipper fold of the dead man's trousers. A secondary point of curiosity was the long-healed ding in the corpse's forehead.

Meanwhile the media had been roped off in an area beside Soldier's Creek, where the TV reporters could stage their stand-ups with the death scene in the background. They were also well positioned to observe a dirty white Dodge van being cranked onto a flatbed truck.

Angie, Ryskamp and Crosby stood together, all in sunglasses, apart from the central cluster of onlookers.

"How long's he been up there?" Angie asked the chief.

"At least twenty-four hours. Inside the van they found a note confessing to robbing and murdering Mrs. Fitzsimmons. Keever Bracco, too."

Ryskamp yawned. "Burns didn't write that."

"No shit," said Angie. "He didn't kill himself, either."

Crosby went on: "The note said he knew he wouldn't get away with it and didn't want go to back to jail. Said he'd rather die first, whatever."

Ryskamp asked if the faked farewell had been written by hand. Crosby said it came from a home laser-jet printer. "Burns didn't own one," he added. "Or if he did, they haven't been able to find it yet."

"In one of his many palatial residences." Ryskamp laughed emptily. "You saw this 'note' with your own eyes?"

"I did. Got a picture, too."

Angie said she wanted to go look at the dead man's body. Crosby asked why.

"Because he's one of the cockheads who broke into my apartment. I need closure, Jerry."

Ryskamp said, "You're taking this very personally."

"I fucking well am," Angie snapped.

"Oh, she definitely does," the chief said to Ryskamp. "However, she should be aware that Mr. Burns soiled himself while expiring, adding to other unsavory elements."

Angie remarked that nothing could smell as bad as the decaying buzzard carcass she'd removed the previous day from a dairy barn in Moore Haven. "So, Jerry," she said, "let's have a peek at the deceased."

Uric Burns was in nasty shape though Angie had seen worse—week-old floaters, pulled from the swamp—during her time as a wildlife officer. From such experiences she'd learned when not to inhale. Burns's face was shapeless and mottled; both eyelids had swollen shut and were turning black. The rope had elongated his grimy neck like a snapping turtle's.

"You sure that's him?" Ryskamp asked.

"Fingerprints match," Crosby replied. "Also, the dent in his head."

"What's that on his wrist?"

"His coded ID for the Fitzsimmons hotline. He probably wrote it there the day he phoned in the tip. See how the marker ink's faded."

The chief's phone rang, and he moved out of earshot to take the call. During their few moments alone, Ryskamp surprised Angie by asking if she was free for dinner. She surprised both of them by saying yes.

"Seriously?" Ryskamp said with an endearing look of relief.

"Long as you're not married."

He held up the bare fourth finger on his left hand. Angie had already noticed.

"Maybe the ring's in your pocket," she said.

"Nope." He turned his front pants pockets inside out.

"Fine," said Angie, "I'll meet you at Nikko at seven. Let's keep it casual."

He smiled. "Next you're gonna tell me we're splitting the tab."

"Dream on," she said.

Up on the bridge, two stocky attendants from the medical examiner's office were struggling to pull the corpse of Uric Burns over the rail and onto the roadway, where a uniformed woman waited with a bright yellow tarp.

When Jerry Crosby got off the phone, he was steaming. "Anybody bring a laptop? Never mind, I need to get back to the office."

"What's wrong?" asked Angie.

"He did it again. Same shit as before."

"Who did what?" said Ryskamp.

"That dysfunctional hump in the White House. Your boss."

At that moment Ryskamp's phone lit up; his ringtone was "Life in the Fast Lane." He glanced down at the caller ID and muttered, "Aw shit. What now?"

"I won't spoil it for you," said the chief.

As their newly assigned Secret Service agents stood like totems outside the Poisonwood Room, the surviving Potussies stayed late drinking after lunch. Fortunately, none of the women had driven themselves to Casa Bellicosa, for by mid-afternoon their blood-alcohol levels far surpassed the legal limit. Fay Alex Riptoad would have blown .12 on a roadside breathalyzer; Dee Wyndham Wittle-field, .14; Kelly Bean Drummond, .15; Dorothea Mars Bristol, .17; and for both Deirdre Cobo Lancôme and Yirma Skyy Frick, a tee-tering .19.

Their degrees of incoherence varied due to dosage differences in their prescription meds, none of which was recommended to be taken with cocktails. Of the group, Fay Alex was the least impaired and therefore the best equipped to interpret the President's latest Twitter commentary. (It was a ritual among the Potussies to pause all social meetings when there was a new tweet stream.)

"Listen up, ladies," said Fay Alex, standing. She adjusted her Cha-nel readers and raised her smartphone almost to her nose. Slurred chatter persisted at the table, so Fay Alex barked: "That's enough, please! Put down your goddamn drinks!"

As the group fell silent, one of the Secret Service agents opened the door and peeked into the room. Fay Alex waved him off, and began to read:

"This is direct from the Presidential Twitter account, as of six minutes ago:

 'I'm delighted to report the death of a second suspect in the robbery and murder of my dear friend, Katherine (KIKI PEW) Fitzsimmons. The Attorney General just informed me that Uric N.M.N. Burns of West Palm Beach has hung himself. Burns knew cops were closing in fast and escape was impossible. A suiside note confessing to his terrible crimes was found in the dead coward's van . . . He also tried (BUT FAILED!) to scam reward money from Fitzsimmons family. So, folks, bottom line: two bad guys down and one to go! All our law-enforcement resources can now focus on prosecuting the final suspect, Diego Beltrán, for his role in Mrs. Fitzsimmons' death. Or should I say *aledged* role (JUST TO KEEP THE LIBERAL LAWYERS HAPPY!) . . . This notorious outlaw—who snuck into America illegally—remains locked down at Palm Beach County jail. Thanks to all my supporters for turning out in HUGE RECORD numbers to rally for justice there and other places around the country . . . As your President, I won't rest till Diego receives ALTIMATE PUNISHMENT allowed by law. I also promise to protect you from all future Diegos that are conspiring to cross the border to rape, kill and muttilate other innocent citizens who happen to believe in my beautiful vision for this fantastic nation. NO MORE DIEGOS!!! And God bless America!' "

The Potussies clapped as spiritedly as their wooziness allowed. Fay Alex Riptoad considered the recitation to be one of her finest and by no means easy, since the President clearly had fired off the multi-segmented tweet without waiting for his full-time proof-reader. The "N.M.N." in his identification of Uric Burns was cop-speak for "no middle name" and should have been deleted on the first edit, but more problematic was the higher than usual number of spelling errors that Fay Alex defensively referred to as typos.

Once the Twitter presentation was finished, the gathering dissolved into a nasal cacophony of overlapping conversations that from outside the Poisonwood Room must have sounded like crows on a road kill. An immodestly beaming Fay Alex was interrupted on her way to the powder room by her personal Secret Service agent, whose name was William something. He said that the Cornbright brothers, who were also lunching late at Casa Bellicosa, wished to meet with Fay Alex in the Gumbo Limbo Room. They said it was an urgent matter.

Fay Alex found Chase and Chance in cordovan armchairs at a bay window overlooking the impeccable croquet lawn, upon which a quartet of geriatric billionaires in shin-high socks spastically flailed candy-colored mallets. The slow-motion melee was being watched with cruel glee by the two Cornbrights. They wore crested navy blazers, button-down Oxfords, creased linen pants (beige and twilight blue, respectively), and Ferragamo driving shoes that had never tapped the accelerator of an American-made vehicle. The young men rose in tandem to greet Fay Alex Riptoad, and Chance immediately asked if she'd heard the big news about Uric Burns.

"Certainly," she said. "I've been in constant contact with Chief Crosby."

When Chase asked to speak privately, she signaled for Secret Service Agent William to wait outside. His arctic nod suggested that he'd rather be waxing his nut sack than trailing Fay Alex around.

As soon as he was gone from the room, Chance spoke up: "So, the man who committed suicide is the same one who called in the tip about Mother's body?"

"That's right," said Fay Alex. "He was one of the three killers, just trying to cash in. The police were waiting outside the bank to arrest him, but by then he'd already hung himself off that bridge. As POTUS himself said: Two scumbags down, one to go—"

"So Burns never collected any of the reward?" Chase asked.

"Of course not. That wasn't ever going to happen." Fay Alex sighed to herself, thinking: *No wonder Kiki Pew gave up on these two stains in the gene pool.*

Chance pressed on with pursed-lip intensity. "So, what about our hundred grand? Is anyone else trying to claim it? Is there a time limit?"

"Chief Crosby says none of the other tips were legitimate."

"Then we, like, get to keep all our money?"

Fay Alex said, "Yes, Chance. The family can, *like,* keep the money."

The Cornbright brothers emitted a lupine howl, knuckle-bumped each other, and called out for more drinks. Fay Alex excused herself and, in more or less a straight line, headed for the double doors of the Gumbo Limbo Room.

Her white Mercedes was idling in the shade of the portico. William opened a rear door for her, but then he sat in front with the driver.

Fay Alex said, "I don't understand why you won't ride back here next to me."

It was the third time that day she'd brought it up. The agent patiently repeated his explanation: "Because I can see more when I'm up here, Mrs. Riptoad."

"But Kelly Bean says her Secret Service man sits right beside her everywhere they go!"

"It's a judgment call, Mrs. Riptoad." William turned his attention to his sunglasses, thumbing a microfiber cloth in practiced circles over each mirrored lens.

Fay Alex, who'd assumed that a Secret Service escort would obey orders as unquestioningly as all her employees, sulked all the way home. There she retreated to her bedroom, shut the door, and endeavored to nap her way out of the steep vodka migraine that would ultimately delay her appearance that evening at the Bath Club, which was hosting a Disney-themed mixer for Peyronie's Syndrome Awareness Week.

Angie knew Paul Ryskamp wasn't thrilled that she'd invited the police chief to join them on their first date. However, the President's inflammatory new tweet had so badly aggravated both Ryskamp and Jerry Crosby that Angie thought a group dinner could be venting therapy—and, for her, a way to get a few questions answered.

Beginning with: What can be done for Diego Beltrán?

"By us? Nothing," the chief said with half a shrug. "It's a goat wedding."

Ryskamp agreed. "The kid's more or less ass-fucked, for now."

Angie finished her beer and ordered another. She said, "Having a pearl in his pocket isn't enough to indict him for the old lady's murder. No way. There's not a jury in the world—"

"Don't you think the prosecutors know that?" Crosby cut in. "They don't want a damn jury trial. They don't want this case going *anywhere*. All they want is a time cushion, and an excuse to keep Beltrán locked up like the President wants."

"But for how long?" Angie asked.

"Until another poster villain comes along," said Ryskamp. He reminded her about Mastodon's gerbil-like attention span; eventually the man would get bored with the No-More-Diegos spiel. "Might take a week, a month, who knows," Ryskamp added. "All depends on the media play he's getting."

A basket of hot rolls arrived. Angie grabbed one and smeared it with maple butter. She said, "You guys are okay letting this kid rot at county with all the no-bail shitbirds? Because I'm really not. Jerry?"

"I asked the state attorney about dropping the stolen-property charge, if Beltrán agreed to return to Honduras. He told me he couldn't do it right now—too much blowback from the White House, Breitbart, the whole drooling mob."

"What does he care about them?"

"For Christ's sake, Angie, he's up for re-election."

"So's the sheriff," Ryskamp noted.

Angie stewed as the Secret Service agent and the chief continued eating. She took another swig of beer and grumbled, "Two sworn officers of the law, I swear to God."

Crosby turned. "What was that?" he asked her crossly.

"Are *you* up for re-election, Jerry? No, you're not."

"But I serve at the pleasure of the town council, which—"

"Never mind," said Angie. "Listen, it just occurred to me—I never got the story on that other pink pearl you showed me."

Ryskamp's fork halted halfway to his mouth. "What other pearl?"

Crosby quietly told them about his field trip with Diego Beltrán to the railroad crossing. Before Angie could add a word, he made a hushing gesture.

"There's more," the chief said. He took out his phone and showed them the street-cam video of the dead python flying from the trunk of the stolen white Malibu after it vaulted the train tracks.

Ryskamp merely nodded, but Angie erupted: "What the fuck, Jerry? What *the* fuck? How can Beltrán still be locked up? Did you not share these juicy little shit bombs with the prosecutor? That you found another pearl right where Diego found his? That you've got freaking *video* of the stolen car at the scene?"

"Hey, dial it down," Crosby said sharply. "I've told the state attorney everything. He knows Beltrán doesn't belong in jail but—for the reasons I already explained—he wants the dust to settle."

"Did you also tell him you'll go straight to the TV stations if he doesn't cut the kid loose immediately?"

"No, I did not," the chief replied stonily.

Angie turned a fierce stare on Ryskamp. "What do *you* think, Paul? If you can pry yourself away from your precious Caesar, I mean. Did you get enough anchovies, by the way? Jesus Christ."

The agent made her wait until he was finished chewing.

"Obviously I didn't know about the second pearl," he began, "but it really makes no difference. The Secret Service doesn't have the authority to order a state prosecutor to spike a case. Neither does Chief Crosby. The evidence is secondary to the politics. It sucks, Angie, but that's how it works."

"Thank you, Mr. Georgetown Law."

"Young Señor Beltrán will remain Public Enemy *Numero Uno* until the President gets tired of ranting about him," Ryskamp said, "which he will, one of these days. I guarantee it."

In a low voice, Crosby added: "And if I did the hero thing and ran to the media on my own, I'd be out of a job. Or busted down to bike patrol, staking out the parking meters on Worth Avenue. For you it might not be a life-wrecking decision, Angie, but I've got a mortgage, two car payments, and three kids who are talking about college. Cue the violins, right? Well, guess what. I can't afford to flush my career down the tubes for Diego Beltrán, or anyone else. Not right now."

Angie backed off. "Last time I took the hero road," she said, "I lost my job, too. Actually it was more like the crazed-avenger road. Point is, Jerry, I get your point. But this kid could get hurt in jail."

The chief stood up. "Just for the record, it makes me sick to my stomach, knowing he shouldn't be there." He opened his billfold. "How much do I owe?"

"Put your money away," Angie told him. "But give me five more minutes."

"What for? There's not a damn thing to be done."

"Please show me the fake suicide note."

The chief found the image on his phone. Angie and Ryskamp moved their chairs around for a better look:

To Whoever Finds Me:

Please tell my family I'm real sorry for what I did. It was me along with Prince Paladin that grabbed that rich old lady from the party on the island. There was no plan to hurt her, but sometimes shit goes down and all of a sudden it's too late. Me and the Prince had a big fight about it, so I had to do him, too.

I know the cops and feds are all over this—I'm number one on their radar, and it's stupid to keep running when there's no place to hide.

BTW, that Diego dude everyone's talking about, he didn't have anything to do with killing that woman. What they're saying about him is total bullshit. I never even met the dumb bastard. And why the hell would me and Prince split a big jewelry score with some wetback straight off the boat?

Anyhow, tell my mom and dad it's not their fault I turned out this way. They didn't fuck up my childhood. I fucked up my own self, big-time.

But there's no way I'm going back to jail alive. I'd rather be dead and free.

U. Burns

"Nice try, Mr. Teabull," Angie said.

Ryskamp allowed that the note had some nice touches. Crosby said a horseshit fake was still horseshit.

"But not necessarily worthless horseshit," Angie said. "Who else besides us knows that Burns didn't write this?"

"The fuckstick who *did* write it," Ryskamp replied. "Same fuckstick who killed him."

"It's Teabull, Paul. The manager of Lipid House. You're allowed to speak his name."

Jerry Crosby said, "Doesn't matter. Nobody gives a shit if Uric Burns was murdered."

Angie didn't disagree. "All I'm saying is the phony note is a gift."

"How?"

"Because it says straight up Diego Beltrán is innocent. Teabull wrote it that way because he's desperate to end the Fitzsimmons investigation. As long as Beltrán is being hyped as the last surviving suspect, the case won't be closed. Reporters will keep trying to dig up more details about the death of the President's favorite Potussy— and that's the last thing in the world Teabull wants."

Neither Ryskamp nor Crosby interrupted her. They knew what was coming.

"So, what if this note got leaked?" Angie tapped Crosby's phone screen. "I mean, here's one of the bad guys swearing in his dying words that he and his partner never met the Honduran kid. If the media got hold of that, the prosecutors wouldn't have any choice except to drop the case against Diego."

Crosby pocketed his phone. "He hasn't been charged with murder. They caught him with a stolen piece of jewelry." Again he stood up. This time he dropped some cash on the table. "I'll text you the screen-shot of the note, Angie."

"Good man," she said.

"But only if you promise to leave me out of it. Don't say a word about the second pearl or the Malibu video, because then they'll know the leak came from me."

"Deal."

"One more thing," said the chief. "Don't get your hopes up."

Once he and Angie were alone, Ryskamp said, "Jerry's right. I don't think you appreciate what's at play here. It's all goddamn theater, and the people behind the curtain don't have souls. You don't know these creeps."

"Honestly, Paul, that patronizing tone does *not* make me want to fuck your brains out."

The agent gave a startled blink. "Was there even a chance of that happening?"

"I was beginning to like you."

"Well, shit."

"Burns was your first homicide, wasn't it? Your first scene? I'm betting the Secret Service doesn't offer much training in that area."

"Low blow," said the agent.

"Well, that wasn't *my* first scene. You know what a dead body looks like after a week in the Everglades? Let's say middle of August. Let's say a stoned pig hunter flipped his airboat at fifty fucking miles an hour."

Ryskamp conceded the point.

"Would it help salvage your opinion of me," he said, "to tell you I don't have the same career concerns as Chief Crosby? I'm cleanly divorced, childless, no mortgage (I rent), and my personal vehicle's paid for. More importantly, I plan to retire soon and—short of espionage, counterfeiting T-bonds, or recreational cannibalism—there's practically nothing a senior agent at my pay grade can do to screw himself out of his pension."

"Translation, please."

"I wouldn't mind putting my ass on the line to spring Diego Beltrán."

"You mean your smirking, self-important ass," said Angie.

"Was that a wink? Pretty sure it was."

"Congratulations, sir. You're back in play."

"I can't promise that anybody'll listen to me. At least anybody who matters."

Angie was a little drunk, so she leaned over and kissed him on the cheek. "Let's go to your place."

"Really?"

"Really. But no sex yet."

Once again the agent was jolted by her candor, and he tried to recover: "That's all right. It's only our first date."

"No, you don't understand. We're not doing it until the day Diego Beltrán walks out of the county jail."

"Uh . . . okay."

"And is publicly exonerated," Angie said.

"Holy Christ, you're serious."

The server brought the check, which Angie handed to Ryskamp. He said, "So, your plan is to leak the Burns note to . . . whom?"

"Local media. Cable news. Politico. The networks. "

"No, pick just one. Make it an exclusive. Much bigger impact."

"You mean like Maddow or Anderson Cooper?"

"That's the idea. Prime-time audience."

"And after the story breaks," Angie said, "you, my friend, will go straight to the state attorney to point out that the suicide note cripples his case against Beltrán and, by the way, where's his proof that the kid belongs to a 'terrorist group' targeting supporters of the President? Tell him the Secret Service needs to know everything he knows. And since he doesn't have jackshit, you'll be duty-bound to advise him to clear Diego's name."

"Duty-bound might be pushing it."

"What's the matter, Paul? You said they couldn't fire you."

"No, I said was planning to retire early."

"And you'd still collect your pension, right?"

"Yeah, but—"

"Sounds like you're having second thoughts," Angie said. "That's fine. Then we'll just stay friends, you and I."

"So let me see if I've got this right: You're proposing a straight-up trade—me helping a random border-jumper in exchange for the possibility of sleeping with you."

"Poor baby. I'm sure you've had worse offers."

Ryskamp raised his cup. "Way worse," he said.

MUSCLE OF LOVE

FIFTEEN

On the night of March 13th, chilly and moonlit, an itinerant trans-mission mechanic named Ajax "Hammerhead" Huppler disap-peared from his boat while casting for snook along the Intracoastal Waterway, within sight of Casa Bellicosa.

Huppler, who grew up near West Palm, had since childhood spent most of his free time with a fishing rod in his hands. His parents preferred to explain this obsession as a love for the wild out-doors, though Ajax himself was never heard to express such feelings. More manifest was a corrosive antisocial streak; Ajax detested the company of other people, including his relatives. Only when he was alone on the water did he feel at ease.

At age thirty-six, Ajax lived by himself in a townhouse devoid of family photographs. His core furnishings were an XBox console, a 60-inch plasma, a motorized recliner, and a secondhand ironing board. For sex he relied upon paid escorts, who were required to come dressed as cockney chambermaids. He was an excellent car mechanic though his contemptuous attitude never failed to get him fired; over the years he'd worked in the repair shops of a dozen major dealerships between Miami Gardens and Fort Pierce. He was a power-train virtuoso—he could fix anything from a plug-in Prius to a vintage Corniche—yet he was always undone by garage politics. On the night Ajax went missing he was unemployed, embittered, and bombed on Budweiser.

It was nearly midnight when his seventeen-foot skiff was spotted drifting toward the seawall of the Winter White House. A Coast Guard speedboat made the interception and dropped off two athletic ensigns, a man and a woman. Seconds later they both dove off the transom and swam rapidly back to their patrol vessel. Other crafts in the presidential security force were summoned, and soon the waterway was a-twinkle with so many red, green, and blue lights that it looked a Christmas flotilla.

Mockingbird stood watching the scene from her second-story bedroom. She wore only a lacy white thong and a pair of pink conch-pearl earrings, five carats each. After setting her glass of cabernet on the windowsill, she took an unauthorized disposable phone from a makeup drawer and dialed Special Agent Keith Josephson.

He was sound asleep at a hotel on the mainland.

"Hi, hon, it's me," the First Lady said. "What the hell is going on behind the house?"

"Uh, don't know. I've been in bed for an hour."

She described what she was seeing from her window. "There's helicopters all over the place. How fast can you get here?"

"Why? Where's Strathman?"

Strathman served as the lead agent on Mockingbird's Secret Service detail when Josephson was off-duty.

"He's right where he always is, sitting in the hallway sexting one of his girlfriends," she said. "But I don't need anything from him, Keith. I need you."

Josephson swung his feet to the floor. "Let me see what I can find out."

He first called Paul Ryskamp, who'd also been sleeping and knew nothing about the incident on the waterway behind Casa Bellicosa.

"Try Strathman," Ryskamp advised Josephson. Then he said: "Are you somewhere you can talk?"

"My room."

"That'll work. So, Keith, you know what I've got to ask—"

"It's Ahmet." He was fully awake now. "Come on, man. A little respect."

Ryskamp said, "Sure. As long as nobody's listening in."

"How'd you like if it they changed your name to Osama?"

"On the other hand, you didn't have to say yes. You could've stayed 'Ahmet' and gone back to TSD."

TSD was the agency's Technical Security Division, which monitors the intruder sensors and explosive-detecting devices on the White House grounds.

"But you wanted to move up the ladder, and who doesn't?" Ryskamp continued. "Still, can we agree it was a poor decision to start boning the First Lady? We've talked about this."

"Talked as friends, you said. Off the clock, off the record."

"Yeah, and as a friend I'm asking if it's still going on between you and her."

"Honestly, I'm not comfortable with that question."

Ryskamp groaned. "Honestly, you both must have lost your minds."

"I really care about her, Paul. She's nothing like the person you read about in the media. She's funny, really smart, warm—"

"Okay, let's also agree a magnetic, beautiful woman. Can't you find one who isn't married to the goddamn President of the United States?"

"She says they haven't done it in years. Not even a handy."

"You promised to end this."

"I did. I mean I tried. She's lonely. Bored out of her mind. And it's not like we do it in the Lincoln Bedroom. We're careful. We pick our moments."

"In what universe," Ryskamp said, "do you see a happy end to this story? Soon as it hits the *Times* or *Politico*, your career's finished—

and then, P.S., the agency gets raked by every whistle-dick subcommittee chairman in Washington."

"That won't happen."

"Oh really?"

"Paul, this thing between her and me won't ever get out because it *can't*. Mastodon would go high-octane batshit, as in suddenly-I-feel-like-bombing-Iran batshit. His people in the White House will do whatever it takes to keep a rumor like this buttoned up—and that includes paying off the tabloids."

"Love your optimism, Ahmet."

"Gotta go. That's her calling back."

"Mockingbird?"

"I bought her a burner phone."

"True love," Ryskamp said. "Shakespeare was born too soon."

"Let me know when you find out what's going on behind the Casa. I'll be up."

"Oh, I'm sure you will."

The ensigns who'd boarded Ajax Huppler's boat thought it was empty, but it wasn't. They leaped off because they saw a huge snake coiled in the bow.

A Special Forces diver attached a rope to the vessel, and the Coast Guard runabout slowly towed it to a marina. The reptile didn't move during the ride, nor did it react to the helicopter spotlight that illuminated Huppler's skiff until it was secured to the dock. At that point a uniformed Palm Beach cop wearing black gloves and night-vision goggles stepped aboard and shot the animal nine times with a semiautomatic. The casting deck was penetrated by numerous slugs, some of which went all the way through the hull with predictable consequences.

By dawn, when Chief Jerry Crosby got there, the skiff was sitting perilously low in the water. None of the well-armed first-responders had been brave enough to touch the dead snake, which Crosby recognized as the same species that had swallowed Kiki Pew Fitzsimmons. He recruited two unenthusiastic officers to help him transfer the python to a large garbage can. Angie Armstrong arrived within an hour to examine the remains.

She peered into the can saying, "You're right, that's another big Burmese. Fifteen-footer, easy."

A crime-scene tent had been erected to block gawkers from taking photos. Crosby told Angie that the registered owner of the vessel was missing: "Ajax Huppler. White male, thirty-six. He went out fishing alone last night. They found his truck and trailer at the Curry Park ramp."

"Does he happen to own a python?" Angie asked.

"No pets, according to his mother. Not even a potted plant. She describes him as a solitary soul. His father says creepy loner."

"How tall?"

"Five-ten."

"Weight?"

"An even deuce," Crosby said.

Together they overturned the garbage can and spread the bullet-riddled snake on the dock. Stepping back from the gore, Angie said, "Good news. This one didn't eat anybody."

"You're sure?"

"See, no lump. Also, it's not big enough to swallow someone as beefy as your missing angler."

"Then what happened out there?"

"Well, pythons do love water," she said. "I'm guessing it got tired from the long swim and crawled up into Huppler's boat for a rest. If he's not a fan of snakes, he probably freaked the fuck out and jumped overboard."

Crosby said, "They counted nine empty beer cans on the skiff."

"The contents of which would not improve one's judgment, or endurance."

"None of the life vests are missing."

"Supporting the theory of a sudden exit." Angie shrugged. "Let's hope the poor guy's clinging to a piling behind one of these mansions, waiting to be rescued."

"Doubtful," said Crosby. "The feds had an armada out there all night, plus three choppers."

"Why the feds?"

"Because the wind blew Huppler's skiff toward Casa Bellicosa."

"Ah. That means our fearless leader's in town."

"No, but the First Lady is. Are we done with this damn thing?"

"Yes, sir, we are."

The chief helped Angie fold the bloody reptile back into the garbage can. She snapped on the lid and said, "It's weird, though. This part of the coast is definitely not their usual habitat."

She'd chalked off the Burmese that grabbed Katherine Fitzsimmons as a geographic outlier, yet here was another jumbo edition straying out of its established range, crossing a busy waterway on a chilly winter night when it should have been dozing in a faraway swamp.

"How do you think it got here?" Crosby asked.

"Maybe they're bailing out of the Everglades to find more prey."

"I wish they'd wait until the season's over."

"These are encroachments, Jerry, not an infestation."

"Thanks for clarifying. I feel so much better."

Together they lugged the can of dead reptile to her new pickup truck. Angie waved goodbye and headed for the Turnpike, where a state biologist with a casket-sized cooler was waiting at the service plaza. On her return drive to the city, Angie called the jail and asked if she could see Diego Beltrán. After a lengthy hold, a deputy came on the line and said Mr. Beltrán would be available for a ten-minute visit.

Angie was resolved to stay upbeat. She still felt bad for raising the young man's hopes so high after she'd leaked the Uric Burns suicide note to MSNBC. Rachel Maddow had gone beast-mode, condemning the "No More Diegos!" campaign as xenophobic propaganda, calling for Beltrán's immediate release, and demanding monetary reparations be paid to him and his family.

For his part, Special Agent Paul Ryskamp had kept his word and paid a discreet visit to the state attorney, who murkily refused to budge.

Meanwhile the White House had shot back with a counter-leak so clever and slick that it couldn't possibly have been devised by the President. Attributed to sources in the Justice Department, the story fed to Fox News and OAN asserted that Uric Burns had falsely exonerated Beltrán in his suicide note in order to protect Burns's own loved ones, who feared a violent retaliation by Beltrán's fellow terrorists—the same brutal gang that had "abducted and assassinated" presidential loyalist Kiki Pew Fitzsimmons. The Fox exclusive said Burns believed his family would be spared if, in his final act, he pretended never to have met the murderous Honduran outlaw.

Every word of the leak was fiction, and Angie naively had hoped that someone in the Burns family would step forward to debunk it. Instead a bespectacled lawyer-spokesperson went on CNN, saying Uric's parents and siblings were still grieving for him and his victims, and collectively would have no comment.

So, months later, Diego remained in jail. The cell beside his was now occupied by a loose-fingered accountant, the llama molester having posted bail and fled the jurisdiction. Wyoming was the rumor.

Diego forced a smile as he entered the interview room. He looked listless and thinner than the last time Angie had seen him.

"That's not what paralegals wear," he said of her khaki capture garb. "I can't believe they let you in here like that."

"Gotta be the briefcase." She opened it to reveal a stack of legal-sized file folders padded with blank copy paper. Diego made a sound like a deathbed chuckle.

"Unfortunately, I've got nothing new to report," Angie said.

"Well, I do. I'm on my third set of lawyers. All the others quit because of death threats."

"Maddow mentioned your case again on her program last night."

"Whoopee," said Diego. "The President tweeted about me seventeen times in the last sixteen days. Your friend in the Secret Service said this would be over by now. He said the lazy old bastard would get bored with the 'narrative' and forget about me."

Angie said, "All of us were hoping that would happen."

"Those maniacs are still demonstrating out front. Didn't you see them?"

"Yes, but not as many as before."

"*One* is too many," Diego said in a raw voice.

The President's political-action committees were still hawking "No More Diegos!" merch on their websites—hoodies, caps, pennants, coffee mugs, tumblers, and other kitsch featuring a crude, sneering likeness of Beltrán's face. That very morning, Angie had spotted one of the bumper stickers on a Range Rover with dealer tags.

She told Diego that she'd deposited a hundred dollars in his commissary account. "You're losing weight, dude. Buy yourself some candy bars."

"Protection is what that money will buy, and not much, but thanks. How's the raccoon-wrestling trade?"

"I got a dope new truck," Angie said. "Camo rims."

Diego actually laughed. "You should have your own TV show."

"I swear you'll get out of here soon. Too many people know the truth."

"Thanks for stopping by, Angie."

She drove home, showered, and tried to nap. Spalding called and asked her to meet for lunch at the Breakers. When she pointed out that she couldn't afford lunch at the Breakers, Spalding said he was buying and told her to wear anything except those butch safari clothes.

She arrived early and took a seat at the Seafood Bar, overlooking the Atlantic. Beside her was a well-fed couple from Montreal counting and recounting their oysters. They had ordered three dozen, and the husband fiercely suspected they'd been shorted. Angie turned her eyes to the ocean, which was royal indigo and regimented with whitecaps to the horizon.

Tonight would be her sixth date with Paul Ryskamp, who had so far been rewarded with nothing more intimate than hand-holding and breezy good-night kisses. Yet still he kept asking her out, hoping she'd cave, even though Diego Beltrán remained behind bars.

Angie was seriously considering it. She liked the agent, and their pact had begun to feel punitive. His supervisor had chewed him out for intervening with the case prosecutor; a letter of reprimand was being drafted. Paul tried not to act bothered, but he confided to Angie that if he continued lobbying for Diego's release he'd be probably be transferred to a desk post in Washington—a dull, demeaning end to an otherwise solid Secret Service career. The man deserved better. He also deserved to get laid. Angie held her phone under the edge of the bartop, where the oyster-slurping Canadians couldn't see it, and sent a breakthrough text to Ryskamp: "Change of plans. Bring condoms tonight."

"Condoms plural?!" he messaged back.

Angie mic-dropped the phone into her handbag. Spalding entered the restaurant followed by Christian, the height-lacking tanning bed technician, who greeted Angie with a hope-filled smile. The three of them went to a table and Spalding ordered a round of mimosas. Christian said he'd flown down to Palm Beach in advance of the President's arrival later that week. Spalding complimented Angie on her white satin jeans and joked that she ought to dress like a heterosexual more often.

"Kiss my white satin ass," she replied.

Soon they were joined by a third man that Christian introduced as The Knob. His shaved head looked like a cypress stump. He was tall and wide enough to cast shade over the table. One chubby hand clutched what appeared to be a taxidermied Pekingese, but was later disclosed to be a vividly lush hairpiece attached to a skull cap. The Knob wore ample slacks and a too-snug golf shirt that tragically failed to conceal the outline of floppy, simian breasts. Both his cheeks were freckled and peeling, while his squinty eyes sat in odd circles of milky-white skin. In a flat voice he said hello while rocking slightly from one thick leg to another.

Angie was looking forward to an explanation of his nickname. When none was offered, she asked, "You must've played pro football."

"Nope," said The Knob. "I hate organized sports."

Christian pointed at the empty chair. "Saved you a seat, bro."

Spalding told Angie that The Knob worked closely with Christian.

"Tuning the presidential tanning bed?" she asked.

"No, testing it," Christian said.

The Knob had nothing to add; he was already immersed in the menu. The subject of his unconventional occupation didn't arise again until after they'd finished lunch, which took longer than expected because The Knob, acting alone, devoured three orders of lump crab cakes, two plates of linguine, and half of Christian's fragrant scallop entree.

"He's got basically the same height and frame as the President," Christian explained, "so we use him for the trial tan, just to make sure there's no temperature issues or electrical glitches."

The Knob glanced over at Angie. "Thirteen minutes on my back," he said with a salacious hitch of an eyebrow. "Easy money, babe."

"Has the bed ever malfunctioned?"

"Like how?" He guffawed and licked the scallop drippings from his lips.

Christian said, "The President's weight goes up and down, and The Knob's supposed to match it pound-for-pound. Some days he needs to drop a few, and other times—like today, obviously—he's got to pack it on."

"What's your current target number?" Angie asked.

The Knob said it was top secret. Christian chuckled and, behind The Knob's head, he flashed two fingers, then six, then nine.

Angie also intended to inquire about the freaky wig, which the tanning-bed test pilot had hung on the corner of his chair, but Spalding asked first.

"It's made from the President's real hair," The Knob revealed. "I shit you not."

Christian elaborated: "It's part of our testing protocol, so we can check off the flammability box."

Angie heard the phone vibrating in her handbag. She didn't answer the call but peeked at the frantic follow-up text: A woman from Boca said an errant hawk was trapped inside her daughter's birthday bounce house. It was a life-or-death crisis, of course. Angie texted back and said she'd be there in forty-five minutes.

The Knob left the table to go weigh himself. When the check came, Spalding grabbed it, as promised.

Angie said, "What's the occasion? You win the scratch-off?"

"No, I brokered a big deal. My cut was eleven hundred bucks."

"Drugs?"

"Jewels, actually."

"Would not have been my second guess."

"Conch pearls from South Africa. My brother sent two beauties and we split the commission."

Angie had never seen a conch pearl. Spalding found the photos on his phone.

Christian leaned in and said, "Tell her who the customer was."

Angie struck a comely pose, chin in hands. "Let me guess—Duchess of Cambridge? Diana Ross?"

"No, it's that Secret Service dude I told you about," whispered Spalding. "Mockingbird's private joy stick."

"Back up. Who's Mockingbird?" Angie said.

"It's the agents' name for the First Lady."

"The guy's totally in love with her," Christian cut in. "Can't get enough."

Spalding confirmed with a lewd hand gesture. "He was bummed the pearls didn't get here in time for Valentine's Day, so he made 'em an early birthday present. Word is some famous jeweler in Pensacola did a rush job on the earrings. Last night Mockingbird wore 'em to a pig roast for the Uzbekistan minister of antiquities. You don't believe me, she's all over the Shiny Sheet."

The first time Angie had heard Spalding's rumor about the First Lady's fling, she hadn't believed it—and hadn't cared enough to press for verification. However, now that she was dating Ryskamp, the story made her curious. She asked Spalding for the agent's name.

"Keith is all he'd tell me."

"What's he look like?"

"Middle Eastern. Tall. Ripped. Early forties."

Angie laughed. "A Middle Eastern 'Keith'?"

"Hey, I didn't ask to see a bloody birth certificate."

"Does the President know what's going on?"

Christian sniggered. "How could he *not*?"

"Well, he doesn't," Spalding declared. "That's the word in the kitchen, and the kitchen's never wrong. So neither of you better say a damn word."

Christian raised his hands like a teller in a bank robbery. "Don't worry, bro. I need my job."

Angie smiled innocently at Spalding. "Oh, come on. Who on earth would *I* tell—and why?"

But of course she'd already thought of someone.

SIXTEEN

Katherine Fitzsimmons was the only person whose approval had mattered to her sons, for it was she who'd controlled the money and, thus, their future lifestyles. Consequently, her unexpected death liberated Chase and Chance from the chore of maintaining a responsible-appearing adulthood; the probate of Kiki Pew's estate was moving along smoothly and, as anticipated, the brothers alone stood to inherit the fortunes left by their mother and both husbands who predeceased her. The final sum promised to be obscene, and the young Cornbrights waited only a short time after the funeral before they started pissing it away.

Their first brainless purchase was a one-hundred-and-sixteen-foot yacht that came with a crew of seven and a pair of coal-black Jet Skis powered by supercharged inline four-strokes. Like most watercraft, Jet Skis have no brakes, though theoretically the Ultra 310s acquired by the brothers could safely be piloted at sixty miles per hour—if the surface was flat calm and free of obstacles. However, that was not the prevailing maritime condition when Chase and

Chance decided to race each other, unencumbered by life vests, on the morning the President returned to Casa Bellicosa.

The Intracoastal Waterway was choppy and crowded, yet the two cackling yahoos drove at full throttle, jumping wakes and spraying rooster tails as they swerved recklessly among the other vessels. Chance took the lead from Chase, but then he picked the worst possible moment to turn around and raise his middle finger. He failed to see in his path the pallid, bloating form of Ajax "Hammerhead" Huppler, which his Jet Ski struck mid-torso before flipping with a roar, catapulting Chance like a sack of potting soil. A split second later, his brother went airborne in a similar arc when his water bike smacked the dead fisherman in the same place. Partiers on a nearby catamaran hooted and clapped, believing the young men were performing stunts for a Yamaha video.

The crew of a passing tug plucked the injured fuckwits from the current. They were lucky to be alive—Chase displayed only a fractured kneecap and a few chipped teeth; Chance had torn both rotator cuffs. Because the accident happened near the secure marine perimeter behind Casa Bellicosa, Coast Guard and ICE vessels were swiftly on-scene, circling slowly. The mewling Cornbrights were transported to a hospital, while the nude corpse of Ajax Huppler— entangled in the rope of a crabber's buoy—was winched onto the stern of a police boat.

An autopsy confirmed that the damage to Huppler's body had been caused post-mortem by the speeding Jet Skis. Drowning was the official cause of the angler's death, with a contributing factor of alcohol intoxication. There was no indication he'd been bitten, constricted, or harmed in any way by the large python found aboard his skiff. Huppler's lack of clothing raised a suspicion of foul play until his parents informed the medical examiner that he often fished naked at night. Police Chief Jerry Crosby was glad to close the file, and happier still that the media missed the story.

Since Kiki Pew's sons were involved, news of the messy accident in the Intracoastal quickly reached Fay Alex Riptoad, who tried leveraging it to extend her time with William, the terse but handsome Secret Service agent. Fay Alex had been basking in the prestige of being escorted everywhere by a young, armed lawman, but the agency had recently decided to terminate the Potussy detail due to plummeting morale.

Fay Alex argued that a dead body floating toward Casa Bellicosa was cause for heightened vigilance, and she implored the President's under-assistant chief of staff to intercede with the Secret Service. An hour later, the aide called back to report that the victim was a local resident named Huppler who'd drowned after diving off his boat while drunk.

"There's no security issue, Mrs. Riptoad," he said. "It wasn't a homicide."

"How do you know the DBC-88 didn't murder that poor man and make it look like an accident?"

"What's the DBC-88?"

"Seriously, are you not on Breitbart? It's the Diego Border Cartel."

"Yes, of course," said the aide. "And remind me what the '88' signifies."

"How the hell I should I know? It's probably gang code."

"But why would they target an unemployed transmission mechanic?"

"For his political loyalties!" Fay Alex snapped. "Same reason they killed Kiki Pew Fitzsimmons—for standing loudly and proudly with POTUS."

"According to our information, Mr. Huppler had no involvement in politics. In fact, he'd never registered to vote."

Flustered, Fay Alex shot back that she intended to discuss the Potussies' Secret Service needs with the President himself that evening at Casa Bellicosa.

"Well, enjoy your dinner," the aide said.

"It's just a damn shellfish buffet!"

"Goodbye, Mrs. Riptoad."

———

Angie was home, lying in bed next to Special Agent Paul Ryskamp, waiting for the sun to come up. He'd been telling her how amazing she was, which is what gentlemen were conditioned to say after sex. Angie knew it hadn't been her best effort—she couldn't clear her thoughts of Diego Beltrán in the county jail. Additionally she'd been distracted by Ryskamp's glossy Silk Rocket condoms; Angie had never heard of the brand, and verbalized some concerns about reliability. Ryskamp had assured her there was nothing to worry about; Silk Rockets were the world's finest prophylactics, manufactured by quality-conscious, hyper-precise Swedes. Five stars on Amazon.

And they didn't break during intercourse, so that was good.

The experience had been more than fine—not mind-bending, not Top Ten—but very encouraging for a first night together. Angie hadn't let on that she wasn't fully engrossed. After they were done, Ryskamp's first breath was: "You were amazing."

And naturally she said, "So were you, Paul. Wow."

The "wow" being a tender reflex, because she really did like the guy.

"Hey, I need to ask you something," she said, bunching a pillow under her head.

"Uh-oh. What'd I do wrong?"

"Relax. New subject."

"Then fire away."

"Is there an agent named Keith guarding the First Lady?"

Ryskamp sat up and turned on the light. "Why do you ask?"

Angie groaned and buried her head. "You're totally killing the afterglow. Can't we talk in the dark?"

"No, this is important. What've you heard?"

"He's screwing the First Lady. A.K.A. Mockingbird, right?"

"Don't ever use that name for her," Ryskamp said. "Please."

"What about Agent Keith?"

"Let it go, Angie."

"He bought her a pair of pink pearl earrings, which she wears in public. Did you know that?"

"Where'd you get all this?"

"And her husband, the most powerful human on the planet, doesn't have a clue," said Angie. "That's the word in the kitchen."

Ryskamp slumped and murmured, "Fuck me."

She peeked one eye from beneath the pillow. "Paul, when is your official retirement date?"

"What's that got to do with this?"

"Promise not to freak."

But freak he did, when she told him her idea. He was dressed and gone from her apartment in three minutes and twenty seconds, tying the record set by a pharmaceuticals rep that Angie had Tazed on the thigh after he'd said she should consider a boob job and offered to line her up with a cosmetic surgeon who also happened to be his uncle.

The morning passed with no follow-up texts or phone calls from Ryskamp, so Angie assumed she'd run him off. She left an apologetic-sounding voicemail that drew no response. At noon she drove to a stable in Wellington to remove what the owner described as a "seriously fucked-up squirrel." He claimed it was terrorizing the show horses.

Angie parked beside a long, flat-roofed barn where she was surprised to see Alexandria, her ex-husband's girlfriend, who was in a state of florid agitation. Pursued by a rake-wielding groom, the squirrel had taken refuge inside one of Alexandria's imported riding boots, which she'd left in a corner of the stall.

"How's your pelvis?" Angie asked nicely. "Have you returned to the soul-soothing universe of yoga?"

"Please help. We didn't know who else to call."

They hadn't spoken since a chance encounter at a craft store, months before Alexandria's riding accident. It was awkward then, and awkward now.

The stable owner and groom hovered by the stall door, poised to dive aside if the deranged squirrel bolted for daylight. Alexandria's horse, a bay warmblood, snorted and pawed at the hay.

"Which boot?" Angie said.

"The left one. Do you think he's pooping in there?"

"Oh, absolutely. How's Dustin?"

"Fine. Just fine."

"Yeah?" Angie knew from Joel that her ex had hit bumpy times and been forced to unload his latest sports car, a trite yellow Lambo. The chicory-edible company that employed Dustin had gone bankrupt after several shipments were found to have cat litter as an additive.

As Alexandria sidled protectively between her horse and her eight-hundred-dollar footwear, Angie observed a limp and she momentarily felt shitty for having harbored such mean thoughts. Nor was she proud of noticing that the hobbled equestrian must have dined well during her recovery, for she had acquired a double chin.

Angie approached the squirrel's hiding place and peeked inside. Then she turned to the young stable groom and said, "May I borrow your shirt?"

Unhurriedly he set down the rake, peeled off his sweaty tee, and handed it to her.

"What are you doing?" Alexandria asked Angie.

"Hush, princess."

She balled up the groom's shirt and crammed it into the shaft of the occupied boot, trapping the frightened rodent. With Alexandria trailing at a faint-hearted distance, Angie carried the chittering animal to her truck and transferred it into a small travel kennel. She snapped the door shut, tossed the shirt back to the groom and held out the vacated boot for Alexandria, who shook her head disgustedly saying, "I don't want that thing now! Throw it away, please."

Angie placed the boot upright in her pickup, next to the kennel, where the squirrel sat panting on its haunches, twitching its bottle-brush tail. The stable owner blurted a question that Angie heard on practically every wild-mammal call: "Is that damn thing rabid?"

"Naw, just lost," she replied.

Alexandria thanked her for the swift, bloodless capture. "Hope it wasn't too uncomfortable seeing me here. I'll tell Dustin you asked about him."

"My fee is three hundred dollars," said Angie.

"Okay. Fair enough."

"What size shoe do you wear?"

Alexandra smiled warily. "Eight. Why?"

"Close enough. I'll take the other boot, too."

A mile from the stable, Angie pulled the truck off the road and freed the squirrel near a stand of Florida pines. When she got back to her apartment, Joel was stocking the refrigerator. She told him about Alexandria summoning her to Wellington.

"A little creepy," he said.

"Is that the same horse that threw her?"

"No idea. She owns a bunch."

Angie said, "Well, I hope your ankle's healing better than her pelvis."

"Almost as good as new."

"Want a sandwich? I see you loaded up on Boar's Head."

"I'm meeting Krista in Delray. Why don't you come along?"

Krista was Joel's latest girlfriend, and they were together nearly all the time. Angie didn't see Joel as often as before, but she approved of the relationship. She simply wasn't in the mood for a group lunch.

"Rain check," she said. "I need to clean my new boots."

It didn't take long. After vacuuming the squirrel droppings from the left one, she applied Lysol liberally with a rag. The right boot was sanitized the same way, after which Angie spritzed perfume inside both. While waiting for them to dry, she watched an episode of *Fleabag* and ate a turkey sub with pickles and mustard. Then she put on a black tank top, denim cutoffs, and two pairs of thick socks, because Alexandria's feet were a size-and-a-half larger.

The riding boots felt mighty fine when Angie did a runway walk down the hall of her apartment. She got in the truck and drove to the Lake Worth Pier, where she sat on a bench and watched shivering tourists fake-frolic for Instagram in the chilly surf. Now that Ryskamp had bailed, Angie needed someone else to help execute her plan for freeing Diego Beltrán. One person came to mind as both trustworthy and connected. She thought about it a while before she returned to her pickup and made the call. Jerry Crosby suggested they meet at the Brazilian Court.

He grinned when Angie walked in.

"What's so amusing, Jerry?"

"It's the first time I've seen you out of uniform."

"This is my jaunty alter ego," she said. "I do have a life, you know."

They took a table in a warm panel of sunshine on the patio. Angie ordered a Bloody Mary and the police chief had a raspberry iced tea. He told her the body of the missing Alex Huppler had been recovered in the Intracoastal.

"He got plowed by a couple of morons on Jet Skis, which made extra work for the medical examiner," he said. "Ironically, the morons happened to be Mrs. Fitzsimmons's sons."

"What a colorful little town you have here," Angie said.

"There was no snake-related trauma on the dead fisherman."

"Can't we call that good news?"

"On another subject: Your least favorite stalker dropped off the radar. Has he been in touch?"

Pruitt had remained in jail for only a few nights after Crosby had him arrested back in January. Angie hadn't heard a peep since the asshole had made bond.

"No more phone calls," she said, "but he's poaching again. Deer and gators."

"Who told you that?"

"One of the wildlife officers I used to work with. Evidently Pruitt has broadened his prosthetic talents to cocking a rifle."

"Let me know if he makes contact. I'm serious, Angie."

"Yes, sir."

"Are you still seeing Paul Ryskamp?"

"Who?" she said.

"Right. None of my business."

"Did you ever interview Tripp Teabull about my two murdered burglars?"

"Teabull's gone. I thought you heard," the chief said.

"Dead?"

"No, fired."

It had happened shortly after No-More-Diegos.net, an anti-immigration website inspired by the President, posted a shocking, wholly invented "reconstruction" of Kiki Pew Fitzsimmons's last night. The graphic animation depicted the doomed Potussy being snatched from the grounds of Lipid House by the homicidal border jumper, Beltrán, accompanied by his two burly white followers, Uric Burns and Keever Bracco. Viewed by more than two million people, the video featured a drone shot of the lush walled estate overlaid by the imagined path of the black-clad kidnappers through the festive topiary to the koi pond.

Within hours of the posting, more than a dozen major galas and balls scheduled at Lipid House had been canceled. The events were quickly re-booked at Casa Bellicosa, the President having big-heartedly offered their sponsors a five percent discount on the standard one-night rental fee. Reeling from the catastrophic loss of revenue, the board of the Lipid House Trust blamed Tripp Teabull's complacence for the belated blast of negative publicity about Mrs. Fitzsimmons's death. Teabull had been hustled out the gates by a replacement security team, and was now rumored to be working as the caretaker at a fly-in hunting lodge in Newfoundland.

"So he got away with it," Angie said to Crosby.

"He did a good job covering his tracks. Plus, nobody gives a shit that Burns and Prince Percocet are dead."

"Because of those two, Diego's still in jail. Because of the damn stolen pearls."

"Unfortunately, I can't do anything about that."

"But you can, Jerry. Absolutely."

"We had this talk before. The answer's still no."

"I've got some new information that you need to hear." Angie dropped her voice to tell him about the First Lady's daring affair with the Secret Service agent named Keith.

The chief said, "First of all, I don't believe it. Second, how in the world does that help Diego Beltrán?"

"Are you kidding?" Angie laid out her plan, step-by-step, then whispered, "Your job would be totally safe. All you've got to do is hook me up with the right person at Casa Bellicosa."

"Now you've lost your damn mind," Crosby said.

"It'll work. I know it will."

"No way, Angie."

"Meaning no way will it work?"

"Meaning no way will I get involved."

She said, "I don't need an answer right now." She purposely hadn't told him about Paul Ryskamp's reaction to the plan, or the last thing he'd said before he walked out of her apartment: *What you're proposing, Angie, is an actual crime.*

"Please, Jerry," she said.

"Back off. I can't help you."

"But, deep down, you wish you could?"

"Deep down, I wish I had a vineyard in Bordeaux. Goodbye."

He got up and left. Just like that. Didn't even offer to pay for his damn tea. That was two walk-outs in one day.

When the server brought the bill, Angie looked up and said, "Can I ask you something, Philippe? When did testicles go out of style?"

The young man paled, and went from chipper to chastened. "I'm super sorry, ma'am. Was, uh, the service unsatisfactory?"

"Not at all, sir. I'm just venting."

Angie paid the tab, exited proudly in her boots, and drove home determined to think up a new strategy.

SEVENTEEN

Mockingbird ate lunch alone—tuna salad with kiwi crescents—at a corner table in one of Casa Bellicosa's informal dining rooms. Keith Josephson and two other agents were triangularly positioned nearby. Between bites, the First Lady would look up and wave mechanically at gawking club members and their guests. She didn't like sitting alone, but the alternative was joining her husband at a raucous patio barbecue for a mob of TV wrestlers who'd performed in his latest anti-impeachment commercial.

The night before, he had called Mockingbird to his suite and asked her to arrange a photo session with the women who called themselves the Potussies. At first she had declined.

He said, "Come on, baby. Be a team player."

"I'm not your baby. Is that what you call the pole dancer you're sleeping with?"

"I have no idea what you're talking about."

"Liar," said Mockingbird. "You got her a cabana over at the Breakers. Anyway, I can't stand those rich old vultures and I'm not doing their selfies."

"Hell, no, use the White House photographer! Two minutes and you're done. Christ, they've been trying to get a picture with you for years," the President said. "I need to throw 'em a bone. They donate a shit-ton of cash."

He wore silk burgundy pajamas and sat barefoot on the edge of the bed. His feet were like moist loaves, the tiny toes appearing more decorative than functional. Mockingbird sometimes found it hard to believe this was the same man she'd married; he looked like a different person now—as if someone had put a fire hose up his ass and inflated him with meringue. His ego seemed to have swollen proportionally.

It wasn't that long ago when she'd fallen hard for him; now he was a raging, gaseous oaf. Gone was any trace of the sly charm and tenderness. In their early years he could actually laugh at himself, but Mockingbird couldn't recall the last time she'd seen an honest smile on his face.

"Come on," he said, "I don't ask you for much."

They both knew what he meant.

Mockingbird said, "All right. One group photo, that's it."

"Good girl. I like those earrings, by the way."

She felt her cheeks flush.

"Didn't even know pearls came in pink. Did I buy those for you?"

"You did," she said, which was true in a roundabout way. Keith Josephson got a government salary, and her husband was the head of the government.

"The Potussies will be here for lunch tomorrow," he said. "We'll set up the photo op for when they're done."

"And probably drunk."

"Sure, but you're a pro at this shit."

"The best," Mockingbird said thinly.

"Listen—whatever you heard about that woman at the Breakers, it's a total fake lie. She's not a stripper, she's my nutritionist."

"And doing a fine job, I can see."

Mockingbird had returned to her room and sobbed, though not

as loudly as she had on that first election night. She hated the emotional cage, the brittle charade. Her romance with Keith was the only
unscripted part of her life, and she felt grateful that he was reckless
enough to fall for her. The seduction had been a challenge—like all
the Secret Service, he was conditioned to be steely and methodical.
It had taken weeks just to make him smile, but that was the moment
she knew the deal was done.

Several of her friends cheated on their cheating husbands, but
they weren't surrounded by handlers and media every time they
stepped outdoors. For Mockingbird, it would have been impossible
to sustain a secret affair anywhere but inside the hermetic orbit of
the White House; the only men with whom she spent private time
were those assigned to protect her. She was lucky that the one she
loved was just a little bit weak.

When she was done with lunch, Keith approached her table and
said, "The Potussies are ready for their photo-up."

"Oh, are they now."

"Would you like to see the list of names?"

"God, no," the First Lady said.

The White House photographer had arranged the women in a
standing semicircle before a decommissioned fireplace in the Poisonwood Room. Mockingbird positioned herself in the middle and
was nearly overcome by a riotous clash of odors—perfumes, hair-
sprays, and top-shelf booze. The Potussies were tipsy though not
incapacitated.

"I'm Fay Alex Riptoad," said the one on Mockingbird's immediate right. "We've met a few times before."

"Why, of course. So lovely to see you again."

"Your husband is a great, great American hero."

"That's very . . . kind." Mockingbird gave the photographer a
look that could not be misunderstood: *Hurry up and take the fucking
picture.*

"As a matter of fact, I saw the President here last night at dinner,"
the Riptoad creature continued, "but couldn't catch his attention. I

was hoping to speak with him about the termination of our Secret Service protection—it seems terribly risky, given all that's happened. I'd be surprised if he was even aware of the decision."

"What? I'm sorry—Secret Service?"

"Oh yes. Each of us had our own personal agent, ever since Kiki Pew was butchered by that horrid Diego gang."

"Your own *personal* agent," Mockingbird repeated, incredulous and also appalled at the waste of manpower. Silently she counted all the tinted little heads—there were six of them. It was unbelievable. Surely Keith would know the full story.

The photographer aimed his camera. "Say 'brie,'" he chirped at the women, and snapped off a dozen frames.

Afterward Mockingbird dutifully shook hands with each of the Potussies, who as they dispersed were cordial if not especially warm. Fay Alex hung back to make one final pitch:

"Could you please share our security concerns with the President? Sadly, we all know this threat is real—I'm sure he'll agree that our loyal little tribe can't endure one more senseless attack."

With a well-practiced nod, the First Lady said, "I'll speak with my husband."

"The agents can be a tremendous comfort," Fay Alex added with a sly whisper, "as you know."

"Uh . . . yes. They're the best at what they do." Mockingbird managed to hold a steady gaze though her nerves were jangling.

She mumbled goodbye to the Riptoad gargoyle and followed her Secret Service detail out of the room. It wasn't until she got in the elevator that she realized she was standing besides Strathman, not Keith.

"Agent Josephson was called into a meeting," Strathman explained.

"Oh. All right."

"We're clearing the gym now. Your regular workout is scheduled in forty-three minutes."

Mockingbird said, "No, I think I'll have a nap this afternoon."

She was vaping in the tub, admiring a chevron of pelicans skimming gracefully over the Intracoastal, when Keith knocked lightly. He came in, shut the bathroom door and haggardly leaned his back against it. His face was drained, his jaw set.

"What's wrong, hon?" she asked.

"They know."

"Calm down. Deep breaths."

"I can't go on with this. *We* can't go on."

"Come here," said Mockingbird, sitting up. "Right now."

The Knob stood on the scale and hit the day's mark, two-hundred-and-sixty-nine pounds. Christian told him to put on the wig made of Mastodon's hair and lie down in the tanning bed.

"It's not a fuckin' wig, it's a piece," the Knob shot back. "Wigs are for chicks."

"Hurry up," said Christian, and set the timer.

The Knob donned the skull cap and adjusted the hairpiece in the President's iconic style. Then he squeezed into the acrylic cylinder and lowered the canopy cover. He wore small reflective goggles, a black tee-shirt, sweat pants, and socks. Only his face and arms were exposed to the UVA rays, because that's how Mastodon did it. There was no need for full-body shading because the commander-in-chief never permitted himself to be photographed shirtless, or in shorts.

As soon as the timer went off, the cover of the Cabo Royale swung open and The Knob emerged. The complexion of his cheeks and nose had darkened from marbled salmon to fawn.

"All done," he said, peeling off the goggles. "I'm gonna go binge some porn."

"Hold on—what's that smell?" Christian asked.

"Maybe I farted. So what?"

"No, this is different."

The Knob said he didn't smell anything. Christian told him to remove his wig.

"It's not a wig, goddammit!"

"Let me see that, bro."

Toward the front of the hairpiece, on the crest of the swooshing peach forelock, Christian spotted a discolored area the size of an M&M. He sniffed it and said, "Oh shit."

"Whassa matter?" asked The Knob.

"It's singed."

"You mean burnt?"

Christian fingered the charred strands. "Something must've thrown a spark. I don't know what, or how."

The Knob said he hadn't noticed anything unusual. "But my eyeballs was shut the whole time."

Christian leaned into the tanning chamber to examine the fixtures holding the fluorescent tube lamps.

"Can I go now?" The Knob said.

"Not yet. We need a do-over."

"But I gotta piss like a drunk donkey."

"Get in and give me another five minutes," Christian said.

"I don't want my face gettin' cooked!"

Like that would change your social life, thought Christian. He gave The Knob a microfiber sun mask of the type worn for protection by fishing guides.

The Knob tried to tug the stretchy fabric down over his head but it kept getting snagged on the skull cap's Velcro patches.

"What's the damn SPF on this thing?" he bleated at Christian.

"Fifty."

"Big deal. Fuck it." The Knob tossed the face mask on the floor.

"You're only doing five more minutes, anyway," said Christian.

"Unless I fucking catch on fire."

"Seriously? Okay, make it four."

The Cabo Royale operated perfectly during the second trial, but Christian replaced one of the ballasts anyway. Mastodon showed up late and undressed alone, thrusting his suit, necktie, and shoes through the doorway to his butler, who stood waiting with Christian and the Secret Service detail. It was routine for the President to demand total privacy during his tanning sessions, which—upon orders of the White House dermatologist—was never to exceed thirteen minutes.

"He'll need to hydrate," Christian reminded one of the agents, who told him that fluids were on the way.

Spalding soon arrived with a tray bearing two unrefrigerated cans of Dr. Pepper, which another agent popped open and tasted. The tanning-room door cracked and one of Mastodon's hands materialized, motioning for his clothes. Minutes later he walked out freshly bronzed except for the stark white eye circles, which served to project the presence of an immense albino raccoon. He grabbed both cans of soda and lumbered upstairs, a half-step ahead of his security phalanx.

"That's Pepper *numero* eleven and twelve for the day," Spalding told Christian when they were alone. "The man's basically mainlining corn syrup and caffeine."

"Least he doesn't smoke or drink."

"No, but he gobbles Adderalls like jelly beans. That's how he stays up all night tweeting. The pills, man."

"Do they also make you forget how to spell?" Christian said.

"In other breaking news, guess what the cleaning staff found under the First Lady's bed?"

"Jesus Christ, not so loud."

"Italian panties," Spalding whispered. "Cosabella."

"So what?"

"They were torn!"

"You need a girlfriend," Christian said, shaking his head.

"What's in the pail?"

"Hospital-grade sanitizer—it's for the Cabo." The cleansing sequence had been ramped up since the pandemic. For applicators Christian employed pressed beach towels embroidered with the Casa Bellicosa logo. "Gets pretty damn toasty in the tanning chamber," he explained. "The big guy, he sweats buckets."

"Gross me out."

"Does that mean you won't help me wipe it down?"

"Fuck no," said Spalding as he departed with the empty tray.

"I'll remember this," Christian called out, laughing, "next time your visa's up."

Joel called and asked to meet for lunch. Angie, who'd just finished relocating a litter of wild cottontails, didn't have time to shower and change. They sat at the bar in Applebee's, each with a burger, fries, and a cup of black coffee. Joel wore a jacket and tie because he had a job interview.

"Assistant manager at Staples," he said. "See, fantasies do come true."

"Try to be a ray of positivity." Angie pinched a brown tick from her shirt, crushing it between her fingers. "Little bastard," she said, and went to the restroom to wash her hands and check herself for more job-related parasites. When she returned to the bar, Joel said he had some news.

"Krista and I moved in together," he said.

"Sweet! Her place, I assume."

"Yeah, the condo in Palm Beach Gardens."

"She seems like a good one. I'm happy for you, Joel."

"Thanks. But there's something else I couldn't talk about in front of her. I've been getting some phone calls."

"Oh shit," Angie said. "Pruitt?"

"Six o'clock sharp, every evening."

"Ass. Hole."

"I didn't say anything because I didn't want you to freak. Krista doesn't know yet, but I've got to tell her."

"No need to scare her. I'll deal with it."

"This has been going on a week or so," Joel said.

"And what does he say when he calls? The usual?"

"That's the thing. At first he'd just rant and rave and hang up, but last night it got real. He said he knows where Krista lives so she better watch out. He said I ought to make you start her car every morning."

Angie pushed her plate away. "Did he mention the actual address?"

"No, so he's probably been bluffing. But still . . ."

"The phone numbers he uses, they're all spoofed?"

"Yup. Different area code every time."

"Okay, I'm on it."

"What're you going to do?" Joel asked.

"Go find him, what else."

"That's nuts, Angie. You've got cop friends—let them handle it."

She said, "You guys should go stay with your dad and the equestrian."

"What's our cover story?"

"The condo's getting painted. Or tented for fleas, I don't care. Bedbugs?"

Joel nodded pensively and took a sip of coffee. Angie called for the check and got up to leave.

"Yo, finish your burger," said Joel.

"Next time lunch is on you, when you're a big shot at Staples."

"Where are you going? See, this is exactly what I was afraid of."

"Good luck with the job interview," she said. "Then go talk to your girlfriend and get packed. Tell her the bedbug crew is coming tomorrow, whatever. You're a bright young fellow, you'll think of something."

From the truck Angie tried to call Jerry Crosby. He didn't pick up, so she left a message saying that fucker Pruitt was back in action. Next she tried to reach Paul Ryskamp in the hope he was finished sulking. Since he didn't answer the phone, she drove to the building where the Secret Service had its West Palm office. Without the keypad code to the agency's private elevator, Angie found herself staking out the lobby. Her khaki ensemble made it impossible to blend in, and before long an agent appeared, handed her a clip-on laminate and led her upstairs. Ryskamp was dressed in total tiki-bar mufti, including flip-flops.

"I'll have an apple margarita," Angie said, "with a floater."

Ryskamp pointed at the bank of surveillance monitors upon which her movements had been tracked from the moment she'd parked the pickup.

"I tried calling first," she said. "I figured you were still pissed."

"I wasn't, and I'm not."

"Once again, you're a terrible liar."

Ryskamp's smile wasn't quite the same as before. "I'm not mad, Angie. But if you're here to discuss the subject we've already exhausted, then Agent Frey will be taking you back downstairs."

She said, "Don't worry, I'm not here about Beltrán. This is personal."

"Have a seat."

"Man, when you hit the Off switch, you hit it hard."

"So, what's up?"

Angie told him about Pruitt's phone calls to Joel. "Supposedly he moved out of the county and vanished. I need some help, Paul."

"He doesn't sound smart enough to vanish."

"Even if he did, you people can find *anybody*. That's your thing. Some meth-head living under a bridge says he's gonna pop the President, you guys have the crazy fool locked up by the end of the week."

"Sometimes," said Ryskamp.

"Pruitt might be in Iceland for all I know, but he's still gotta pay rent and utilities, or at least have a credit card. For sure his name and address are in a database somewhere."

"Has he ever done anything worse than make phone calls?"

"Look, he's threatening my stepson and his girlfriend. I can't take a chance that he hasn't suddenly stripped his gears."

"Say I was able to locate him. Tell me what you'd do with the information, Angie."

"Notify the authorities that have legal jurisdiction?"

"Give me an effing break."

"Paul, I promise not to feed any other part of his anatomy to a gator."

"Honestly? I don't give a shit if you do, as long as the trail doesn't lead back to me. Let me see what I can dig up."

"For real? You're gonna help me out?"

Ryskamp said, "Go home and do some laundry."

Angie glanced down, frowning at the stain on her shirt. "It's just bunny pee. Want to meet up later for a drink?"

"Sorry, I'm working. The President's in town."

"No offense, but what are you trying to pull off with this Parrothead look?"

Ryskamp laughed. "Carefree island dude who doesn't get noticed."

"Then you need to gain about twenty pounds."

"Uh, okay."

"That's a compliment, sir. Means you're too cut to be wearing a baggy shirt covered with palm trees."

As he walked her to the elevator, Angie asked, "Are you and I done, Paul? Date-wise, I mean."

"I believe so."

"God, was my Diego plan really so terrible? Before all that, things were going peachy. You even told me I was great in bed. Not just great—amazing."

"Sssshh," he said.

"My new plan is cleaner. You don't have to be involved in any way."

"We're on camera," he whispered without moving his mouth. "And our people can read lips."

"Uh-oh," Angie murmured.

As the elevator doors opened, she shook Paul's hand and said in a clear firm voice, "I appreciate you taking the time to meet me with me, Agent Ryskamp."

"You're welcome, Ms. Armstrong. Thank you for dropping by."

———

They turned up her Pandora playlist to cover their voices, and they held each other for a long time in the darkness. Mockingbird kept telling him everything would turn out all right, and Keith Josephson kept saying no, it wouldn't.

"Some of the people who work here know about us," he said. "They're talking."

"Cheap gossip, Keith, that's all. Nobody can prove a thing." She didn't tell him about Fay Alex Riptoad's loaded remark at the Potussies photo session.

"The agency's sending me back to D.C."

"Not happening," said Mockingbird.

"A special agent named Jennifer Rose will be replacing me on your detail."

"*Definitely* not happening."

Keith said, "The last thing you need is a public scandal."

"I told you, hon. My husband's people would do everything and anything in their power to cover this up. And it's my word against whose? Some nosy busboy from Belgrade?"

"If I don't go back to Washington, I'm done." Keith sounded frayed and desolate.

Mockingbird said, "You don't get it. The Secret Service won't do anything the White House tells them not to."

"You're wrong. And even if for some reason they agreed to leave me where I am, my career's basically over. Besides, your husband won't want me around, especially if he finds out what I am."

"Oh great. Let me guess: You're a spy."

"Worse, actually in his eyes." Keith confided to Mockingbird that his real name was Ahmet Youssef, and explained why it had been changed. "I agreed to do it only because they said they needed me on this detail. Don't cry."

"Shit, *Keith,*" she said, wiping her eyes with the corner of a pillowcase.

"This is all on me. I should've been . . . I don't know. Stronger."

"Meaning you should have said no when I hit on you. Right?"

He walked over to the window. "I'm on a flight out of Lauderdale tomorrow night."

"You could quit and go to work for Black Eagle." Mockingbird was talking about a private security contractor with which the administration had unsavory ties. "I could set it up with one phone call," she said, then quickly added: "Never mind. That won't work."

"No, ma'am."

Both of them knew their affair couldn't survive if he left the agency. They would never get to see each other.

"I should head back to the hotel now," he said.

"Not yet."

"Strathman knows I'm here. So do the other agents on the shift."

"Of course they do." Mockingbird reached up and turned on a light. "So what? You're still officially on the job, right?"

"As of tonight, yes."

"Then please open that bottle of shitty Chablis."

"Not allowed," he said.

"The wine's for me, not you. Stay awhile. Please, Ahmet."

EIGHTEEN

The Key Lime pie that Mastodon devoured punctually every night came from a mom-and-pop bakery in Marathon. When the President was in Washington, the pies arrived in lots of a dozen on a Grumman C-2 based at the Boca Chica Naval Air Station near Key West. During his vacations at Casa Bellicosa, the pies were delivered by refrigerated truck directly to the mansion. The trip from the Middle Keys to Palm Beach took roughly four hours on the Turnpike, depending on traffic. Typically the driver made a bathroom stop at the Pompano Beach service plaza. He was away from the truck for fewer than six minutes on the afternoon of the security breach, but there was no video because the camera posted in that quadrant of the parking lot had been disabled by someone with a pellet gun.

Later, the director of the Secret Service would be summoned before a Senate subcommittee and questioned about why Mastodon's Key Lime pies hadn't been transported in an unmarked vehicle. The director would explain that the small bakery didn't own any trucks without signage, that the cost of using a government rig would have been exorbitant, and that in any case the hardworking couple that made the pies felt it was good advertising to have the bakery's name on display, especially when delivering to such a prestigious zip code.

The time was five-twenty p.m. when the tangy shipment from Marathon arrived at the service entrance of Casa Bellicosa. Two white-clad Brits on the kitchen staff stood in wait while the driver, whose name was Guppo, backed up the gaily painted Betancourt Pastries chariot. It was he who noticed that the truck's cargo compartment wasn't locked, but he assumed he'd forgotten to do it. He rolled up the door, stepped into the cooler, pulled the wide tray from the rack, and let out a sound that changed from a quizzical hum to a terrified shriek.

A long mottled snake had threaded itself among the delicacies. It wasn't moving because reptiles become dormant in cold temperatures, a herpetological fact unknown to Guppo. He reasonably feared he was about to get chomped and possibly squeezed to death.

So he dropped the heavy tray of presidential pies and ran.

The British kitchen workers resisted the impulse to follow him. They knew Mastodon would go raging apeshit without his beloved dessert, though the pies scattered in the truck looked unsalvageable. When the tray had fallen, the plastic containers popped open. Now the silky coils of the great python were smeared with citrine filling, whipped Chantilly cream, and crumbs from the fractured graham-cracker crusts.

However, in a lone corner on the other side of the motionless beast, sat a single, intact Key Lime pie. The lid of the container had been sprung, yet the fluffy treat looked perfect.

"I'm going for it," one of the workers announced.

"Are you crazy?" said the other. "Let the fat toad eat ice cream!"

"My visa's up next month. If I do this, I'm golden," the brave one said. "Maybe I'll even get a raise."

"Or maybe you'll get your dumb ass strangled," said his co-worker, and took off.

The brave one pressed his back to the inside wall of the bakery truck, edged nervously past the torpid snake, and picked up the miracle pie. He balanced it one-handed over his head as he sidestepped out of the cooler, and he continued carrying it that way as he hurried to the Casa Bellicosa kitchen, where he arrived beaming.

"This is fun," Angie said. "The Three Musketeers, together again."

They were gathered in the dark around her pickup, which she'd parked next to the Betancourt Pastries truck at the delivery ramp of the President's mansion.

Chief Jerry Crosby asked, "Did you bag the damn thing?"

"Yes, sir. Wanna see?"

Special Agent Paul Ryskamp was all business. "In your professional opinion, how did this happen?"

"Someone put the snake inside the bakery vehicle," Angie said. "There's no natural way it could have gotten there."

"Maybe it crawled in through the cooling system."

"No, it's way too thick to fit. Anyway, pythons hate the cold."

"So the person who did this," said Crosby, "knows how to handle those things."

"And also where the President gets his pies." Angie looked at Ryskamp. "Wasn't there a big write-up about the bakery in *USA Today*?"

"Two weeks ago," the agent acknowledged tightly.

"Paul, at first I didn't recognize you out here. But, dude, you are rockin' that charcoal suit."

"Enough, Angie."

The chief said, "Can we all agree that monster snakes aren't all of a sudden showing up in Palm Beach just because they're bored with the Everglades? Some sick son of a bitch is targeting this community."

"Looks that way," said Ryskamp, "but let's hear from the expert."

Angie wasn't positive she detected sarcasm, so her response was straightforward: "I agree—there's no way this is random. This third one clinches the deal."

"It's not number three," Crosby said bleakly. "It's number five."

"What the fuck, Jerry? Why didn't you call me about the other two?"

"Because I didn't need you to come catch them. They were already dead. One got chopped to pieces by the Revlon yacht last night while it swam through the inlet. The other was hit by an asphalt truck on A1A at dawn this morning, only a thousand feet from the front gate of this place."

"Sweet Baby Jesus," Angie said.

It was another crisp, clear night, and there were trim men in gray suits all over the place. Like Paul Ryskamp, they were armed.

Angie had never been to the Winter White House before, and she was impressed. Even the service driveway had a postcard view of the Intracoastal, bathed by the tropical lights of the West Palm skyline. The Casa's croquet lawn was even more pristine than the one at Lipid House, although no club members or guests were playing. Likewise, the tennis courts and sapphire swimming pools sat empty. Angie knew it was because the President was in residence. Tonight he was dining privately with his nutritionist, according to Spalding's sources, and wanted quiet on the grounds. A couple of long-scheduled events had to be rescheduled, including a Humane Society fundraiser featuring rescue cats dressed as figures from Persian mythology.

"How large were the other pythons?" Angie asked Jerry Crosby.

"Double XLs."

"If this were a natural population shift, we'd be finding all different sizes," she said. "So it's not a migration, it's an unleashing."

The chief looked stricken. "Please find another word for it."

Ryskamp, holding a finger on his earbud, said, "You can't weaponize a damn python. They hardly ever go after humans, correct?"

"One of 'em sure as hell went after Mrs. Fitzsimmons," Crosby cut in mordantly.

"No, Paul's right," Angie said. "Maybe somebody's just trying to scare the shit out of people. Somebody who gets off on all the panic, like a firebug."

Crosby said hiding a python in the presidential pies was more than a prank; it was a message. Ryskamp agreed, saying, "Whoever did it knew the route and destination of the bakery truck. That is of serious concern to us."

Several members of the wait staff emerged on a vape break. Ryskamp motioned for Angie and the police chief to follow him down to the seawall. When they were out of earshot, the agent said: "Here's what's happening tomorrow in my world: At nine sharp I'll be patched into a video conference with Washington, and a person making way more money than I do will ask me—dead seriously—if these snakes pose any threat to the President and his wife. And my answer will be . . . ?"

"A qualified no," said Angie.

"Despite what happened at Lipid House?"

"Paul, I don't know a single documented case of a Burmese swallowing anything—man or beast—as gi-normous as the President."

Crosby, who'd made the mistake of googling "fatal python attacks," described a grotesque video supposedly taken in an Indonesian rain forest. "The victim was a logger at least six-two. They found his body when they cut open the snake with a chainsaw."

"No, that whole thing was fake," Angie said. "Same for all those anaconda videos from South America."

Ryskamp stared up at the constellations and took a long, quiet breath. "Okay, what about the First Lady? She weighs a hundred and twenty-one pounds."

"The python would have to be exceptionally large and hungry," Angie explained, "and the First Lady would have to be exceptionally unlucky. These things aren't like Rottweilers—you can't train 'em to seek and attack." She smiled grimly. "Can you guys believe this fucked-up conversation?"

Ryskamp remained focused and unflappable, which Angie found attractive; the man had his act together.

He said, "The three of us know one key fact my superiors don't know, and probably don't wish to be told: An eighty-eight-pound woman that the President claims was murdered by terrorist immigrants was actually inhaled by a mutant reptile. So the challenge for me is how to do my job and protect the boss without exposing his Diego riff as total bullshit, which would infuriate him and undoubtedly jeopardize the careers of the folks I'll be speaking with tomorrow. Angie, being the expert, I bet you can't rule out the possibility that a python larger than the one at Lipid House would be capable of eating a human that weighed more than the late Mrs. Fitzsimmons."

She said, "Maybe. But a whale like POTUS is definitely safe."

"Still, there are guests and visitors to Casa Bellicosa who could be, *theoretically*, on the menu."

"Size-wise? I guess it's possible."

"Ever heard of a python killing somebody and *not* eating them?"

"Yeah, Paul, but in most cases it's a neglected pet that gets aggressive and strangles the owner. Hell, a ten-footer's big enough to choke somebody," Angie heard herself saying, "just not big enough to swallow 'em."

Jerry Crosby pressed his knuckles to his temples and walked away mumbling.

Ryskamp said he was done, too. He took out an unmarked envelope and handed it to Angie. She grinned and said, "That was fast. Thank you, sir."

"Don't do anything that could put you back in prison."

"Who, me?"

"One more thing," the agent said. "Since I'm ninety-nine-point-nine-percent sure the Secret Service has no profiling formula for individuals who drive around 'unleashing' giant snakes, my last question is: What kind of psycho should we be looking for?"

"I have no idea, Paul. But if I were you—"

"Oh, absolutely. We're taking the President and First Lady back to Washington."

But the President and the First Lady refused to go.

The daily deluge of death threats had dropped to a trickle, but Diego Beltrán knew better than to relax. Now that the venture capitalist charged with making child pornography had fallen seventeen times on his fork in the cafeteria, Diego was the highest-profile inmate at the Palm Beach County Jail.

Held alone in a cell, he felt scalding stares whenever he walked down the corridor. He was the only prisoner branded a killer terrorist by the President of the United States, and there was no Honduran brotherhood to protect him while he was in custody. The other inmates derisively called him "Pinky" because of the conch pearl he was alleged to have stolen from the rich old woman he was alleged to have slain.

Diego kept his mouth shut. Every few days the garrulous scumbag in the cell next to his would be replaced by a new garrulous scumbag, who immediately would try to initiate incriminating conversation. It was from one such aspiring snitch that Diego first heard of DBC-88, the Diego Border Cartel, a nonexistent alien gang of which he supposedly was the leader. Diego couldn't stop himself from chuckling when the snitch—an addled fentanyl mule from southern Mississippi—asked if he and his friends could join the group.

The other prisoners knew little about Diego except what they'd heard, and they were suspicious of his unwillingness to open up. One of many personal facts that he chose not to share was that he'd learned how to box while in college, won several amateur matches, and on two occasions had knocked a larger opponent unconscious. That information would have been useful to a man named Tuck Nutter. He was doing eight months for stealing Amazon packages from the porch of a group home for seniors, though he considered himself first and foremost an American, and a thief second.

One day Nutter was approached in the chow line by an inmate who said a group of patriots on the outside was offering serious bank for the death of Diego Beltrán. When Nutter asked who those people were, he was told they were part of a small but well-connected organization dedicated to saving the country from a takeover by dark-skinned, non-English-speaking foreigners.

Nutter, a fledgling white supremacist who shared similar views, asked how much money was being offered.

"Six thousand dollars," the inmate whispered, and handed him a shiv.

"Tell 'em I'll do it for fifty-six hundred. Aryan discount."

Although he'd never killed anybody, Tuck Nutter was under the misimpression that it happened all the time in jails and would be easy to get away with because prisoners didn't rat each other out.

The weapon was the sharpened handle of a plastic soup ladle. Nutter tested it by stabbing his mattress and was satisfied with the damage, although the rounded spoon end of the shiv proved awkward to grip. For days he continued to rehearse by goring his bedding, and then one afternoon he contrived to be in the shower area at the same time as Diego Beltrán.

It was a galloping ambush, and poorly executed. Nutter slipped on the wet tiles, clipped a faucet with his hip, and dropped the shiv. While fumbling to retrieve it he left his upper body unprotected and Diego, wearing only a towel, threw a flurry of upper cuts that flattened the hapless porch pirate. He awoke with swollen eyelids and a cracked sternum in the medical wing of the jail.

The next morning, when Diego met with his defense lawyers, he told them what had happened. They promised to try to get him transferred to a more secure facility.

"How about ICE detention?" he said. "I was safer there."

"We're still working on that."

"Is the President's mob still outside?"

"Not very many."

"It's definitely trending the right direction," the other attorney added. "At least nobody spit on us today."

"Finally some good news," Diego said tonelessly, staring at his bruised knuckles. "That's so encouraging."

NINETEEN

Pruitt was staying at the first-floor apartment of a divorced sister who was away for the winter, working as a pansexual escort in London. Paul Ryskamp was able to locate the poacher because the genius had gone online and ordered ten boxes of Remington bullets on a stolen AmEx card. The ammo was delivered by UPS to the sister's address, signature required.

Angie Armstrong arrived before dawn and found an unlocked sliding door in the back. After shooing Pruitt's Bichon and Labradoodle out of the apartment, she carried the hissing travel kennel to the threshold and set loose the occupant—a robust male bobcat weighing twenty-four pounds. Angie had captured it at an orchid farm where it had been feasting on the owner's juicy domestic ducks.

She watched as the nub-tailed cat darted down the hallway seeking an escape. There was a cry, and Pruitt emerged at a run wearing only tartan boxer shorts and his mechanical hand. He was searching for the deer rifle that Angie had already kicked underneath the sofa.

Pruitt looked up and shouted, "The fuck are *you* doin' here?"

"I heard you were in need of a specialist." She stood blocking his way and wielding the long-handled noose. From the bedroom arose a low, feral rumble.

Pruitt said, "Get that goddamn cat outta here."

"First we need to reach an agreement."

"Just 'cause I only got one hand don't mean you can take me, bitch. I'll go all Jaime Lannister on your ass."

Pruitt grabbed a mop and charged back down the hall. Angie heard tables overturn and lamps crash as he flailed at the agile intruder. Moments later he lurched out of the bedroom and flung the mangled mop.

"I'm gonna call the cops!" Pruitt rasped. "Say you busted into my place."

"Great idea. When they come, they can bring your outstanding warrants."

Through a doorway Angie could see the bobcat. Agitated but unharmed, it was crouched on the handlebar of a Peloton bike.

Pruitt himself looked wobbly and distraught, his pale legs striated with bleeding claw marks. He shook his polymer fist at Angie and told her to go fuck herself with the catch pole.

Without blinking she slipped the noose around his neck and jerked with sufficient emphasis to put him on his knees.

"Ever bother my stepson again, I'll kill you," she said, "and not in a statutorily humane way."

Pruitt shook his head back and forth, swiping at the capture pole. Angie hung on easily and waited for him to tire. Soon he fell wheezing on the carpet; his watery eyes were half-open, his cheeks the color of ripe turnips.

"Listen up, Señor Fuckwhistle," Angie said. "I'm about to remove the noose from your neck and chase after the bobcat. I suggest you shelter."

Pruitt grunted. "Don't trash this fuckin' place. It ain't even mine."

As soon as he was freed, he crabbed into the bathroom, climbed up on the toilet seat, and knee-shut the door. Angie put on her canvas gloves and entered the bedroom, which had been newly redecorated in rose, pale blue, and white, as if a little girl lived there. The soft décor reflected charmingly on Pruitt's worldly sister, though it also reminded Angie that she herself hadn't gone on a shopping spree in years, possibly because she didn't have any close female friends. Still there was no aching void in her life. She probably would have met some interesting women had she learned to play tennis, joined a gym, or gone down the yoga path, but she'd always preferred the unstructured Zen of solitary boat trips through the Ten Thousand Islands, or camping alone in a cypress forest. Moreover, she'd chosen a predominantly male occupation, and in any case covered so much territory that there was no central after-hours gathering spot to connect with colleagues and develop relationships. At the end of a day as a wildlife wrangler, all you wanted to do was go home, scrub off the stink, and dress your wounds.

When Angie stepped forward to extend the capture pole, the bobcat bounded from the Peloton to a bookshelf to the pleated window drapes, which turned to shreds during the struggle that followed. Afterward she hauled the thrashing animal through the apartment, pausing momentarily to rap on the bathroom door. Pruitt peeked out and quailed at the sight, a tawny blur of fangs and claws.

"Remember what I told you," Angie said, "or I'll come back here one night and put something way worse than this thing under your sheets."

Pruitt answered with a slam of the door. Angie loaded her snarling detainee into the transport kennel and drove out the Bee Line to a stretch of pine scrub near the motorsports track, where she let it go.

Then she went home, showered, put on some normal clothes, and went to meet a man who was rumored to know a man who was rumored to be unusually comfortable among snakes.

He lived alone on a small tree island, surrounded by shimmering Everglades marsh. His camp couldn't be seen from the air or water. Tall, lush hardwoods shaded the hammock when the weather was hot, and shielded it from biting north winds during the short so-called winter. The funky black soil that anchored the ferns and gumbo limbos stayed moist throughout the year.

Although the old man had only one good eye, he could navigate comfortably in the dark, sometimes guided by the lights of the big jets lining up to land at Miami International. He traveled in a flat-bottom johnboat powered by a small outboard, so it ran shallow and quiet through the creeks and saw grass prairies. There was nobody else for miles, anyway.

The man owned a diesel pickup, elevated for off-roading. He kept it at a Miccosukee village on the Tamiami Trail, a historic cross-state highway which the government belatedly was elevating in sections, to let more needed water flow south. The Indian settlement was only forty minutes by boat from the tree island. On Mondays and Fridays the man tied up to a piling, got into his truck, and drove to Dade Corners to meet his connection for frozen rabbits, which were shrink-wrapped on pallets over dry ice.

Other nights he cruised slowly up and down the narrow dirt levees, lamping the wetlands with supercharged LEDs racked on the roof and bumper of his truck. If he saw other hunters he pulled off to the side, rolled up his windows, yanked the shower cap down over his face, and pretended to be asleep. Often wildlife officers patrolled the same dikes, but they knew who the man was and they let him be. He owned none of the required licenses or permits; the only identification he carried was a counterfeit Arizona driver's license bearing a photograph of Jackson Browne and the name George W. Hayduke Jr.

The predawn return drive to the Miccosukee settlement was usu-ally devoted to collecting fresh road kills, mostly small gators and coons, that the old man would skin and salt for his own meals. If the bed of the truck was full, he piled the bloody carcasses next to him on the passenger side. Occasionally, when the traffic thinned, he would stomp the accelerator and lean his six-and-a-half-foot frame out the window crooning while he emptied a pistol into the sky. On those nights his silver beard was clotted black with mosquitoes by the time he reached the Indian docks. There he carefully transferred his cargo, living and dead, to the johnboat. Because of the added weight, the ride back to the tree island always took longer. Once ashore, the one-eyed man used a sled made from mahogany limbs to move the frosted pallets and holding containers inland to his hidden campsite.

Only one person, his sole lifelong friend, had ever visited him there. The friend didn't stay long. He was shaken by what he saw.

"You're too old for this shit," the friend said.

"I've been working out."

"They could kill you in your sleep."

"So could a heart attack," said the one-eyed man. "Haven't you been following the news? The country we both fought for is getting ass-raped by a paranoid, draft-dodging, whore-hopping—"

"There's no TV out here. How the hell do you even know what's going on?"

"Because I've got a generator, a laptop, and my very own Wi-Fi hotspot. These days I stay painfully informed, watching rat-toothed politicians drag the planet into a smoking death spiral."

"You told me you gave up a long time ago," the friend reminded him.

"It's no longer possible to look away and live with myself."

"So this 'operation' is how you cope?"

"Oh fuck, no. I cope by micro-dosing."

"What's that?" the friend asked.

"LSD 25. Fifteen micrograms, every other day."

"Now you're scarin' the shit out of me."

"Like old times." The old man grinned and lifted the denim patch where his left eye used to be. A mottled, whitish form protruded from the scarred socket.

"What've you done now, captain?"

"I'm incubating an iguana egg."

"Lord Almighty," the friend murmured.

"I get bored out here. The acid helps."

"That's some cage you built."

"Let's call it an enclosure," said the one-eyed man. "Tell the truth: Do I look as ancient and damaged as you do?"

"Way worse—and I can still kick your sorry white ass."

"Assisted living agrees with you, Jim."

The friend was too troubled to smile at the joke. He couldn't stop staring up at the tree canopy, which at first he'd thought was decorated with long streamers of dingy crepe. Now he realized that the garlands in the boughs were made of something else.

Nor was the scene on the ground reassuring: Hundreds of books that the old man had accumulated over the years were now stacked high with their spines facing outward, makeshift bricks that formed a square of connected walls domed by a roll of chicken wire.

The visiting friend's view of the back wall was blocked, though by moving closer he was able to read the titles on the others. One had been constructed with political biographies—Lincoln, Churchill, Huey Long, Teddy Roosevelt, Joe McCarthy, most of Caro's LBJ series, Reagan, the Kennedys, the Bushes, the Clintons, all the way up to Obama. The opposite side had been fortified with fiction, from Dickens to Rushdie, including multiple editions of every John D. MacDonald novel. A third, east-facing wall appeared to be reference volumes—several old sets of encyclopedias, the *Florida Statutes*, dictionaries, gazetteers, medical textbooks, even a 1987 edition of the *Federal Criminal Code and Rules*; in the center of the partition was a space barely large enough for a grown man to squeeze through, and fitted with a removable panel of clear aquarium glass.

"That's quite a structure," said the one-eyed man's friend.

"Not up to code, I admit, but it serves the purpose."

The books were dank and blackening with mold, and the old man's friend could smell the rotting paper. It made him feel sad.

He said, "Put an end to this nonsense, Clint. Please."

"It's my last motherfucking rodeo, I promise."

"I'd better go now. I got another damn CT scan this afternoon."

The friend began walking down the path toward the water, but the tip of his cane got plugged in soft dirt. The one-eyed man helped him to the airboat and told the driver about a shortcut back to the Miccosukee village.

A week or so passed before the friend decided to do something about what he'd seen at the tree island. He made the call from his handicap-accessible apartment at the Rainbow of Life Senior Center, one of those "compassionately structured" settings where elderly widows and widowers transitioned from ambulatory to bedridden to dead.

He didn't know if the phone number he dialed was still good, but the kid answered right away and said, "I'm glad to hear from you. It's been a while."

"Sorry, but I need a favor."

"Anything, of course," the kid said.

"It's time for your stepmother to meet my friend."

"I never said a word to her. She doesn't even know his name."

"And he appreciates that. We both do."

"But why all of a sudden does he want to see her?"

"It's not his idea, it's mine," replied the one-eyed man's friend. "She'll understand as soon as she sees what's going on."

"So this will be a surprise for both of them?"

"Oh yes, Joel."

Mastodon reacted scornfully when the Secret Service informed him of a possible python threat at Casa Bellicosa. He said that it sounded like the plot of a shitty horror movie, and that he'd look like a pussy for fleeing to Washington just because a snake or two turned up.

The mansion would soon be hosting the season's most sensational event, Mastodon added, and he wouldn't miss it for anything. He was, after all, the star attraction.

Mockingbird had a different reason for refusing to leave Palm Beach, and she had no intention of revealing it. She summoned

Special Agent Paul Ryskamp to a one-on-one brunch at her private beach cabana and offered him fresh fruit and stone crab claws, which he declined. As soon as he began discussing python scenarios, she reminded him about the headless one that had turned up along the route of her motorcade.

"I wasn't scared then. I'm not scared now," she said.

"Until the individual responsible for the snakes is in custody, we believe it's best if you and the President return to the White House."

Mockingbird plucked a strawberry from the sterling platter and nibbled off the tip. "I know Agent Josephson's real name," she said. "What do you think the media would do with a crazy story like that?"

"How would such a story get out?" Ryskamp asked mildly.

"Oh, who knows. But what a scandal for the Secret Service."

"It wouldn't be great, I agree."

"What's that cute pattern on your shirt? I like it—so, *so* tropical."

"Turtles," he replied. "Baby sea turtles."

"Where is your gun, by the way?"

"Under my shirt."

"It's not a very big one then, is it?"

The agent smiled with perverse equanimity, a man with retirement squarely in his sights. "My duties are mainly supervisory," he said.

"I know, Paul. That's why I asked to meet with you." Mockingbird moved closer and told him how it would be:

Special Agent Jennifer Rose would be allowed to join her security detail, but only if Keith Josephson remained the leader of the team. A rumor would be circulated among the staff at Casa Bellicosa that agents Rose and Josephson had rekindled a past romance, and were hooking up—strictly during off-duty hours—at a Comfort Inn out by the interstate.

Mockingbird said, "There's a name in your business for this kind of thing, isn't there?"

"Disinformation."

"That it is. Meanwhile my husband is screwing a stripper who's masquerading as a nutritionist, of all things. I'm sure you people know about this. She's got an ass like a Volvo sedan."

Ryskamp answered only with his eyes.

"It would mean a great deal to me," she said, "if his relationship with that sloppy whore stayed secret from the public. And, yes, I can tell what you're thinking."

Ryskamp turned slightly in his beach chair and made sure the other agents were standing far enough away. To the First Lady he said, "I'm thinking exactly what you think I am."

She frowned and reached for a slice of Bucheron. "Whatever's going on in my *own* private life, Agent Ryskamp, in the future I promise to be much more careful about, you know, appearances. None of the blame for all this stupid gossip belongs anywhere but on myself. Do you understand?"

"I've always liked Agent Josephson."

"You mean Agent Youseff."

"He took one for the team," Ryskamp said.

"All because my husband doesn't trust anyone with an Islamic name. Or Jews, or blacks, or Asians, or Hispanics, or Mormons, or whatever. God, it's exhausting to keep track. With my accent, I'm amazed he married me."

"No, you're not."

She leaned closer. "It must never, *ever* get back to him as a true thing—this kitchen talk about me and Keith."

"How can you be sure he doesn't already know?"

"Because you and your bosses haven't been fired."

Mockingbird was wearing a black one-piece swimsuit under a forgivable Lilly Pulitzer cover-up. Ryskamp interpreted her flame-red toenails as playful mutiny.

"One last thing," she said. "Those old vipers who call themselves the Potussies—by the way, how trashy is that?—apparently they've all had Secret Service protection?"

"Until recently. For a number of reasons, the decision was made to terminate those assignments. The President was informed, and he signed off."

"Yes, I get it, the whole idea's outrageous. But the women really miss having their dashing young agents around, so I need you to call Washington and make it happen again, before the big ball."

"Can I ask why?" Ryskamp said.

"One of the ladies, a Mrs. Riptoe or something like that, spoke to me personally. Her group raises lots of money for my husband."

"Lots of people raise lots of money for your husband."

"Mrs. Riptoe was very persuasive. It's possible she's heard that sleazy rumor about me and Agent Josephson." Mockingbird put on her sunglasses, stood up, and tucked her crocodile clutch under one arm. "I've got my deep-tissue in five minutes. Let me know what Washington says."

"We're doing a teleconference this afternoon."

"I like those flip-flops, Agent Ryskamp. Where'd you find them?"

"There's a new Ron Jon's on A1A," he said. "What's your size?"

The Commander's Ball had been staged every spring since Mastodon's election. Lovingly organized by the Potussies, it was a giddy, feisty, celebrity-packed tribute to the forever embattled chief executive, and had become his most lucrative political fundraiser. Tickets started at ten thousand dollars a seat, but for only twice as much you got photographed at the President's side. For thirty thousand he would personally sign the photograph; for forty grand he would shake your hand in the picture; for fifty he'd place an arm around your shoulders. (When advised to avoid physical contact due to the lingering virus threat, Mastodon had berated his doctors and said the risk of a lung infection was less important than the gusher of cash generated by the photo operation.)

Those who paid a hundred thousand dollars to attend the gala were called Legacy Friends, and each received a full bear-hug in their posed photo; a sleeve of new Titleists bearing the presidential seal; a liter of vodka from a Chernobyl distillery half-owned by Mastodon's grown sons; an autographed teleprompter script for the first inaugural address, complete with "Pause for Applause" placements; an empty Dr. Pepper can, flattened, framed, and stamped with the time and date it had been hurled across the Oval Office; and two tickets to the after-party featuring a top Lee Greenwood cover band.

The theme of this year's Commander's Ball was "Big Unimpeachable You," based on an original ditty commissioned by Fay Alex Riptoad and the other Potussies, who would be performing the song onstage. (The mid-range baritone part, originally written for Kiki Pew Fitzsimmons, had been posthumously reassigned to Kelly Bean Drummond and Dee Witty Wittlefield.) Glossy programs for the ball had been revised to include a short homage to Kiki Pew that featured a photo of the radiant widow flicking lint off POTUS's suit collar during the inaugural Commander's Ball. Omitted from the program text was any reference to Kiki Pew's gory demise at the hands of Diego Beltrán's border cartel, Fay Alex not wishing to darken the carefree mood of deep-pocketed partiers before the live raffle.

Typically about half the guests at the ball were year-round members of Casa Bellicosa who simply wanted to be seen at the season's biggest bash, and the other half were political mega-donors who had G-5s and tall favors to ask. The chore of screening the list fell to the Secret Service, though seldom were more than a handful of persons denied entry. The wealthier the rejected ticket-seekers were, however, the more detailed was the justification demanded by the White House.

This year, Stanleigh Cobo, idle bachelor brother of one of the Potussies, had wanted to bring as his date a Chinese citizen whose uncle's company was the world's largest manufacturer of digital meat thermometers. Unfortunately, the niece herself reported directly (and often) to the Ministry of State Security, China's version of the KGB.

When Stanleigh Cobo was informed that he'd have to find a new companion for the President's gala, he broke down and begged the Secret Service agents for a security exemption. He confided that the woman, who lived in Guangdong Province, had promised to bring five grams of powdered narwhal tusk, his last hope for a presentable erection. The agents were unmoved, so Stanleigh Cobo tearfully called his sister Deirdre, who called the President's under-assistant chief of staff, who called the Secret Service director, who called the deputy director, who called the West Palm field office, where Paul Ryskamp answered the phone, listened to the pitiable plot of Stanleigh Cobo's romance, and said, "Bottom line, she's a spy."

"Oh, definitely," said the deputy director. "But their date is just for one night. Can we put someone with her while she's on the property?"

"I don't have any spare bodies. They're all assigned to Potussies, including Cobo's sister."

"Well, she gives a mountain of money to Mastodon's PACs. The brother is a harmless dolt."

"Who happens to be dating a spy," Ryskamp reiterated.

"That's so helpful, Paul. Any bright ideas?"

"I'll bet Mr. Cobo could survive breaking up with his date if we can find him some narwhal tusk."

"How? No, actually, I mean how the *fuck*?"

Ryskamp explained that Palm Beach was an epicenter of E.D. panic. "This is a place where you can score any kind of miracle boner potion, from scorpion wine to a tiger penis. Money's never an issue, obviously."

"I'm not sure how we'd expense it," the deputy director said mirthlessly, "but what does five grams of whale horn cost on the street?"

"Let me check that out. Meantime, is there no way to convince Mastodon to skip the event?"

"Not a chance. He's already rehearsing a big duet with Roseanne Barr. They're singing 'Leather and Lace,' right after the huckleberry mousse."

"Bloodbath," said Ryskamp. "Poor Stevie Nicks."

"She ought to sue," agreed the deputy director. "Regarding the Agent Josephson problem, I agree with your recommendation. We'll leave him on the First Lady's detail, for now."

"It's a fraught set of circumstances."

"A fucking disaster waiting to happen. Literally."

"Mockingbird's holding all the cards."

"Again, Paul, no shit."

"What did Mastodon say when he learned about the pythons?" Ryskamp asked.

"Christ, he thinks it's just a political prank. He blames the Speaker of the House for the pie truck . . . whatever you call it."

"Sabotage?"

"An 'unexplained contamination' is how we decided to file it."

Ryskamp still hadn't briefed the deputy director about what had really happened to Katherine Fitzsimmons, because then the deputy director would have been obligated to tell the President, who would freak out and order the information classified as secret. He was still balls-deep in his anti-Diego crusade on social media.

"So, Paul, what do we do about these damn snakes?" the deputy director asked.

"I've reached out to a specialist."

"Good. Make sure he searches the property thoroughly before the Commander's Ball."

"It's a woman."

"Really? How weird is that. You check her out?"

"I did," said Ryskamp. "She's clean."

TWENTY

The Knob was supposed to avoid natural sunlight during periods when he was testing one of the presidential tanning beds. Usually he spent his daytimes watching porn in his motel room, and at night he went out to gorge and drink. In spite of his somewhat off-putting appearance, he almost always attracted female company. He never wasted a moment trying to understand how or why. The women who approached him seemed genuinely curious; often they asked if he had a circus background. Sometimes one would get a friend to snap photos while she smooched the knotty crown of his head.

For having such a large body mass, The Knob was easily impaired by alcohol. He carried a pair of Vic Firth drumsticks wherever he went, and after only two Rum Runners he'd start channeling Keith Moon, pounding madly along to whatever style of music would be playing, or to no music at all. The Knob wasn't a fighter or a belligerent drunk, but he could be ungainly and destructive. On one such night, at the bar of an upscale restaurant in Jupiter, he upended a table occupied by several famous professional golfers. Having zero interest in sports, The Knob didn't know who the men were, or why he was being asked to leave. It was just an accident, after all.

Still he found himself being escorted to the parking lot, where—with California surf music twanging in his skull—he couldn't restrain himself from drumming "Wipe Out" on the hood of a gleaming new Bentley GT. The vehicle happened to belong to one of the pro golfers, who popped the trunk, snatched a three-wood out of his bag, and furiously began pummeling The Knob.

Twelve hours later, he awoke sprawled half-nude on Juno Beach. Bruised, blistered, and hungover, he was also momentously sunburned and therefore unfit for duty in the Cabo Royale. The Knob looked at his watch and thought it must be broken. There was no sign anywhere of his billfold or phone.

A slight blond woman wearing Daisy Duke cutoffs and a Patriots jersey snored beside him on the sand. It was a project to rouse her. When the Knob asked for a lift to Palm Beach, she laughed and threw up on his lap. He washed off in the ocean and walked dripping to A1A and stuck out his thumb. The first vehicle that stopped was a police cruiser, which took him to the emergency room.

As soon as Christian arrived at the hospital, he realized the gravity of the situation. The Knob was swollen and buttered with aloe, his skin as raw as carpaccio. Mastodon had scheduled a tanning session for mid-afternoon, and now there was no one to pre-test the bed. Finding a club employee the right size—and then obtaining a security clearance—would be nearly impossible on such short notice. Christian called Spalding and asked him to scout the service staff, but the search proved futile. The only fit candidate, a bartender who topped six feet, had a body odor so pungent that it posed a respiratory risk inside the tanning chamber.

So, upon returning to Casa Bellicosa, Christian—who weighed only a hundred and sixty pounds—put on three cotton bathrobes for padding, donned The Knob's wig and eye protectors, climbed into the Cabo Royale, and closed the canopy. It was an act of courage, for Christian had been fiercely claustrophobic since the age of five, when his older sisters had put him inside a recycle bin and duct-taped the lid.

Christian was hoping that the sun lamps inside the Cabo would ease the suffocating sense of confinement, but the eerie bluish glow made him even more anxious. As the temperature rose he tightly closed his eyelids and began worrying that the goggles might melt to his face. The instant he began to hyperventilate, a familiar thrash of panic took hold. Both legs began to kick uncontrollably and the canopy flew open. Christian lay there gasping, clammy, and ripe with perspiration.

He tore off the hairpiece and hurled it across the room. Once his heart stopped hammering, he rolled out of the bed and checked the digital clock on the machine. Unbelievable—only four minutes and forty-two seconds. He felt sure his eyes were shut most of that time, yet it seemed like the sun lamps had flickered at some point.

Christian wiped down the Cabo and went outside to catch some fresh air. He sat on a chaise by the pool, toweled off the sweat, opened a Gatorade, and wondered: *Did I see something, or not?*

The tanning bulbs wouldn't blink on and off unless one had loosened, or there was a wiring issue. Christian hurried back inside and, as a precaution, replaced each of the tubular lamps. When he re-started the Cabo, the lighting was uniform and constant. He decided that the flash he thought he saw must have happened in his own frenzied brainpan.

Goddamn claustrophobia.

He still hadn't forgiven his sisters.

Angie went to meet the man Joel had told her about. His name was Jim Tile, and for most of his life he'd been a road trooper with the Florida Highway Patrol. Now he lived at a West Boca senior center called the Rainbow of Life. That was all Angie knew about him.

He was sitting at a table in the dining room; a wooden cane hung on an empty chair beside him. There was a foam cervical brace around his neck, though his shoulders were still broad and straight. He had thick arms and snow-white hair and tinted wire-rimmed glasses. Angie noticed he was the only black person in the place who wasn't wearing caregiver scrubs.

She introduced herself and sat down across from him. He smiled and said he knew who she was; he'd seen her before.

"Where?" she asked.

"At your sentencing hearing."

"Are you kidding me?"

"I was in the back row."

"Wait. Why?"

"An old friend asked me to be there. He took an interest in your case. Want somethin' to eat? They say the food's decent, but I can't taste a damn thing." He showed her the bandaged crook of his left arm, where the morning IV attached.

She said, "I know you're tired, Mr. Tile. I won't stay long."

"Doesn't matter. I don't sleep hardly at all."

"How did you and Joel connect?"

"I met him in the courthouse the last day of your trial."

"By accident, or on purpose?" Angie asked.

Tile seemed amused by her intensity. "We were both in line at the water fountain. He's a good kid. Worries about you, naturally."

"He says you've got information about the python outbreak."

"Now *there's* a fine word. 'Outbreak,'" Tile said. "My friend's the one you need to speak with, Ms. Armstrong. I'm about to tell you where he is, and how to get there."

"And his name, too, please."

Tile chuckled. "His actual Christian name, or what he answers to?"

"Either," said Angie. "Or both."

"Skink is what they call him."

"That's your friend? Please don't bullshit me, Mr. Tile."

"Young lady, do I look like a bullshitter?"

Angie knew the legend. So did every wildlife officer past and present, going back decades. She said, "Just to be clear: You're talking about Tyree? The missing governor."

"Yes, ma'am."

"So he's not dead, like they say."

"Far from it," said Jim Tile.

Angie hadn't yet been born when Clinton Tyree fled the governor's mansion in a fever of despair, later re-launching himself as a vagabond saboteur, striking out at everything he believed was going wrong in Florida. Since then, the man who became known as Skink had been blamed for many acts of eco-vengeance he didn't commit—and had gotten away with those he did. Never was there enough evidence to prosecute, and he remained perpetually at-large, unavailable for questioning. Nothing had been heard of him for so long that those who remembered his unglued heyday assumed he must have died of old age, or heartache.

"Where's he hiding now?" Angie asked Jim Tile.

"Tree island deep in the 'glades." He unfolded a handmade map and placed it on the table. "I can't draw worth a damn," he said, tapping a long, bent finger on the paper, "but right there is downtown Miami, and way, way out here is him."

"Does the hammock have a name?"

"Whereabouts Unknown is what he calls it."

"Have you been there?"

"I got the GPS numbers. You'll need an airboat."

"That's not a problem. What else should I bring?"

"Nerve," said Tile.

A server brought each of them a plastic glass filled with tap water and one whole cube of ice. Angie said she wasn't hungry; Tile ordered a pork chop, steamed broccoli, and whipped potatoes.

"And black coffee, please," he told the server, who was young and pretty.

"She's from Jamaica, *mon*," Tile whispered to Angie afterward. "I'm a sucker for that accent."

For a while he talked about his late wife, how much he missed her, the last trip they took together before she got sick. A cruise to San Juan, or maybe it was Nassau. He told a story about her gaily unscripted style of cooking—a meat loaf that even the dog wouldn't eat—and laughed until he was out of breath. Then he spoke joyfully about his daughter, who worked for the Justice Department but still called him every day. Well, almost every day. She had a law degree from Stetson . . .

Although Angie was in a hurry, she didn't interrupt. She liked listening to the man, and didn't bring up the subject of Skink again until after he'd finished eating.

"How'd you and the governor meet?" she asked.

"I was his driver in Tallahassee. Back then the FHP was in charge of security."

Angie would have loved to hear the retired trooper's version of what had happened in the capital that sent Clinton Tyree skidding over the edge, but she knew better than to push. Tile had been watching out for his wild, haunted friend during all the fugitive years, and he wouldn't lower his guard now.

She asked, "How much of what I've heard about him is true?"

"A fraction," Tile replied, "but that's enough."

"They say he wears a bat-wing eye patch and lives on road kills."

"Ha! He's not a fan of bats."

"I'd never put you on the spot, Mr. Tile."

He patted her arm. "I'd never tell you anything, anyway."

"But how does he know me? And why did he send you to my court hearing?"

"Ask him when you get there, Angela."

She bit her lip. The last man to call her Angela was the judge who sent her to prison.

"Fine," she said. "He knows I'm coming, right?"

"Hell, no. If I told him that, he'd be gone."

"So what's he going to say when I suddenly show up at his hideout?"

"Probably 'Get the fuck outta here!'—pardon my French. Then it'll be up to your charming, green-eyed self to calm his rude ass down."

Tile slid the map toward Angie. She re-folded it and put it in her handbag. "Does the governor have a gun?" she asked.

"I'd be amazed if he didn't. Now, you don't mind, I believe I'll have a piece of pecan pie."

Angie had one more question: "Is your friend alone on that island?"

"If he was," said Jim Tile, "you and me wouldn't be having this conversation."

Mockingbird continued to call him Keith in front of the other agents. When the two of them were alone, he was Ahmet.

"We don't have much time," he told her.

"What else is new," she said, locking the door.

They disrobed, oiled each other up, and got on the massage table, Mockingbird having feigned a migraine and instructed her deep-tissue guru to take the afternoon off. She hadn't told Ahmet about her productive chat with Paul Ryskamp, but he suspected that she'd made a major, behind-the-scenes move; otherwise he would have been on that flight back to D.C.

He muted his microphone but left his earpiece in place, as always, in case a threat surfaced elsewhere on the property. During fore-play the curled tube dangled distractedly from the side of his face, along with the wire to the pocket radio unit that he'd propped on a corner of the table. The apparatus always bothered Mockingbird but Ahmet refused to unplug it, so they'd become skilled at having sex in an orderly way that wouldn't dislodge his earbud, or send the receiver tumbling to the floor.

Over time their stealth intimacy had grown more and more intense, almost Tantric except for the speed—they never had more than a few minutes alone together, and other Secret Service agents were always nearby. Mockingbird kept a playlist of meditation tunes for her deep-tissue sessions, but she didn't use it with Ahmet because he said sitar music was a buzz kill. Instead she put on Post Malone, keeping the volume loud enough to muffle what few moans they inadvertently made.

Afterward they took turns showering, in case somebody knocked on the door. Ahmet rinsed only his lower half so as not to drip water in his sensitive earpiece. As he was getting dressed, Mockingbird asked what he thought of Jennifer Rose.

He said, "Smart and steady. She's a good agent. Why?"

"Maybe you should flirt with her a little. You know, just to put the idea out there."

"What idea?"

"To make them quit gossiping about you and me," Mockingbird said.

"Are you out of your mind? There's no flirting in the Secret Service."

"Calm down," she said. "You're putting your underwear on backwards."

"I can't believe you're serious. What's left of my career is already hanging by a thread."

"Just think about it, please."

Ahmet buttoned his shirt and said, "I'm pretty sure Jen's seeing somebody."

"Oh, so what." Mockingbird was still wearing only a towel. Her hair was pinned up, and the conch-pearl earrings he'd bought her shined like hibiscus dewdrops.

"You don't have to *do* anything with her. In fact, you better not," she said. "All I'm talking about is a smile or a laugh when you're in the same room. Body language, Ahmet, that's it. A fake show for all those snoops on the kitchen staff."

"I'm no good at acting. I can't fake—"

"Here, hon, let me help you with that."

As she reached up to knot his necktie, her towel came undone and dropped.

"Oops," she said.

He took her by the arms and pulled her close. She still smelled like her special massage oil—eucalyptus and bacon mint. Ahmet stifled a sneeze and said, "Are you sure the President doesn't know about us?"

"Nobody around him would have the guts to tell him. Even if they did, he's too damn vain to believe it."

"Yes, but what if—"

"Hush," said Mockingbird. "He can't accuse me of anything, not while he's got that pole dancer stashed in a cabana down at the beach. Suzi, the phony nutritionist. Have you seen the thighs on that woman?"

"No, ma'am."

"I love that you still call me that."

"Reflex," Ahmet said self-consciously.

He had never imagined himself capable of having a thing with the First Lady of the United States, much less falling in love with her. The agency's rules against such entanglements were inflexible and unambiguous; instructors at the Rowley Training Center devoted an entire afternoon to the topic:

Do NOT fuck anyone you are guarding, male or female. NO intimate contact of any type, with any part of your body, under any circumstances! Do not initiate, do not accede, do not even contemplate! ARE WE CLEAR?

Sometimes Ahmet wondered if he was subconsciously trying to get himself fired. Perhaps he was cracking under the pressure of the job, and secretly wanted to bail. As a teenager he'd aspired to be nothing more complicated than a pro hockey player. It was too late for that, but there was still woodworking; Ahmet enjoyed making household furniture, and he was good at it. His specialty was Shaker media cabinets.

In college he'd played well as a first-line forward, but no NHL teams drafted him. He joined the Boston police and was on Boylston Street when the bombs went off during the marathon. Afterward Ahmet and other Arabic-speaking officers got assigned to an anti-terrorism squad, but he never felt at ease despite being half-Irish. The day he applied to the Secret Service, his longtime girlfriend dumped him because she didn't want to move to Washington; she owned a pottery studio and had only four payments left on the kiln.

As a special agent, Ahmet had limited free time. He dated sporadically, rarely following up, and even his cabinetry output declined. He hadn't slept with a woman in almost a year when Mockingbird made the first move—a furtive pinch on his ass while he escorted her through the private entrance of her favorite botox-and-enema salon on Blue Marlin Lane. Ahmet had been careful not to react, but weeks later it happened again in the hallway outside her suite at Casa Bellicosa. When she surreptitiously tugged one of his fingers, he turned and fell into eye contact. The next night, she called him into her wardrobe closet on the pretense of being unable to reach a certain Panama hat on a certain high shelf.

And when she kissed him, he kissed her back.

The affair was reckless, nerve-racking, and utterly addictive, made more thrilling by the impassive role that each of them was forced to play in public. Although they never spoke about devising a future together, Ahmet wanted to believe that, beyond the heat of the moment, Mockingbird cared for him as much as he cared for her. He understood it was likely the biggest mistake of his life; it was also the biggest rush.

When she kicked her towel away, he said, "No, we're supposed to have you out on the croquet lawn in seven minutes."

"For what?"

"Make-A-Wish photo op."

"Oh, right. That poor child." She let go of Ahmet and asked, "Is she in a wheelchair?"

"I don't have that information."

"I'll start crying if she is. I can't help it, hon. I'll break down and sob."

"That's all right," he said. "This was her wish, to visit the Winter White House and meet you in person."

"But why?" Mockingbird asked.

"Obviously she's a fan."

"God, if she only knew."

"Don't talk like that." Ahmet put on his suit jacket, slipped the radio receiver into an inside pocket, and smoothed his sleeves.

Mockingbird gave a frustrated sigh. "Seven minutes? My hair's a nightmare!"

He kissed the tip of her nose. "Now we're down to five," he said, "and you look perfect, ma'am."

TWENTY-ONE

Angie dreamed she was still a veterinarian at her father's clinic. There was another cocker spaniel on the operating table, another swallowed ping-pong ball on the X-ray. Angie made the first incision and then ran out crying. Her dad chased after her, but she was too fast. She heard him yell that she was a quitter, a weakling, an ingrate. He shouted for her to come back and finish the surgery, but she kept running.

Her eyes were dry when she woke up, which was surprising. She called Joel to find out if he'd heard anything more from Pruitt.

"Nothing," he said. "What did you do to him?"

"Noose and a bobcat."

"You mean a bobcat bulldozer."

"No, a *bobcat* bobcat. As in *Lynx rufus*."

"Holy shit, Angie."

"I was careful not to hurt the pussy, or the cat."

"Are you trying to get arrested again? You miss that delicious prison food, or what?"

Angie said it would be best if Joel and his girlfriend stayed at

Dustin's house a little while longer, until they were sure Pruitt had been spooked off.

"No, Krista wants to be back in her condo ASAP," Joel whispered into the phone.

"Wild guess: Because of the equestrian?"

"She will *not* back off that yoga shit. Krista's been faking cramps to get out of doing the classes."

"Just a few more days, Joel. Hang in there."

Angie hung up, ate a bowl of dry Frosted Flakes, and re-read the all-caps text from Chief Jerry Crosby. Then she put on a long-sleeved shirt, bush pants, and hiking shoes, and drove to Sunrise Avenue on the island to remove a seventeen-and-a-half-foot Burmese python from a designer beachwear shop where the First Lady recently had purchased several swimsuits. A panicked security guard had fired four times. One bullet fatally struck the snake, and the other three took down a mannequin in a Missoni tankini. Once on-scene, Angie spent time commiserating with Crosby and the agitated store owner before loading the deceased reptile in her truck.

On the way to the Turnpike, she stopped at the county jail to visit Diego Beltrán in the medical wing, where he was being treated for stab wounds.

"You look better than expected," she told him, "all things considered."

Actually, Diego looked terrible. He lay ashen and heavy-lidded, cuffed to a hospital bed. There was an oxygen tube in his nose and a drainage tube in his chest. He said he had a punctured lung.

"Who did it?" Angie asked.

"Ayran Brotherhood."

"How many?"

His breathing was shallow but controlled. He held up two fingers and said, "They saw my face on TV this morning. Fox News did an update on my case. Guess the bored white boys wanted to be heroes."

"By shivving you."

"Yeah, with sharpened bed springs."

"Valiant, God-fearing patriots," said Angie.

Diego looked away. "I'm never getting out of here alive."

"You will. I promise."

He said, "There's nothing anyone can do for me. Don't you see?"

Angie was raging inside. She thought of arranging a painful payback for the racist shit-sticks who tried to murder Diego, but she knew they'd be well-protected on their cell block.

She squeezed Diego's hand. "All I can say is, don't you fucking dare give up."

He turned back, smiling sadly. "Why? You know somebody at the top?"

"I will soon," she said with a wink. "I got invited to a special party."

"Yeah? Will you be dancing?"

"Get some rest, *amigo*."

The Turnpike was a mess, so Angie crossed back to the interstate. She cranked up the radio hoping to take her mind off the attack on Diego. This was a problem, her dogged temper. It was the only reason she had a rap sheet. Feeding a poacher's hand to an alligator was more than a mad impulse; locating that particular reptile had required deliberation, and a detour.

Calm the fuck down, Angie told herself, speeding down the highway.

She jumped off on the Palmetto, which was, miraculously, clear all the way to the Tamiami Trail. The airboat driver had said to meet him at the S-333 spillway, a few minutes west of Krome Avenue. His was the only truck in the parking lot when Angie pulled up. She walked down the launch ramp and smiled at the sign warning visitors not to feed the wildlife.

The airboat driver shook her hand and said to call him Beak.

"Like a bird's?" Angie said. "I don't see that. Your nose looks fine."

"My real name's Ivan. I had to try on something else."

Angie handed over three hundred dollars cash, Jim Tile's hand-drawn map, and a paper napkin on which she'd written the GPS numbers for the tree island.

"What's in the sack?" Beak asked.

"Rope."

"Looks heavy."

"Not really," Angie said.

"Okay, hop in."

He was late-twenties; good smile and no visible ink. Tangled blondish hair, Brad Pitt-style shades, and a camo cap turned backwards so the wind from the ride wouldn't blow it off. Also, he was clean-shaven, one of Angie's requirements. She found herself thinking unprofessional thoughts.

Before flipping the ignition switch, Beak handed her a set of noise-suppressing earphones with a microphone arm. The airboat's propeller was a big two-blade Whisper Tip, the same type Angie had on her engine when she worked for the state. She knew what Beak's answer would be if she asked to take the stick, but the thought of driving stirred good memories; crossing thin water at crazy speeds was one of the things she missed about her old life.

The afternoon was mild, with a rippled mackerel sky and a touch of northwest in the breeze. Herons, purple coots, and warblers scattered ahead of the roaring airboat—the marsh still attracted lots of birds. Angie spotted a young eagle circling and, much higher, a line of turkey vultures weaving like a black kite string in the thermals. Beak tapped her shoulder and pointed to a pair of anhingas perched on a log, their coat-hanger wings spread wide. Angie was disappointed that the mic in her headset didn't work; she was nervous about meeting the ex-governor, and would have liked the distraction of chatting with her young, attractive guide.

Jim Tile's coordinates were solid. It took twenty-four minutes to reach the tree island, and Beak circled twice before steering slowly through a gap in the reeds. As they glided toward the bank, Angie spotted a long, metallic form that had been covered with hand-cut branches—an aluminum johnboat. From the air it would have been invisible.

She put on her backpack, picked up the knotted bag, and jumped ashore.

"Come back in an hour," she said to Beak.

"Why don't I just hang here and wait?"

"No, sir, I'll be fine."

"Are you lookin' for 'shrooms?" Beak asked. "'Cause I know some way better spots."

Angie waved and then turned to follow Clinton Tyree's footpath to his hideout in the shadows.

Paul Ryskamp found Stanleigh Cobo behind a peach-pulp mask at the Casa Bellicosa spa. The agent introduced himself, showed his badge, and asked the aesthetician to step out. Cobo plucked the peach pits from his eyelids and sat up inquiring, "Did something happen outside? Is there a shooter?"

Ryskamp tossed him a towel and said, "We can't have a serious conversation until you wipe that crap off your face."

"But it needs ten more minutes."

"Do it now. I don't have all day."

"Where did you get such a bad attitude?" Cobo sniffed as he scrubbed away the fruit paste. "I never heard of a Secret Service officer behaving so arrogant. You people work for *all* of us, remember?"

The agent said, "I don't need to be polite with you, Mr. Cobo. I know things about you that you definitely don't want your family to learn—especially your sister Deirdre, her being so prominent in political circles. And I'm not just referring to your Vegas debts or the hookers or the drugs, or even your bulk purchases from BondageOverstock.com."

Cobo went pale as he stiffened. "I thought this was America. What happened to our constitutional right of privacy?"

"Down the shitter," Ryskamp said. "Clearly you haven't been paying attention. Try reading a newspaper once in a while."

"Oh, I see. You've gone rogue."

"Wake up, Stanleigh."

"So, what else have you got on me that's so awful?"

"You currently employ four—or is it five?—individuals who are undocumented aliens. Correct? From Guatemala, I believe."

"Hold on, please, they're okay," Cobo protested. "Decent, docile people. And wizards at shrubbery!"

"Imagine the embarrassment to the President if this got out—that a brother of one of his Palm Beach Potussies was harboring five illegal Diegos?"

Cobo caved without a pause. "Fine, I'll arrange for all of them to be deported. That's easy. Deirdre knows the head honcho at Homeland Security. One phone call, boom."

Ryskamp was too jaded to be disgusted. Cobo had recoiled in the treatment chair—bony legs drawn to his chest, the flaps of his neck slick with sweat.

"I don't want a damn thing from you," the agent told him, "and personally I don't give a shit about the Guatemalans, as long as you're paying a fair wage. Let's talk about the Commander's Ball. Your Chinese date is a spy."

"Megan? No way."

"That isn't her name. Not even close. *Megan?* Seriously? Point is, she's a foreign intelligence operative and you cannot bring her to a presidential residence."

Cobo began to weep. Ryskamp had been forewarned. He reached into his suit pocket and took out the plastic baggie.

"Guess what I've got here, Stanleigh."

Cobo sucked in his breath and toweled the snot off his chin. "Is that blow?"

"Even better," Ryskamp said.

"What the fuck? Heroin?"

"No, Stanleigh. This is what your darling 'Megan' was going to bring you. Remember?"

Cobo's bloodshot eyes grew wide. "Tusk?" he croaked hungrily. "Is it, uh, the good stuff?"

"All the way from Baffin Bay."

"Fucking narwhal!"

"Fucking narwhal," said the agent.

That was a lie. Ryskamp had not wasted a minute of his time trying to score narwhal tusk in Palm Beach's tight-knit underground E.D. community. The substance in the baggie was an improvised blend of baking soda and cupcake mix, cut with jock-itch talc from Ryskamp's personal gym bag.

"One thing, Stanleigh: You didn't get this shit from me."

"Of course not!" Cobo sang out. "We never met."

He grabbed for the baggie but Ryskamp held it out of reach.

"First, you've got to break things off with your spy girlfriend," the agent said.

"Right this minute?"

"Yup." Ryskamp gave the powder a teasing little shake. "And try not to be an asshole about it."

Cobo licked his upper lip and said, "We've got a deal."

He made the call in front of Ryskamp. It didn't last long, or end well. Afterward Cobo put on a heartsick face, though he didn't take his eyes off the baggie. Ryskamp handed it over and walked out of the spa.

On his way to the Breakers, he called the deputy director in Washington to tell him the Cobo situation was resolved. Next he tried to reach Angie Armstrong, but her phone went straight to voicemail. Ryskamp didn't leave a message.

The door of the nutritionist impersonator's cabana was open when he got there. After multiple knocks, he stepped inside. It was more spacious than the First Lady's beachside bungalow, though in stale disarray. A glitter-flecked stripper's pole had been erected in the sitting area, the furniture shoved to one side. A suitcase lay agape on the divan, and women's clothes were strewn about the floor. The mussed bedsheets featured an empty wine bottle, a rolled-up copy of *Pro Wrestling Illustrated,* and several incriminating Dr. Pepper cans, drained and crumpled. The whole place smelled like the exhaust vent at a Burger King.

Ryskamp tracked down Suzi Spooner on a lounge chair down by the ocean. She was wearing black Ray-Bans, a white plastic nose guard, and a canary bikini. A surprisingly dainty icicle pendant dangled from a piercing above her navel.

Suzi knew from Ryskamp's gray suit and earpiece that he was Secret Service.

"Oh, God, no!" she cried. "Was it a stroke?"

"What?"

"Heart attack? Is he dead yet? Take me to see him!"

"The President's fine, Miss Spooner."

She produced a credible sigh of relief and flicked off her nose guard. "Then what are you doing here? Nobody's supposed to know about me."

"Well, that's the problem. There's too much talk."

"Is this really part of your job?"

"Fair question," Ryskamp said.

His visit to Mastodon's mistress was unofficial. The agency hadn't sent him to speak with her; he merely wanted to confirm for himself that the commander-in-chief was banging the same exotic dancer who was secretly shopping a racy book proposal to half a dozen publishers in New York. Ryskamp's sister-in-law, a literary agent, had read him a page of the synopsis in which the author scathingly compared the executive gonads to "desiccated chickpeas."

When Ryskamp asked Suzi if she'd ever written anything under the pseudonym Gillian LaCoste, she got so agitated that the silver tray of sliders flipped off her lap.

"I'll get your ass fired if you tell anyone!" she said.

Ryskamp informed her that his ass would be out the door in a few weeks, anyway. "Besides, it's not my concern what people say about the President, unless there's a threat of physical harm."

Suzi looked insulted. "Hey, I don't hurt him. I've *never* hurt him. Soon as he's out of breath, we stop."

"Okay, fine, but that's not what I meant."

The voice in Ryskamp's earpiece reported that Mastodon and Mockingbird were on the move; the President's motorcade was heading to the golf course, the First Lady's was going to a jobs fair in Riviera Beach.

"I really, really care about the man," Suzi went on. "I always tell him, 'Baby, get more cardio. Try a spin class. Zumba. Whatever.'"

"The mind reels," said Ryskamp.

"Don't judge me, bro. You know how many women out there would trade places? For the chance to bone a President, any President—are you kiddin'? How 'bout supermodels. Preachers' wives. Even Costco cashiers."

"If you care about him so much," Ryskamp said, "explain why you're doing a book."

"I bet he'll like it."

"Oh, yeah. Especially the part where you say he snorts like a wildebeest when he comes."

"No, *baby* wildebeest," Suzi said. "And I didn't write that line, swear to God! The dude that's helping me with the words, sometimes he's such a smartass."

They stopped talking while a white-clad attendant retrieved the fallen mini-burgers and buns from the beach sand around Suzi's chair. When the young man was gone, Ryskamp said, "I don't have to tell you about the President's large temper."

She sighed and rolled her eyes. "You're right. He will *totally* lose his shit if he finds out about the book."

"It won't be from me."

"So how much you want in order to keep your big mouth zipped?"

"That's funny. You're the second person today who thought I was trying to blackmail them when I wasn't." Ryskamp put on his sunglasses to watch a dark-haired woman on a paddleboard catch a nice wave. She was good.

Suzi said, "He told me he and his wife haven't done it in forever. Is that true?"

"Were you planning to be at the Commander's Ball? I didn't see you on the list."

"Not as Suzi Spooner. My birth name's different. He said he's gonna get me a fake date, so it's all cool."

"Oh."

"I never been to his mansion, the Casa Whatever. You gonna be there?"

"I will," Ryskamp said emptily. "Should be quite an evening."

TWENTY-TWO

Angie took a bite. "Not bad. What is it?"

"Coyote," her host replied.

"From where?"

"Eastbound lane, mile marker nineteen. Years ago, you never saw those gnarly fuckers around here. Now they're a-thriving."

He had grilled the stringy hind quarters over an open fire. Angie could hear a generator running on the far side of the camp; that would explain his internet connection, and the heat lamps that warmed the big strange cage at night.

"Not a cage—an enclosure," he said without irony.

After everything she'd heard about him, Angie still wasn't pre-pared for the live, in-person experience. His height, for starters. The funky pink shower cap that clashed with his military camo and boots. A beard as unruly as Spanish moss.

For someone his age he displayed a freakish vitality; the soothing cave-deep voice and movie-star smile, which were part of the leg-end, failed to offset the thrumming, unsettled force of his presence.

Then there was the damn iguana egg that he was attempting to hatch in his empty eye socket. One of the first things he'd done was flip up the patch and show the speckled white bulge to Angie. If that was a test, she assumed she passed. At least he hadn't chased her off the island.

When she'd told him her name, he had seemed surprised. "Jim Tile sent you?"

"He told me it was okay to call you Skink."

"There's no reason to call me anything. You won't be staying."

"Can I see them? Please."

"What—my books?" Wryly he had gestured toward the library-styled walls of the enclosure. The fissures of his face put the hard years on raw display, the corrosive sorrow and anger.

"Let's eat," he'd said, and cooked up the road-kill coyote, which actually tasted terrible. It was another test Angie passed. The only beverage that the governor offered was dark rum in a Dixie cup.

After they were done eating, he scrubbed the pan with swamp water while Angie doused the fire. She asked him what was in the large freezer, and he said frozen rabbits, sorbet, and expired hemorrhoid suppositories.

She said, "I'm actually on your side. You're aware of that, right? And I know you're not insane."

"Do you now?" He laughed and laughed.

"Come on, Governor. Show me what you've been up to."

Angie pointed at the trees, festooned with crispy, translucent snake sheds that fluttered whenever a breeze snuck through. "You should rent this place out for Halloween parties," she said.

Skink grunted. "Let's get on with it."

Angie unknotted the bag that she'd brought, depositing the dead python in smooth flaccid coils at his feet.

"One of yours?" she asked.

He knelt to examine the snake's bullet-punctured head. "The bikini shop on Worth Avenue," he said.

"Not just any bikini shop—the First Lady's bikini shop."

"I guess my intel was solid."

"And sneaking one of these suckers into the shipment of presidential Key Lime pies—that was slick, too," Angie said. "Who told you the bakery truck always stops at the same gas plaza?"

"What can I say?"

"Start by telling me why. Is there a particular political point you're trying to make?"

"If you were truly on my side, you wouldn't need me to spell it out."

Angie stood back while he skinned the python, which he proclaimed would make a "sporty" vest. Afterward he hacked up the meat, wrapped it in wax paper, and placed the pieces in the commercial-size freezer.

She said, "I'm not here to stop you, Governor. I doubt if I even could. Still, out of professional courtesy, maybe you can give me a sense of what's coming."

Skink tossed his head back and roared. "You, my dear, are cute as a button!"

Angie followed him over to the enclosure. From the front wall of books he removed a rectangle of tempered glass. After wriggling through the aperture, he called back to her: "No sudden movements, *por favor*."

The sight inside the cage was jolting. Angie had never been afraid of snakes, but she'd never seen so many enormous constrictors in one place, confined together. For habitat Skink had constructed a web-like scaffold of stripped tree branches—cypress, live oaks, mahoganies—covered by chicken-wire mesh that let in the sun and rain. The pythons in the boughs shined like blown glass; some were crawling, some were balled up asleep.

Angie tried to count them all but quickly she became dizzy. Through the chicken-wire dome she spotted a jet high in the sky making a marvelous rainbow-colored contrail. Meanwhile the eyes of the pythons draped in the tallest branches began throbbing like embers, which was impossible.

Skink said, "Is this the first time you've ever done acid?"

"What?"

"I micro-dosed your ass. It was the rum."

"That's not funny, Governor." Angie looked for a safe place to sit down.

"Relax. I'm tripping, too." Skink steadied her in his arms. "It's legit head therapy. I've been reading all about it in medical journals. A euphoriant that helps fight depression, they say."

"Let go of me," she said, though she didn't mind being held.

"Also good for anxiety."

"What's the biggest python in here?"

"Twenty-three feet, eleven inches."

Angie whistled. "World record. Nice work."

For some reason she was clutching the front of his Army shirt. Her fingernails glinted like candy ice, which intrigued her. She cleared her throat saying, "I take back what I said about you not being insane."

The pythons in the scaffold were becoming more active.

"They think it's supper-time," said Skink. "That isn't a joke, by the way."

"Not even a twenty-four-footer can swallow that fool in Palm Beach."

"Hell, I know. I'm just havin' a little fun."

"Well, you got the Secret Service all worked up," Angie said.

"Harmless capers."

"Uh, *no*."

Now there were snakes on the ground around them. Angie didn't flinch. She thought they were beautiful, the way they kept changing colors. She wanted to feel their feathery tongues flick at her skin, making sparks.

"How long does a micro-dose last?" she asked Skink.

"Depends on the participant. Usually a couple hours."

"Ah. Okay. Wow."

He was still holding her. "It was better when I was hiding from all human contact. For a while I couldn't tell you what year, month or day it was. The setback, God help me, was deciding to reconnect. Once I turned on the goddamn internet, no more sleep. President Shitweasel never fails to light my fuse. Just last Thursday he let a coal barge unload ten thousand tons of toxic ash at the port of Jacksonville. Dumped all of it in a landfill upwind from a playground. You shouldn't have wasted your time at vet school, Angie. Pediatric oncology—that's the future!"

She said, "Maybe you should ditch the laptop."

"Lord, no! What's left of my soul would shrivel without Pandora. They've got a whole station for Buffalo Springfield!"

"How did you know I went to veterinary school?"

"Your court file is public record, as with most felons." Skink's sigh had a sympathetic tone. "I'm waiting for you to remind me that the pythons don't belong in Florida, that they're devouring every native animal in sight—opossums, coons, bobcats, deer, all the lovely wading birds, even the crocodilians. But my specimens don't do that, sweetheart. They get frozen entrees."

Angie let go of his shirt and looked up at his scarred brown saddle of a face. "But the ones you're turning loose in Palm Beach, they're all going to die. You know this, right? It's shoot to kill. The winter's too cold for them up there, anyway."

"Every year's getting warmer," he said. "Thanks to geniuses such as our climate-denier-in-chief, the biggest Burmese are movin' north."

"This is light-years beyond crazy. What can you possibly hope to accomplish?"

"Maybe scare him out of Florida."

"The President?"

"I'm pleased, actually, that the Secret Service has taken notice. I wouldn't be surprised if they advise him to vacation elsewhere."

"Then what?" Angie was grinding her jaws in exasperation.

"Look," he said, "these frothy projects keep my spirit from flaming out. Now it's time for you to leave."

"No, not just yet—"

"I hear the airboat coming, Angie."

"Jim Tile said you sent him to my sentencing hearing."

"True. I'd been following your case."

"Can I ask why?"

"I liked how you dealt with the asshole fawn poacher."

"It wasn't very original," Angie said. "Plus I got that poor old gator killed."

"You did the best you could with what was available." Skink spun her around and aimed her toward the portal in the wall of books. "Now, scoot," he said.

Gingerly she stepped through the gathering snakes and wormed out the exit hole. The ex-governor was close behind. On the other side of the wall he paused to refit the piece of aquarium glass into the entry space.

Angie stood transfixed by the skin sheds streaming overhead in the treetops. "Can't I stay longer?" she asked.

"Your ride's here. Come along, dear."

Skink began walking her down to the shore. Angie concentrated on setting one foot in front of the other. She jumped when a cardinal, bright as a rose, streaked past.

"You drugged me, Governor. That's a social misfire," she said.

"It wasn't enough to hurt a kitten. You're doing great, by the way."

To avoid being seen by the airboat driver, Skink stopped in the shadows halfway down the path. When he told Angie goodbye, she found herself squeezing his hands. "Oh shit," she said. "Of course, of course, of *course*. Now I get it."

"What?"

"You're the one who paid for my lawyer!"

He smiled. "For all the good that did. What a lazy dick he was."

"Still it was eighteen thousand bucks. Shit!"

"Why 'shit'?"

"Because I've always wanted to pay back the person who did that for me," Angie said, "but I don't have the money right now."

"Pretend you never saw all this, and we'll call it even."

Then he kissed the top of her head and stomped back toward his secret, teeming camp.

Beak got his nickname in fourth grade when a dog named Tucker leaped into his lap and bit his nose, which resulted in weeks of the boy wearing a splint secured by a white pointy bandage. The mutt, which belonged to his stepbrother, attacked several other family members before succumbing to a heel kick delivered by a no-nonsense postal carrier who'd once played collegiate soccer.

Since then, Beak had been leery of domestic pets even as he grew into an amateur naturalist and avid outdoorsman. The airboat gig was the coolest job he'd ever had. Most of his customers were tourists or birders who were attentive to the surroundings and appreciated Beak's knowledgeable patter. He lived off of tips, which he'd learned were proportionate to the number of alligators, eagles and spoonbills sighted. Normally he didn't allow riders to leave the boat, but Angela Armstrong obviously was at ease in the Everglades and, more importantly, had happily overpaid for the charter.

"Where's your bag of rope?" he asked when he picked her up at the island.

She pointed at her ears and said, "Can you find me a headset with a mic that works?"

On the trip back she seemed different—way more chill—humming tunes he didn't recognize and asking him about his work. She had a sharp eye for wetland fauna, correctly naming every species of bird they saw, including a juvenile black-crowned night heron. Beak was impressed. He wasn't the brightest bulb in the chandelier but, after Angie touched his knee and laughed a little too hard at his Zika mosquito joke, he wondered if she might be putting the moves on him.

"Beak, how old are you?" he heard on his headset.

"Twenty-seven."

"Yikes," she said.

"How was your hike through the hammock?"

"Kaleidoscopic."

"Yeah? Is that good?" he asked.

"I'm still processing the experience. You married?"

"Nope."

"Girlfriend?"

"Negative."

Angie swayed in her seat as he turned the rudder hard, skirting a stand of cattails. She said, "FYI, I am likewise unattached."

"Hard to believe."

"You're a smooth one," Beak heard on his headset. "Do you have plans for dinner?"

They wound up at a barbecue joint where alligator *croquetas* were on the menu and derisively avoided by the locals. Beak had a plate of pulled pork while Angie ordered a rack of ribs and a stuffed potato. For a small woman she seemed to have a big appetite. When she asked if he'd ever taken LSD, he thought she was joking.

"I'm such a lightweight," she murmured before chugging a jumbo tumbler of unsweetened iced tea.

Beak said, "I got some excellent bud at home."

"Let's get a drink instead."

They found a decent bar, where he held her hand and listened to a thumbnail version of her life story. He said he couldn't picture her locked in a prison cell. He liked how she'd rigged her pickup truck, and he had lots of questions about the wildlife-relocation business. He was surprised that it didn't pay better.

"Was that tree island trip one of your jobs?" he asked.

Angie answered no, it was personal business.

"Was anyone else out there?"

"Don't be ridiculous," she said.

"But what about that johnboat hidden in the grass?"

"Who knows. Maybe a poacher?"

"Yeah, probably," said Beak.

They went back to his doublewide, Angie following in her truck.

She fell asleep while he was in the shower, and he had no luck trying to wake her. In the morning she apologized, combed out her hair, and made pancakes.

"Are you booked today?" she asked him.

"Nope. Wish I was."

"You are now," she said. "I need to go back to that island. I'll give you five hundred bucks."

So Beak took her back, and this time Angie told him to wait at the shore. She was gone only a few minutes, and she seemed upset when she returned.

"What's wrong? What happened back there?" he asked.

"Forget it. Let's get the hell out."

Beak said, "No, I'm gonna go look for myself."

"You are *not*," she snapped. "There's nothing to see."

Which was the wild and dumbfounding truth.

TWENTY-THREE

Fay Alex Riptoad gathered the Potussies at the club library in order to quell an uprising about the Commander's Ball. The Italian gown designer most worshipped by the group had fallen behind in his work and assigned a straight young assistant to finish the patriotically themed dresses of Dorothea Mars Bristol, Yirma Skyy Frick, and Kelly Bean Drummond, all of whom were outraged by what they perceived was second-tier attention. Since there wasn't enough time to start from scratch with another designer, the three demoted Potussies insisted that—to level the social playing field—every member of the group should come to the ball in a previously worn gown.

That radical proposal was jeered by Dee Wyndham Wittlefield and Deirdre Cobo Lancôme, both of whom were already drunk and feisty. Fay Alex Riptoad cast her vote with the tipsy traditionalists, asserting that the President and First Lady would surely notice—and be offended—if the women didn't show up wearing something new and spectacular. Fay Alex cited her own chiffon Statue-of-Liberty ensemble from the previous year's gala as particularly unforgettable—the toga-like gown fitted daringly to bare a shoulder, and hemmed precisely to ankle-length so as not to conceal Fay Alex's one-of-a-kind, tri-colored Louboutin slingbacks. The outfit was so distinct that it couldn't possibly be recycled, even for the cause of friendship.

Dottie Mars, Yirma, and Kelly Bean were so incensed that they vowed to boycott the ball, a threat Fay Alex didn't take seriously. The group was to be seated at the same table as the executive producer of *Fox & Friends* who was bringing as a guest his sleep-disorder therapist, wealthy and single. Since Dottie Mars was the one who'd gifted the tickets, there was no chance of her staying home. Still, seeking to mollify the mutineers, Fay Alex announced that anyone who was dissatisfied with the dress from the apprentice designer could seek reimbursement from the fashion slush fund controlled by the President's eldest daughter, a size 8 with exquisite taste.

Once the matter was put to rest, Fay Alex offered to treat the group to a conciliatory brunch. The Potussies collected their respective Secret Service agents, who were posted outside the library, and headed for the Sabal Palm Room, a members-only lounge overlooking a garden of fiberglass bamboo. Along the way they passed the First Lady with her own Secret Service entourage, led by her tall, dark, alleged lover and an attractive female agent that Fay Alex remembered seeing occasionally on the grounds of Casa Bellicosa.

The President's wife, wearing a long-sleeved tee and slate-gray leggings, had offered her trademark unbreakable smile but avoided eye contact with all of the Potussies except Fay Alex, who responded with the slightest of conspiratorial nods. Fay Alex had told none of her friends how she'd persuaded the First Lady to reinstate their Secret Service protection.

"What in God's name has that woman done to her hair?" Kelly Bean sniped.

"She fired her colorist is what I heard," whispered Yirma Skyy.

It was Dee Witty Wyndham who later, over lobster rolls, brought up the subject of the affair. "POTUS deserves someone who appreciates him," she said, "not someone who carries on like a common tramp."

"Or even an uncommon one," added Deirdre Cobo.

"Well," Fay Alex said. She paused cruelly to polish off her Tito's and beckon for another.

"Well *what*?" honked Dottie Mars.

Fay Alex smirked and dropped her voice. "I heard it's over."

A trenchant glee rustled through the room. One of the Potussies asked Fay Alex if the juicy bulletin had come from her own Secret Service man.

"Ha! William barely says good morning," said Fay Alex. "No, I got this from someone on the staff of the club, very reliable. Apparently the First Lady's special 'friend' broke up with her this week. Now he's all hot and heavy with one of the other agents. Supposedly they're hooking up at some trucker motel out by I-95."

"Ughhh," was the tablewide reaction, Dee Dee Wittlefield emitting the loudest and following with: "Which agent is it, Fay Alex?"

"Rose is her last name. It's the blonde we just saw him walking with in the hallway."

"That skinny thing with the retro bangs?" Yirma Skyy yipped. "For Heaven's sake, what kind of man dumps the President's wife for *that*? And how has he not been transferred to Bumfuck, Alaska?"

"No, Arkansas," said Kelly Bean. "That's *my* prediction."

"For both him and the blonde whore," Dottie Mars added coldly. "Bumfuck, Arkansas."

Fay Alex understood that the group was torn over which revelation would humiliate their beloved President more—that his gorgeous spouse had been cheating on him, or that her lover had rejected her for someone else.

Like she wasn't hot enough!

Dee Wyndham said, "No wonder the First Lady didn't look happy today."

When does she ever *look happy?* Fay Alex wondered.

"Obviously she doesn't have the warmest personality," Deirdre

Cobo cut in, "and she definitely needs to re-think some of her col-lagen choices—but, still, no man in his right mind would say nay to those incredible legs!"

Fay Alex agreed, though in the absence of fresh details she'd grown bored of discussing the scandal.

"Ladies, we have our big show number to rehearse. Now, who's been practicing? Raise your hand!"

Large-print lyrics to "Big Unimpeachable You" were distributed around the lounge and, with Fay Alex leading, the Potussies com-menced to harmonize.

Typically there was an uptick of trespassing at Casa Bellicosa in the days before the Commander's Ball—curious tourists, daredevil spring breakers, brainless Instagram dolts, and mumbling psychos in bathrobes.

Secret Service agents would turn the harmless ones over to the Palm Beach Police Department, and Jerry Crosby's job was to make sure they remained locked up until the morning after the gala. The chief didn't mind his secondary role; managing security for presi-dential events was a pain in the ass. His officers actually preferred working traffic outside the gate, overtime pay being the sweetener.

The chief happened to be southbound on A1A when Paul Rys-kamp called to say that two belligerent men had been arrested in the foot tunnel between the oceanfront and the Casa's parking garage. Claiming to be VIP friends of the First Family, the trespassers had demanded that Crosby be summoned to vouch for them. Reluc-tantly, he did.

Both young Cornbrights bore evidence of their Jet Ski injuries—Chase had gleaming new dental veneers and a Burberry-pattern cast on his broken knee, while Chase sported matching shoulder braces that not only stabilized his reconstructed joints but markedly improved his posture. The sons of Kiki Pew Fitzsimmons had been confined to a half-renovated powder room on the mansion's second floor, where they tag-team bitched at Paul Ryskamp while waiting for Jerry Crosby.

Chase and Chance had been catching some rays on the beach when they decided to drop by the Winter White House for a late lunch and Bloody Marys. Agents had intercepted them in the tunnel and asked for ID. The Cornbright brothers had become infuriated when they learned that their club privileges had terminated with the recent death of their mother, whose membership slot at Casa Bellicosa had already been re-sold to another widowed heiress on the waiting list. Chance and Chase had refused to leave the property, and vowed to have the Secret Service agents fired. The young men had felt insulted by the agents' impassive response, and were still unloading on Ryskamp when the police chief arrived.

"You know these two?" Ryskamp asked Crosby. "Would you please take them home to their nannies?"

"Hold up!" Chase protested. "We came for lunch, and by God we're having lunch—"

"You're not members here, Mr. Cornbright, and you're not on the guest list for today," Ryskamp said. "No lunch. No snacks. No breath mints."

Because his shoulders were injured, Chance could only wag a finger. "Mister, you've got no idea what kind of shit blizzard is rolling your way."

Crosby and Ryskamp left the powder room to speak privately. They agreed that the Cornbright brothers were spoiled young shits, and that the dispute over their membership status should be dealt with by the club manager, not law enforcement.

"Their mother had met the President only a few times," the chief said, "but he's taken a major interest in her death. He mentions her name all the time in his tweets—that No-More-Diegos thing."

"I'm well aware, Jerry."

"The other Potussies are gonna flip out when they hear that Kiki Pew's kids got thrown off the property."

Ryskamp put a hand on the chief's shoulder. "Would it make your life easier if we let these two assholes hit the buffet line?"

"Yeah, it would."

"Then what the hell. I'll call downstairs."

"And don't worry, Paul, they're bluffing. They'd never try to get you fired."

Ryskamp chuckled. "I don't give a flying fuckeroo if they do."

Jerry Crosby enviously wondered if the day would come when he didn't give a flying fuckeroo, or at least could afford not to.

"Can you let me know if the Cornbrights are on the list for the Commander's Ball?" he asked. "Because I guarantee you they *think* they are."

"You want me to clear them?"

"If they get stopped at the door, it'll be an issue."

"Then I'll take care of it," said Ryskamp, "but only because they just lost their mom."

"Their mom thought they were useless."

"Yes, and they'll fit in beautifully at this event."

Crosby wished he could get away with saying things like that. Tragically, keeping his job depended on sucking up to the Kiki Pew Fitzsimmonses and Fay Alex Riptoads of the island. Special Agent Ryskamp clearly had no such obligations.

"What do you hear from the elusive Ms. Armstrong?" the chief asked.

"She'll be on duty at the gala. Will you be there, Jerry?"

"Yeah, but not in the ballroom."

"Lucky bastard," said Ryskamp.

Mockingbird took a hit off the vape pen before going to her husband's suite. He was occupied in the bathroom, so she waited with her security team in the sitting area. It was impossible not to notice Keith-slash-Ahmet and Jennifer Rose quietly exchanging words;

Mockingbird was almost certain they smiled at each other. Obviously Ahmet was following her instructions to fake-flirt, and his performance was subtle enough to be convincing.

Earlier that morning there had been another moment—an amused-seeming whisper that passed between him and Agent Rose in the presence of Spalding, the young server from South Africa and Ahmet's conch-pearl connection. Spalding, who'd delivered a tray of star fruits and CBD-infused hummus to the First Lady, had undoubtedly hurried back to the kitchen to report on Ahmet's wandering eye. Mockingbird saw that her disinformation scheme seemed to be working.

Up close, Jennifer Rose appeared thinner and even more attractive than Mockingbird remembered, but that meant she probably had a man in her life and wasn't looking for a new lover. In addition, the Secret Service strongly disapproved of romances between its special agents. Nonetheless, Mockingbird considered asking Ahmet to turn down the charm dial a few notches, just in case.

After an awkward wait, Mastodon emerged from the bathroom breathing hard and red-faced from exertion. He snapped at his butler to fetch more fucking laxatives.

"That's what red meat does to your system," Mockingbird remarked. "Have you thought about cutting back to, like, two pounds a day?"

On cue the agents filed out and closed the door. Mastodon was still fumbling to belt his pants, groping blindly for the buckle below the rolling sea of his gut.

"We need to talk about the Commander's Ball," he said to his wife. "What are you wearing?"

"Tom Ford."

"Not so much sky in the cleavage department, okay? Last year, well . . . you know what happened."

"One dried-up old hag complained," said Mockingbird. "So what?"

"That dried-up old hag is the reason I won Wisconsin."

"Yes, you've told me."

"She forked out three million bucks on phony Facebook ads," Mastodon went on. "And since she'll be sitting at the main table on Saturday, you should show a little respect and dim those headlights."

"Fine. But the gown has a thigh-high slit."

"Yeah? Maybe I'll drop my napkin and sneak a peek." Mastodon's smile these days was more of a wormy sneer, the product of too many press-conference performances.

He said, "Know what else you should wear? Those new pink pearl earrings. Very sexy."

His wife responded with granite indifference. She asked if his "nutritionist" would be attending the gala.

"Yep," said Mastodon, "with her date."

"Nice try."

"You'll see."

"Are we done here?" Mockingbird asked.

"Not quite." Her husband told her what the Secret Service said about the rise of the pythons.

"Yes, I was briefed," she said curtly.

Mastodon snorted. "Well, just so you know, it's complete total horseshit. Another fake hoax by the Deep Staters."

"But there was a big one dead in the road not long ago. They had to stop my motorcade."

"Goddammit, can't you see what these people are trying to do?"

"Who?" said Mockingbird. "I don't understand."

"Never mind. Someone will be patrolling the estate during the ball—a snake expert, they tell me. Not my idea but, hey, we ain't the ones payin' for it."

Mastodon popped a handful of Adderalls, checked his watch and saw it was time for his tanning session. Mockingbird rose to leave. She was curious but not worried; Ahmet would give her the latest python update.

"One more thing," her husband said. "You might want to keep little Bagel on his leash for the next few days, just to play it safe."

"Bagel?"

"Your dog." Mastodon arranged his koala-sized hands to approximate the dimensions of an overfed Yorkie. "Isn't that his name?"

"*Was* his name," said the First Lady. "He passed away the Christmas before last."

"Aw shit. Really? What the hell happened?"

"Old age."

"Well, then, let's get a new one!"

"You're such a dick," Mockingbird said, and stalked off.

"I can't wait to see your new dress!" Mastodon called hopelessly after her.

The Knob insisted he was good to go. Christian said no way; the man's face and torso still looked like shrimp-skin since passing out with the bimbo on Jupiter Beach.

"She wasn't no bimbo. She's a cheerleader for the Patriots."

"Of course she is. And I'm Dwayne Johnson's stunt double."

"Yo, man, I can definitely do this," said The Knob, who suspected he wouldn't be paid until he went back inside the presidential tanning tube.

Christian was in a jam. The Secret Service always required the Cabo Royale to be tested the same day Mastodon was scheduled to use it. Christian asked The Knob if there was any sector of his body that wasn't sunburned.

"Bottom of my feet," he replied.

"That's it?"

"My ass cheeks, too. I guess me and that chick didn't take our underwear off."

Christian forlornly realized what had to be done. "Let's have a look," he said, bracing himself. The presentation was even nastier than he'd feared.

"My God, have you been to a dermatologist?" he cried.

The Knob said, "What for? It's just acne scars."

"No, I don't think so. I really don't."

"Yo, maybe some heavy-duty UVs would knock that shit down."

Christian had to look away. "Let's get on with this," he said grimly.

Following directions, The Knob donned the Mastodon wig, goggles, a sun mask, bicycle gloves, dive booties, a hooded long-sleeve tee, and Lycra-blend leggings altered by scissors to expose his chalky pitted buttocks. He entered the Cabo on his knees, lay forward on his belly and waited for Christian to shut the canopy.

Thirteen minutes later, when the lid opened, The Knob heard a loud whoosh and felt a blast of frigid air on his rump.

"Hold still!" Christian yelled as he unloaded the fire extinguisher.

"What the fuck? What the motherfuckin' *fuck*?"

"Don't move, man! Do not move."

"Whassat goddamn smell?"

"You."

The Knob let out a wail. "I'm on motherfuckin' fire?"

"Just your ass hair," Christian said.

Later the President's personal physician would examine The Knob and determine that in fact he had suffered curlicue first-degree burns on each buttock. A cooling unguent was applied while Secret Service agents took Christian aside and quizzed him about the Cabo Royale's untimely malfunction.

What caused it? Christian wasn't sure.

Could it be repaired? Oh, absolutely.

How soon? He couldn't say. With luck he wouldn't need to order any parts.

But how *soon*? Well, maybe tomorrow. Maybe longer.

We need an answer as soon as possible, the agents told him. The President has an important event this weekend.

He could go to a regular tanning parlor, Christian suggested.

Absolutely out of the question, the agents said. Now get to work.

TWENTY-FOUR

Angie tried not to think much about politics. It didn't seem to matter who was in power—nothing got better in the besieged, breathtaking world she cared about most. The Everglades would never be the lush unbroken river it once was; the shallows of Florida Bay would never be as pure and sparkling with fish; the bleached dying reefs of the Keys would never bloom fully back to life. Being overrun and exploited was the historical fate of places so rare and beautiful.

Every year, Angie diligently wrote checks to the Nature Conservancy and World Wildlife Fund, but she was too much of a loner to jump into the fray. No meetings, no rallies, no Facebook petitions. Never once had she fired off an angry letter to a congressman or a county commissioner. Sometimes she wondered if she was too cynical, or just too lazy.

The sitting President of the United States was a soulless imbecile who hated the outdoors but, in Angie's view, at this point Teddy Roosevelt himself couldn't turn the tide if he came back from the dead. All the treasured wilderness that had been sacrificed at the altar of growth was gone for all time. More disappeared every day; nothing ever changed except the speed of destruction, and only because there were fewer pristine pieces to sell off, carve up and pave.

Surely the old ex-governor knew this. Angie found herself envying his capacious anger and high torque after a lifetime of crushingly predictable futility. The man was seriously bent, but he also was high-functioning.

The tree island—abandoned. What the fuck?

Gone were his walls of great books, his laptop, the generator, the cooking pans, the freezer packed with dead rabbits. Also gone were his pythons, of course, even the skin sheds that he'd strung throughout the treetops. Gone was his boat, as well.

And somehow he'd done it in one night, cleaned out the whole damn camp—like he'd been planning the move, like he'd hung around just long enough to give Angie a peek.

"And he never told you his name?" Paul Ryskamp asked.

"No, sir," she said, which was technically true.

Jim Tile was the person who'd divulged Skink's identity, but the retired lawman wasn't available to be interviewed by the Secret Service. After Angie's second visit to the island, she had driven directly to the assisted-living facility. There she'd been told that Tile had been taken to the hospital after complaining of chest pains. And when she'd arrived at the hospital, she learned he wasn't there and that nobody fitting his description had been treated in the emergency room.

By then she'd already made up her mind to shield both of them, Skink and his ailing old friend. Giving up their names wouldn't stop whatever was about to happen in Palm Beach.

"How'd you track down this nut job?" Ryskamp asked her.

"A tip."

"From what, a swamp informant?"

"A highly placed swamp informant," Angie said.

"You're not telling me even half of what you know."

"I've told you the important parts, Paul."

"Thanks, I suppose. But now what?"

"I don't know. Prepare for a plague of pythons?"

"Shit, Angie."

"Major fuckage," she agreed, "from a party planner's perspective. But from a professional standpoint, the situation is containable."

"Containable to *what*?"

"The category of nuisance. Burmese don't want to be around human activity. They'll be hiding, not roaming the ballroom."

Ryskamp whistled dismally and sat up. "God, I hate snakes."

"Not as much as I hate your Silk Rockets. They actually squeak," Angie said. "Or was that you?"

He wasn't listening. She flicked the condom wrapper off the nightstand and said, "One star out of five, comfort-wise. Also, that color? Mighty distracting."

"I've got to call Washington." He rolled out of bed and put on his robe.

"Wait, Paul, one thing I forgot to tell you."

"Uh-oh. What?"

"You were *amazing*," Angie said.

He broke into a grin. "Stay right there."

"Dream on, sailor boy."

Angie had phoned him late in the afternoon to say she had major python news. To her surprise, he suggested meeting at Pistache, a French restaurant with patio seating on Clematis. All during cocktails and dinner, they didn't talk business; Ryskamp told stories from a long-ago trip to Paris, and Angie offered theories on the provenance of the escargot. Never had she seen him so relaxed, and she was puzzled that he didn't hound her for the promised information. He didn't even ask for an update on her frowned-upon plan to clear Diego Beltrán—she'd been looking forward to bragging that she no longer needed any covert help from him, or from Jerry Crosby.

Afterward it had been Ryskamp's idea to go to his place, where there was reggae music and pinot noir. He was peeling off her jeans when she'd decided to ask him why he changed his mind about seeing her.

"It's simple. You're different, you make me smile, and life's too fucking short. Also, I missed you."

"When did this thunderbolt strike, Paul? And, by the way, 'intriguing' would sound way better than 'different.'"

"I'm retiring next week," he'd said.

"So this is why you're on cruise control."

"Not just yet, Angie. Big weekend ahead."

She had waited until after they made love before telling him what she'd seen on the Everglades tree island, and what she believed it portended.

The phone call to Washington went on for a few minutes. Ryskamp returned to the bedroom cupping his hand over his phone. "They want to know how big," he said.

"The longest was nearly twenty-four feet."

"Damn."

"Still not fat enough to swallow your man," Angie said, not mentioning it was the largest Burmese she'd ever heard of.

The agent left the room to finish speaking with his supervisors. When he came back, he said, "They want you to wear a gown to the event."

Angie laughed. "I don't own a gown."

"Shocker."

"That's not very nice, Paul."

"This is straight from the President's vice-assistant deputy chief of staff. He thinks your regular workday outfit will spark unwanted curiosity." Ryskamp sat on the edge of the bed and took her hand.

"Screw the gown," Angie said.

"Just between us, they'd love an excuse to hire one of your competitors for the job."

"Because I'm a woman."

"Duh," said Ryskamp. "I were you, I'd go buy the most expensive dress I could find. Your rich Uncle Sam will pay for it."

"I'm kind of liking this new attitude. But, seriously, retirement?"

"The timing's right, Angie."

"In six months you'll be bored out of your skull."

"Possibly not. I rented a place in Key West."

"Good choice," she said. "You've already got the wardrobe."

"Tomorrow I start packing my shit."

"But I'll see you at the ball Saturday night, right?"

"Yes, indeed," said Ryskamp. "Call of duty."

Then he slid under the sheets beside her, and they talked some more.

Sedated and bandaged heavily, Diego Beltrán was surprised when they moved him from the jail's hospital wing to his cell. One of the older Hispanic deputies advised him not to come out.

"Word is they want you offed before the weekend," the deputy said, "as a present to the President."

"Is it El Rotundo's birthday?" Diego asked.

"There's a big party for him on the island. I don't know what for."

"So who's supposed to kill me?" Diego's ribs ached when he inhaled. "The Aryans again?"

The deputy whispered, "No, it's the Neo-Christian Cawks."

"The Cucks? Isn't that a sex cult?"

"No, man, the *Cawks*. As in Caucasians."

"Lamest gang name ever," Diego said.

"Just stay in your cell, dude. I'll bring you some books and magazines."

"But I need a shower. Bad."

"You wanna be dirty and breathing," said the deputy, "or squeaky clean and dead?"

"How much are these racist assholes getting paid?"

"Ten grand is what I heard. Eleven if they cut off your nut sack, too."

Diego felt wobbly. The deputy helped him get on the cot.

"Big crowd out front today," the deputy said. "They want your balls on a fork, too."

Diego wondered what had stirred up the loonies. Lately there had been so few demonstrators that even the local Fox affiliate had lost interest. The deputy reported that the TV crews were back in force along with the protesters, who were wearing crimson tee-shirts that said "No More Damn Diegos!" and practicing their chants between live feeds. He said some carried signs with black-bordered pictures of Kiki Pew Fitzsimmons and the words: WE WILL NEVER FORGET.

Diego stared despondently at the crusted gray ceiling. "I don't get it. Why now?"

"There was a radio contest, I heard, for who could yell the loudest."

"What's first prize?"

"Christmas for life at Olive Garden. Whole family eats free." The deputy closed the cell door, which locked automatically.

Diego lifted his head. "Hey, did my lawyers ever call back?"

The deputy said an envelope from the Public Defender's Office was tucked in the pages of his Bible. When Diego opened it, he found a copy of a Motion to Withdraw from the case. His latest team of attorneys had informed the judge that they'd been receiving "graphic" death threats online and "ominous" items sent by mail. The disturbing deliveries included a disrobed and crudely altered Mickey Mouse doll, a bullet-riddled target with the lawyers' faces pasted to the bull's-eye, and a blood-stained cockatoo feather that arrived without clear explanation. Another anonymous package featured a photo of one of the defense lawyer's daughters kissing a "nonwhite" high-school classmate at a football game; the word "HORE" had been written on the picture with an orange crayon, scratched through, and replaced with "SLUTT."

Diego saw a second envelope inside the Bible—a handwritten letter from his mother in Tegucigalpa. The letter had been opened and inspected by an officer at the jail, and the last page—his mother's loving sign-off—was missing. This had happened before. Diego knew somebody was screwing with his head. The first time he had complained, but now he let it go.

The deputies continued to go through the motions of protecting him, but Diego sensed they were tired of the extra effort. Upon his return from the medical unit, he'd noticed that a new leather belt had been placed on top of his neatly folded jumpsuit. He processed it as a strong suggestion, if not a warning.

Suicide once had seemed cowardly and unthinkable, but the idea had been drifting on the periphery of Diego's thoughts since the stabbing. There was no reason to believe that Angela Armstrong—as fiery and resolute as she might be—had the juice to get him freed from jail. Even if he was released, for the rest of his life he would be the border-jumping Diego who ignited the No-More-Diegos movement, the Diego made notorious by the President of the United States.

Where could a man run to escape such infamy? How could he hide from the global talons of Twitter and Instagram? Diego had been told his name was now well-known in his hometown, and all Honduras. If he returned, who would risk being a friend? Or lover? Or wife? It was overwhelming to contemplate the chore of erasing his past, inventing a new identity and starting over someplace far away.

Engulfed by hopelessness, he closed his eyes and heard the rabid red-shirted fanatics screaming his name. They were either outside the jail, or inside his head. He felt like it didn't matter.

An unfamiliar deputy, a middle-aged white dude with a bleached soul patch, came to Diego's cell and rolled a prescription bottle of pills on the floor through the bars.

"Nurse said you should take those," he said, "for pain."

Diego shook the bottle. It sounded full.

"You should get some sleep," said the deputy.

"What a good idea."

Mastodon was livid after he learned his tanning session had been postponed because of equipment problems. He bemoaned his halibut complexion, head-butted his bathroom mirror and canceled several afternoon appearances, including the dedication of a seniors-only pickleball complex named for his pal Geraldo Rivera.

Christian worked on the Cabo Royale nonstop for hours, replacing every part for which he had spares. With The Knob singed, sidelined and threatening to sue, Christian had turned to his friend Spalding, who agreed to fill in as the test dummy. To replicate the President's physique, Spalding climbed into a padded K-9 trainer attack suit that the Secret Service had purchased secondhand from the sheriff's department.

Fortunately, the tanning cocoon operated perfectly; no flickering, no sparks, no hot spots. An elated Christian offered to buy Spalding dinner, and they ended up late in a corner booth at Echo.

"Why doesn't the dumbass use bronzer instead?" Spalding asked between bites of wahoo sashimi. "It's way easier."

"He won't touch that stuff anymore," Christian said. "No personal gels whatsoever."

"Strange dude."

"He had a really bad experience at a pro-am in Tahoe."

"Okay, not while I'm eating," Spalding said.

"Grabbed the wrong tube—"

"Yeah, I get it. Can we please move on?"

Christian ordered more sake. He asked Spalding for the latest gossip about the First Lady's romance. "Did she really get dumped by her studly Secret Service man?"

"Uh, dumped *hard*."

"Man, I was rooting for those two."

"Word is he's boning one of the other agents," said Spalding. "You know that tall blonde?"

"When you're my size, bro, they're all tall."

"I talked to her in the kitchen once and she is *nice*. I've seen her and the dude together and, yeah, it's definitely on."

Christian smiled half-drunkenly. "So, what I hear you saying, the President's wife is now available."

"She's five-ten, douchebag. You better learn to pole-vault."

"Aw shit." Christian was checking his texts. "Hey, I've gotta re-test the Cabo first thing tomorrow. Can you swing by at eight?"

"Maybe nine," said Spalding.

"Eight-thirty at the latest. The big man himself is coming at ten."

"Can I stay for the show?"

Christian shook his head. "Speak of the devil," he murmured.

He was staring past Spalding, who turned to see. It was the First Lady entering the restaurant behind a small wedge of Secret Service agents. She sat down alone at a corner table.

"God, you're right," said Christian. "She's a bloody stork."

Spalding turned back and attacked the last slice of raw wahoo. He said, "I feel sorry for the lady."

"Sweet tan. It's bottled bronzer, though. You can tell."

"Is the agent dude with her now? The ex."

"I don't know which one's him. Anyway, it's too dark," Christian said.

Their server appeared with the check and said the restaurant was closing early. As Spalding and Christian made their way to the door, they peeked sideways at the President's chic wife, skimming the menu and sipping Chablis.

As soon as the place was empty, Mockingbird stood up and went to the ladies' restroom, which had been cleared earlier by Agent Jennifer Rose. Posted solo in the vanity area was Keith Josephson, who within moments was summoned inside one of the stalls.

"Ahmet, what the hell?" Mockingbird said, angrily poking his chest with a finger.

"You're the one that told me to flirt."

"Everyone on the property is talking about you two."

"I know, but wasn't that the point?" Ahmet said. "To stop the rumors about us?"

"No, you're enjoying this way too much. The woman who does my peddies, she says one of the housekeepers overheard you and Agent Rose chatty-chatting the other day. By the way, she does *not* have a steady boyfriend. I checked up on that."

Ahmet was caught off guard by Mockingbird's jealous outburst, yet still it felt good to be standing so close to her. She was wearing a perfume that smelled like a minty alpine waterfall.

"Are you sleeping with her?" she asked, further startling him.

"No, ma'am, I'm not. No!"

"Do you want to sleep with her? What if she asks for it? Tell the truth, Ahmet. Not even a quickie?"

"Same answer: No! But, again, this whole crazy thing was your idea, not mine."

"And you told me you were a lousy actor."

Ahmet realized he was trapped in conversation purgatory. All he could do was ride it out. A voice in his earpiece inquired about the First Lady's prolonged restroom visit. He replied that she was retouching her mascara.

Then to her he said, "I was being honest. I *am* a terrible actor."

"Are you now?" She crossed her arms and glowered. "Men are all the same. You, my pig husband, no difference."

Ahmet bent down to kiss her, but Mockingbird turned her face away. He was hurt to see her pluck off the conch pearl earrings and theatrically drop them in the toilet, one at a time.

He fished them out and dried them with a handkerchief.

"So, *Keith*," Mockingbird said, "when did you plan to tell me about the maple armoire?"

"The what?"

"The Shaker piece you promised to make for Agent Rose."

Ahmet rocked back against the stall door, an involuntary reaction he perceived as self-incriminating. He theorized that the wood-working intel had come from the eavesdropping housekeeper.

"It's not an armoire, it's a writing desk," he said thickly. "And all I told her was pine, not maple. Ordinary Georgia pine."

"Asshole!" Mockingbird cried. The word seemed to ring off the tiles as Ahmet rushed to follow her out of the restroom.

Because Angie had no close girlfriends, she dragged Joel along the next morning when she went to Worth Avenue. Shopping for gowns was a new but not unsatisfying experience. Eventually she picked out a sleeveless jungle-print Versace that Joel noted was actually a dress, and probably too short for the Commander's Ball.

"Not if I have to climb a fucking tree," Angie said. "Do you like it or not?"

"Yeah, it's pretty hot."

"Eeewww, stepson."

"Just buy the damn thing so we can get out of here," he said.

The dress cost eighteen hundred dollars, which almost maxed out Angie's credit card. She texted a photo of the receipt to Paul Rys-kamp saying a prompt reimbursement would be appreciated.

Joel was up for tacos so they went across the bridge to Rocco's, where Krista met them. She and Joel had moved back to her condo; they reported that Dustin and Alexandria weren't getting along. Angie was proud of herself for not feeling uplifted by the news.

"She's bugging him to build her a new horse barn," Joel said, plainly taking his father's side, "and attach a yoga studio."

"Might cost be an issue?" asked Angie, without mischief.

"They'll work it out," was Krista's assessment.

"Or strangle each other," said Joel with a shrug.

Angie inquired about the sling on Krista's right arm.

"What happens when ashtanga vinyasa is taught by an amateur," was her weary reply. "The woman is possessed."

"You're a good sport," Angie said.

They ordered beers and toasted Joel's new assistant-manager job at Staples. He said he was scheduled to start the following week. Krista wanted to hear more about Angie's upcoming gig at the Commander's Ball, but Angie said she wasn't supposed to talk about it, which was the truth.

"Are you bringing a date?" Krista asked.

"No, a machete."

Joel said, "She isn't joking."

"I'm not allowed to have a gun," Angie elaborated. "It's the law."

"Okay. Wow." Krista had no follow-up questions.

After lunch, Angie got in her pickup and headed out Okeechobee Road toward the interstate. Joel and Krista were in the same lane, directly ahead in Krista's VW sedan. They'd all stopped at the railroad tracks, waiting for a half-empty passenger train to pass, when Angie noticed who was driving the green minivan behind her.

It was Pruitt, the dumb lunatic. He had a stranglehold on the steering wheel with his good hand—gloved—and his bare prosthetic. His disguise was neon-framed shades, a dark knit cap, and an unfortunate Rasta-style beard. Under different circumstances, Angie would have burst out laughing. But clearly Pruitt was on the hunt, undaunted by the interactive bobcat experience that Angie had arranged at his sister's place.

The crossing gates went up and traffic began to move. Angie grabbed for her phone but it fell down the crack between her seat and the console. She was taken by surprise when Pruitt flew past her and then suddenly cut back, forcing her to stomp the brakes. When she caught up to him, he was tailgating Krista's VW.

Angie got a chill down her neck. Krista and Joel were probably busy talking, unaware of what was happening. They'd be going north on I-95, and the entry ramp was already in sight. Angie considered sideswiping Pruitt's minivan but she decided to wait; she couldn't risk causing a crash that might hurt other drivers.

Maybe Pruitt was putting on a show, or maybe this time he'd really unraveled. There was no way to know if he was armed, and the thought of him shooting at Krista and Joel—even if only to rattle them—terrified Angie.

She rolled up close and began tapping the minivan with the front bumper of her pickup. The poacher looked in the rearview, shaking his fist. Angie responded with a spirited double flip-off and continued bumping.

Pruitt was no longer paying attention to Joel and Krista in the VW, which was pulling away. To challenge Angie he sped up erratically, slowed down, then accelerated rapidly again. She wouldn't back off. The next time she made contact, she heard one of her headlights shatter. By now Pruitt was so upset that he was bouncing like a beet-faced toddler in a high chair. When Angie motioned with a mocking forefinger for him to follow her, he shook his head heatedly at the mirror.

So she rammed him again and stuck out her tongue as she passed on the left side, in the crosshatched pavement between the road and the northbound interstate entrance. She was betting that Pruitt couldn't resist chasing her, and she was right. He veered off and tailed her to the second ramp, which looped to the highway's southbound lanes. Angie was hoping other motorists on Okeechobee were dialing 911, though she also knew that road rage was so common in South Florida that incidents falling short of a point-blank homicide were not a police priority.

Once the two vehicles merged into the torrent of cars and trucks on I-95, Pruitt dropped back so far that no one except Angie would have known he was pursuing her. Like a plump green bee, the van flitted in and out of view in her mirrors. She groped beneath her seat for the phone but couldn't extricate it. Her next hope was to flag down a cop car—as luck would have it, she saw exactly zero on the drive between West Palm and Lake Worth.

Pruitt was less than a quarter-mile behind when Angie wheeled into the apartment complex where she lived. She didn't park in the lot but drove headlong across the sidewalks and over the grass, mowing down a ponytail palm before stopping a few feet from her front door. She dashed inside and hurriedly assembled the most serious-looking weapon she owned: the tranquilizing rifle that she saved for bears, wild boars and other large, noose-resistant critters.

When Angie ran back out, she saw the green minivan parked behind her truck. She approached from the passenger side, the dart gun raised to her shoulder.

The van's engine was running, the windows were open, and the radio was blasting Outlaw Country on Sirius. Nobody was in the front seat.

She called Pruitt's name several times before stepping closer. Drops of fresh blood were visible on the gray upholstery, and a revolver lay on the floorboard between the accelerator and brake pedal. Dangling like a severed claw from the steering wheel was a clenched prosthetic hand.

Angie backed away, got the phone from her pickup truck, rushed inside, and called Chief Jerry Crosby. A few minutes later, when she peered out the window, the minivan was gone.

TWENTY-FIVE

"It was a rental," the police chief informed Angie when she went to see him later. "The county dragged it out of Lake Mangonia this morning."

"And Pruitt?"

"No corpse in the van. No gun, either. He hasn't turned up at any hospitals."

Angie sniffed the air. "I believe I smell cannabis."

"No, you don't."

"Oh, I'm pretty sure."

They were alone in Crosby's office at the police department. The door was shut. He looked different, like the off-switch had been flipped.

She said, "I get it, Jerry. You're stressing big-time, and that's allowed. I sure wouldn't want your job."

He took the bong out of a drawer and offered her a hit. She declined but encouraged him to fire up.

"Don't tell anyone," he said. "I'd be sacked in two seconds."

Angie asked if Paul Ryskamp had told him about her trip to the

Everglades. The chief said yes, he'd been advised that a mentally unstable individual might be freeing multiple pythons on the island to disrupt the Commander's Ball.

With a drowsy shrug he added, "The information has been shared with my officers, at least half of whom will crap their pants if they see a snake."

"Have them call me right away. I'll be on the property."

"Yes, I heard," said Crosby.

In fact, he'd just returned from the Winter White House, having been summoned to escort a woman named Suzanne Carhart Brownstein off the property through a maze of private hallways. Ms. Brownstein, an adult entertainer whose stage name was Suzi Spooner, had been fucking the President cross-eyed inside his private suite when the First Lady arrived to show him the gown she'd chosen for the Commander's Ball. The President himself had requested the fashion preview but soon thereafter lost track of time, precipitating an awkward scenario in which the First Lady and her Secret Service agents were forced to wait outside his locked door, squeamishly enduring a chorus of bovine rutting.

Mockingbird's composure had dissolved somewhat quickly, and she'd made her presence known vocally and also by hammering on the wall with a five-inch stiletto heel. No Secret Service personnel were available to transport the disheveled stripper—all agents from the backup teams were on Potussy duty—so the decision was made to call Chief Jerry Crosby, who was known as reliable and savvy. He used an unmarked police car to transport Ms. Brownstein from the presidential estate to a waterfront cabana at the Breakers, which she confided had been visited by the leader of the free world. After dropping her off, the chief had gone back to the station, retreated to his office, and, for the first time in his police career, got baked while on duty.

"What's your guess on what happened to Pruitt?" Angie asked.

"Maybe he shoots himself by accident in the front seat."

"But—"

"Injuring the same arm the mechanical hand is attached to."

"So he leaves it hooked on the steering wheel? What's with that?"

"Say he yanks it off his arm 'cause of the pain," said Jerry Crosby. "Say the gunshot's just a flesh wound, no major organs. He sees you coming with a rifle, bolts from the van and hides somewhere till you go back inside."

"Maybe. But it's still ultra-weird."

"He *will* be found, one way or another. Until then, you be extra careful."

"Yes, sir," Angie said.

"How's Beltrán holding up? I heard he got stabbed pretty bad."

"And you're surprised?"

"I'm sorry. I truly am." The chief put the bong back in his desk. "The President of the United States wants the kid to stay locked up—a guy in my position, at the local level . . . you think the White House would ever listen to me? Hell, they basically gagged the state attorney."

Angie knew Crosby was hoping for her to say she understood his dilemma, but she wouldn't let him off the hook that easy. He could have done more; he had all the proof he needed that Diego was telling the truth—the second conch pearl from the railroad tracks, the Chevy Malibu videos. When the prosecutors had refused to act, Crosby should have gone to the damn governor.

"Diego won't be in that jail much longer," Angie said matter-of-factly.

"How do you know?"

"Because I'm meeting with somebody that can make it happen."

"Tell me who."

"Nope. Can't do that."

"Aw, come on, Angie Armstrong."

She said, "You need a cup of coffee."

The chief felt looser than a bobble-head doll. He planted both elbows on his desk to self-stabilize.

"Well, okay, how soon is soon?" he asked. "When's your big meeting?"

"This weekend," Angie replied, "at Casa Bellicosa."

"What?"

She smiled. "Why do you think I'm going to the ball, Jerry? Not for those damn snakes, I promise."

Mastodon's day was thrown off-schedule by the Suzi Spooner incident. The thirteen minutes he'd set aside for tanning were instead spent getting reamed by his irate wife. By the time she stormed out of the suite, Mastodon was late for a long-sought meeting with a surf-crazy Turkish tycoon and prospective hotel investor. The next morning the President would be flying to Alabama for a tour of tornado damage followed by eighteen holes at Augusta and then private fundraisers in Chapel Hill, Hilton Head and Sea Island. He would not re-occupy the Cabo Royale until he returned to Casa Bellicosa on Saturday, before the Commander's Ball.

Christian was glad for the extra time to re-inspect and re-test the temperamental machine. The second run-through using Spalding in the chamber had gone off without a hitch, but then a douche identifying himself as a lawyer for The Knob called demanding access to the tanning bed—he wanted photographs and of course all the maintenance records. Christian told him to contact the manufacturer's corporate office.

The lawyer said, "You should know that my client's in bad shape after the accident."

"And *you* should know," replied Christian, "that being in bad shape was the only reason your client got this gig."

Later he went to hang with Spalding on his lunch break. The talk of the kitchen was Mockingbird's interruption of Mastodon's noisy tryst. Depending on which version of the episode was circulating, the stranger in the President's bed was either a retired Olympic gymnast, the revenge-minded wife of a promiscuous Cabinet secretary, or a professional stripper.

Both Spalding and Christian voted stripper. Whoever she was, she'd been smuggled in and out of the Winter White House without being seen by any of the staff. That was impressive.

Another topic of Casa gossip was the raunchy behavior of a club member named Stanleigh Cobo, who in a single swoop through the grounds had supposedly propositioned a breakfast buffet attendant, an aesthetician, a laundry sorter, a tennis instructor and three female guests, including the married daughter of a well-known Mafioso. In each instance, the offer had included an unseemly fanning of cash.

When confronted by the manager while crossing the croquet lawn in orange Crocs, Cobo had indignantly denied approaching any of the women. Then, after being led to the unmarked salon reserved for the embarrassingly drunk or high, he'd collapsed in weepy contrition, blaming his offensive actions on an unspecified "diet supplement" that he'd taken for the first time. He was examined by the club physician and then sent home with a bottle of spring water and a reprimand.

"The dude looked like a rabid dog. I served him myself," said Spalding.

"What the hell was he drinking?" Christian asked.

"Virgin coladas, swear to God. I'm gonna go grab a smoke."

Christian followed his friend outside to the pretend bamboo garden. A cold front was blowing through, the sky piled with gray-shouldered clouds. Spalding lit a cigarette and said rain was in the forecast. Christian said it was snowing up North.

A surreal warbling arose from a room on the other side of the bay window.

> *Roll on, roll on*
> *You big unimpeachable you*
> *They lie, they scheme, they plot in the dark*

Like all deep-state traitors do
But they ain't as smart, and they ain't as hungry,
And they don't know how to stage a coup.
Unbendable, unbreakable, unstoppable,
You big unimpeachable you!

Christian grimaced and said it sounded like macaws in a microwave. Spalding told him it was the Potussies rehearsing a song they'd written in honor of the President.

"To be performed live at the Commander's Ball," he added, "which lucky you won't have to suffer through."

When the second verse began, Christian spun and said, "Let us motor the fuck *out* of here."

It had begun to drizzle, so they relocated to a latticed gazebo used for waterfront weddings and the occasional renegade bris. From there the off-key Potussies could not be heard. The breeze had picked up and Christian felt the temperature dropping. Spalding heretically flicked his cigarette butt into a flawless hedge and asked about Mastodon's tanning session that morning.

"He canceled after getting busted with that chick," Christian said. "He won't be back here till Saturday afternoon. Can you break free then, for one last test flight?"

"No way. We'll be slammed all day, prepping for the ball."

"Come on, man. Thirteen bloody minutes is all I need."

"Sorry," said Spalding.

"Well, to quote my dear old granddad, shite."

"The Cabo's working great, bro. You kicked its hinky ass, so just chill."

"Yeah," Christian said. "I kinda did."

The deep-voiced man who called said he needed a large air-conditioned storage unit with an electrical outlet. An hour later he drove up in a box truck.

Mazzelli, the owner of the warehouse park, was waiting at the office. The man was very tall, and he had a sun-beaten face like an old cowboy. Oddly, he was wearing a bolo tie and a pin-striped suit. His silver hair had been combed back, only half of his beard was groomed and one eye was covered with a black satin patch. For ID he produced an Arizona driver's license; Mazzelli had no expectation that it was legitimate, and he didn't care one way or the other.

"How long you need the space for, Mr. Hayduke?"

"Couple days."

"We got a two-month minimum."

"That's fair." The one-eyed man signed the lease and counted out three hundred dollars in twenties.

"Access is twenty-four-seven," Mazzelli told him. "Your gate code's the last four digits of your Social."

"Outstanding." The man pretended to re-read the last page of the lease. Mazzelli knew he was memorizing the made-up Social Security number he'd written down.

"You got a padlock for the unit?"

The man said, "Yes, but unfortunately there's only one key. I misplaced the spare."

"Not a problem." Mazzelli had to smile. "We don't ever go inside unless the cops show up with a warrant. Then we just bust off the lock with a hammer."

"I'm storing only personal items. Mostly books."

"Honestly? None of my business."

"Are you a reader?" the man asked.

"Me? Naw. I don't have time."

"Do you vote?"

"Huh?" said Mazzelli.

"It's the bare minimum," the man said, "assuming you believe in democracy. Voting, reading, paying attention—those would be the fundamentals."

Whack job, thought Mazzelli. He lied and told the man he'd recently moved to Florida from Detroit. "I haven't got around to switching my registration yet," he said.

"There's plenty of time before the next election."

"Right. It's at the top of my list." Mazzelli showed him a map of the property. "Your unit is 626-Y. Third building, middle door."

"What about the power outlet?"

"Basic one-twenty, so no heavy appliances."

"Ha! The only thing I'll be plugging in is a heat lamp," the man said with a startling grin. "The next few nights are supposed to be nippy."

A heat lamp for books? Mazzelli thought. *What a fag.*

After the man unloaded his truck, he came back to the office seeking restaurant recommendations. "I'm not used to city dining," he said.

"What kinda food you like, Mr. Hayduke?" Mazzelli had almost slipped and called him Mr. Haywire.

"I'll eat almost anything dead," the man answered, which was true in a way that Mazzelli could not have imagined.

"Try the Longhorn on Belvedere," he said.

"Thanks, brother." The man amiably snapped his eye patch and walked out the door, which Mazzelli immediately locked.

A few days later, after the gay psycho had cleared out, Mazzelli went to inspect the storage space. It was as spotless as a surgical suite, and empty except for one item—a small leatherbound book in the middle of the bare floor. Mazzelli circled cautiously before picking it up.

The title of the book was *The Zurau Aphorisms,* written by somebody named Kafka. It had been left open to a page upon which two sentences had been underlined with a green ballpoint:

> **The mediation by the serpent was necessary. Evil can seduce man, but cannot become man.**

Mazzelli was no Bible scholar, hated snakes, and his only experience with mediation was a pauperizing day spent with a future ex-wife and two divorce lawyers. He had no idea what fucked-up message the one-eyed freak was trying to send, and no intention of trying to figure it out.

He closed the door of the warehouse and sailed the book into the nearest dumpster.

TWENTY-SIX

A snide cease-and-desist letter from lawyers representing Ms. Stevie Nicks snuffed Mastodon's planned duet with Roseanne Barr at the Commander's Ball. In response, the President defiantly ordered an instrumental version of "Leather and Lace" added to the set list, which already included several songs written by performers who despised him. The house band at Casa Bellicosa was The Collusionists, a versatile quintet unfazed by last-minute changes before major events. Often the lead guitarist would sneak in a number by the Dead or even the Chili Peppers, as Mastodon seldom stopped schmoozing long enough to listen to the music.

Among the first guests to arrive were Stanleigh Cobo and his new date, a saucy whirlwind named Suzi Spooner. Cobo was delighted to be escorting such a woman, handpicked for him by the President, who in exchange had asked Cobo to share his new E.D. antidote. The delivery took place out of earshot of Suzi and the Secret Service agents, in a hallway leading to the President's private tanning room.

"Where'd you get this?" Mastodon asked when Cobo handed him the small baggie.

"It's the tusk from a narwhal."

"Whales have tusks?"

"They say this shit's incredible, Mr. President."

Cobo had no firsthand testimonials yet because none of the women he'd propositioned at the club had wanted to sleep with him. If Mastodon had gotten wind of Cobo's serial lechery, he didn't let on.

"You chop a line and snort it like coke?" he asked.

"Preferably off some angel's ass," Cobo said.

"Beautiful, fantastic." The President pocketed the powder. "One more thing, that girl you're with?"

"She's so hot. Thanks for teeing me up."

"Don't lay a finger on her. She's my personal nutritionist."

"What?" Cobo squeaked.

"Keep your goddamn cock in your pants," Mastodon said. "I'd like a word with her now, please."

Suzi was already coming down the hall toward the tanning room. She walked past Cobo saying, "I'll meet up with you in the ball-room, Stanny. Order me anything with vodka."

He was waiting with a warming martini when she showed up ten minutes later wearing freshened lip gloss and a gopher-sized bite mark on one shoulder. "The President and me do a daily calorie count," was the best she could do.

"It's working. He's definitely dropped a few," Cobo said.

As dim as he sometimes could be, Cobo had quickly sized up the Suzi situation and was already scouting the crowd for new pos-sibilities. The glass of bourbon in his other hand was his third. He and his fake date slipped outside so he could sneak a cigarette. She wasn't exactly aglow, so he was curious to hear her review of the nar-whal erection dust. In the end, he couldn't muster the courage to ask.

The sprawling back lawn of Casa Bellicosa had been lavishly illu-minated by amber floods. A chilly breeze blew across the water, from the west.

"Stanny, I'm cold," Suzi said.

"Then you should go back inside. We're at table seven."

"What about you?"

"I'll be there soon as I finish my smoke."

Cobo waited until Suzi was out of sight before he approached the attractive ash-blond woman in the short, jungle-print dress.

"What are you looking at?" he asked.

The woman was aiming a flashlight at the top of a towering royal palm.

"I dropped an earring," she said.

Cobo chuckled. "I get it. None of my business. What's your name?"

"Go away," said Angie Armstrong.

Stung, the man walked off. Angie moved to the next palm tree along the seawall. Pythons were climbers, but when hiding they favored thicker foliage.

From behind her, another male voice: "Lady Tarzan?"

It was Spalding in his Casa monkey suit, balancing a tray of champagne glasses.

"Lord, I cannot believe my eyes," he said with a hungry look.

"Believe it. I'm working."

He winked. "I don't know about you, but the *dress* is definitely working."

Angie shook her head. "And that's all you got?"

"Hey, listen, there's an after-party."

"Wild guess. Your place?"

"Great idea!" said Spalding.

"Go away."

Angie's next stop was a cocoplum hedge that squared the croquet field. Her removal equipment—including a new machete—was laid out in the back of her pickup truck, parked at the service ramp behind the mansion. Inside the Fendi knockoff bag on her shoulder was a clean .22 Ruger fitted with a suppressor. It was strictly against the law for Angie to be carrying any weapon—much less a silenced semiauto—and strictly against Secret Service regulations for Paul

Ryskamp to have given it to her. However, based on her visit to Clinton Tyree's tree island, Angie had prepared for multiple targets.

The cocoplum hedge yielded no snakes though she spooked several iguanas. Walking past the swimming pool, she said yes to a vivid rum drink offered by a server whose name tag said she was from Sarajevo. The woman showed no reaction when she saw the military-grade camo flashlight in Angie's hand, as if it was a perfectly normal accessory.

A knot of guests stood appraising a life-size ice sculpture of the President swinging a golf club. One of them, a distinguished-looking man with a cane, spotted Angie and began walking toward her. He had close-cropped white hair and wire glasses. She didn't recognize him until he got close.

"You look nice, Angela."

"What are you doing here?"

"Beautiful evening. Good music. Interesting conversations."

"Horseshit," Angie said. "How'd you score an invitation?"

Jim Tile laughed. "I didn't."

"Tell me what's going on."

"Aren't you cold in that dress?" he asked guilelessly.

They moved to a place where they could talk, next to a statue that was supposed to be Julius Caesar though it looked more like John Goodman in *Raising Arizona*. Angie asked Tile how he'd made it past all the security.

"Look at this crowd, young lady," he said. "You think these rich proper white folks gonna make a scene and turn away a fine-looking black man in a tuxedo, the only black man in this whole damn zip code? Especially when he's old and a little confused, and then he drops a few names they've heard before. Names of people he actually knows—political types, and so forth."

Angie said, "But there's a guest list."

"You should see all the characters outside, trying to crash this party. Scammers, posers, pouty-ass billionaires that didn't get an invite. I feel sorry for the Secret Service tonight."

"Mr. Tile, I need to know if he's here. And what about the snakes?"

The old man motioned around the grounds with his cane and said, "This is a damn big slice of habitat. You should get back to work, Angela."

It had turned into the weirdest, most frenetic shift of Jerry Crosby's law-enforcement career. While most of his officers were working traffic control and perimeter security at the Commander's Ball, other large though less-exclusive galas were underway all over the island. The police chief was sitting in his SUV in front of Casa Bellicosa and monitoring the dispatch calls when the shit totally demolished the fan, shortly after sunset.

The first big python interrupted the Carpal Tunnel auction at the Alabaster Club. The second snake derailed the Scoliosis raffle at the Founders Club. A third Burmese appeared in a gin fountain at the Pilgrim Club, then another at the Plymouth Club, then the Sailfish Club, then the Marlin Club, then the Snapper Club, then the Bath Club, and finally the Salt Club.

Angie Armstrong was tied up at the Winter White House, so Jerry Crosby went and killed each of the pythons himself. All the event managers begged him not to further disrupt their festivities by using a gun, but Crosby had no experience wrestling lethal reptiles and no time to debate other options. He left the dead snakes lying where he shot them, and was assured more than once that he'd be out of a job the following Monday. After a certain number of threats, he no longer gave a flying fuckeroo.

A text from Agent Paul Ryskamp brought the chief speeding back to Casa Bellicosa, where the Cornbright brothers had been intercepted stepping onto the seawall after arriving on an inflatable outboard. The boat was the tender for their new yacht, the *Inheritance,* which Chase and Chance had inconveniently anchored near the main channel of the Intracoastal Waterway, for maximum exposure.

The Secret Service had whisked the Cornbrights from the sea-wall to a secure storage room filled from floor to ceiling with boot-legged Canadian toilet paper. When Crosby walked in, the young men and their wives were loudly griping that they'd been humiliated in front of the other members and guests. The chief informed them that it was he who'd gotten their names on the ticket list, and that everyone else but them understood that Casa Bellicosa was to be accessed only through the front portico, where armed agents were overseeing the ID checkpoints and metal-detectors.

"So what if we came in a boat instead of a car? That's no reason to treat us like we're Al-Qaeda!" Chase snapped.

With narrow-eyed reproach, his brother added, "Chief Crosby, what do you think our mother would say about all this?"

"She'd say you're acting like spoiled little turds."

The chief led the stewing young men and their spouses to the Grand Ballroom, where the other guests had congregated in antici-pation of dinner and POTUS's arrival. Crosby saw that sequin party masks were being distributed at each table. He overheard a server say they were leftovers from Mardi Gras Night.

A confused Cornbright spouse said: "Is this a costume ball? Nobody told us!"

"What if they re-themed the event?" fretted her counterpart.

The room went dark, and The Collusionists started playing "Hail to the Chief." Crosby slipped out through the kitchen and headed back to his SUV, so he missed Mastodon's entrance. Later, he and 18.4 million other Americans would watch the viral YouTube video, almost all of them wondering why the President of the United States was holding a Bakongo tribal fertility mask over his face, how he had come to choose such an unusual artifact, and whether it was a safe alternative for an N95.

In fact, the wooden mask was a replica that for decades had hung between the genuine head of a snow leopard and the genuine horns of a greater kudu on an oak-paneled wall in the club's Safari Room. Christian himself had volunteered to fetch the mask following the accident, when Mastodon had refused to go to the hospital and bellowed that nothing would stop him from attending the Commander's Ball.

Days later, on the long flight home to Copenhagen, the newly unemployed tanning-bed technician would rack his brain trying to figure out why the Cabo Royale had malfunctioned yet again. It couldn't possibly have been sabotage—the machine had been locked down under guard since Christian completed the final tune-up. Had one of the replacement capacitors been faulty? Or one of the new relays? Also, against Christian's advice, the President had applied to his skin a pungent cream advertised as a miracle bronzing accelerant, and promoted by one of his groveling right-wing radio stooges.

Whatever had gone wrong inside the Cabo, the result was arresting. Mastodon's complexion was the color of eggplant when he punched his way through the canopy. His goggles were fogged, his signature forelock was spiky and charred, and the Velcro base of his skull cap emitted an audible sizzle. He came out raging.

Christian spent the rest of the night being interrogated by the Secret Service. The next morning, Spalding called to tell him what had happened during the Commander's Ball. Christian said he was relieved not to have been there, though he would have loved to see Lady Tarzan in that skimpy Versace.

"My fellow Americans," the President began, "thank you so much for coming to show your support. I can't think of a more beautiful night in a more beautiful place to celebrate the beautiful achievements of my administration. Pause for applause."

The last sentence wasn't meant to be read aloud, but Mastodon's view of the teleprompter cues was narrowed by the tribal mask's slit-like eye holes. Regardless, there had been no burst of applause because the mask was also blocking the projection of the President's voice—only a husky, muffled singsong reached the microphone, leaving the audience adrift. Some guests theorized that the President was attempting an authentic African dialect, to match his col-orful face piece.

"Before we go any further," he said, "I'd like to recognize two amazing young men who are here with us tonight, Charles and Chauncey Cornbright. Where are you, fellas? Stand up!"

The Cornbrights, Chase and Chance, didn't move. They couldn't make out a word the man was saying.

"Come on, guys, stand!" prodded Mastodon impatiently. He'd once played a round of golf with the brothers but he couldn't recall what the hell they looked like. Neither of the snots had broken 100—*that* he remembered.

An aide crept to the podium and asked Mastodon to position the mask a few inches out farther from his face. He did, and it helped.

"As many of you know, not long ago, Chuck and Chandler trag-ically lost their mother in a horrible, violent crime," he went on. "Kikey Pew Fitzsimmons was a close personal friend of mine and a founding member of the Potussies, my favorite bunch of badass Palm Beach gals. Where are you ladies? Stand, please."

Seated at a front table, the Potussies arose shimmying and twirl-ing imaginary lariats—a raucous detonation of red, white, and blue. Each of their gowns was more elaborate and blindingly tasteless than the last. When the women attempted to croon the President's name, he cringed behind the mask thinking: *These broads are already shit-faced.*

"I want the Cornbright brothers to know," he continued, "that we haven't forgotten, and we'll *never* forget, what happened to our precious Kikey Pew"—this time the mispronunciation drew uneasy murmurs—"and it's my sworn promise to you, Chip and Christo-pher, that justice will be done, and justice will be harsh! Pause for applause!"

The crowd clapped with a vigor that sounded compulsory.

"These two outstanding boys were left orphaned by a vicious for-eign criminal," Mastodon growled on, "who is now rotting in a hot, stinking jail cell only a few miles from here. And guess what? He ain't gettin' out! And the rest of his bloodthirsty gang, the DBC-77s or 88s or 69s, whatever the hell these thugs call themselves, they're not gettin' across our borders, either. Not on my watch, folks. No more Diegos! Come on, let me hear you send that message loud and clear: NO MORE DIEGOS!"

The chanting lasted so long that the President grew weary of holding the wooden mask, but he would have crawled under the cauliflower boiler before letting the crowd see his lobsterized face. It was aggravating that so many guests—including his own daughters—had snubbed the impromptu Mardi Gras theme by not donning their own party masks, which had been rounded up on short notice after the tanning-bed misfire. The two seats reserved for his sons were unoccupied; an ice storm had stranded them at an illegal hunting camp in Antarctica, where they'd been stalking emperor penguins.

His face still afire, Mastodon hurried to wrap up his pep talk so that he could slip away for more numbing ointment. "Folks, I'm going to let you relax now and enjoy your prime sirloin or grilled mahi—both dishes are fabulous, congratulations as always to Chef Roger! But first I want to introduce someone you know very well, one of the most smartest, articulatest and hottest women in the whole world, my tremendous wife—"

Only when the President turned to present the First Lady did he realize that her chair at the table was empty. "I guess she's still in the powder room," he said with a brittle stage chuckle, "but please give her a big hand when she gets here."

As he and his Secret Service phalanx departed, Mastodon was surprised to spy through the mask's eye slits an actual black person in formal wear, indicating he was a guest and not on the wait staff. The President detoured into the crowd and conscripted the amused-looking fellow to pose for a photograph, promised to send him an autographed print, and complimented him on his steadiness with a cane.

"Make sure you get a picture with my wife, too," Mastodon said. "She'll be back any minute."

But Mockingbird wasn't in the powder room. She was still in her suite, on the vintage Chesterfield sofa, riding Agent Ahmet Youssef cowgirl-style.

When he had arrived to escort her downstairs, she'd stepped from her dressing room wearing nothing but Margaritaville flip-flops.

"Wow," Ahmet had observed helplessly.

"Agent Ryksamp gave me these. Aren't they cool? I love the little parrot on the logo."

"Paul got you those? Why?"

Mockingbird had smiled teasingly, and in an instant Ahmet had swept her up and carried her to the Chesterfield. They went at it so hard and for so long that his earpiece got ejected. For once Mockingbird made no effort to be quiet, knowing Jennifer Rose was waiting outside in the hallway with the other agents.

"You think they heard us?" Mockingbird whispered afterward to Ahmet.

"I don't care anymore," he said breathlessly, music to her ears.

The next morning, the First Lady's housekeeper would surreptitiously remove the tropical flip-flops from the bathroom trash basket, where Ahmet had jealously tossed them, and smuggle them home for her teenaged daughter.

Fay Alex Riptoad had overdone the Tito's. That was the most obvious excuse for what was happening. Also, those two milligrams of Xanax.

Bad idea.

Or possibly it was the stress—she was justifiably nervous about performing with the Potussies in front of POTUS and a thousand other people. The rehearsals had been fractious, and good harmonies elusive. Fay Alex had been up late every night, losing sleep—so that could be a factor, too.

She had never cared for Deirdre Cobo Lancôme's deadbeat brother, Stanleigh, and Stanleigh had never paid attention to any woman older than fifty. Yet here the two of them were, making out on a padded bench in the secluded Meditation Pavilion beneath a trellis of lush red bougainvilleas.

They were alone because Fay Alex's Secret Service escort, William, had been recruited by Paul Ryskamp to help deal with a disturbance at one of the crystal Purell stations—a fistfight between coal barons had turned hairy when one of them pulled a plastic pistol, fully loaded, that he'd manufactured on a 3D printer. Such a weapon normally would have been detected by the state-of-the-art body scanner at the first security checkpoint, but Mastodon had banned such screening at the Commander's Ball in order to spare his wealthiest supporters from embarrassment, as many of them had artificial joints, partial skull plates, or penile implants.

At first Fay Alex Riptoad had been irked when William rushed off, but at the moment she was glad for some privacy. She had detailed herself as a flamboyantly statuesque version of Abigail Adams, and now Stanleigh Cobo's nose was planted in her bunched, powdered cleavage. Sniffling like a French bulldog, he fumbled somewhat brutishly to unfasten the front of Fay Alex's sparkly, one-of-a-kind gown.

"Down, big boy," she teased.

"I'm jacked up on narwhal," he said. "It's now or never."

"Jacked on what?"

"Check this out." He grabbed one of her hands and placed it on his groin.

"Whoa, Stanny." It had been a long time since Fay Alex had heard herself giggle.

"At your service, Mrs. Adams."

"If you rip the dress," she said, closing her eyes, "I'll yank your goddamn nuts off."

It was only moments later, after Cobo had pulled Fay Alex on top of him, that while sucking on one of her emerald-studded earlobes he noticed movement in the bougainvillea vines above.

A bronze-striped head, as big as a cocaine brick, poked out of the leaves. Cobo's cry died in his throat. Petrified, he watched foot after foot of the colossal body unwind from the trellis beams while the beast's stone-eyed face—probing night scents with a gossamer tongue—levitated over the lovers' bench.

Ultimately it was Fay Alex who shrieked, Cobo having clamped his jaws together in terror. He was gone by the time Angie Armstrong reached the pavilion. She found an older woman with a shredded ear sprawled on the paving stones. The woman's hair had been styled and dyed as a Continental-era flag, and the front of her spangled gown was unbuttoned.

"Stanleigh, you asshole!" she yelled in the direction of her companion's cowardly flight.

"Don't move," Angie said.

"Why are you just standing there? Get over here and help me up!"

"Do not fucking move."

"You know who I am?"

"A damn fool," said Angie, "if you don't listen to me."

Fay Alex sat upright and finally saw the snake—it was descending fluidly from the bougainvilleas, arranging itself on the meditation bench one muscular coil after another. Calculating that she was within striking range, Fay Alex shut up. Anxiously she glanced back and forth between the endless-seeming reptile and the rude young woman in the jungle-print Versace.

Guests were streaming out of the ballroom to see the tumult, forcing the club's security guards to hastily erect a velvet-rope perimeter. The Collusionists gamely tried to halt the exodus by cranking up their amps and delivering the tightest cover of "Sugar Magnolia" that Angie had ever heard.

"What's your name?" she asked the woman on the ground.

"Fay Alex Riptoad."

"What happened to your ear?"

"Some horny idiot bit me."

Mrs. Riptoad was still bleeding, and would likely need stitches. She added, "He got my emerald stud, too. It's an heirloom!"

Angie spotted the green gem lying on the pavers where the fleeing boyfriend must have spit it out. The crowd surrounding the
scene parted for Paul Ryskamp, running ahead of William and two
other Secret Service agents. After ducking under the velvet ropes,
they were quick to heed Angie's warning not to come any closer.
After she'd tipped off Ryskamp about the tree-island menagerie,
all the special agents assigned to the President's ball had received a
crash course on python behavior.

"Jesus, how big is that?" Ryskamp asked, short of breath.

"Twenty-three feet, eleven inches," Angie said.

"So it's one of his."

"Yes, sir. The grand prize."

"Wait," one of the other agents cut in, "you know this snake?"

"Oh, I believe it's a new world record," said Angie.

Suddenly the Burmese lashed out with a hiss, snapping the empty
air inches from Fay Alex's nose. She rolled to the side, yeeping.

Like a hoodless cobra, the upraised python struck again wildly
and then again. Without moving her eyes off the snake, Angie took
the gun out of her handbag.

"That big fucker is seriously whacked," she informed Ryskamp.
"Get these people away from here."

TWENTY-SEVEN

Buttered with aloe, Mastodon put on a top hat to hide the scorched remains of his state-of-the-art mane. Stoically he returned to the Grand Ballroom to greet his admirers, who couldn't make sense of his Lincolnesque headwear in the context of the tribal mask.

The President was moving from table to table when unrest began to rumble through the audience. Guests were murmuring and pivoting in their seats to eye the doors; a handful of people in the back of the room got up and darted out, emboldening others to do the same. Fuming, Mastodon barked at The Collusionists to play louder, but hardly anyone was paying attention to the music. As the place emptied, only diehards such as the Potussies held their positions.

In a fit, the President charged outside to locate the source of the buzz-killing disturbance. He was as unstoppable as a water buffalo, and his Secret Service detail shoved aside fan after fawning fan—donors and ass-kissers alike—in a rush to keep pace. The flying wedge halted at a velvet cordon separating onlookers from an elegantly dressed young woman pointing a handgun at something that looked like a theme-park creation.

One of Mastodon's agents reflexively took him to the ground as the others whipped out their P90s.

"I can try the machete," the armed woman said, "but it's gonna be messy."

On Paul Ryskamp's order, all weapons—including Angela Armstrong's illegal Ruger—were put away to avert a friendly-fire calamity. Fay Alex Riptoad's agent, William, rushed forward and dragged her to safety, inadvertently kicking her missing emerald into a thorny hedgerow.

There was a collective gasp when Mastodon, having lost his top hat and Bakongo mask while being tackled, arose with his baked ham of a mug uncovered. No further incentive was needed to make the crowd shrink back, but the retreat accelerated when the giant python began writhing wildly, like a broken hose.

"I think he micro-dosed the damn thing," Angie whispered to Ryskamp. "All we can do is back off and wait."

"The snake's tripping?"

"It's, uh, not inconceivable."

"Okay, Angie, just to be clear," Ryskamp said, clearing his throat, "you're telling me the crazy old fuck fed LSD to a twenty-four-foot killer python?"

"Look, I know you guys don't train for situations like this."

"There's never *been* a situation like this. Anywhere. Ever."

She said, "Please send someone to get the machete from my truck."

Slowly the Burmese stopped flailing, and became as still as a moonbeam. Its elevated head overlooked the now-distanced crowd, though its eyes seemed fastened on one burly figure standing well apart but ringed by other men in constant motion.

Mastodon stared back with a bewitched, child-like expression. Even as his Secret Service team hustled him away, he continued raptly gazing over one shoulder at the surreal, unblinking behemoth.

Later, crossing the north courtyard, the President and his security detail encountered the First Lady with her retinue.

"My God, what happened to you?" Mockingbird said to her husband. "Your face looks like a baboon's ass."

Thereby establishing beyond any doubt that she hadn't forgiven him for subjecting her to Suzi Spooner's sex yelps while she'd waited in her new Tom Ford gown outside his suite.

"It was the goddamn tanning bed," he mumbled swollenly. One of his agents handed him the replica tribal mask. Another produced the top hat, slightly dented.

Mastodon took both items and said, "All right, now we can go back to the ballroom."

His wife shrugged. "Sure. Fine."

"No, Mr. President, it's too risky," his lead agent interjected. "You and the First Lady should return to your quarters until the grounds are secure."

"Aw, fuck that shit," Mastodon said. "I'm not missing my own party."

Mockingbird turned to Agent Ahmet Youssef. "What do you think, Keith?"

Ahmet, who had a crick in his neck from the Chesterfield romp, refitted his earpiece so that he could better hear the ongoing chatter about the reptile in the pavilion. He reported that the situation appeared to be under control, and that there was no longer a threat.

Mockingbird testily motioned for her husband to line up at her side for their standard amicable-couple entrance. Hoping for a thaw in attitude, he said, "The pink earrings look fantastic with that gown."

"These pearls? They're my faves," she said. "Give me your hand. Let's get this over with."

That's a shame about your dress, Angie heard over and over in the bathroom.

"Will those stains come out?" one woman asked.

"Unlikely."

"Listen, dear, I've got a phenomenal dry cleaner on the mainland."

"It's snake blood," Angie said. "But thanks anyway."

She washed up as well as she could. The decapitation had been clean—one hard swipe of the machete—but she still got splattered.

Fuck the Versace. That animal was so big and beautiful.

She sat in a stall and cried for a while. The python's problem was being on the wrong continent; her problem was being in the wrong state of mind. A job was a job.

Using the pistol would have been easier but way more dangerous; Paul Ryskamp was right—there were too many bystanders. Angie had waited to make her move until the crowd grew bored and started filtering back toward the ballroom. After a while the snake rose higher—tilting its nose upward, as if sniffing the flowers in the trellis—and remained fatefully extended in that surreal, perpendicular pose. Angie wondered about the acid trip it was experiencing, what kind of hallucinations might visit such a primeval brain.

Oh well, she thought. The end was quick.

She dried her tears, fixed her eyeliner, and walked out of the restroom. Ryskamp was pacing outside, speaking into his sleeve. He accompanied Angie to her pickup so she could stow the gun and the machete, and retrieve her first-aid kit. Along the way they could hear the President's reboot of the Commander's Ball, a second "Hail to the Chief" melting improbably into "Bennie and the Jets."

After locking the truck, Angie followed Ryskamp to Casa Bellicosa's storied billiard room. There she began stitching up the violently pruned left ear of Fay Alex Riptoad, who was too vain to let herself be seen by any of the prominent physicians attending the event, especially the widowers.

"You look too young to be a plastic surgeon," Fay Alex commented from the antique snooker table upon which she'd been placed.

"Hold still, please. This won't take long," Angie said.

"Where'd you go to school?"

"The University of Florida."

"And where'd you intern?"

"At a spay clinic in Daytona," said Angie. "I'm a vet. Well, *was*."

"Very funny." Thanks to Fay Alex's disproportionate intake of alprazolam and vodka, she barely noticed the needle pokes and suturing.

"The hell happened to your dress?" she grumbled at Angie.

"I guess I got my period."

"That's disgusting. Would you make a joke like that in front of your mother?"

"Mrs. Riptoad, did you see the second Tyson-Holyfield fight?"

"What on God's earth are you talking about?"

"Check it out on YouTube," Angie said. "Just one more stitch, okay? This one might sting."

Later she and Ryskamp took a walk to the farthest end of the seawall. The outdoor speakers, laboriously disguised as foliage, were now blaring The Collusionists' intrepid take on "Climb Every Mountain," the President being a fan of Broadway show tunes.

"It took five guys to carry the damn thing," Ryskamp said to Angie, "but the dead snake's in the back of your truck."

"Have any more shown up tonight?"

"Not here." He told her about the pythons at the other private Palm Beach clubs.

"Give me the addresses. I need to go."

"No, you don't. Jerry Crosby shot 'em all."

"Personally?" Angie was trying to envision it.

"I'd be lying if I told you I wasn't impressed," Ryskamp said. "There's no sign anywhere of your mad hermit, by the way. Nobody's got a clue how he pulled this whole thing off, but it's already blowing up on social media. The mayor's freaking."

"Jerry's a good guy."

"They'll fire his ass anyway."

"He can do better," said Angie.

"Sorry about your Versace."

"Are you shitting me, Paul?"

"I've got a confession to make."

"Don't tell me you guys aren't really paying for it."

Ryskamp thought that was funny. "You will *definitely* be reimbursed. No, Angie, this is something else."

"Hope your mic's off."

"It is," he said, stepping closer. "Nobody on the President's staff ever said you couldn't wear your Steve Irwin outfit tonight. That was just me."

"You made it up? Why?"

"Because I knew you'd look incredible in a dress like that, and you do. Well, you *did*."

"Fucker." Angie felt herself blush; at least he didn't say she looked *amazing*. "You tricked me," she said, "and for that I deserve a hot lingering kiss."

"Later. Promise." Ryskamp tapped at his earpiece. "The First Lady's lead agent just contacted me."

"Her lover, you mean."

"For some reason, she wants to meet you," Ryskamp said.

"Oh, does she?"

"Like right now."

"What an honor," said Angie.

As Mockingbird took her seat at the table, her husband went to the men's room to snort the last of Stanleigh Cobo's secret dick powder. The first bump had failed its hydraulic mission and, according to Suzi Spooner, smelled like jock-itch talc.

Still, she had gamely promised Mastodon a chance to rebound.

He laid out the rails on the top of his hat, took two sniffs, and sat down on the toilet to scroll through all the adulatory tweets he was receiving. An audio clip of his fiery opening remarks had been posted on the White House website and was now exploding on the internet. Mastodon cackled as he read one worshipful comment after another from his easily incited fans.

Among the places that the broadcast caused a stir was the TV room of the Palm Beach County Jail, where inmate Diego Beltrán had listened to the President's words, swallowed six hundred milligrams of Ambien, and passed out lifeless on the floor. The news was relayed first to Police Chief Jerry Crosby, who chose to share it selectively.

When Mastodon returned to the ballroom to join his wife, the patriotically bedecked Potussies aligned on stage to perform their tribute. Those who'd been bold enough to ask Fay Alex Riptoad why she'd put on a veil had been told it was a historically accurate re-creation of an Abigail Adams favorite. If anyone noticed her bandaged ear beneath the burgundy lacing, they didn't mention it.

Behind his tribal mask, the President beamed as the Potussies began to sing.

Roll on, roll on
You big unimpeachable you

Mockingbird leaned toward her husband and, without moving her lips, whispered, "They sound hideous."

"Are you kidding? It's a fantastic song."

"Pure torture." She reached for her purse and stood up.

"You can't leave in the middle of their big number!" Mastodon protested. "You and I are supposed to have the first dance."

"Ask your nutritionist," Mockingbird said. "Or does she require a pole?"

Outside, the Intracoastal was flat, the cloudless sky sprayed with stars. Crossing the west lawn, the First Lady felt a chill and wished she'd brought a wrap. Ahmet Youssef and Special Agent Jennifer Rose led her entourage, and no flirting was observed—in fact, the two hardly exchanged a word. Mockingbird allowed herself a bittersweet smirk; Miss Blondie would have to find someone else to build her a Shaker writing desk.

They walked all the way to the end of the seawall, where a pair of figures stood beside a flickering tiki torch. One of them turned out to be Paul Ryskamp. The other was a tired-looking younger woman in a sleeveless, bloodstained Versace.

"Are you the one who sent me the note?" Mockingbird asked her.

"That's me. Thanks for coming."

"What note?" Ahmet said.

The First Lady held up a Casa Bellicosa cocktail napkin, folded in half to cover the message. "I found it under my soup bowl."

"May I see it?" Ahmet held out his hand.

Mockingbird shook her head. "No, you may not."

"Oh, relax," the young woman said to the agent, "it's not like I spit in the lobster bisque."

"Can I have your name, ma'am?"

"Yes, sir, it's Angela Armstrong. I prefer Angie."

Paul Ryskamp spoke up: "This is the wildlife expert we brought aboard to handle the python fuckery. She's been cleared."

Mockingbird told Ahmet that she wished to speak alone with the woman. "This concerns you, too," she said to him under her breath.

The agents stepped away, all except Ahmet and Ryskamp forming a wide, protective half-circle on the grass. A patrol boat flashing its lights slowed to an idle no more than fifty yards off the seawall, in case the President's wife somehow wound up in the water.

Ahmet and Ryskamp positioned themselves at the next tiki torch down the line and muted their microphones.

"Your tie's crooked," Ryskamp said.

Ahmet's face reddened but he kept his eyes fixed on Mockingbird. She liked to knot his necktie for him when they got dressed after making love.

"You're not my problem anymore," Ryskamp told him. "This is my last week."

Ahmet nodded. "I heard. Why are you retiring? They pushing you out?"

"Hell, no. I just can't work for this ignorant clown anymore."

"Yeah. I get that."

"You see what he did to his face?" Ryskamp said. "He looks like one of those gargoyles in *Ghostbusters*."

"They said it was an accident in the tanning bed."

"There was no evidence of tampering but, still, what the fuck?"

Ahmet laughed quietly. "Where'd he come up with that awesome African mask?"

"Unbelievable," Ryskamp agreed. Then, after a pause, he said, "Look, man, I hate to see a career like yours go down in flames, but that's your future if you don't break it off with Mockingbird."

"You don't understand how it feels to fall this hard."

"I've been with women who wouldn't leave their husbands for me, and she ain't leaving him for you."

"Just wait," Ahmet said.

"Jesus Christ, I give up."

"When's the last time you fell in love, Paul?"

"I don't know. A few days ago?" Ryskamp turned and fondly looked down the seawall toward Angie Armstrong, whose torch-lit expression indicated she wasn't the least bit intimidated by the First Lady of the United States.

She was absurdly tall, gorgeous and poised, but Angie saw turbulence in her eyes.

"That's a shame about your dress," the First Lady said.

"Have you ever been blackmailed before?"

"Is that what's happening here?"

"I'm not judging you. Agent Keith is a great-looking guy," Angie said. "Sorry, I mean Ahmet. Plus, your husband's screwing a stripper who's writing a book about it. That's never good for a marriage."

Thinking: *Thank you, Paul.*

Mockingbird said, "The dumb whore couldn't write a Post-it note."

"Oh, but I smell a best seller."

Angie was trying to be civil, and falling short. She was upset by Jerry Crosby's phone call. The sight of Venus, a bright amber twinkle in the western sky, made her feel a little better. So did the sound of randy Cuban tree frogs screaking to one another in the bromeliads. Then a school of frantic mullet detonated like a pinwheel beside the seawall, chased by a hungry tarpon.

The First Lady said, "What do you want? Money?"

"Not a dime."

"Then it's not really blackmail, is it?"

"Hard bargain sounds better. That work for you?" Angie took another napkin from her shoulder bag and handed it to the President's wife. "I'm pretty sure you know who this is, but I also wrote down his inmate number and cell block. At this very minute he's in the medical wing at the jail, and I haven't heard if he's dead or alive. All I know is he tried to kill himself, thanks to your lying puke-bucket of a husband."

Mockingbird read the name aloud: "Diego Beltrán. Isn't he the one who—"

"Quiet!" Angie raised a finger. "The man had *nothing* to do with the death of Kiki Pew Fitzsimmons. The prosecutors know that. So does the police chief and the Secret Service. So will everybody else, soon enough."

"But what's this got to do with me?"

"I know you're not a stupid person, so why would you ask such a stunningly stupid question?"

The look on the First Lady's face confirmed that she hadn't been spoken to that way in a long, long time.

Angie said, "You know TMZ, right? The tabloid website."

"I've seen their TV show."

"Excellent. Now, if you do what I ask, I promise that nobody at TMZ will get a detailed, anonymous tip about your relationship with Agent Keith-slash-Ahmet, or the President's sloppy affair with Suzi Whatever-the-hell-she-calls-herself. That's my end of the bargain."

Mockingbird blinked once, slowly. "And what's mine?"

"First: If Diego Beltrán pulls through tonight, you make sure he's released from jail within twenty-four hours. Second: You get Immigration to fast-track his application for political asylum. Third: A statement comes out that exonerates him completely—doesn't have to come from the White House. DHS is fine."

"DHS?" Mockingbird said.

Angie rolled her eyes. "Department of Homeland Security. Read much?"

"You don't have to be such a cunt."

"Girl, this is me being nice."

"What about the stripper's book?"

"Write her a check for an outlandish sum," Angie suggested, "in exchange for shredding the manuscript."

Mockingbird's cheeks burned and her throat was as dry as ash. She said, "So, you want me to speak with the President about Beltrán."

"Yes, ma'am."

"What if he refuses to do anything?"

"Here we go again with the dumb questions," Angie said impatiently. "Apparently, Ahmet-slash-Keith is crazy about you, and I bet you care enough about him that you don't want to wreck what you have together—or ruin his life—which is just the beginning of what will happen if this avalanche of shit breaks loose. I predict media frenzy and a royal goat fuck. Him. You. The President."

Mockingbird touched a tissue to the corners of her eyes. It wasn't an act.

She said, "Why do you care what happens to some random Diego? I mean, who *are* you?"

Angie gave her a business card.

The First Lady looked annoyed, as if she were being punked.

"'Discreet Captures'? Is this, like, a joke?"

"Nope. You got skunks in your garbage, I'm the one to call," said Angie. "Now please go talk to your husband."

She turned and waved an arm at Paul Ryskamp and Ahmet Youssef, who came striding side-by-side down the seawall.

"All done?" Ryskamp asked.

"I believe so," the First Lady said.

"We are," said Angie. "Where's Jerry? Never mind, I'll find him."

She went to the Grand Ballroom and peeked through a doorway. The band had taken a break while servers poured coffee and cleared the remnants of the huckleberry mousse. Some guests were milling about the dance floor, and many more were standing in line at the open bars. Fay Alex Riptoad and the Potussies had posted up near their Secret Service escorts at the foot of the stage, soliciting raves for their performance. Angie didn't see the President at the head table; she assumed he was in mingle mode, milking the donors. She tried to call Chief Jerry Crosby but he didn't answer.

A hand touched her arm lightly, and a voice said, "What do you think of the party, Angela?"

It was Jim Tile. He looked tired, and he was leaning heavily on his cane.

"Aren't you going to ask about my dress?" she joked.

He chuckled and said no, he knew what had happened.

"Mr. Tile, I've got some questions. Can you spare a minute?"

"I'm on my way out," he said. "Walk with me."

The minute Mockingbird had left the room, Mastodon had begun scouting the crowd for Suzi Spooner. She was easy to find, even through the slits in his tribal face guard. He schmoozed his way toward her table, where she greeted him with a formal-appearing handshake.

"Where's Stanny?" he asked.

"Went home," Suzi reported. "Something he ate, I guess. Maybe the shrimp."

"Naw, the shrimp's fantastic. Probably just a flu bug."

She shrugged. "Whatever. I didn't let him get close enough to breathe on me."

"Have you ever seen the Palmetto Room? There's a Picasso and a Hopper, all kinds of classic shit on the wall."

"Cool."

"Why don't you meet me there? I'll give you a tour," Mastodon said.

"Fun stuff."

"See you in five minutes."

Which turned out to be longer than the actual hookup.

Put off by the President's blistered countenance, Suzi insisted on doing it doggy style, which for girth-related reasons wasn't his favorite position. He was counting on Stanleigh Cobo's exotic boner dust for deliverance, yet again it failed to trigger even a tip-twitch.

Suzi's response lacked understanding—there was none, in fact—so, while she was muttering in the bathroom, Mastodon buttoned his tuxedo trousers, grabbed the African mask, and slipped out the door. He didn't expect to see his wife waiting in the hallway.

"We need to talk," she said.

"Right now? I've got to get back to the ball."

"No, you don't."

Peevishly Mastodon propped his mask against the wall. Both sets of Secret Service agents, well-schooled after so many marital quarrels, repositioned out of earshot. One of them was hovering outside the Palmetto Room to whisk Suzi away when she emerged, though Mockingbird saw the whole thing.

"I can explain that," Mastodon said.

"Don't even bother."

"She was checking my BMI. That's all."

"It's hard to take you seriously right now," Mockingbird said. "Have you even looked in the mirror?"

"I told you—the damn tanning machine shorted out. What's this all about, anyway?"

"There's a rumor going around that I'm sleeping with one of my Secret Service agents. It would be bad for both of us if that ever got past these walls."

Mastodon appeared genuinely startled. Mockingbird wasn't surprised, cluelessness being a chronic symptom of his self-absorption.

With an air of reproach he jerked his chin toward a watchful quartet of tall, fit agents. "Which one is it?"

"Wake the fuck up," she snapped. "What if *your* latest fling hits the media? How many more scandals like this before the evangelicals turn on you?"

"They won't. Not ever," he said smugly.

"Can you say the same for me?"

Mastodon pursed his scabbing lips. "What's the whole point of this conversation?"

"To avoid disaster," said Mockingbird. "For once, you're going to shut up and listen to me."

And he did.

When she finished, he scowled and asked, "Why all of a sudden do you give a shit about some border-jumping beaner?"

"Beltrán didn't kill anybody. Your people know that."

"He's still illegal," Mastodon huffed, "which means he's supposed to be locked up."

"Not for something he didn't do."

"Oh Jesus, don't go all snowflake on me. I'm sending a message that needs to get out there in a big way—no more Diegos, and so forth. Haven't you seen my Twitter feed? I'm on fire."

Like a sack of flaming pig shit, thought Mockingbird.

"I want Beltrán out of jail," she said. "Make the fucking phone call."

Mastodon's white-ringed eyes narrowed. "And what are you going to do if I say no."

"Divorce your cheating ass."

It wasn't an entirely empty threat. Mockingbird had been daydreaming about moving back to Manhattan and starting her own fashion label. And Ahmet? He could get any job he wanted; all the top security firms had offices in New York.

"Going to court would be a shit show for both of us," she told her husband, "but you've got the most to lose."

Mastodon puffed up. "I am *the* President of *the* United Goddamn States of America," he snarled, "and you're just a fading runway model who hit the jackpot. Don't ever forget it."

To his bewilderment, the First Lady didn't flare. Instead she coolly cocked her head and said, "You watch TMZ, don't you?"

"What? Fuck, you can't be serious."

"Totally. It would be my first one-on-one interview."

"But you signed an NDA," Mastodon hissed, "*and* a pre-nup!"

"Oh, we'll get everything straightened out. Like you say, that's why God created lawyers. By the way, your fake nutritionist is writing a book about you. From what I hear, nothing's off limits."

"Not Suzi. She'd never do that. No way."

"Oh really?" Mockingbird said with a lacerating wink. "I bet she got inspiration for a whole new chapter tonight. You might want to pay off the bitch, before it's too late."

The most powerful person on the planet had nothing to say as he helplessly watched his ball-busting wife march off with her Secret Service team.

Angie and Jim Tile stood under the portico. A line of couples carrying go-cups and Mardi Gras masks waited for the valets to bring their cars.

"Those people are staring at us," Tile said.

"It's because of the damn blood on this dress."

"No, Angela, it's because they think we're a couple."

"Well then, hell, yes." She pressed her head against his shoulder.

"Lord Almighty, what are you doing?"

"Messing with these dickheads. Am I making you uncomfortable?"

Tile laughed softly. "Just the opposite."

"Why are you here?"

"My friend wanted a firsthand report."

"What are you going to tell him?" Angie asked.

"That the President of the United States asked for a picture with me."

"It's probably up on his website already."

"No shit?" Tile said. "Does that mean I've been to the mountain-top?"

"Where's your friend now?"

"I know you feel bad about killing that snake."

"Just another payday," she said.

"I hope that's not true. My ride's here, Angela."

A sleek Genesis G90 rolled to the front of the valet line.

Angie whistled. "Look at you, getting chauffeured around like a movie star."

"I had to spring for a black one," Tile said wryly, pointing to the Uber sticker on the windshield. "Not too shabby for an old fart on a state pension."

She held his cane while he eased into the back seat. The sound system was cranked so loud that she wondered if he heard her say goodbye. She recognized the song, though it took a moment to register.

By then the sedan was moving down the driveway toward the gates, but not fast enough. Angie kicked off her heels and ran until she got alongside, banging on the roof.

The driver stopped, opened his window, turned down the volume, and lit her up with his smile.

"Buffalo Springfield," she blurted, half out of breath.

"That's right! With Mr. Stills kicking ass."

She said, "Governor, you are officially out of your freaking mind."

"For what it's worth." His laughter boomed from the car. "Get it?"

"Tell me the truth. Did you dose that python?"

"Just a sprinkle, Angie. I wanted her to be soaring at the end."

He looked shockingly different, and not only because of the bolo tie and pin-striped suit. His jaw was shaved as smooth as teak; his silver hair had been trimmed, groomed and stylishly raked back; and his funky denim eye patch had been replaced with one made of black satin. He flipped it once, revealing that the socket was empty.

She said, "Wild guess. The egg hatched."

He smiled down at the breast pocket of his suit jacket. A little bright green head was peeking out.

"We're working on our manners," Skink whispered.

Angie heard a thump and looked past him, into the back seat. Jim Tile's eyes were half-closed; the old man was dozing off.

"What was that noise?" she asked Skink.

"What noise, dear?"

"Oh, come on. The pounding."

Outbound cars were stacking up behind the Genesis. Somebody in a Range Rover flashed the brights and started honking. Skink acknowledged the communiqué by thrusting a middle finger skyward. The honks ceased as soon as the other driver saw the size of the hand that was flipping him off. Meanwhile Angie noticed a pair of the club's security guards peering intently from their post at the members-only Purell station.

The thumping in the Uber car got louder, like a bass woofer.

She said, "Governor, how can you not hear that?"

"Oh, yeah, I forgot. There's a man in the trunk."

"No fucking way."

"Your pesky Mr. Pruitt," said Skink.

Angie threw her arms around her head. "Oh God, what are you going to do with him?"

"I believe he'd benefit from some alone-time in the Big Cypress." The ex-governor yawned like an old wolf. "See you in the next life, dear. Wake me up for meals."

He reached for the radio dial and took his foot off the brake pedal. The G90 began rolling toward the mansion gates.

"What about Pruitt's dogs?" Angie shouted.

"They're safe and sound," Skink called back, "at your apartment."

She couldn't take her eyes off the car as it peeled out of Casa Bellicosa, disappearing in the stream of southbound headlights on old A1A.

Chief Jerry Crosby walked up behind her and said, "Who was that?"

"Some smart-ass Uber driver."

"Jesus, look at your dress."

"Yeah, a real tragedy," Angie said. "I heard you had a busy night, too."

"Probably my last shift in this uniform. I'm going back to the office, clean my gun, and get toasted. What about you?"

"I've gotta go stock up on Purina," she said.

UNCOILED

"Where'd you get this?" asked Giardia, fingering the large emerald.

"Found it in a flower bed where I work," Spalding said.

"Bullshit."

The pawnbroker spun around to lock the door. Spalding was nervous; the man's crusty red tuxedo jacket had a gun-shaped bulge under one arm.

Giardia said, "The hell am I supposed to do with one earring?"

"The stone's worth twenty grand."

"Says who, fuckstick?"

"I got it appraised at a Jared's," Spalding said.

"Ho! And that's how stolen gems get priced?" Giardia's grin was disturbing. It looked like he'd brushed his teeth with tapioca.

He said, "I'll give you a thousand."

"Fifteen hundred," Spalding came back.

"Twelve-five, and motor your amateur ass out of here."

Giardia handed over the money and placed Fay Alex Riptoad's emerald earring in the safe.

"How about a receipt?" Spalding asked.

"Sure." The pawnbroker blew his nose into a Kleenex and dropped the moist wad in front of Spalding. "There's your mother-fuckin' receipt, junior."

When Spalding got into his car, he re-counted the cash and then laboriously swabbed his hands and arms with Clorox wipes. He was late arriving at Angie's apartment, where she'd been waiting to introduce him to her new rescue dogs.

"Fritz is the Labradoodle. The Bichon is Marcel, but don't call him that," she said. "Call him Spike."

"Because?"

"Marcel is no name for a dog. I think it fucked him up."

"Does he bite?" Spalding asked.

"Not anymore." Angie opened the kennel doors and the dogs galloped to Spalding. They were wagging their butts, sniffing his slides, licking his toes.

"Hi there, guys!" He knelt laughing and stroked their heads.

Angie was smiling, too. Joel and Krista were supposed to be dog-sitting, but they had spontaneously decided to go to Nassau and get married.

"You're a natural," Angie said to Spalding. "Fritz gets a cup-and-a-half of the dry food in the morning, same for dinner. Only three-quarters for little Spike. He's got gout. I left his pills on the counter."

"When will you be back?"

"I'm not sure. Couple of days."

"Key West is super chill," he said. "I wish I was there."

"Paul's loving it. Thanks for watching the pups."

"Anything for Lady Tarzan."

"And thanks again for the soup-bowl sorcery. Very smooth."

Spalding had been one of the servers assigned to the head table at the Commander's Ball; it was he who'd hidden Angie's note to the First Lady at her place setting. He hadn't expected anything in return, so he was happily surprised when Angie gave him Fay Alex Riptoad's lost earring, which she'd retrieved from a hedge at Casa Bellicosa before departing.

"Don't worry, that old buzzard will make out like a bandit," Angie had said when she put the emerald in Spalding's hand. "Jerry Crosby says the rich always over-insure their jewelry."

Spalding hadn't decided what to do with the pawn money. He was thinking of flying home to Cape Town for a surf trip, since he now had some free time. Like all the clubs on the island, Casa Bellicosa had been furloughing staff since the night of the python apocalypse. Cell-phone video of Chief Crosby shooting a thirteen-footer out of a kapok tree at the Pilgrim Club had gone viral, killing the Palm Beach social season as dead as the Burmese. Every scheduled gala had been canceled, or re-booked in a competing county. It was almost worse than the pandemic. Now the membership at Casa was in revolt, lawsuits raining down like dung-tipped spears on Mastodon's company.

"Here we have the doggy treats," Angie said, shaking the box. "Only two per day, no matter how pitifully they beg."

Spalding asked if she had Hulu.

"Yeah, but no porn. In your honor I turned on the parental controls."

"Rude," he muttered.

"Also, this is a skank-free zone. You'll have to take your babes somewhere else to hose off."

"Okay, that's enough. Have a great trip, drive safe, and bring me some fritters from Louie's. Now let me carry your bag to the truck—"

"No, sir." She hugged Fritz and Spike, and promised Spalding she would Skype him one night from Mallory Square.

"Angie, I've got a question. You're going to the Keys, right? As in 'romantic getaway'?"

"That's the plan."

"So how come you're wearing those same old ugly-ass khakis?"

"Because I've got to make a stop on the way down," she said, hoisting her duffel bag. "Oh, and this is important, Spalding—do *not* let those dogs poop on the shuffleboard court."

On the way to the airport, Diego Beltrán asked the ex-police chief about the cloth jewelry bag sitting on the console in the car.

"Have a look," said Jerry Crosby. "It's for my wife. Tomorrow is her birthday."

Diego took a slender box from the bag. Inside was a thin gold necklace with a cream-pink conch pearl—the one Crosby had plucked from the sooty gravel in the train tracks on that day with Diego.

"That's pretty cool, Chief," Diego said. "She'll love it."

He didn't ask about the other railroad pearl, the unlucky one that had turned him into a hated homicide suspect. It had been released to the heirs of Katherine Pew Fitzsimmons in a sealed baggie indelicately stamped EVIDENCE.

When Diego thanked Crosby for the lift to the airport, the ex-chief said, "It's the least I can do. Can I ask why New Jersey?"

"Lots of other Diegos up there. Easy to blend in."

Crosby didn't bring up the young man's suicide attempt at the jail. He considered it a minor miracle that someone was on duty who knew how to pump a stomach.

"You got a job lined up?" he asked.

"I'm going to work for the Census Bureau," Diego said.

"Perfect."

"Now that I'm legal, right?"

"Welcome to the American dream," said Crosby.

The county had freed Diego Beltrán thirty-two minutes after prosecutors received a call from Homeland Security, which had received a call from the Justice Department, which had received a call from the White House. Deputies had hidden Diego in the back of a Stanley Steemer van and smuggled him out through a rear gate; the demonstrators, not knowing he was gone, continued chanting themselves hoarse.

Diego never returned to the ICE detention center where the other boat migrants were being held; instead he was transported directly from the jail to a Holiday Inn Express in Delray Beach. The next morning his lawyers informed him not only that the State Attorney's Office had dropped the stolen-pearl charge, but also that immigration officials had pre-approved his yet-to-be-completed request for asylum, due to the political violence in Honduras that had claimed the lives of his uncles.

A short statement buried on the Department of Homeland Security website said Diego Mateo Beltrán was released from custody after "a thorough investigation produced evidence indicating he was not involved in the abduction or homicide of Katherine Pew Fitzsimmons, nor is he a founder or member of an organized criminal enterprise referenced variously as the DBC-88, DBC-77 or DBC-69."

Dumbfounded by his sudden release, Diego feared it was either a mistake or a government trap. He'd remained hunkered in his darkened motel room half-expecting ICE agents to come crashing through the door any moment.

The next morning he turned on CNN just as the President of the United States began addressing a convention of Christian firearms manufacturers. Diego's stomach roiled as he waited for the President's version of how the sensational murder case against him had dissolved. He didn't expect a public apology for how he was demonized, but he figured the President owed some sort of explanation to his restless, impressionable base.

Yet Diego's name, and what had happened to him, was never mentioned. Instead the commander-in-chief launched a rant about a new villain that he referred to, variously, as Bang Lo Sinh, Li Sonh Bang, or Lee Roy Bangston—a "diabolical Chinese espionage agent and self-infected virus carrier" who'd allegedly snuck across the Texas border, traveling with a vaccinated mob of Asian gang members.

"These ruthless foreign invaders have come here to rape our great nation, but our great nation stands prepared to rape them first," proclaimed the President, distractingly caked with apricot-colored makeup. "I promise you, folks, we will track down Bang Lo, we will capture Bang Lo, and we will send Señor Lo *down* below!"

The convention erupted in cheers. Diego turned off the television. From the phone in his room he called Angie Armstrong and thanked her for getting him out of jail—saving his life, actually—and told her he was leaving nuthouse Florida as soon as possible. He had a second cousin in Union City who'd said he could sleep on her couch until he got his own place.

Jerry Crosby had bought him a one-way ticket from West Palm to Newark. As they drove down Congress Avenue toward the main terminal, Diego asked the ex-chief if he planned to stay in law enforcement. Crosby said he already had interviews scheduled with the police departments in Coral Springs and Key Biscayne.

"There's also an opening up at The Villages," he added, "but who wants to drive a golf cart with a siren?"

He had resigned before the town of Palm Beach could fire him. The council needed someone high-ranking to blame for the calamitous night of the pythons, during which Crosby had discharged his service weapon more times than the whole police force had in the previous decade. The shrillest advocates for his dismissal were Fay Alex Riptoad and, naturally, the Cornbright brothers.

During the tense and embarrassing week that followed, seventeen additional snakes—all jumbos—had turned up in random locations on the island. They were captured and later euthanized by experienced reptile wranglers summoned from all parts of Florida and paid from a hurricane fund tapped by the apoplectic mayor.

As Crosby pulled over in the JetBlue drop-off lane, he apologized for the third time to Diego Beltrán for not doing more to help him.

"Hey, we're both damn lucky to get out of this place," the young man said, using the visor mirror to check the fit of his wig and fake mustache. "Good luck, Chief."

"You, too."

Crosby went home and gave the conch-pearl necklace to his wife. She had tears in her eyes when she put it on. He told her she looked amazing.

Which was true.

Mockingbird was sunning on a private beach at Parrot Cay, enjoying a watermelon margarita, when she opened her laptop and saw an email from one of her husband's many lawyers.

"Per your request," he wrote, "please find the secure bank documentation attached."

It was the copy of a wire transfer of $266,666 from Casa Bellicosa's food-and-beverage account to the trust fund of a Reno lawyer representing one Suzanne Carhart Brownstein, also known as Suzi Spooner and Gillian LaCoste. Minus attorney fees, the sum received by Ms. Brownstein more than doubled the advance money she had returned to a New York publisher after abruptly canceling her book contract.

"Well, that one's done," Mockingbird said, closing her laptop.

Ahmet Youssef, who was reading a book on the chaise beside her, cupped a hand to the side of his head and said, "What?"

"He paid off the pole dancer."

"I'm sorry, what?"

"HE PAID OFF THAT NASTY POLE DANCER!"

Ahmet winced as he nodded. He couldn't hear much from one side because of a ruptured eardrum. When the doctor at Walter Reed had asked how it happened, Ahmet said there was a freak mishap in his wood shop, the circular saw spraying a splinter of black maple into his right ear. Although the doctor had been unable to find the tiny fragment, he could see that the tympanic membrane was indeed perforated. The Secret Service immediately placed Ahmet on medical leave.

In truth, his hearing loss was unrelated to his furniture-making hobby. One afternoon at the White House, during a lusty coupling in the cramped Lincoln Bath, Mockingbird had clutched at Ahmet's face with both hands, trying to draw him toward the V of her panties. Unfortunately, in the fervor of that moment, she had inadvertently mashed his agency-issued earpiece deep into the auditory canal. The pain, instant and epic, had put Ahmet on the floor.

He was feeling somewhat better a few days later when he'd boarded the plane to Providenciales. The long flight wasn't as discomforting as the incredulous stares from Jennifer Rose and the other agents when he'd stepped out of the taxi at the resort. Ahmet understood that his arrival there was essentially an announcement; this was the choice he'd made, and he was prepared to be pegged as a reckless, lovestruck fool.

Yet he was also aware—after a call from the newly retired Paul Ryskamp—that the Secret Service was in a sticky bind. The agency director had received a handwritten note on the First Lady's stationery inquiring about a recent incident at a retro-Swedish massage parlor in Bethesda involving at least three off-duty agents, a bag of edibles, and a rechargeable Swiffer.

The director didn't know how the First Lady heard about the escapade, which had supposedly been well covered up, but he found himself more relieved than offended when she offered not to tell anyone, including the media, as long as Special Agent Ahmet Youssef retained his position on her security detail. The director had replied with an eyes-only memo assuring the First Lady there were no plans to reassign Agent *Josephson,* who had a spotless record and was highly regarded by his supervisors.

A screenshot of the memo was stored on Mockingbird's phone, which was now inside her beach bag. With the other agents posted nearby, she didn't want to keep raising her voice, so she texted her hearing-impaired lover from two feet away:

"They let that Diego person out of jail, too."

"Deported?"

"No, he gets to stay."

"Wow," was Ahmet's response.

"Yeah, wow. Snake Babe should be super—" and here Mocking-bird inserted a smiley-face emoji.

"4 sure," Ahmet texted, raising his margarita glass with his other hand.

Mockingbird raised hers, too, then typed: "Think she'll keep quiet about us, like she promised?"

Ahmet replied with a shrugging-dude emoji.

Mockingbird mouthed the words: "I hope so."

"What if she doesn't?"

"We deny everything," she texted. "Oops. I mean ME."

"4-ever?" Ahmet asked.

The First Lady took off her sunglasses and blew him a secret kiss. Then she typed:

"Patience, hon."

The new tree island was farther west than the other one. Angie had found it on Google Earth after Jim Tile provided the GPS numbers and told her about a Miccosukee who rented airboats for cash. She would have hired young Beak to take her out there, but Skink's message said to come alone.

Even though the boat was old and the engine was loud, Angie loved driving it. Going fast reminded her of the best parts of her old job, pre-Pruitt. She missed the exhilaration of hurling at a deranged speed through the Everglades, snaking through the subtle twists and runnels, the flat hull hissing across the skimmed-down saw grass. She missed riding with her cap turned backwards so that the wind wouldn't catch the visor. She missed having to dodge the sleepy gators and jump the dry hummocks, and the tickle of broken spiderwebs on her arms. She even missed the sting of the bugs hitting her cheeks.

As the airboat circled the island, spooking snowy egrets, Angie spotted a bareheaded figure sitting on a high branch in a tall cypress, playfully kicking his legs like a boy on a swing.

When she walked into the camp, he was back on earth, waiting for her. His chin showed stubble, and long twists of hair were poking like silver pipe stems from under his new petunia shower cap. He wore an eye patch fashioned from the shell of a small mud turtle, and a faded fatigue jacket with c. TYREE stenciled above the pocket.

"Want a beer?" he asked.

"Thank you, Governor."

He gave her a bottle of Stella and opened one for himself.

"Jim calls me captain," he said.

"I know. Is that how—"

"He had another round of chemo today."

"Damn," said Angie. "Hey, he's a tough dude. He's got a few good miles left."

"Hope so." Skink sat down on the ground beside the fire pit. "The White House sent a picture of him and Lord Bumblefuck at the poser ball."

She laughed and said, "Yeah, I saw."

Jim Tile had texted a screenshot of the President's inscription: *To my old pal Morgan Freeman—you've come a long way since driving Miss Debby!*

"We are *so* fucked," Skink said quietly.

Angie sat down beside him. There was a rifle propped against a gumbo limbo near his sleeping bag. All his cherished books were stacked in tall neat rows, not walls, and covered with sheets of clear plastic; it had rained like a mother the night before.

"Why the hell Key West?" he asked.

"Meeting a friend," Angie said. "Okay, a *good* friend."

"Lucky prick."

"We'll see how it goes."

Skink looked wistful. "I always loved that town, but I can't go back. All those cruise ships with their porky pilgrims, I might end up rooting for the goddamn virus."

"Paul's house is actually on Angela Street," she said.

"Ha, that's a slick move! He *must* be smitten."

"No, it's just a funny coincidence."

"But what a sweet story to tell your kids."

Angie felt herself blush. "Just for that, I'm going to bring you one of those classy tee-shirts from Duval."

"With which I will wipe my surly white ass," he said.

She noticed a red light blinking on a small device piled among other electronic equipment on an oilskin tarp. Skink said it was a telemetry receiver.

"For the tracking collar I strapped on Pruitt," he explained. "Same size they use for panthers. Last time I checked, the dumb douche was about six miles from Copeland."

Holy shit, Angie thought. *He wasn't joking.*

"Governor, that's the middle of the Big Cypress swamp."

"In all its glory," Skink said. "I gave him chlorine tablets, a Randall knife, waterproof matches, and a volume from my personal library."

"Which book?"

"The Sporting Club."

"You really think a mouth-breather like Pruitt can recognize irony?"

"Oh, there *will* be a test." Skink looked away smiling.

Angie figured he still had the freezer because the beer was cold, and she could hear the rumble of the gas-powered generator. She opened her backpack and took out an object wrapped in a plastic Publix bag.

"For you, sir," she said.

He tore it open thundering, "Oooohhhh, baby! *Zuppa del giorno!*"

Inside the bag was a road-kill armadillo that Angie had collected on the Turnpike extension in Homestead. Skink ran off to place the curled-up remains on ice. Angie scanned the tree canopy and saw no snake sheds.

When he returned, carrying two more beers, she asked about the pythons.

"They're gone," he told her. "I trucked every one of 'em up to Palm Beach, and now they're all dead."

"And you don't feel shitty about that?"

"Sure I do, but they already had a price on their head when I caught 'em. At least with me they got a few pampered months and five-star dining. The truth is they'd been doomed since the day they crawled out of their eggs. Damn things don't belong here, dear, and they're a ravenous menace. Agree or not?"

Sharply Angie said, "That little Caribbean iguana you hatched doesn't belong here, either."

Skink clicked his teeth. "Sadly, a hawk took him yesterday. Pythons are too big to have such worries."

"And you saved the biggest for the President's party."

"Maximum impact. She was a beauty, wasn't she?"

"What the fuck, Governor? The man weighs two-hundred-and-seventy pounds!" Angie exploded to her feet. "There isn't a snake on this planet fat enough to swallow that moose and you know it. So what was the point? Why did you do all this?"

"To imbed the idea," Skink said. He seemed amused that she didn't see the big picture. "'The mind, once stretched by a new idea, never returns to its original dimensions.' That's from Emerson, by the way. All I was hoping to do is stretch some goddamn minds."

Angie closed her eyes and murmured, "Jesus H. Christ."

She sat down again, and he put his arm around her.

"No harm done," he said.

"Really? Tell that to the family of Katherine Fitzsimmons."

Skink's good eye squinted. "What do you mean?"

"The woman that got eaten at the Lipid House!" Angie said angrily. "Don't pretend you don't know who I'm talking about."

"Of course I do."

"The very first python."

"Oh, that wasn't one of mine," he said.

Angie pushed his arm away and stared at him hotly. "Don't bullshit me, Governor."

"I'm dead serious. That big glorious beast motored up there all by herself."

"No. Freaking. Way."

"I swear, Angie. Where do you think I got the inspiration?"

"Shit," she said, keeling against his shoulder. She wanted to cry and she wanted to laugh.

Skink poured the rest of her beer on the ground.

"You need something stronger," he said.

"Yes, sir, I do."

Acknowledgment

I will forever be grateful to Sonny Mehta, my editor of almost thirty years, who passed away in December 2019. Working with Sonny was a gift I never took for granted, and he was also a good friend in difficult times. If it weren't for his understanding and encouragement, this novel might never have been written. I will miss him, as will so many other writers and editors who benefited from his grace, extraordinary perception, and maddeningly infallible instincts.

C.H.

A NOTE ABOUT THE AUTHOR

Carl Hiaasen was born and raised in Florida. He is the author of fourteen previous novels, including the best sellers *Bad Monkey, Lucky You, Nature Girl, Razor Girl, Sick Puppy, Skinny Dip,* and *Star Island,* as well as six best-selling children's books, *Hoot, Flush, Scat, Chomp, Skink,* and *Squirm.* His most recent work of nonfiction is *Assume the Worst,* a collaboration with the artist Roz Chast.

A NOTE ABOUT THE TYPE

This book was set in a modern adaptation of a type designed by the first William Caslon (1692–1766). The Caslon face, an artistic, easily read type, has enjoyed more than two centuries of popularity in the English-speaking world. This version, with its even balance and honest letterforms, was designed by Carol Twombly for the Adobe Corporation and released in 1990.

Composed by North Market Street Graphics, Lancaster, Pennsylvania

Printed and bound by Berryville Graphics, Berryville, Virginia

Designed by Anna B. Knighton